The Boy With The Thorn I₁

Acknowledge

A huge thank you to my family, friends and supporters.

Copyright © 2015 by Chantelle Atkins
Published by Pict Publishing
All rights reserved. No part of this book may be reproduced, stored in a retrieval system or transmitted in any form or by any means, electronic, mechanical, photocopying, recording or otherwise, without the prior permission of the author.

Printed in the United Kingdom
Third Edition

The characters and events in this book are fictitious. Any resemblance to actual events or to any persons, living or dead, is entirely co-incidental and not intended by the author.

Chantelle Atkins

Author's Note

Dear Reader,
I first published The Boy With The Thorn In His Side in 2014 and in two parts. Part One and Part Two. In 2015 I decided to merge the two parts together and publish it as one (very) large book. During 2016 I started getting ideas for alternative endings. To put it briefly, this story and these characters would not leave me alone. As they've been in my head since I first wrote the story aged 12, they are part of me and my life, and as real to me as anyone else. They carried on talking, so I listened. This resulted in me writing an alternative ending and including it in my 2016 short story collection, Bird People and Other Stories. This should have ended things, but it didn't. I now had a lot of new material in my head, and started penning a screenplay just for fun. This new material started at the end of Part Two, delaying the original ending and creating a whole new book. This screenplay has been my obsession since then, with me scribbling into various notebooks at any given opportunity. Finally, I came to a decision. Perhaps a risky one. I did not want to make the book any longer, but I could not leave this new material alone. Their story was not finished. So, I made the decision to split The Boy With The Thorn In His Side back into two books, using the new material for Part Three, and turning what was the sequel, This Is The Day, into Part Four. Changes to Part Four have led rather inevitably to ideas and a plot outline for a Part Five...Therefore, you are about to read the second book in a five-book series and I truly hope you enjoy it.

Part 2
1

December 1996

I have written three letters, but I suppose I could easily write more. There are probably things I should write down for my mother and my brother, but I don't have the time or the energy now. I place the letters into the envelopes and write the names on each one. I leave them on the kitchen sideboard, spread out evenly, so that there is little chance of them being missed. I check my pocket for change, to make sure I have enough to catch the bus. I pause and scratch at my head and for a moment fuzzy confusion floods in on me, jumbled lyrics and disjointed melodies, and I am not even sure what I am doing. *The boy with the thorn in his side,* I hear the song in my head, the boy and his murderous desire... I don't have my headphones on yet, but the music is always in there. I have a constant walking soundtrack to my life you see. There is a song for everything. For every bit of pain, for every bit of joy, for every single moment I can see in bright clarity in my mind, for people's faces and people's words, and for all the things left unsaid...

There is an open bottle of wine on the side, next to the kettle. Looks like there is about half left, and the cork has been stuffed back in at a wonky angle. I reach out for it. I see my hand travelling slowly and thickly through the air, before my fingers touch the cold glass and curl hesitantly around it. My breathing has slowed right down again. The fog in my head has thickened, and intensified, and I can feel my eyes staring, and my heart rate accelerating again, as my grip on the wine bottle tightens. I find myself focusing my gaze on the floor, on the faded green lino that has curled up and receded away from the doorway. I can see the dusty grey tiles that lay beneath. I can see a cigarette butt, a ball of soft brown fluff and some bright orange crumbs that look like broken Doritos. I pull weakly at the bottle, lifting it away from the surface, and somewhere at the back of my wrecked mind, I can hear one of the voices, the aggressive snarling one, asking me what fucking good I'll be if I don't snap out of it.

Chantelle Atkins

My throat attempts to swallow and the back of my mouth feels like it is coated with grit. The bottle falls from the side, just within my feeble grasp. I feel it bang against the side of my leg and it seems to jolt me, just a little bit, as I blink, and finally swallow and drag my eyes away from the peeling lino. But my body is still so very heavy, weighed down by a million things, my mind so full of everything that it seems to want to shut down on me. My arm moves upwards, lifting the dead weight of the wine bottle, until it reaches my face. There is another voice now, trying to push through the others, this poking, needling, pinching voice, struggling through the heavy mist, trying to call out to me. I lift the bottle to my lips and reach in to taste the wine. It rolls back with my tongue, sweet and sharp.

I can hear a slow, steady snoring from the other room. I want to be drawn in by it, I long to move towards it, this crushed and lonely part of me still yearning for warmth and safety, still reaching for hope. The snore rolls out and then in again, whistling slightly on its return.

I lick my lips. I feel the alcohol rushing through me as I continue to guzzle the wine. A brutal kind of warmth thunders through my veins. The squeak of a voice has died down again now, been forced silent by the tangled mess of my mind. The Stone Roses smoothly crooning Shoot You Down. I think yeah, yeah, he's got it coming, he's always had it coming...I wipe my mouth with my other hand. I think I am completely and totally fucked. So, I drink more wine, and my body is bracing itself for something even before I know what it is going to be. My body is always ahead of my mind, I think, and it has been true. It always lets me know when trouble is close. It has sung out its warning bells on many an occasion and has reacted accordingly to the most extreme of human emotions; pain, fear and hate. I have closed my mind down so many times that now I wonder if it has shut up shop for good, if it has gone, and only basic animal instincts now remain.

I suck on the wine bottle like a thirsty baby, images of violence and galloping voices and music swirling and crashing around in my brain. Jim Morrison telling me that music is my special friend...until the end, and I want to laugh and toast him with the wine and tell him

The Boy With The Thorn In His Side-Part 2

that he was fucking right about that. Bob Dylan, he chips right in as well, pushing Morrison out of the way to tell me that a hard rains' a gonna' fall. Well Bob you might be right. I feel close to sleep as I gulp the wine, and in dull curiosity I raise my other hand and gaze at the skin on my wrist. I've thought about opening it up so many times, and I wonder what it will be like, if I scratch away the layers of skin, what would be revealed to me? I guess, whatever it is, it will be with me forever.

Forever. My mind seizes on this word and tosses it around. Forever is a weird concept. I frown a little, smile slightly and drain the bottle of wine. I place the bottle carefully back on the side. People talk about forever, not knowing what it means. I don't think forever is a pleasant thing. It just means until you die. Forever ends when you cease to exist. Forever is your choice. I nod a little, mulling it over. Forever is there until you don't want it to be anymore. I don't want to live like this forever, I think, and there it is, astounding in its simplicity.

Okay then.

I've always wondered about the nature of violence. What it is and where it comes from. I used to worry that the violence would infect me, that it would somehow worm its way inside of me, and find a place to become entrenched, a place to take root and spread. Maybe it has. Maybe it's been growing like a disease inside of me all this time. Maybe that is what this is. An inevitable explosion of the violence that has been breeding within me for so long. So, in which case, the bastard only has himself to blame. He has to be stopped. I nod vigorously, in complete agreement with myself.

If I don't stop him, it will just go on. How many more people will he infect and ruin? His disease will just spread, becoming rampant. I will pass it on myself. I know it. It will begin with my friends, with the people who would stand by me and excuse my behaviour. I will snap and lash out and lose my temper. I will feel better about myself when my fist collides with one of their faces. It will make me feel bigger and better and stronger, and once I see that withered and fearful look upon someone else's face, who is to say what effect that will have on me? That is how it starts. I am telling you. I know about these things. Once you find that power and own it, you feel better. Once it has lifted you up above the shit and the humiliation, then you would want more of it. It would be friends first. And then lovers. Kids, if I was stupid enough to have any. It is horrendous and it must be stopped.

Okay then.

I pat myself down and snap back into action. The knives are there, all in place, awaiting instruction. I check the side, the three envelopes laid out neatly. I pat my top pocket where my Walkman sits, and I reach in and press play. I smile instantly and brightly when the music fills my ears. It is always good to return to a first love, to something that meant something real, something that kicked your arse along.

I pull on the headphones. Righteous anger and the desire to fight back stir violently inside of me. I take a deep breath and walk out of the kitchen. I am thinking about one thing and one thing only. Revenge. Violence. Blood. I'm coming to get you, I sing inside my head, I'm gonna' knock on your front door and slice your throat right open! I'm going to dice you up and piss on your bones!

Okay then. It is okay. It is okay because it has to be done. What else is there? What else can I do? No one knows that bastard like I do, no one. And it will never end. It will never ever end, not until one of us is dead.

2

September 1994

I was feeling good. Satisfied. Everything was finally as it should be. During the months that came after the wedding, I had become the sole owner of Nancy's nightclub. Phillips had become seriously ill and his doctor had told him his liver was calling time on him. In a fit of snot and tears he had begged me to buy him out and take the club off his hands for good. I had been waiting patiently for the moment, and when it arrived, I savoured every second of it. I renamed the club K. It was my name above the door. The honour and the adulation were all mine. The success as word spread, the queue of people outside that grew longer every night, the money that rolled through in larger and larger quantities; it was all mine. I suppose I had an extra strut to my walk, a brighter gleam in my eye, but it had been a long time coming. My bank manager was as happy as I was, practically wringing out his sweaty hands in glee. The house came next. The deeds signed and sealed and delivered into my beautiful wife's hands on the morning of her fortieth birthday. The house, the club, the woman, all mine. All as it should be.

Every now and again I had to make myself pause, just to appreciate the glory, just to bask in it a little. Even the boy was in line. Oh yeah, he knew the line all right and he did not cross it. He had turned fifteen and started his final year at school. Kay murmured constantly in my ear about his attendance and his truanting and his crappy grades, but they were not major concerns of mine. He behaved for me, so I was happy. He worked hard at the club, so I increased his hours and his workload. He would come along and open up, and help collect and wash glasses until closing time. He seemed to prefer coming along on a Friday night, which I assumed was something to do with the Friday night DJ being better for some reason. I often spotted him leaning in to chat to him.

I watched him closely though. You had to with kids that age. They're open to so many other suggestions you see. There were bad influences everywhere, so I had to keep an eye on things. I hadn't been lying when I told him that I kept tabs on him and his friends. Damn fucking right I did. Currently it seemed that he did not mix with his friends much, but was usually either at the beach, the record shop, or Jack's flat. I kept an eye on it all. Where he was, what he was doing. I taunted him with the possibility of everlasting peace. I taught him that if he stayed beneath my wing, everything would be fine. I didn't miss the wondering look of hope in his eyes when I questioned him about his opinion on bands I was thinking of hiring for the club. There was the edge of fear and caution, just slightly softened by his desire to be needed, and valued. He would offer up his opinions then, and if I was receptive, he would come out with suggestions too, and this gentle hue of red would spread across his cheeks when he talked about music he really loved. I never pretended to understand any of it. He had been right when he had accused me of not liking any music. I didn't really. There was nothing that particularly called out or spoke to me like it did to him. But it amused me, the desire in his eyes, the innocent belief he held onto that he could convince someone that some band, or some song was really important, really life changing.

  He still dressed like a homeless person most of the time. With ripped jeans, checked shirts, band t-shirts and shapeless jumpers, but Kay and I had noticed he had some new heroes these days. At one point we had joked that he would never come out of the mourning he had gone into after that idiot singer shot himself. But then he started putting up these Oasis posters, playing their music, and one day he even went and got his hair cut a bit shorter. We had to hide our giggles until he had left the room. It was amusing though. The way his music filled the house, and sometimes you could hear him singing over the top of it, and I liked the look Kay got on her face then, sort of fuzzy and dopey with love. We had a normal teenager in the house, and all was fine. All was as it should be.

  Kay was always relieved when he came scurrying back from Billy's house or the record shop with an armful of tapes and records. She would breathe out her relief, and I would feel the grateful love pulsing from her when she curled into me on the sofa. Sometimes she got a little worried about where he was, who he was with, but I knew there was nothing to be concerned about. Most of the time he was at Jack's flat, smoking weed and getting high, having the time of his life. It was fine by me, and I let them get on with it. It kept things calm, I suppose, subdued and in order. I didn't have to worry anymore

The Boy With The Thorn In His Side-Part 2

about him kicking off and threatening to stab me in the eye. He was too fucking out of it to care. Jack and I had a mutually beneficial friendship all right, although sometimes I did wonder how he could possibly see it the same way, being confronted with sweet temptation like that. His greedy eyes lit up when he told me if the Anderson boy had shown up. It always put my back up a bit, because I didn't trust that boy at all. He had a major problem with me. A big axe to grind. But Jack liked him coming over and waved my concerns away dismissively. They're just stupid kids getting high and talking about music, he would inform me, nothing to worry about here. And so, things were rolling along nicely. I had not had to clench my fist in a long time.

3

I was in a little routine. I would go to school, try to get through as much of it as possible, and then leave and walk into town. On the way to Jack's I would stop in The Record Shop. I would stay in there for as long as Terry allowed me to. It was all that occupied my mind at school and at home. The boys still asked me to go to the base with them, or the park, or the café where Jake worked, but I usually shrugged them off. Those places felt out of bounds to me for some reason. The base and the park, the things they talked and worried about such as girls and school and exams, all seemed childish and pointless to me. They moaned about their parents, and talked about TV programmes I never watched. In some ways, I felt sort of unburdened and free compared to them, because I rarely worried about anything. I turned up at school when I could be bothered. I faked sick notes from my mother, and slipped out unnoticed when the day was taking too long to pass. The rest of the time I put in hours at the club, which generally made me feel too tired for school anyway, and I went to the record shop, and I went to Jack's flat.

Terry seemed to tolerate me more as time wore on. Maybe he even liked me just a bit. He'd bring out two cups of tea instead of one, and he'd sling magazines at me when I walked in, ordering me to read the reviews section. Sometimes, if he was too comfortable on his stool, he would send me out the back to make the tea. We would talk and argue endlessly about which was the greatest Dylan album, or the greatest Smiths. I continued to consume music, old and new on a daily basis, as if on some great quest, as if attempting to quench some great and endless thirst I had.

I discovered that there was very little music that did not have some kind of effect on me. When I had enough money to purchase music, I tried to always buy something old and something new. One week it would be Captain Beefheart's Safe as Milk and Radiohead's Pablo Honey, and the next week Frank Zappa's Hot Rats alongside Blur's Parklife. I'd buy them in any format, tape, vinyl or compact disc. It didn't matter, because I could play them all at Jack's. I still listened to Nirvana at some point every day, out of pure respect. I just

The Boy With The Thorn In His Side-Part 2

had to. But I had managed to move on, I mean, it was inevitable when new music was getting so exciting.

I tried to tell anyone who would listen how important Oasis were. 'For one, they're British, they're just like us,' I'd insist while Billy laughed at me.

'They're from Manchester,' he'd say, as if this was another country altogether.

'It doesn't matter,' I would shake my head. 'It's just a place, it's just a town, like millions of other towns, just like this one! Where there's nothing to do and no jobs and everything is shit and boring! And they're singing about getting out! About being rock and roll stars!'

I'd watch them on the TV, transfixed to Top Of The Pops, feeling like I was watching a slice of history being made. What amazed me was how such stillness from a frontman could still convey so much arrogance, so much self-belief and passion, so much of everything. I'd kneel on the lounge floor right in front of the screen to watch him sing. I wanted to be him, I wanted to sing like him, and feel like him; invincible and snarling. And the songs, they spun electric tingles down my spine, they followed me about as I trudged through my days, they thrummed and hummed and beat at my mind at night, they made me imagine what I could be one day. I sometimes just lay on my bed, or sat on the floor, with my eyes closed, so it was like the lyrics and the vocals were made just for me, and it felt like with every song they were speaking to me, about me, like they knew me, knew everything. I mean, Cigarettes and Alcohol? Has there ever been a better song written for teenage layabouts? I'd laugh my fucking head off, light up a smoke and slosh a measure of whisky down my throat, just to agree, just to feel it.

I bought or borrowed music from Terry every day, then took them over to Jack's to listen to. His flat was overcrowded with randomly placed furniture. There were three tatty sofas, two arm chairs, two coffee tables, various mismatched bookshelves and fold down tables. He blamed the mess on his late mother. He had to get all her furniture out of her home when it was sold, and he hadn't got around to selling or dumping any of it yet, or so he said. I had never seen so many books in one home before. They were everywhere. He even had a little bookcase in the bathroom, within reach of the toilet, no less. It was in there that I discovered Hubert Selby Jr's Last Exit To Brooklyn. He made a bit of a face and laughed at me when he saw me with that one.

'Did you know they took that book to fucking trial?' he asked me, with a wheezy grin. 'It was banned for years! For being so indecent.'

Of course, that only made me want to read on, and so I did, and by the end, I could well believe him.

I read J.D Salinger's Catcher In The Rye one day when I should have been at school. When I'd finished it, I went right back to the beginning and read it again. I think that was the first time I fell in love with a book. I wanted to crawl into it. I wanted to be poor old Holden's friend, and to tell him not to worry so much. I got it though. I mean, when he was going on about fakes and phonies and how depressing people were, I really understood what he meant. On the rare occasions that I made it into school, I just found myself increasingly disgusted with these children I was supposed to have things in common with. I looked at them and didn't understand them one little bit. They were all the same, I thought, flashing fake smiles at people they despised, constructing gossip to pass the time, making up filthy rumours to destroy the people they walked home with. The fake concern they showed each other made me want to writhe in embarrassment. The constant never ending mantra that this was the last year, that they would stay friends forever and never forget the best years of their lives...it was bullshit!

I discovered that Jack had loads of good books, interesting books, naughty books, books they would never let you read or study at school. Books that were like good songs, books that pulled you in and held you tight and didn't let you go free again, even after you had finished reading them. Charles Bukowski became a literary hero of mine around that time. I just loved the man. Every word he wrote was poetic self-destructive beauty, and fucking hilarious. I devoured Post Office and Tales of Ordinary Madness. I wanted to write like him; fuck the rules and the grammar and the useless tedious soulless shit they pump into you at school, just write! Just let it come! And he was right too...you did write better when your veins were full of booze,

The Boy With The Thorn In His Side-Part 2

because you just didn't give a shit, and you just *felt*...William Burroughs was another, and Jack Kerouac. I read On The Road so many times that Jack let me keep it in the end. It drove me wild, that book. I got caught up in the mad and restless energy of it, the scrapes they got into, the characters they met, and the beautiful way he described ordinary, mundane things...It made me dream, just like the music did, about escaping, about getting away and being someone, living a life on my terms, a life full of adventure and joy.

Jack remained a man of few words. He came and went, shuffling about as if lifting his feet was too much effort. He survived on takeaways and cups of tea and whisky. Unlike Howard, mess and rubbish did not offend him. The flat remained in a constant sticky and mucky state. The coffee tables were always covered in food wrappers, which he would simply sweep to the floor to make space for the next greasy meal. The tiny kitchen had a smell of its own; stale sweat and warm whisky, mingled with sweet and sour chicken balls, and dead flies. On the nights that I stayed over, I made myself a bed on one of the sofas, always the grey one that sank in the middle so that you slept in a c shaped position. It had pale yellow stuffing spilling out of one arm. I would cover myself in blankets that reeked of smoke, or my own jacket, and fall asleep with the record player on softly.

Jack rarely bothered me. We had a simple relationship which I appreciated. I only thought about how little I knew the man, when Michael turned up occasionally, firing his dark eyed questions at me. What did it matter? I would shrug at him and say, who knows? Who cares? It was cool that we had somewhere private to go. Somewhere we would not be bothered by parents, or little kids, or anyone else. There were no rules. We could smoke a little weed, drink some booze and listen to music. Michael was always so bloody suspicious. If it was just the two of us, he would start to relax after a while though. We would roll a joint or two, neck some lagers and put music on. For a while maybe, we would laugh and joke like we used to, before there were so many unsaid things between us. But if Jack rolled in, Michael would change. He would become dark and surly and tense. I would just try not to notice, try not to let it get to me. I was always so pleased to see Michael. It meant a lot to me that he still looked me up.

One night, a few days before the new school year started, I was alone at the flat, relaxing on the grey sofa, with my feet up, listening to an early Dinosaur Jr album Terry had passed to me earlier in the day.

'If you like it, you can pay me later,' he had said, as usual barely glancing up from his music magazine, 'and if you don't like it, just bring it back.'

I was two songs in and already hooked when there was a knock at the door. I instantly recognised it as Michael's knock and rushed to let him in. He was smiling for once, really smiling, bright light dancing in his dark brown eyes as he bundled excitedly past me and into the flat.

'Guess what?' he asked, following me over to the collection of knackered sofas. 'Guess what? I've got some good news Danny! Some amazing news!'

'Yeah?' I grinned. 'What is it?'

'Anthony gets out next week!' He clasped his hands together and jumped up and down like a little kid. His face looked manic, with his wide eyes and this big grin plastered from ear to ear.

I shook my head, disbelieving. 'No way! Does he really?' I tried to think back in my head, how long it had been. How many weeks and months had passed since that terrible, confusing day.

'Yep,' he informed me proudly. 'Sentenced reduced for good behaviour. It's all definite. I didn't want to say anything until I knew for sure. But he's coming back Danny...he's really coming back!'

I couldn't help but smile of course, but inside I felt a mixture of emotions. I sat back down and picked up the joint I had started to roll. I twisted one end up and popped the roach into the other.

'So, it's been about a year?' I asked, unable to look at him as I spoke. I picked up a lighter lying on the coffee table and sparked up, shaking my head. 'Fuckinghell Mike. I can't decide if it's gone fast, or slow.' I stopped then, halting my words for fear of saying the wrong thing.

'Can't believe it,' Michael said dreamily, as he jumped down beside me and dropped one arm lazily over the back of the sofa. 'Gonna' be so amazing to have him back Dan. I can't wait.' He looked at me, and his smile was hesitant, so I looked down, and there

The Boy With The Thorn In His Side-Part 2

it was again, as usual; all the things left unsaid, all the things that were never spoken of. I thought of something then. I was just desperate to end the silence and liven things up, so I passed him the joint and swept my little tin up from the table.

'Hey, this calls for a celebration!'

Michael toked on the joint a few times and passed it back. I took it from him and placed it in the ashtray to smoulder. He was eyeing me curiously. 'What you got there?'

'Something very cool.' I took out a small package of Clingfilm, unwrapped it in my palm and showed him the delicate pinkish white power that sparkled inside.

He recoiled from it, frowning. 'What the hell is that?'

'Speed. You want to do a speed bomb with me?'

'A what?'

'A speed bomb. Look.' I pinched some of the powder between my fingers, picked up a cigarette paper, dropped the powder into the middle and screwed it up into a tight little ball. I held it up between my thumb and forefinger to show him. 'You eat it. See.'

He was looking concerned. 'Speed? Since when did you start doing speed?'

'I dunno,' I shrugged. 'Since whenever. Someone gave it to me. I don't wanna' waste it. Come on, you gonna' do one with me?'

'You've done this before?'

'Yeah, a few times. It's no big deal, honest. What do you say?' I held the ball out to him and he took it and rolled it between his fingers, before placing it on his other palm and poking at it with his index finger.

'Who gave it to you then?' he asked me. 'Oh, let me guess. Your amazing new friend Jack.'

'So what?' I shrugged again. 'It helps keep you awake. Makes you wanna' talk and talk for hours! The characters in On The Road did stuff like this! Just stayed awake for days and days and days, just talking and learning!' I made another one and looked back at him. 'What do you say?'

'I'm not sure about this,' he replied, peering distrustfully at the ball in his hand. 'Weed is one thing you know. This is something else. Anthony always warned me not to, you know? He said nothing

15

else is safe, not ever. Why is Freeman just giving this to you Danny? Why didn't you have to pay?'

'It doesn't matter,' I laughed at him, rolling my eyes. 'If you don't like it, you don't have to do it again do you? Come on, it's meant to be fun! Don't you want to have fun Mike? Just live life by your own rules and not give a fuck!' I laughed, hoping he would laugh with me, but he didn't. He eyed me sternly, his forehead furrowed under his hair.

'The guy's a drug dealer then?'

I sighed and turned around to change the record over. Jack had a fold down table behind my sofa with the record player set up on. I got on my knees and flicked through some records before deciding it couldn't be anything else other than Definitely Maybe.

'This place is a shit hole and it stinks,' Michael complained huffily beside me. I held up the twelve inch Definitely Maybe.

'Look I got it on vinyl too!' I told him. But he didn't care. He didn't care about music like I did. It didn't make him feel better, or make him feel like he wanted to laugh out loud, or like he wanted to hold someone and cry tears into their eyes. It was just me. Maybe I was mental.

'So, he's a dealer then? That's what he does?'

I jumped back down and grinned when the opening chords of Rock and Roll Star kicked in behind us.

'I dunno and I don't give a shit,' I told him. 'Look are you gonna' do it or what? 'Cause I am. We've only got one life Mike, then we're dead and gone forever. We might as well try everything once. I fucking am!'

He watched me as I popped the small ball into my mouth and swallowed it. 'Oh shittinghell,' he groaned then promptly did the same.

I wanted to slap him on the back and congratulate him, but I didn't. We just smiled at each other dopily, and then rested our heads back on the sofa, waiting for something to happen.

'I'm gonna' kill you if this fucks me up,' he warned me with a half-smile.

I nodded and tapped his knee. 'You're gonna' love it Mike.'

The Boy With The Thorn In His Side-Part 2

Next thing I knew, we were having this strange and animated conversation about what songs we would want played at our funerals. It happened to be a subject I had put a lot of thought into. Michael was sat cross-legged on the floor, swaying from side to side with the music and tapping his open palms against his knees as if drumming them.

'Live Forever, obviously,' he was saying. 'But I bet everyone chooses that from now on.'

'You'd have to have it, wouldn't you?' I agreed passionately, sweeping a sweaty hand through my hair so that it all stood on end. 'Fucking Live Forever man! I love that song Mike, God I want to hear it every day, I think it might be my favourite song ever, you know?' I was scratching at the same spot on my head, back and forth with my fingers, while trying to decide if this was a massive betrayal of Nirvana or something. 'It is joyous,' I said then, biting my lip. 'That's what it is...lifts you up, like The Stone Roses too, just joyous and uplifting, I don't know how they do it though…But at my funeral I'd have Lithium too, course I would, it's so amazing that song. Every line! Brilliant, I have to listen to it every day out of respect for him you know? Hey, what do you reckon he had played at his funeral?'

Michael didn't answer me. His eyes looked huge. 'I'd have Supersonic or Cigarettes and Alcohol as well,' he was saying, sort of talking and babbling over me. His voice suddenly sounded very down and low and far away. For some reason he found himself funny, threw back his head and hooted laughter at the ceiling.

I got up and stood on the grey sofa. I was waving my arms about to keep my balance as I stepped from one sagging cushion to the next.

'Christ! I nearly forgot! How could I forget? I'd have I Am The Resurrection as well! Love that song! Hang on I'm gonna' put it on, we have to have it on Mike, right now, have to have it really fucking loud to appreciate every genius part of it!' I turned around and started scrambling through the records to find it. 'Wait,' I was saying breathlessly. 'Wait for this, wait for the drum intro...' When it started I whirled around, back on my feet and playing the drums in the air while Michael curled up with laughter on the floor. I started singing along loudly, before bouncing down onto my bottom, sweat now pouring from my forehead. When the chorus kicked in I screamed along with it. I went into the air guitar, holding aloft an invisible one, plucking the strings, and then back to the drums again.

'I need water,' Michael announced and got onto his knees to grab a can of coke from the nearest coffee table. 'Is this safe to drink?'

'I'd have some Dylan too,' I started to ramble again, and somehow, I don't know why, but somehow, I felt just so desperate to make him understand about the music. I kept looking over my shoulder at the record player, panicking about what to put on next, about how to make him feel as I felt. 'Positively Fourth Street,' I was nodding emphatically. 'Or maybe Forever Young...I have to write these down! Billy, fucking Billy, if he takes the piss out of Bob Dylan one more time I'm gonna' thump him one...Stupid, stupid, he won't even listen! How can you dismiss a whole catalogue of work without even properly listening to any of it! Oh, and The Smiths. Got to agree with Terry. Just *genius* Mike. Hilarious. The Boy With The Thorn In His side, that's me that is!' I pointed to myself happily as I stared down at Michael. His face had gone very pale, making his eyes look even darker, like lumps of black coal shining in his face. 'That's what they call me you know, those bastards...you're a bloody thorn in my side! Oh, I'd have loads...Panic, and There Is A Light That Never Goes Out and Stop Me If You Think That You've Heard This One Before.'

'Don't know any of them,' Michael said, looking blank.

''Cause you don't listen, you don't listen!' I insisted, my voice rising high above the music. 'I keep playing you stuff, all the time, I keep trying and you don't listen! You've got to give it a chance! Oh, at my funeral it's gonna' be one huge party!' I turned back to the records and the tapes, hunting through them. I was frantic and it was getting worse. I was realising with dawning horror that there was not going to be enough time in my stupid little life to listen to all the music, that I would never be able to hear everything, and that it was endless, because new stuff, amazing life changing stuff was coming out every day, and I didn't want to miss a thing! 'I have to just lie down and listen to it sometimes,' I was saying, my back to Michael. 'So, I can properly listen to it, properly concentrate. I lie down and put the speakers to my ears and turn it up really loud...oh anyway, until shit face comes and tells me to turn it down!'

The Boy With The Thorn In His Side-Part 2

Michael was drumming his hands against his knees again. 'Oh right,' he said. 'God, he would, wouldn't he? How are things with him mate?'

'Oh, I'll show you,' I said enthusiastically, spinning back around and standing up with my chest puffed out and my hands on my hips and my head cocked to one side. 'I can do a really good impression, get this...*Turn that fucking shit down you bastard! Sit down when I'm talking to you! Stand up when I'm talking to you! Look at me! Don't look at me!*' I laughed helplessly and tugged at my own hair in frustration, while Mike looked on, his eyes slowly narrowing. 'I can't do anything right...He took the lock off my bedroom door a while ago, you know. So now he can come in whenever he wants, 'cause now he owns the place you know, it's his house!' I rolled my eyes and laughed. Michael was watching me uneasily from the floor. He had stopped drumming his knees and pulled them up under his chin.

'All your shit is here,' he said, looking around. 'Do you practically live here now or what?'

'Well,' I shrugged and rubbed at my face. I was so hot I felt like my insides were ablaze. 'I just come here as much as I can to get away from the arsehole.'

'Doesn't he give you the creeps though?' Michael asked, shivering suddenly and wrapping his arms firmly around his legs. 'I don't think I could stand it. He's like a dirty old man, creeping about, and this...' he gestured to the room, and the mess. 'It's such a shit hole.'

'Who cares about stuff like that? You don't normally care about stuff like that.'

'But he's creepy Danny, I'm telling you, there's something about him! He's always watching us for one thing. I can't believe you haven't noticed!'

'Who, Jack?'

'Yes! The way he just comes in and doesn't say anything, but then he just sits there and looks at us.'

I laughed. 'Mike, it's his flat, he can do what he wants. He's just not a talkative person.'

'But it's creepy,' Michael said rather miserably, glancing at the door. 'Why'd you have to be here so much?'

'It's better than home that's why!' I yelled, with a laugh. I turned back around, uncomfortable with his questioning eyes. I started rummaging through my music again, looking for something that would get us on our feet and feeling wild. 'He lets me do what I want,' I said. 'He leaves me alone. That's why Mike. I can relax here. He's hardly ever here anyway!' I looked back at him, this huge smile eating up my flushed and sweaty face. I put on a record and turned back to him. 'Hey, listen to this. I really like this.'

'Who is it?' Michael shrugged. I started to bounce up and down on my backside again. I felt too wired up, too crazed to sit still, I just wanted to keep listening to music, keep talking about it.

'James Taylor,' I told him, sniffing. 'You like it? I want this at my funeral too please.'

'Listen, what you were saying, about Freeman.'

'What was I saying?'

'He's Howard's friend, Danny.'

I frowned, still bouncing. 'Yeah, so?'

He shook his head at me. 'So, this is all weird crazy bullshit, and you need to be careful Danny.'

I stopped bouncing and stared at him in wonder. 'Do I?'

'Yeah. *Really* careful. Look, I know we haven't talked about it in ages, but we both know what an evil bastard Howard is, so you need to be careful, right?'

'Careful?' I threw back my head and snorted laughter. 'Okay Mike. I'll be careful, I promise, I really will. Actually, I have been very careful for ages now. Haven't had any falls off that stupid bike, have I?' I looked at him and winked and grinned, whilst feeling like I was shrivelling up with guilt on the inside. I didn't want him looking at me too long then. I felt like if he looked at me too long, he would see the truth of me and how wretched and pointless I really was, and then he would leave. He would get up and stalk out of the dirty flat he despised so much and I would never see him again.

'You know what I mean,' he said, with this awful, sad sigh, as he tore his eyes away from me and gazed around the room. 'You should know what I mean.'

The Boy With The Thorn In His Side-Part 2

It was all fine and good, like most things, until we woke up the next morning feeling like death. It was a horrible way to wake up, believe me. It was like a slow misery awakening inside of you and your body. I could see it on Michael's face as he groaned into life on one of the other sofas. I felt an instant slam of guilt. I had done it to myself, that was one thing, but I had roped him in as well, and now he looked and felt like shit and I was swamped with self-loathing. I wanted to turn over and go back to sleep and wake up when I was feeling normal again. Michael sat up slowly, his nostrils twitching, his lips curling up. He looked at the blanket lying over him and punched it away as if it suddenly and violently offended him. He looked pale and sick and angry. I smiled at him weakly from my sofa and he shook his head at me.

'I am never doing that again,' he said.

'It's not that bad.'

He raised his eyebrows at me and looked amazed. 'Fucking is! I need to go home.'

He shuffled to the edge of the sofa, pressing one hand to the side of his head as he moved, closing his eyes briefly against the pain. Then he looked across at me and I felt scared when I saw his face, because it looked for a moment like he really and truly hated and loathed me. I was lying on my back with my hands laced on my chest. I was trying not to move too much because everything seemed to hurt.

'Did he come back?' he whispered. 'Freeman? Is he here? I don't remember him coming back.'

I nodded. 'It's all right. It was really late. He just went to bed.'

I watched him shiver and he got to his feet quickly, as if knowing Jack was somewhere in the flat made him want to get out of there even faster. He stretched out his limbs one by one and picked his leather jacket up off the floor.

'Are you coming with me?'

I tugged the blanket up to my chin and shook my head. 'Nah. Think I'll stay here for a bit.'

'What for?' he groaned, slapping a hand against his forehead this time and wincing dramatically.

'Just to hang around,' I shrugged.

'Oh, okay fine, suit yourself,' he snapped, rolling his eyes and rubbing aggressively at the small of his back. 'You always do,' he added, heading for the door.

I blinked in hurt and surprise and said nothing. He stopped though, and looked back at me as if waiting for something.

'What does that mean?' I heard my weak voice asking him. Though of course I knew, I knew what it fucking meant and he was right.

'Nothing. It's just...you always do what you want...Fuck anyone else.'

'I don't.'

'Yeah, you do, look at you! Just gonna' hang around this place all day with your creepy drug dealer friend!'

'He's not my friend,' I replied childishly, scowling at him and his accusing eyes.

'Why'd you hang about with him then?' Michael cried, throwing up his arms in frustration. 'He's an old man Danny. It's not right! And you and that bloody club!'

I felt myself shrinking under the blanket. I could see it all in his face, everything I had known was there all along, everything that I deserved. 'What about it?'

'You working for Howard. I don't get it.'

'He pays me.'

'There is no amount of money worth working for him for,' Michael snapped. 'You hate the guy, or you should do after what he did to Anthony. I don't know how you can stand to be around him.' He slipped his arms through his jacket and zipped it up. He looked so dark and angry and sulky, he reminded me of the boy I'd watched from the window all that time ago. I just stared down and said nothing. What the hell could I say? I'd just fucked him up with drugs and he was taking his bad mood out on me. No problem. Come on, I felt like saying, give me some more. Come over here and pound my face in. It's no less than I deserve.

He sighed and opened the door. 'It's just..look I'm sorry Danny okay? It's just I think there's something going on here, but you just don't wanna' see it. You just wanna' stay high and not talk about anything. We never talk about anything anymore.'

'What do you mean, something's going on?' I asked him quietly.

'It doesn't matter, forget it,' he said, shaking his head and stepping out onto the yellow landing outside the door. 'Look I'm gonna' find Jake and Billy and go down the beach or something. That's where we'll be, if you can tear yourself away from this wonderful place.'

I didn't say anything else. I just watched him go. And then I was alone. The flat was cold and silent and my bones throbbed under my skin. I closed my eyes and let it all go because I had to. I turned my mind to other things. Like music, and a little shot of whisky to warm me up. Anything to make it all go away.

4

It was kind of horrible knowing that Anthony was back. I showed my true cowardly colours and stayed away. I knew neither of them would come to the house with Howard around, so I was safe. I took a few days off school and spied on them from the bathroom window. If I stood on the toilet and cracked open the top window, I could see their house. I watched the day he arrived back home in the back of a yellow taxi and Michael burst out of the front door to receive him. I held my breath, watching them. It felt like I was sharing the moment with them. Michael threw himself at his brother and they stood like that on the front path, locked and still. I could see Michael's black hair waving in the wind. Anthony had his head lowered on top of his. Mrs Anderson paid the taxi driver and carried two bags into the house. They all went inside together, Michael with his arm around Anthony's waist, and then the door closed on me.

I knew he would call me soon after and I was right. The phone rang in the hallway while I was still in the bathroom. I came out onto the landing and saw Howard stood there, a strange look upon his face.

'They hung up,' he said, and he started coming up the stairs towards me. 'Funny that.' He nodded to the open bathroom window. 'Close that, you're letting all the cold in.'

I walked back into the bathroom and reached up to pull the window shut. He made his move while I had my back to him, his fist shooting into my kidneys. I grunted and hit the floor, pain exploding up the back of me. He used his cowboy boot to push me over onto my back, and so I lay there and stared up at him, dazed and numb.

'I wouldn't think about going over there if I were you,' he said, his voice a dreamy drawl, his beady eyes all glassy. 'That man's a criminal. People like that never change. He'll be up to no good again before long. You stay away, right?'

I nodded back at him. I wanted to tell him that Anthony was no criminal. I wanted to scream up at him to leave them alone, to never go near them again. He held his hand out to me, and I took hold of it reluctantly and let him pull me up to my feet.

'Good boy,' he said, and patted the back of my neck. There was a loose and drowsy smile upon his face and his eyes looked far away. 'Washing machine just finished,' he said. 'Go and get it out on the line while it's sunny.'

I did what he said, but when it was done, I ran up the stairs and back to the bathroom window. I stood there and watched for hours, and if I heard Howard or my mother, I would just flush the toilet and come back out. Towards the end of the day I saw them all out the front. Anthony was leaning against the wall and lighting up a cigarette. Michael had his hands in his pockets and this endless burning smile upon his face. Jake and Billy were there, laughing and grinning, all of them chatting animatedly. It put this pain inside of me which grew and grew, and it was far worse than the blow to my kidneys. I was completely on the outside and Howard had made it very clear that I needed to keep it that way. They looked like they were heading back inside, but at the last moment Anthony stopped and stared right back up at my house. I was sure he couldn't see me. But he smiled.

I avoided them and kept my distance. Billy showed up after school one day, looking all nervous and jumpy as I let him in the back door.

'Mike's worried about you,' he hissed, his freckled hands tightly gripping the strap of his school bag, as his eyes shot about the kitchen anxiously. Howard and my mother were in the lounge watching TV. I shrugged at him, conveying my confusion. He rolled his eyes. 'You're not at school. You can't be sick all the time. What's going on?'

'Nothing,' I said. 'How's Anthony?'

'Fine,' he grinned, his shoulders relaxing slightly. 'He wants to see you, but he can't come over here can he? What about you meet us at the base, or the beach or something?'

I thought about it for a moment. I wondered if any of them knew that Lucy and I met at the beach every Sunday without fail, and had done since the day of my mother's wedding. It was a secret, though I didn't exactly know why it was.

'I'll try,' I said, just to appease him. He looked like he wanted to say more, but then decided against it. I didn't feel the same around Billy and Jake anymore, and I had a hunch that it was a mutual thing. They didn't know what to say to me half the time. They didn't like to smoke weed anymore. Jake was always busy, rushing from school to his job, and then to his flat to get his school-work done. He was taking it all very seriously, I suppose, life and school and work and getting somewhere. I was sure he thought I would drag him down somehow. He was pensive in my presence, and gave me the feeling that he was biting his tongue the entire time, not telling me what he really thought. It's all coming to an end, I thought, and said goodbye to Billy.

Two days later I had to go back to school. I went in alone, as ever. Headphones on, eyes down. I didn't get very far across the playground before Michael caught up with me, grabbing my elbow and bundling me away from everyone else. I caught a glimpse of Jake and Billy lingering in the background, hands in pockets and expressions cautious. Michael held onto my arm and looked very serious, so I pulled off my headphones.

'All right?'

'We know why you haven't been around, but that's fine,' he said.

'Right. Okay.'

'Look, Anthony wants to see you, he *needs* to see you. I've filled him in on everything!'

I frowned at him and started walking again. He walked with me. 'What's everything?'

'You know, Howard marrying your mum, buying the house and the entire club, and about the way Freeman turned up exactly the day Anthony was set up.' Michael glanced over his shoulder at Billy and Jake who were following from a safe distance. 'It's all very convenient, don't you think? And then Howard keeps you away from us, and Freeman gives you drugs and shit. I was telling Anthony, he said for fucks sake, get you over to see him *now*! He's really worried about you Danny, *really* worried. We all need to get together and talk.'

I stopped walking and shoved my hands into my pockets. I nodded at Billy and Jake. 'What's their problem these days?'

'Hey? Oh, forget it, don't worry. They're just being babies. They think you're always high. I've gone mad at them lately.'

'Don't do me any favours,' I retorted angrily. 'Tell 'em it's my life and I can do what I want if it makes me happy.'

The Boy With The Thorn In His Side-Part 2

Michael was frowning heavily. He shifted his bag from one shoulder to the other and appeared restless.

'Forget about that, that's not important. Anthony wants to see you mate. He doesn't blame you, you know, not one little bit. You know that right? He just wants to see you mate, just please, please say you'll come over or something.'

'It's not safe to,' I told him. He opened his mouth to argue, but I put my headphones back on and walked away from him.

That Friday night I felt far away from all of it. I was at the club, out the back, washing glasses with my shirt sleeves rolled up above my elbows. Towers of glasses stood next to me, waiting to be dunked into the hot soapy water. Howard was very particular about the glasses. He would appear in the kitchen sporadically throughout the night, lifting a wine glass up to the light to check for smears or fingerprints.

Every now and then someone would yell at me to go out and collect some more, and so I would dry my hands and roll down my sleeves, and go back out into throng of writhing, bustling punters that filled the club. I would never really see or notice them, as I slipped between their bodies to retrieve the empties. They were nothing more than moving, shifting shadows of people, whose voices became lost beneath the thumping music and whose faces were blurred by the darkness.

The only thing that reached me, the only thing that could sometimes break through, was the music, if the music was good. I hadn't given up trying to suggest songs to the Friday night DJ, although most of the time he just rolled his eyes at me and turned away. That night though, as I reached in between a group of men to retrieve their pint glasses, I heard the opening chords of Supersonic ripping up the speakers. It came out of nowhere, taking everyone by surprise, and as the electricity shot down my spine I could feel the people rushing past me to get to the dance floor. I paused and stared at nothing, my eyes bloodshot and huge, my pulse leaping in my veins. The people knew all the words; they all sung along. They all thought it was about them. They jumped about and roared it into each other's faces; they *needed* to be themselves! Pure rock and roll, I thought, utterly dazed by the simplicity of it.

I bobbed my head slowly up and down, mouthing the words to the song I had requested. And then I felt a presence close behind, and became dimly aware of someone leaning in towards me. I felt a warm, rough hand close around my wrist, tugging and pulling me away. I wanted to resist, because I needed the music, and then I heard Jack's voice in my ear, raspy and hoarse.

'Quick word?'

I felt vague. I'd had a smoke earlier, and the world looked soft and fuzzy around the edges. I let him tug me along, and I could see him looking at me, sort of squinting down at me, as if he needed glasses but could not be bothered to wear them.

'We've got a little problem,' he started to say. 'With our arrangement? Think Lee is getting suspicious and that's no good.' I stared back at his face, trying and failing to absorb what was being said. 'You with me?' he asked. 'Thing is, I can't risk him finding out, so I've found you another supplier, how's that? Nothing changes. It's just you deal with someone else, all right?'

Jack pushed through the double doors that led out to a small corridor. The men's toilets were just to one side, and to the other, a winding staircase which led up to the next floor and the women's toilets. Two young men were talking to each other, leaning up against the wall. When we came through, one of them immediately pulled away and slouched on up the stairs, not looking back. The other man was thin and wiry, with an England baseball cap pulled down low on his head. He wore pale blue jeans, Adidas trainers and a Ben Sherman shirt. He nodded at Jack.

'Jaime,' said Jack, looking down at me. 'Danny, this is Jaime all right mate? He can take care of you, all right?'

I didn't understand. Not one little bit. I just looked blankly from one man to the other. Jack sighed and shook my shoulder a little.

'Tell Jaime what you need yeah? He'll sort you out. I need a drink.' He clapped me on the back and left us to it, pushing back through the double doors.

The young man in the baseball cap leaned towards me in a very conspiring way, with a half-smile on his thin lips. He had a very bony angular face, a bit like a pale rectangle, all sharp corners, and his eyes were a murky sea of grey.

The Boy With The Thorn In His Side-Part 2

'All right mate?' he asked me, but there was no real interest in those grey eyes. 'Danny yeah?' I nodded at him, because this was something I did know the answer to. 'Bit of whizz?' he asked, in a far lower tone. 'That all you need tonight?'

'Oh, yeah,' I said, suddenly finally my voice as I remembered what I had been looking forward to all day. 'That's right, yeah.'

'No problem mate.' He stepped closer to me, until our arms were touching, and then he took my hand and shook it in his, pressing something smooth and plastic against my palm. I grasped it and he pulled back, touched the brim of his cap and winked at me.

'I don't get paid 'til later,' I remembered.

He slipped his hands into his pockets and shrugged his loose, lanky shoulders at me. 'It's all right. I'll still be around later. Tenner yeah?'

'Ten? It's normally five!'

'Tonight it's ten, sorry mate,' he said with another loose limbed shrug, as he turned away from me. 'Seeya' later mate.'

I turned around and pushed my way back into the club. The good song had ended. Some awful banal dance track had replaced it. I worked my way back through the crowds, picking up glasses, until I found myself back in the kitchen. I ran a fresh sink of water and placed the glasses next to it. Then I took the wrap and pushed myself into the small space between the fridge and the window. I didn't have any papers on me, so I decided to just lick the powder off the Clingfilm. I stayed where I was for a few minutes afterwards, and I zoned out, just imagining the speed working its way down through my digestive system. I was not sure exactly what had just happened out there, but as usual I decided to not pay it much thought. What was the point? I had what I needed, that was the main thing.

Moments later I felt better. Brighter. Quicker. I found my Walkman in my jacket pocket and put it on. I had a big smile eating up my face while I washed the dishes singing along to 'Whatever'. Howard was stressed that night. I picked up on it as soon as he barged aggressively into the kitchen to find me. I pulled down the headphones and pressed stop on the Walkman. His big face was flushed red and rolling with beads of sweat. He gave me a withering look, his hands on his hips.

'You need to be quicker! I don't pay you to stand out here fucking dancing! Get back out there and collect some more! Just had a load go crash out there, fucking glass everywhere!'

'Okay,' I said, realising that although I had pressed stop, the music was still playing in my head. How amazing was that? I could still hear those beautiful violins, and it made me sway my head from side to side as I walked.

'What's the matter with you?' he asked me.

I stopped. 'Um, nothing, I'm fine! I'm fine, and having a good time, why, aren't you?'

'No,' he said, slowly and darkly. 'I'm not as it happens. Are you drunk? You're acting like you're drunk. You better not be fucking drunk!'

I couldn't stand still. I was trying not to make faces as my feet danced me from one to the other. 'I'm not drunk,' I assured him. 'I can stay at Jack's tonight yeah?'

'No, you can't,' he shook his head. 'Your mum wants you home.'

'Oh. Why?'

'Because she's had the school on the phone again, complaining that you're never there!' He pushed his face towards mine as he spoke, and his small eyes seemed to roll around in his head like marbles. I stared at them, transfixed. 'The truant's officer and a teacher are coming over at some point to speak to you. You need to be there.'

'Oh,' I said, attempting a sheepish smile. 'Whoops.'

'I haven't got time to discuss this now,' he snapped then, rubbing the heel of one hand into his shiny forehead. 'Get out there and get some more bloody glasses!'

At the end of the night, Jaime Lawler was still hanging about, sat at the bar nursing the dregs of a pint and keeping his slate grey eyes on me the entire time. I started to sweat a bit down my end of the bar, where I was gulping coke like I had never known thirst before. I started to shit myself that Howard wouldn't pay me as he usually did, and this strange sea-eyed fellow would come loping over to me to demand his money.

Just as I was working up a real shaky little panic about it, Howard passed by and dropped two ten-pound notes onto the bar in

The Boy With The Thorn In His Side-Part 2

front of me. Jaime Lawler lolled forward from his stool, and made his move. He slid in beside me, and before I even knew what was happening, he had closed his hand over one of the notes and slipped it into his own pocket. I looked at his face and he met my bewildered expression with an eerie smile and faded eyes that peered out from beneath his cap.

'Thanks mate,' he said. 'Here's my number if you need anything.' He left a piece of paper on the bar and walked out.

I was still happy and buzzing when I got home and fell into bed. My mum was nearly always asleep when we got back. I put my music on low, going for Definitely Maybe yet again, needing to hear it in its entirety after having Supersonic ripped away from me at the club. Nowhere near sleep, I bounced up and down on my bed like an over excited child. I felt wired; every nerve and cell in my body alive and humming with energy. My heart beat like a drum in time with the music. I had about a million really important and intelligent things I wanted to say, to anyone, to everyone! I decided to write them down, and I wrote and wrote until I had rubbed a blister onto my finger. I still felt good. Like the King of Happiness, bouncing around on my bed, playing album after album, just like that. I devoured every single lyric sung, gobbling them up, along with every note played, every screech of the guitar, every beat of the drum. I devoured all of it and I felt myself glowing from the inside.

In the morning my mother started rapping urgently at my door, and as I stared at it, and at the sunshine outside my window, and at the piles and piles of loose paper floating around my bed, it dawned on me with slow and nervous horror, that I had not slept at all. All I could do was stare at the door she pounded on, totally confused, trying to picture myself spread out asleep, or curled up under my duvet, but the pile of tapes on the floor, and the ridiculous amount of paper, told a different story. I had stayed up all night. Okay, I reminded myself, it was okay, it was Saturday. I could sleep all day if I wanted. I would fall asleep at some point. It was just a matter of time. I tried to think then, clawing my way back to the moment in the kitchen. How much had he sold me? The same amount or more? Had I taken too much?

She came in then, suddenly and intrusively, and she hurt my head with her screeching and wailing, as she moaned on and on about how the truant's officer had tracked her down. 'Like a criminal!' she was crying at me, her eyes all wet and running.

'I'm not going there anymore!' I decided to tell her. I screamed it without meaning to. I was feeling all desperate and panicky and she was making everything worse. I wanted her out. I looked in desperation to the window, and thought seriously about jumping out of it, risking broken legs just to get the hell away from her face. I was shaking my head and rubbing my eyes, and trying to tell her that it would all be okay if she would just get the fuck out and let me sleep, but that made her worse. She started crying really hard, and the noise in my head was so bad it felt like the walls were coming down on me, and I had the constant urge to shield my head with my arms. I felt like I was going to be buried, so I started throwing things at her.

And then what happened next was mostly a relief, because Howard came storming in blowing out his breath like a bull, and he told her to get out, and she did, and he kicked the door shut and then I felt his hand around my throat. I laughed at him, because it was all so fucking funny, and he was hissing at me through his little spiky shark teeth, and I could see him changing into this huge wet snake, writhing and gleaming on my bed. I laughed at the snake through my constricted throat, and this sound made him wild, and the fear of it all was eating its way through my bones, one by one, and when the snake pounded me in the stomach, it was a relief. I was relieved, because when the pain arrived, it was familiar, and it was a comfort, and it made sense, and it made everything else just fall away. I finally fell asleep when the snake had gone. The steady throbbing of my gut took over where the music had ended.

The Boy With The Thorn In His Side-Part 2

5

I was in a mess all weekend. I could not eat. I smoked jittery cigarettes out of the window and gulped warm whisky when no one was looking. I felt terrible, like my body and my soul had been wrung out, twisted and distorted. Everything hurt. I felt nervous and on edge, unable to pinpoint exactly why it felt like the sky was about to come crashing down upon all of us. I couldn't concentrate on anything for more than a minute. I pulled my duvet over my head and shivered in the darkness for the entire day, sporadically breaking down into tears for no reason. My mum came in and out, and she was always crying too, and demanding to know what the hell was wrong with me, and should she call the doctor?

I felt my mouth stuffed full of a million things I would never be able to tell her and it felt like I was slowly choking on them, and it was too late, it was all too late. I could always see the shadow of Howard behind her, and I knew that all was lost, that everything was over. I became utterly convinced in my paranoia that they had done this to me on purpose. Jack and the guy in the baseball cap. They'd sold me something rotten and poisoned and now it was eating away at me from the insides. And Howard, he was the puppet master, controlling us all! He had decided chopping me up would be too messy, that poison was a far easier way to get rid of me. I was engulfed in this terrible blackness and could see no way out. The only solution I could think of was going to find the guy in the baseball cap and buying something else from him, something that would put me right, but I couldn't move. I was too terrified to leave the house.

Saturday night I slept badly. I became certain that there were dark people hiding within every shadow in my room. Howard's people. Watching over me. Keeping tabs, in case I thought about escaping. I hid under my duvet, trembling, hoping they would not find me there. On Sunday morning I woke up feeling sick. My stomach kept lurching and heaving, and my mouth kept filling with hot, yellow saliva, but there was nothing in my stomach to bring up. Howard came up to see me when my mother left the house. He breathed his fiery rage into my sweating face.

'Whatever drugs you've got yourself fucked up on, you better not bring it here again!' I sobbed my tears into the duvet while he stalked my room like a tiger in a cage. 'Your mother does not need to see this sort of thing! She does not need the stress! We'll have to ask for help if this carries on, we'll have to get the social involved. They have places for fucked up boys like you, you know. Kind of like prisons. I did warn you, didn't I? I've warned you so many times how close she is to giving up on you!'

'I have to get out,' I croaked, rising slowly from the bed and testing out the floor with my feet. I stood up, stiff and sore from the bruising to my middle, but I had suddenly remembered something, something important. Something that started to fill me up with an almost unbearable level of hope. 'Get some fresh air.'

'Good idea,' said Howard, folding his big arms across his chest. 'Don't come back until you are straight and then I want you to apologise to your mother.'

'I will, I will,' I chanted this gladly, pulling on the nearest jumper. 'I'll give you guys some peace, stay at a friend's yeah? I am never touching that shit again, not *ever.*' I pulled the jumper down and stared at Howard seriously. 'I mean it.'

I put on my headphones and ran all the way to the beach. I don't know where I found the energy or the strength, but it was there somewhere, lurking in my bones, swirling to life when I needed it, setting me on fire. The music helped. It always fucking helped. Liam's voice was in my ears as I ran as fast as I could, my stomach in my mouth, my guts churning as a desperate panic flooded my veins. He was telling me things I really needed to hear; maybe I would never be all the things that I wanted to be, but now was not the time to cry, now was the time to find out why! Why? *Why?* Lucy, Lucy, Lucy, it was her! She was the one, wasn't she? The one, the same as me! We saw things *they'd* never see! That was it, Liam was right! So, I ran and ran, and hoped and hoped, and she was gonna' be the one, me and her, we were gonna' live forever, live forever, live forever...

I was late and I knew it, so I ran faster and faster, gonna' live forever ...gonna' live forever...I was late, she would have gone, she

The Boy With The Thorn In His Side-Part 2

would have got up and walked away by now, she would have gone and given up on me like everyone else.

When I made it to the cliff top, I took the path down too quickly, nearly tripping over my own feet several times. At the bottom, I stopped and scanned the beach. I could not see her in the normal spot. I walked out onto the sand, and my legs felt fucked, like they were calling time, saying no, no, no more. I bent down, clutching my knees with my hands, scooping air back into my lungs as my chest rose and fell rapidly. When I looked up, I saw Michael standing just behind me, leaning against one of the beach huts. My mouth fell open and I gawked at him. He wasn't really there. He couldn't be. I was hallucinating now.

'You looking for Lucy?' he called out to me, and I nodded, dumbstruck, wondering if I was going crazy. I felt wrapped up tight in misery and darkness and I knew none of this was real. I was back in my bed and I was dying. 'At the shop,' he said, and jerked his thumb in the direction of the beach café and shop just to the right. I stared that way, and sure enough, there she was. A slim, brown haired girl coming out of the shop with a plastic carrier bag swinging from one hand. She saw me and waved. I thought she was an angel, a real-life angel, and we were gonna' live forever, me and her... I looked once more at Michael, who was fading out now, and then I looked back at her and started to run again.

When I finally reached her, I could barely stand. The run from home had taken everything I had. There was nothing left. It was all too much, and I collided with her, our bodies smashing together violently, and we fell down onto the sand together, and I saw her bottle of water fall from the bag and roll away. Her eyes were alarmed and she touched my face and pulled me close.

'Are you real?' I was asking her. I could see Michael again. He was standing over us. 'Are you both real?' I buried my head in her shoulder and started to cry. There was no stopping it. I cried like a baby. My face began to ache and my eyes stung and my throat grew raw as my shoulders shook, and still I could not stop crying. But it didn't matter anyway, I thought. It was a dream and I was back in my bed, and just dying. Lucy just held onto me and Michael was saying something softly above our heads.

'Shittinghell mate. Shittinghell.'

In the dream, they got me up and helped me walk. They sounded frightened and Michael kept saying; 'get him to Anthony, get him to Anthony.'

I tried to tell them things as we walked, and I sung some lyrics at them for a while. My feet felt thick and heavy when we stumbled in through the front door, and Anthony appeared like another angel, bright and tall and calm and resolute and he got me onto the sofa and told them to give me some space.

I was awful by then. Just shaking violently, my face screwed up in pain.

'All right take it easy,' he was saying to me. I couldn't open my eyes and look at him, I just couldn't. 'What's all this about then Danny? Eh? What you been doing to yourself mate?' He squatted down beside the sofa, his hand touching my arm. I curled up small, my knees drawn up to my chin, my arms wrapped tightly around my middle. 'Danny, what was it eh? What you been taking mate? Was it speed?'

I managed to nod, although I wasn't exactly sure if this was true. It was poison, I wanted to tell him, it was poison because they were trying to kill me.

'We should call a doctor,' Lucy said tearfully from across the room. 'He's ill!'

'Nah, he'll be all right,' Anthony replied calmly, rubbing my back. 'It's a bad comedown. Speed is the worst. If he took too much, or if someone sold him something dodgy.'

'But he's in pain!'

'He'll be okay soon enough, you'll see. It can take a few days sometimes. Danny, you should leave that shit alone mate. I'm serious. Not worth it eh, is it? Look at the state of you.'

'I did it with him once,' came Michael's voice, tense and guilty.

'Well it better only be once!' Anthony snapped back at him. 'I've told you before Mikey, grass is the only safe thing to mess with, and only then not too much.'

'I know, I'm sorry. I suppose I was just curious.'

'And?'

The Boy With The Thorn In His Side-Part 2

'Not worth it,' Michael said adamantly. 'Felt like shit the next day. Wanted to take someone's head off.'

I heard Anthony sighing beside me. 'Well learn your lessons boys,' he said. 'This is fucking outrageous. These people are evil. He's gonna' get himself killed!'

'What're we gonna' do?' asked Michael in a small voice.

Anthony sighed again. 'Right,' he said. 'Make some tea and toast. Get him to eat and drink. Then he'll feel better. Then just keep him here until he's straight again.'

'What about Howard? What if they come looking for him?'

'We haven't seen him. And I answer the door. Might as well let him know I'm back again. But he can't know we've seen Danny. He can't know we're involved, got it?'

A short while later I opened my eyes, and only Anthony was there. He was sat on the edge of the sofa, right next to me. He smiled down at me and placed his hand on my shoulder.

'You're back,' I croaked at him.

He nodded. 'Time flies, eh? Now I'm back, you don't need to worry okay? You don't need to be doing all this shit again.'

I had to close my eyes. The pain was coming and going in waves. 'Ahhh, shit it hurts...' I moaned, pressing my face back into the cushion.

'It's okay, just relax,' he told me. 'When did you take it?'

'Hurts...'

'I know mate, I know.'

'Anthony?'

He leaned over me. 'What is it mate?'

I wanted to tell him everything then. I wanted to tell him all the things Howard had said and threatened, about how he ended up back in jail, about Michael disappearing, about killing my mum. I opened my mouth and struggled to bring the words up and out, but the pain got worse again, ripping through my stomach muscles.

'It's in my stomach!' I panted, curling up even tighter. He rubbed my back again. 'It's in my stomach Anthony...they poisoned me...it's in there and it's killing me!'

'It'll get better,' he told me very firmly. 'You just have to remember this Danny. Remember how bad this is and never fucking do it again, all right? Who gave it to you eh? This Freeman bloke Mike's been telling me all about?'

'Someone else...' I shook my head. 'It's all gone in my stomach...I can feel it...it's killing me Anthony...'

'It's not killing you, I promise you. You're just coming down really badly. You took too much probably, and you haven't been eating properly by the look of you. You've just got a bad stomach and the comedown is making it worse. You'll be all right, I promise you. Just eat and drink something. Look, Mike's made you toast.'

I didn't want to eat anything, but they made me. They practically forced me, so I gave in. I ate half a slice of Marmite toast and drank half a cup of tea. It hurt even more after that, but Anthony had little sympathy left.

'You'll be all right you little twat,' he laughed and patted my back. 'You'll be just fine.'

I slept after that. It was a beautiful thing. Deep, black sleep that claimed me suddenly and blessedly. Every now and then I rose up out of it, felt the pain subsiding and slipped back under again. I was warm and safe and watched over. I could hear the TV on low, and the murmurs of their gentle voices. I was out cold when Howard came banging on the door, demanding to know where I was.

The Boy With The Thorn In His Side-Part 2

6

By Monday morning I felt better. I was all right again. Michael packed up his school bag and left the house. Anthony cooked me this huge breakfast with bacon, sausages, eggs, the works and came and sat on the sofa beside me while I tucked in. My stomach had finally stopped hurting and it was a massive relief. At one point I'd been completely convinced that I was dying. But Anthony had all the answers apparently.

'Bad drugs, no food,' he said, counting them off on his fingers, while his eyes rested on mine, dark and solemn, and looking at me as if he knew and understood everything. He reached across to me and lifted the edge of my t-shirt. I swatted his hand away instantly, but he made a face that told me he had already seen. 'Couple of right hooks to the stomach.' He shrugged, telling me it was simple and obvious. 'No wonder you were in pain mate. I'm surprised you were able to walk!'

I said nothing. I just stared right back at him, and he passed me a cigarette and lit it for me. I put my half-finished breakfast down on the floor and inhaled slowly, deeply.

'We need to talk,' he said softly. He was still staring at the edge of my t-shirt and his expression was reluctant and pained. I didn't want to talk to him, not really. Just sitting next to him was torturous, knowing what I knew. 'I saw when you were out cold,' he went on. 'So, it's still going on? When he gets mad or wants to lash out at someone? And your mum, she doesn't know?'

I smoked the cigarette, my eyes on the floor. Anthony sighed and stretched his legs out in front of him. What could I say? Yeah, things are bad, worse than you know, but look what happened the last time you tried to help me? I glanced at the door, remembering that Howard was out there, hunting me down as we spoke.

'Those other marks Danny,' Anthony said, nudging me with his elbow. 'Cigarette burns, aren't they?'

I looked right at him then. My bottom lip trembled so I bit down on it hard. 'You can't get involved Anthony,' I told him sharply. 'I mean it Anthony. You can't get involved. You only just got back out. You *have* to stay out of it. Stay out of everything.'

'You're right,' he said to me, smiling gently. 'I shouldn't get involved. I told Howard that much when he hammered on the door last night, looking for you. You know, he asked if I'd learnt my lesson, how do you like that? I told him I had. I told him it pays to mind your own business these days.'

'Yeah,' I nodded at him. 'That's right.'

'It's not right,' he disagreed. 'And I can't do that. I can't ever do that.'

I swallowed and glanced at the door again. I thought about getting up and running out, getting away from him before it was too late. My legs felt weak though, so I dragged on my smoke and tapped it against the ashtray when Anthony held it out to me.

'You have to,' I told him, and when I looked at him I just hoped and prayed that he could see it there in my eyes, how deadly serious I was. 'I mean it, Anthony. You don't know what he's capable of. Do you want Michael to end up hurt? Or worse? He's threatened it you know, and he has people that can do it, he told me.' I licked my dry lips and my hand shook as I lifted the cigarette back to my mouth. Anthony sat forward, waiting for me to say more. 'I'm serious,' I nodded at him. 'I wouldn't joke about this, but Mike could end up dead if you mess with Howard, if you piss him off again. I've got to go. I shouldn't even be here, it'll get you all in trouble.' I stubbed out the cigarette and started to push up from the sofa, but Anthony was having none of it. He caught my arm and eased me gently back down.

'Don't be silly, you're not going anywhere yet. Sit.'

I sagged back into the sofa, pressing my hands against my face for a moment and groaning softly behind them.

'Just stay a minute yeah?' he said to me. 'Just talk with me a minute. He doesn't know you're here.' I nodded and shrugged and dropped my hands down onto my knees. 'We said we hadn't seen you,' he told me. 'And I think he believed me. I said you and Mike don't even hang about together anymore, and he seemed to swallow it. But Mike says that's pretty much true anyway?' I shrugged again. 'Such a shame. You're such good mates. He'd do anything for you, you know?'

'I don't want him to get hurt,' I said, staring at nothing. 'He lost you for an entire year, because of me.'

The Boy With The Thorn In His Side-Part 2

'No, not because of you, you idiot, because of Howard and possibly this other guy Freeman. Tell me about him. Where'd he come from? Who is he?'

'Friend of Howard's. From way back.'

'Jack Freeman, right?' I nodded in reply. 'So, what's he like?'

'He's all right,' I said. 'He's nothing like Howard, I mean. He just lets me hang out at his flat and listen to music and stuff. Most the time he isn't even there.'

'Okay,' Anthony said slowly, nodding at me. 'So, he lets you come to his flat and listen to music and smoke weed and stuff? Okay, but why, why would he do all that?'

I could feel the force of indignation and suspicion behind his gaze, and I shifted uncomfortably on the sofa.

'I dunno,' I replied. 'I dunno why people do things.'

'You should think about it Danny. He's Howard's friend, right? Doesn't that seem weird to you in any way? Does Howard know he gets you drugs and stuff?'

'No,' I shook my head quickly. 'That's why someone else sold me speed on Friday, 'cause Jack thinks Howard is getting suspicious or something. He thinks he'll throw him out.'

'Throw him out? So what, he's in Howard's flat is he?'

'I dunno. Must be.'

'See, weird?' Anthony sounded almost pleased. 'He lets this guy move in his old flat, and suddenly this guy is palling around with you, giving you drugs and shit. Does that not seem weird to you Danny? Don't you see what they're doing?' I stared at the floor again, my mouth tight and my nostrils working. I knew he spoke sense, and I could see what he was doing, putting all the pieces of the puzzle together in his own mind, and his dark eyes were alive with knowing and this fierce kind of energy. 'Who sold you the speed on Friday then? Who was that? You remember his name?'

'Jaime someone,' I told him with a sigh. 'Skinny guy, about your age.'

'I know of a Jaime about my age,' he said, talking faster and louder. 'He's one of the Lawlers. They're this terrible family of losers on the Somerley estate. Jaime is a bit older than me, but one of his brothers was in my class at school. Bunch of crackheads and criminals. Makes sense they'd have someone like him on board.'

'Look Anthony, I really better get going, if he comes back here or sees me leaving...'

'Hang on, we need to figure this out. When did Freeman show up here? Can you remember?'

Of course I could remember. That day was etched inside my mind forever. Me hiding behind the sofa, while they talked and laughed and enjoyed the spectacle of Anthony's arrest from the bathroom window. I felt horrible and sick inside. I wanted to go. I didn't know how he could bear to be near me.

'It was the day you got arrested,' I said then, and even as I spoke the words I wondered what I was doing, giving him that information. His eyes were glowing and his body tensed beside mine. The bad memories were trying to get back into head, knocking on the window of my mind like petulant ghosts. I didn't want to think about any of it. To be honest, all I really wanted to do right then was go and get stoned somewhere. 'I came back from the base,' I said, not looking at Anthony. 'I fell asleep in the lounge and when I woke up I heard Howard and this guy...Jack. I could hear sirens and stuff. I hid. I didn't know what the hell was going on. Then Jack left. And Howard found me.'

Anthony shifted restlessly on the sofa, and for a moment he covered his mouth with both of his hands. 'I've got to think,' he spoke through his fingers. 'I've got to be so careful.'

'You think it will happen again?' I asked him. 'I mean, if they got rid of you like that once, they can do it again, right?' I looked at him and my mouth was sucked free of moisture. Anthony looked back at me.

'It was them,' he said firmly. 'You know that, don't you?'

I nodded. 'He told me. He told me he got rid of you and he'd do the same to anyone else that stuck their nose in. That's why you've got to stay out of it, you *have* to. You can't do anything, Anthony, you really can't. Mike can't lose you again!' I bowed my head, unable to look him in the eye any longer. The tears were swimming, threatening to fall. I sniffed. 'I'm sorry Anthony. I'm so, so sorry.'

The Boy With The Thorn In His Side-Part 2

Anthony twisted to face me and clamped his hand down onto my shoulder. 'You can't let it drag you down,' he told me fiercely. 'You listen to me. It wasn't your fault. Not any of it. Okay?'

'Michael lost you for a year, because of me...you were locked up! Because of me.'

'Because of Howard, not you. And maybe this other guy.'

'I feel so shit about it...If you hadn't tried to help me, if I hadn't told you anything...'

'Listen to me, I stuck up for you because I like you okay? I couldn't stand the thought of that fucking gorilla giving you a hard time. Okay, I'll admit I had no idea who I was messing with...but that's not your fault right? None of this is your fault Danny.' He stared right into my eyes and did not flinch. He stared at me until I nodded back miserably. 'You've got to listen to me mate, or all this is gonna' drag you down and finish you off, I mean, look what's happened to you in a year! You look a mess mate. You look like you don't give a shit about anything. You have to understand something, all right. They're the adults, you're the kid, so none of this, fucking none of it is your fault. That man is evil. And I'll bet we don't even know the half of it.'

I managed to smile and nod at him. There was a sort of lightness filling me slowly. Just knowing that he did not blame me was an amazing feeling. I felt a little bit like I had been untethered, set free.

'Okay,' I told him. 'Thanks.'

'Don't thank me yet,' he replied, getting to his feet. 'We're up to our necks in it. But we've got to figure something out, bring them down somehow. But he can't know we're up to anything. He can't know anything or we're fucked. Maybe we start digging around a bit, yeah? Play detective. Play it smart. I got one idea already.'

'What?'

'I'll track down Lawler. If he's who I think he is he won't be too hard to find. He knows me. Might be able to score some grass off him and get him talking.'

The thought of it flooded me with fear. I shook my head. 'Anthony...'

'Don't worry about it, don't even think about it,' he commanded me. 'All you have to do is keep your head down and stay off them drugs, yeah? You'll feel better then. You'll be useful to us then. So no more silly stuff, all right? Because all you're doing is playing right into their hands, you know. They've had an easy ride for a year, if you think about it. Me inside. You apart from your mates, spaced out, not questioning anything, not fighting back.' He laughed a little and gave me a playful punch in the shoulder. 'What about that eh? You forgot about all that didn't you? The old Danny eh? The boy Mike was always telling me about, getting arrested at school for fighting! Giving people hell. What happened to him eh? We need him back man. You gotta' get him back.'

After lunch Anthony announced that he was going to have a bath.

'Do all my best thinking in there,' he grinned.

He had been up there for twenty minutes or so, when I decided to leave. I should have told him or called up to him, but I didn't. I thought he would try to stop me. I couldn't stay there a minute longer. I'd been growing jumpier by the second, thinking about Howard, still storming around out there looking for me. So, I walked to Jack's, and I took the long way around so that no one would see me.

I walked with my head lowered and my hands in my pockets. The Smiths were playing on my Walkman. It was the kind of song that made me want to wallow in sadness and despair, and that was pretty much what washed over me as I walked. That Joke Isn't Funny Anymore. Listen to it some time. Then you will know. I heard children laughing, and I realised that I had just wandered carelessly through a whole bunch of them on the pavement. I guessed they were heading to the fish and chip shop for their lunch. One of them called out to me and I pulled the headphones down curiously.

'Danny?'

It was Higgs. Eddie Higgs. He was in the middle of the group, and he was staring back at me, his expression wondering, a slow smile lifting his lips. It was weird looking at him. My old adversary, the boy who had been the cause of so many of those explosive fights with my mother. I felt a detached kind of curiosity, nothing more, but it made me see that Anthony was right. I wasn't the same boy anymore. I was

The Boy With The Thorn In His Side-Part 2

a shell. An imprint of who I had once been. I saw him smiling and nudging the other kids. I suddenly felt horribly aware of the clothes I had been wearing since Friday and of how awful I must look. I couldn't bear to see any trace of satisfaction on his face, so I turned quickly and kept walking. I pulled my headphones back on so I would not have to listen to their laughter following me down the pavement.

I let myself into Jack's flat with the key he had given me. He was home. Slumped in one of the tatty sofas, whisky in one hand, fat cigar in the other. He was watching Countdown. I paused at the door, my head suddenly full of Anthony's questions, and Jack and I eyed each other warily across the room. He puffed on his cigar.

'Well you look like hell,' he said finally.

I shrugged at him. 'That guy sold me something bad. I've had the worst comedown ever.'

Jack merely chuckled at me. 'Bit dramatic ain't it? No such thing as bad stuff mate, you just probably took too much. Just ask Jaime for some downers next time. Take the edge off when you come back down.'

I shook my head and walked across the lounge and into the kitchen to put the kettle on. 'I'm not touching any of that stuff ever again,' I said.

He laughed again from the sofa. 'Whatever you say kiddo. It's your life.'

I grabbed the kettle and filled it with water. The area around the sink was cluttered and overcrowded with dirty plates and cups, and piled high with takeaway wrappers and containers. The window was closed, holding the unique smell of boozy sweat and chicken tikka-masala hostage in the airless room. I shuddered and wondered what the hell I was doing back there. Why had my legs walked me there like some kind of robot, instead of walking me somewhere decent, like the record shop, or to Lucy? I found the cup I always used, the cracked cream one with the black Labrador on the side. The teabags lived in a metal tin next to the kettle. I rummaged around in it, found one in the dust at the bottom and dropped it into my cup. I took the milk from the fridge, checked the date on the side and then sniffed it just to be sure. I heard Jack clear his throat of phlegm.

'Lee's looking for you, you know,' he called out. 'You're meant to be at home he reckons, seeing some people to do with school?'

I'd forgotten all about that. I folded my arms in the doorway and waited for the kettle to boil. 'He wasn't very happy with me all weekend. I was in a total mess.'

'You just need downers. Told you.'

'No. Never again.'

'You won't be wanting this back then?' He picked up my little tin from the coffee table. He waved it back and forth in the air. I rolled my eyes, went to make my tea, and then carried it into the lounge and sat down on the sofa. Before he could say anything else, I picked up my tin and shoved it into my pocket. He laughed out loud. I stared at the TV.

'This is Howard's place, right?'

I felt his eyes turn on me, measuring my question. 'Yeah, it is yeah.'

'You rent it off him then?'

'That would be the name of the arrangement, yes young man. Why the sudden interest?' I looked his way to see that ever present soft smile upon his lips and I felt immediately stupid. I had said too much, too soon. We never really talked much, so I had to be careful not to make him suspicious. I drank my tea for a while, saying nothing. When Jack poured himself another whisky, he grabbed the rim of an empty glass sitting on the table and filled that one as well. He passed it to me and I took it without even thinking about it. It was just habit, that's all. Sitting there with him, getting wasted. I couldn't deny the urge was as strong as ever.

'Would Howard kill you if he knew about the speed and shit?' I ventured some time later when the whisky had stoked up my bravado and my curiosity. Jack turned his calm eyes upon me again.

'Who knows?' he replied with a sigh. 'But it's the thought of your mother finding out that terrifies me the most.'

'So why do you then?'

'Why do I what?'

'Why do you sell it to me?'

'I don't. Not anymore.'

The Boy With The Thorn In His Side-Part 2

'But you have,' I argued. 'You did, until Friday.' I knew I was pressing him, pushing him too far, but I felt desperate and impatient. I wanted something to take back to Anthony so that he would not have to risk going out to look for it himself.

'Look,' Jack sighed again. 'I don't give a shit what other people do, as long as it don't bother me, right? Live and let live and all that. Take it if you wanna' take it, don't if you don't, it's no skin off my nose either way.'

'And now you're worried that Howard would be mad? If he knew about it?'

Jack stared at me then, and his eyes were narrowed and he ran his tongue slowly over his lower lip before he broke out into a smile again.

'I think you need to look at yourself Danny,' he advised. 'No one forced you to take anything, not once. If you don't want to do things, then don't. It's your life buddy. But I never heard you complaining about any of it until now, so what's changed? One bad comedown?'

'Howard doesn't know?' I asked him once more. I had finished the whisky and it had loosened my tongue. I felt like I was walking along a tightrope, trying to keep my balance while certain death waited for me on either side. I could sense the danger in the air and I understood it.

'Why don't you ask him yourself?' Jack said. 'He'll be here any minute.'

The air in a room always seemed to alter when Howard walked in. It smelled different and it clung to the skin. I thought about leaving, but where could I go? Not back to Anthony. I couldn't risk leading them back there. My mind wandered helplessly as I sat there. What was to stop them setting Anthony up again? If they had done it once, surely they could do it again?

When Howard finally arrived, he just strode on in as if he owned the place. He walked in big angry strides and tossed his car keys onto the glass topped coffee table with a bang that made me jump. He stood like a tree, legs spread and head cocked.

'Where the fuck have you been?' he demanded. 'I've been everywhere looking for you. You've not been at the record shop, or at

Billy's. You better not have been with those Andersons.' He raised his eyebrows at me questioningly. '' Cause I thought I already warned you about that.'

'I wasn't there,' I said. 'I've been ill.'

'Yeah and that's your own fucking fault! Don't expect any sympathy off me!'

'True,' I nodded, glancing at Jack. 'But it's also his fault.'

Both men were staring at me now. I didn't really know what I was doing, or saying. I thought maybe they would kill me. Maybe they would just laugh at me. But I had to get something from them, anything to make things a little clearer. Howard nodded at the door. 'Come on,' he said. 'The truant's officer and a teacher are on the way over.'

'You don't really want me to speak to them,' I said, and my voice was a whisper, but they still heard it all right. I swallowed nervously as my throat began to tighten. Howard looked intrigued.

'Don't I?'

'I might have to tell them the truth about why I keep missing school,' I shrugged and glanced between them. I suddenly felt horribly small and vulnerable sat there with them staring at me. But I could definitely see the anxiety in their eyes. It was obvious, I thought. Howard knew, and he did not want to talk about it. Anthony was right.

'Come on, let's go,' he said coldly.

I rose up from the sofa. 'So you don't mind that Jack deals me drugs then?' I don't even know where the courage to ask the question came from, but there it was. And all Howard did was head to the door.

'What you two get up to is your business,' he snapped. 'I told you already. Just don't fucking do it in my house.'

'Okay,' I said, as we left the flat. 'I get it.'

We headed down the corridor and down the flight of stairs and I felt this little throb of fire burning in my gut. I wanted to smile and I wished that Anthony could have seen me then. We walked out into the sunshine and towards Howard's car, and I was just about to ask him what mum would think if I showed her my little tin and told her all about Jack, when Howard slipped an arm around my shoulders and pulled me into his side.

The Boy With The Thorn In His Side-Part 2

'You can tell your mum and these other people whatever the fuck you want,' he told me, as a thin cold smile stretched out his lips. 'But if I were you I would think about what happens to you next. 'Cause I know for a fact your mum is on the edge as far as you're concerned. It's only me that keeps talking her out of getting you put into care, you know. So you think what happens if they all know about your drug habits. Kicked out of school probably. Arrested again if the cops are called in. Third offence right? So you'd be up in court little man, with a pretty colourful record going ahead of you. All I have to do is suggest care would be a better place for you, and she'd jump at it mate. I'm telling you.'

He unlocked the car and opened the passenger side for me. He nodded down at the seat, so I slid in and stared back up at him. He grinned and leaned towards me, a glint in his eyes as he spun his car keys on one finger.

'Do you know what happens to boys your age when they go into care?' he asked and waited for an answer. I just stared back at him and shook my head as the heaviness of despair came crushing down on me yet again. My mouth had gone dry and my fire had gone out, and I already knew that I would not be telling anyone anything today. 'Pretty boys like you?' He was laughing at me now, licking his lips hungrily and revealing those neat rows of teeth. 'Let's just say, you'd get a very *warm* welcome Danny, do you get my drift? My brother found that out the hard way when he was a naughty little shit stain. My parents sent him to a place like that, so I know. You'd be eaten alive mate. A little blue-eyed kid like you. You'd be their fucking pet.'

He laughed out loud, slammed the door shut and walked around to his side. He climbed in, still laughing, and turned the key in the ignition. Then he slapped my thigh briskly and winked at me when I looked at him.

'There's something for you to think about anyway mate. That and the fucking shit that will come down on those Anderson cunts if you ever threaten me again.' His eyes burned down, his lips tight and small, all humour dissolved now, nothing but violent promise behind those eyes. 'Now shut the fuck up and be a good boy like I told you to be.'

The Boy With The Thorn In His Side-Part 2

7

When the lectures were over I slunk on up to my bedroom and closed my door on the murmurings that continued downstairs. I sat on my bed for a few strange minutes, staring at the door, the floor and the cracks in the ceiling. I stared at these the longest. I could identify with these. Eventually the silence started to hurt my ears so I leaned over and pressed play on the stereo. I smiled a little when the music started. It was The Doors Strange Days album, one of my oldest tapes. I could still remember where I bought it. A car boot sale back in Southampton, and I must have been about twelve years old. It was one of the very first albums I ever bought.

Listening to The Doors now felt sort of disjointed and nostalgic. It was like being able to see through a window to a younger me. What I remembered most was how angry I had always been back then. How I'd watched my mother spinning recklessly from one stupid boyfriend to the next. How John had just rolled his eyes and ignored it all, letting it all wash over his head. I realised that they were both gone now. I'd lost them both. And a spiteful little voice at the back of my head told me that this was my own fault; that I had pushed them too far too many times and this was why I was now all alone.

I took out my tin and rolled a quick joint. I wanted the pot to fill my head up with warmth and fuzz and detachment from everything. I wanted to lie back on my bed and drift into heavy sleep, not thinking or feeling anything. I wanted the fingers of fear to stop scrabbling inside of me. I got on my bed and smoked, and thought about the scene which had just transpired downstairs. The farce of care that had surrounded me. My distraught mother, wringing her hands and looking at me as if I had just been diagnosed with a terminal disease. Howard had done well. The man deserved an Oscar, the way he played the over protective, slightly stressed out father, with a constant look of strain etched upon his face. I felt like applauding him at times.

I had to put an end to it as soon as possible. I admitted I had tried a few things. I told them how awful it had been. I told them it was really stupid of me and I would never be doing it again. They believed me. I told them I was going to buckle down and do better at school, and stop skiving off with faked sick notes, and they believed me again. My mum even reached across the table to squeeze my hand as I babbled on. It didn't really matter what I said, so long as they bought it.

Back in my room I took deep satisfying drags on the spliff and reminded myself that it was over, and I was safe. I was not being shipped off to care any time soon. And that, I reasoned, was what it was all about at the end of the day. Staying safe. Doing what they wanted so I would be left alone. I felt bad about running out on Anthony and Michael, but I would go to school in the morning and explain it to them.

I fell asleep for a while. I woke up briefly when my mother called up that they were going into town and then I drifted off again. I woke up a second time because someone was banging on the front door. I sat up in bed, rubbing my face awake. I'd done a really stupid thing and fallen asleep with the ashtray and half smoked joint on my lap. I made sure it was out and placed the ashtray down on the floor. There was another knock at the door, followed closely by a female voice which called through the letterbox and trailed up the stairs to greet me.

'Danny? Danny! It's Lucy!'

What the hell? I laughed a little and headed for the door, shaking my hair from my eyes and wondering what she was doing here. I appeared on the landing and could see the letterbox pushed open in the hallway.

'Lucy?' I asked, coming quickly down the stairs. I pulled open the door. 'Hiya'!'

She grinned in relief and stepped quickly into the hallway. She was still in her school uniform with her bag upon her shoulder.

'Anthony's been looking everywhere for you!' she told me. I closed the door and shrugged apologetically. 'He sent me over to see if you were here. To see if you were okay.'

'Will you tell them I'm fine?' I asked her. 'I had to come home and get cleaned up and stuff, then I had a teacher and the truant's officer come over to see me.' I made a face and she made one back.

'Oh. Wow.'

'Yeah. Nightmare.'

The Boy With The Thorn In His Side-Part 2

'What did they say? What happened?'

'Oh, I did most of the talking,' I shrugged. 'I'll be back at school in the morning. You can tell Mike that as well. Tell him I'll meet him out on the main road.'

She smiled and her shoulders relaxed with it. 'Well that's a relief.'

I placed one foot on the stairs and smiled at her cheekily. 'You want to come up and listen to music with me?'

She looked surprised for a moment, her head moving back slightly and her eyes flashing.

'Okay then,' she grinned. 'Why not?' I took her hand and walked back upstairs, with her following behind me. Inside my room, I closed the door and she stood beside the bed, her school bag dangling at her ankles. She stared around, sort of frowning and smiling at the same time.

'What?' I asked her.

'It's just...' She broke off and let the bag thump to the floor. Her eyes ran along the length of my desk, up to my shelves on the wall and down to my bed. 'Wow. It's just so clean and tidy. I've never seen a room this tidy. You should see mine! My mum just closes the door on it. In fact, she tells me off if I leave the door open!'

Lucy laughed rather nervously and sat down on the edge of my bed. She appeared unsure and cautious. I didn't exactly blame her. Looking around my own room gave me the creeps most days as well. The desk was all ship shape, the way Howard commanded it. School books in piles, stereo at one end with cassettes stacked neatly beside. The books on my shelves were organised in height order, with the spines turned outwards. My bedside set of drawers, set out neatly with reading lamp, alarm clock and one book. My bed always made up and tucked in at every corner. No clothes or shoes lying on the floor. No piles of magazines or crumby plates, or half-drunk cups of tea. Everything in its place and a place for everything.

I sat down next to her. 'My step-dad is a bit of a clean freak,' I told her.

Her smile faltered just a little bit. I wondered what Mike and Anthony had told her. Did she know the whole sorry story, or did she just think I was a stupid druggy who took too much and practically had a breakdown on the beach? I looked at my hands resting on my knees and decided I didn't really want to know either way.

'So,' she said then, looking away briefly as her cheeks warmed up. 'You're okay now then? You're feeling better? You look better.'

'I'm fine,' I nodded at her. 'I'm really sorry about all of that. I've been a complete idiot.'

'You don't have to say sorry to me. I was just so worried, you know. Seeing you like that. You're not going to do any of that stuff again are you?'

I shook my head quickly. 'No way. Learnt my lesson. Promise.'

'Okay. Good.'

She didn't say anything for a while. I was glad. I liked that about her. She didn't feel the need to probe or lecture, or preach. You could see everything she was thinking and feeling right there on her face. I leaned towards her ever so slightly, until our arms were touching. We were both staring down at our knees. The Doors were still playing. I found my feet tapping along to the music. Lucy giggled then, and her hair fell over her ears and into her face. I giggled too and bumped my shoulder into hers. I was grinning like a lunatic. I had the urge to grab her and wrestle her down onto the bed. Tickle or kiss her, and try to make her giggle again.

'Who is this?' she asked me.

'The Doors. You heard of them?'

'Think so.'

'Sixties band,' I explained. 'Used to be really into them. Haven't listened to them in a while. Do you like it?'

'Yeah, it's good,' she nodded. 'Sort of…haunting.'

I laughed softly. 'Exactly.'

I moved back, pulling my legs up onto the bed and finding the pillow with my head. I patted the bed with my hand.

'Come on.'

She stared, her hair falling back over her face, her smile widening shyly. Then she took a little quick breath and pulled her legs up too. It was awkward for a moment or two. She was blushing like mad as she lay down beside me. And then I put my arm around her shoulder and she sort of snuggled into the side of me and rested her

The Boy With The Thorn In His Side-Part 2

head down on my chest. I wondered if she could hear my heart going totally crazy. She seemed to fit in so nicely there, tucked under my arm, curled into me. My feet were twitching with the music at the end of the bed. She sighed. We lay like that for a long time. I thought it was the best feeling in the world. I leaned down and planted a clumsy kiss on the top of her head, and she sighed again, and giggled. Look up, I wanted to say to her, look up, and I will kiss you properly.

The next morning, I met Michael out on Somerley road. He was smiling like crazy as I approached, hands in pockets and school bag across my chest. He slapped my back, bumping his body into mine, and then punching my shoulder while I laughed at him.

'For God's sake,' I complained. 'What you doing?'

'Ah it's just so good to see you,' he told me, as we checked the road for traffic and crossed it between cars. 'You know, properly. And being normal!'

I grimaced in regret. 'Yeah I'm sorry about all that Mike. Haven't had a chance to thank you and Anthony. You know. Everything you did.'

'No problem,' he shook his head. 'Any time. Although not again in a hurry please?'

'No way. I was a complete twat. I shouldn't have put any of you through that.'

'Shut up, it wasn't your fault you idiot.' He gazed down at the pavement as he walked and nudged me with his elbow. 'Come on.'

'Yeah, Anthony said that too, but it's not really the truth. No one forced me to take that stuff Mike. I could have said no.'

'Come on, seriously forget about it. You've had a crap year! Who can blame you for wanting to get off your face, right? Think I'd hit the hard stuff too if that psycho was my step-dad! Shittinghell. Anyway, listen, before we get to school, got loads to tell you. Anthony's been a busy boy.'

I looked at him sharply. 'What do you mean?'

'When he couldn't find you he went all over the place looking for you. Not just looking for you as it happens, looking for this Jaime bloke too?' Michael shook his hair from his face and glanced at me. I nodded at him, waiting for more. I started to chew at my lip. I was nervous enough as it was; heading back to school after everything that had happened lately, and now this. I hoped he hadn't placed himself in danger again. 'Well he found him. Jaime Lawler, whatever his name is. Bought a bit of weed off him to keep him happy. Poked around a bit you know? Went to school with his brother, so it was all pretty relaxed. They had a drink in The Ship together.'

'Really?'

'Yep. Anyway, turns out Jaime Lawler is the errand boy for Freeman. He works for him. And Anthony reckons both of them work for Howard.'

'Oh,' I said, stopping and pulling him back by his sleeve. 'That's something I learnt too Mike. Howard knows Jack deals. He knows he deals to me and he doesn't care.'

Michael stared back at me, his eyes penetrating with their intensity. He wettened his lips with his tongue and shook his head very slowly. 'That bastard. That filthy lying drug dealing bastard. We ought to go right to the cops Danny. We should tell them everything.'

I smiled at him gently. He looked so fierce I found it sort of touching.

'I've thought about that a million times,' I told him. 'Jack's a copper Mike. Or he was. I dunno. And Heaton, we already know he's chummy with Howard. I don't trust them. And you don't even want to know what he's threatened to do to you and my mum if we mess with them.' I swallowed the lump that had formed in my throat and started to walk on again.

Michael nodded as he followed. 'I know Danny, I know, I get it. We've got to be careful. Anthony says. He says, if we be careful and tread lightly, we can trip them up somehow. We need proof. That's what he said.'

'Billy and Jake,' I said, gesturing ahead. They were approaching the entrance to school from the other direction, pushing their bikes and talking excitedly. I smiled briefly at the sight of them. I thought how young and excited and innocent they looked. Jake saw me first and did an instant double take, before punching Billy on the arm and nodding in my direction. We met and fell into step together; the four of us again like old times, going through the school gates. I felt different though. I felt tired, and I felt older than them, and I felt a little bit like I wanted to cry, not because of everything that was happening in my life, but because of the looks on their faces. Because they were so full of hope and direction and promise, and I knew it wouldn't stay that way forever because that was impossible. I knew that some day, at some point, they would both face pain, and fear, and disappointment and desperation, and that was what made me sad. That they would change.

'Hi mate,' Billy said, his grin fading in and out as if he was not quite sure if he should even have one or not. 'Long time no see, how are you?'

I gave him a nod. 'Good thanks. You?'

'Fine mate. Fine.'

'You've been like the invisible man lately,' Jake remarked, eyeing me sideways as he pushed his bike along. I couldn't help but get the feeling he was giving me the once over you know, trying to determine if I was high or not. 'We'd nearly given up on you.'

'Well not all of us,' Michael sort of snapped at him. Jake did not respond. He just shrugged very slightly and kept walking.

'Turned over a new leaf haven't I?' I told them all to shut them up. I don't know if they believed me any more than I believed myself, but it closed the subject. Billy groaned at me.

'Got loads of tapes for you man. My dad's been on one. Taping all sorts of stuff for you.'

'Oh wow. Tell him thanks a lot.'

'Why don't you tell him yourself? Come over after school, yeah?'

I looked at Michael. He was smiling and nodding, so I did too. 'Okay,' I said. 'Why not?'

By first break I was already struggling. Double maths was no kind introduction back into school life. I abhorred the subject and always had done. Couldn't see the point in it. Couldn't get excited or interested in numbers. I fought for a while to stay with it, leaning forward over my desk, straining my ears to listen, scribbling notes as fast as I could to help me catch up. The monotonous drone of the teacher didn't help, and I soon became horribly aware of how far behind I had fallen. My mind kept taking me off to other places and I felt too tired to fight my way back. I found my gaze drifting time and time again to the world outside the window. The skies outside were pale and grey, promising nothing, and all of it, the sounds of the classroom, the thudding in my own head, filled me with a grating irritation.

When the bell finally rang, I rushed for the door with Michael at my heels. I was craving a drink, a cigarette, something stronger. Instead I found myself standing in line in the canteen, waiting to buy a crappy can of coke and a Mars bar. I ate the chocolate and drank the coke and tasted nothing. I followed my friends aimlessly around the corridors, reaching out with one hand to drag slowly along the cold beige wall, and I thought about cows being herded in for milking, and I felt the narrow walls and the smell of floor cleaner crushing down on me, squeezing the life out of me and it was getting harder to breathe. I made an excuse and rushed to the nearest toilet.

I sat on the loo with my head between my knees. I scooped in several long breaths of air and told myself to calm down. Beads of sweat had marched out across my forehead and there were damp patches under my arms. There was a prickle of panic coursing through my veins and I hated myself for it. I pulled myself together in time for History, taking my old seat at the back of the class, hoping I could just slump down and get through it. But every time someone looked my way, or whispered to the person next to them, I became convinced they were aiming it at me. It became a battle just to keep my backside in the chair. My arse kept shifting. My legs twitched because they wanted to get me out of there and my feet tapped restlessly, wondering where the music was. I just became overwhelmed and bogged down by this feeling that I was in the wrong place, that I shouldn't be there, that I did not belong. I looked at the other kids and I felt nothing like them. I didn't care about the stuff they cared about. Truth was, all I cared about, all I really wanted right then was music and drugs.

I emerged from History, sweating and wanting to kick something. Michael walked alongside me, asking tentatively if I was all right, and I couldn't even bring myself to answer him, that was how bad I felt by then. I kept staring at the exits every time we passed one. The temptation to walk out was getting stronger and stronger. And then I felt this light little arm slip through mine, and I looked down and it was Lucy, smiling in that giddy way of hers. Right away I felt myself relax. I remembered us lying on the bed together yesterday. I remembered all the Sundays we had spent at the beach, talking, and not talking. I put my arm around her and pulled her close, resting my cheek against the top of her head for a moment and breathing in the smell of her. There was something between us that needed no explaining or defining.

'How's it going?' she asked me.

I sighed. 'Better now I've seen you.'

'Been that bad?'

'Worse than I thought. Much worse.'

'Come on, you can do it,' she told me with a smile that believed I could. 'It's only school. And it's nearly lunch time. Half way there.'

'Can't concentrate on anything. Too much in my head.'

'Don't worry about concentrating,' she laughed at me. 'That will come later. You only have to be here in person, right? To keep them off your back?' I nodded. 'Well then, that's all you have to worry about. Just be here. And if you want help catching up, I'll help you after school. Any time.'

'Thanks Lucy. You are very wise, you know.'

'I know I am,' she grinned. 'You should listen to me always.'

Her words and her smile kept me going through English and towards the end of the day. She sat next to me for English. She squeezed my knee under the table and winked at me when I looked her way. I tried to keep my head down. I tried to pretend I had not seen the watery pitying smiles from Mrs Baker and I tried to push out how sickened, how low and fragile I felt inside. I gazed out of the window again. I doodled in the margins of my rough book. I knew what I was doing; just killing time, and I didn't know if I could do it again. 'Life is killing time' I wrote on my paper. Lucy peered at it, and then put a line through it. 'Life is what you make it...' she wrote underneath before looking at me expectantly, as if daring me to disagree. I clung onto what she was telling me. If she hadn't been there, anchoring me in place, I would have got up and walked out.

At the end of the day, the plan was to go to Billy's to listen to music and do some school-work. Michael and Lucy linked arms with me and led me there. I didn't want to go. Not one bit. I felt exhausted and desperate for a smoke, but I was too weak and shaky to argue. I let them all sweep me along; because it was making them smile and I did not want to let them down again.

Up in Billy's room, he closed his door and switched on the music. I could have laughed or cried then. I was just so relieved to hear some music, and there was this huge collective sigh in the room and we all just dropped and sprawled and spread our bodies around the room. I ended up with Lucy, curled up together in Billy's battered arm chair. I let my head fall back into her shoulder and just listened as the others began to dissect the school day, as they scattered their text books and papers across the floor. I possessed no more energy to join in, or to laugh or comment, but it was comforting enough just listening to them.

There was still a certain level of tension though. You couldn't escape it. It was there in the way that Billy and Jake glanced at each other a lot, as if passing messages not meant for me. It was there in the way they seemed to pause or hesitate before they spoke, as if fearful of saying the wrong thing. Their laughs seemed planned and hollow. Michael was tense for different reasons, I realised. Because he was desperate for things to go well, for us all to get along, for things to be as good as they used to be. The only one who seemed truly and totally relaxed, was Lucy. I held onto her tightly and she held me back. When Slide Away came on, I squeezed her tighter and whispered the lyrics into her ear, making her giggle and blush. She laughed and kissed me on the cheek, and we were shut off from the rest of them then.

'You're crazy...' she whispered into my ear. I grinned and pressed my lips up to her ear.

'All I know is that you take me there!'

'Me too,' she whispered. 'Me too Danny.'

The Boy With The Thorn In His Side-Part 2

8

To everyone's surprise, not least of all my own, I made it to the end of that week without missing a single day of school. It was hard, but made easier by the force of Michael and Lucy, propelling me forward. By Friday though, my will was rapidly fading. The daily walk to and fro to school made me think about hamsters running on the wheels in their cage. They think they're going to get somewhere, they think they're going to get out, but they're not, and they don't realise they are trapped forever. Treadmill, I would think, as I wandered the corridors of school, treadmill.

So, I went through the motions like the rest of them did, and I wondered if any of them knew that all they were really doing was towing the line, obeying the rules. I considered the future they said lay ahead of us with a cold kind of detachment, viewing the day that school became employment, as just the jump from one treadmill to the next. They all thought they would be free but they wouldn't be. I found myself staring around at people wherever I saw them. Were they happy, I wondered? I watched the schoolchildren dutifully following the rules that would lead them into a decent adult life, and I watched the adults that passed us by, driving off to work in their small cars with their suits on. Were they happy about it? Or were they just being good? That was what they were doing, I thought when I watched them; they were being good, staying in line, doing everything the way they were meant to.

It made me wonder whether Howard was doing me a warped kind of favour by encouraging me to stick to the rules and be a good boy. It would serve me well in later life, I reasoned, as I trudged back and forth to school that week, with my head hanging low and my eyes burning into the ground. I would know what to do when the time came. I started thinking about the people who didn't stay in line, the people who skirted around the edges of it all, ducking and diving, running and hiding. People like Jaime Lawler with his shifty eyes the colour of the sea on a grey and dismal day. He scurried around town with his cap pulled low, friends with everyone, yet trusted by no one.

'See you Friday mate,' he said to me one day, as we passed him on the street on the way to school. I felt the weight of Michael's stare on my back then. Jaime Lawler was the scourge of the town, I realised, a hunched-up figure selling his wares in back alleys and teenage bedrooms.

Friday night loomed; something I both feared and desired. Michael did not want me to go back to the club.

'Sneak around to us,' he kept pleading. 'We'll stay in and let Anthony cook for us, he's really good!'

I tried to explain to him that Howard expected me at the club.

'I can't piss him off,' I said, seeing the regret and the disappointment in Mike's eyes and hating myself for it. 'I better not rock the boat.'

I didn't tell him the truth though; that as much as I trembled at the thought of going back to the club with Howard, I was excited by it as well. Maybe it had something to do with the mind-numbing and soul-destroying week I had just endured at school. The pointing and the whispering and the giggles that followed me wherever I walked. The wary look in the teachers' eyes. The strange and uncomfortable feeling of a pen between my fingers.

So, I went. I ran down the stairs when he yelled for me. I caught a glimpse of my mother asleep on the sofa. 'Is she all right?' I asked him as he steered me through the front door and out into the night. 'She's always asleep.'

'Migraines,' he grunted in reply. 'Doctor gave her some stronger stuff for them.'

We drove to the club in total silence. I sensed a dark atmosphere that made my skin crawl with goosebumps. He stared down the road with hooded eyes and rigid shoulders. There had been arguments on and off in the week. I knew some of it was work related, because I had heard him shouting down the phone at people. But some of it was between my mother and him. Slamming doors, and my mother in tears, and my name floating about between them.

Inside the club I moved quickly away from him and approached the DJ as he was setting up. I had a few suggestions for him.

'Just try it,' I told him. 'Try I Am The Resurrection later in the night and they'll go mental for it, I promise you.'

The Boy With The Thorn In His Side-Part 2

The young man offered me a familiar roll of the eyes. 'You should get a job collecting glasses at Chaos, in Belfield Park,' he told me.

'What's that?'

'Kind of club that plays the music you like,' he said wearily.

I retreated to my duties as the club began to fill up. The words rolled around and around inside my head, making me smile and nod. Kind of club plays the music I like. Oh my God. I had never even entertained the idea that such places existed! I slipped quickly and easily back into the routine of the club. The horrors of last weekend seemed a long way away from me then. I moved around the club, collecting glasses, enjoying the way I felt just a little bit older, just a little bit taller than I had done all week at school. Here, no one knew me, so no one was pointing or whispering.

Towards the end of the night, I perched up on a stool at the bar, stack of pint glasses resting on it behind me and my feet swinging just inches away from the floor. I was taking a short break, watching the crowd of drunken people as they swayed and weaved on the dance floor, and I was in a world of my own until I heard the DJ make an announcement on his mike.

'This is for the annoying kid who collects your glasses,' he said dryly. 'He reckons you'll all love it.' I sat up straight, filled with a sudden awe and excitement as he started playing The Stone Roses song I had requested. I thought, they've never played the Roses here before! This is an education for some of these people! The crowd were drunk enough to react wildly to anything, and they seized the opportunity to jump and push, spilling drinks and banging heads. I was just smiling from ear to ear. People looked my way and whooped and hooted and held up their drinks to me. It was amazing. I felt amazing. And it was a fucking good song. I was singing along, drumming my heels against the bar, and tapping my hands against my knees when I felt the shadow fall over me.

Howard bumped against me and stayed there, arms crossed rigidly over his puffed-out chest, his expression full of scorn.

'Look at them going mental,' he sneered, his top lip curling up. 'Did you pick this then?'

I nodded. 'Been asking him for ages.'

'This is not a fucking rock club you know,' he said, his voice growing tight with the anger I could see filling up his face. 'I'll have a bloody riot on my hands in a minute!'

'They like it,' I tried pointing out, with a weak shrug. 'The Stone Roses are still really popular.'

'Only to people like you.'

'They seem to like it too,' I said, and nodded back at the crowd.

Howard was silent then. I felt myself getting trapped in it, as it drew out, longer and longer, dripping with promises. I looked away from him and could still feel his eyes burning into me, just staring and staring, saying nothing and yet telling me everything. I fidgeted nervously on the stool, and then finally I couldn't stand it anymore, so I slipped down from it, picked up the glasses and slunk off to the kitchen with them.

It was a bad move. He followed me.

'Don't you just walk off when I'm talking to you,' his indignant voice warned me from behind. 'You should know better than that.'

I was in the kitchen, and my stomach dropped and my hands began to tremble when he joined me there, slamming the door behind him. Fuck, I thought. It was the only word that filled my head. Fuck, fuck, fuck! I tried to remain calm as the blind panic swamped me. I put the plug in and turned on the taps, and squirted washing up liquid into the sink.

'I thought you'd finished,' I said.

'Like fuck.'

'Sorry then.'

'You're not sorry. I think you need reminding whose club this is, smart arse little prick thinking you can tell my DJ what to play!' He stepped closer to me at the sink, crossing his arms again. My nostrils twitched as the air grew thicker around me. I could smell both whisky and rage spilling from his pores. 'I think you need reminding who the boss is.'

I swirled a limp hand in the water to froth up the bubbles. 'No, I don't.' Steam rose up in front of my face. My stomach was on fire with the pain of fear. I was aware of every single hardening muscle in

The Boy With The Thorn In His Side-Part 2

my body as he stepped closer again and placed his hands down onto his hips.

'You know you really piss me off,' he said in a low, soft, snarl. 'All week you've been doing my fucking head in.' I kept quiet, waiting for him to tell me why exactly. 'Got your mother in my ear, prattling on about how wonderful you are, just for going to fucking school like you're meant to! She thinks the sun shines out your bloody arse for it! Fucking Saint Danny is it now eh? Mister goody two shoes eh? Now I've got to watch you try to take over my club! Getting the DJ to play shit to aggravate the punters!' He was winding himself up, I could feel it. I licked my lips slowly. I wanted to believe there was a way out of this, but I could feel it coming from him, pulsing like a heartbeat; the desire for violence.

'Okay,' I said. 'I won't do it again then. I won't ask for any songs. You didn't mind before, that's all.'

'I mind now.'

'Okay then.' I shrugged a little and braved a look at the ghastly face that was leering closer and closer to mine, and I could see the rage making his small eyes bulbous in their sockets and the ropey veins bulging in his neck. 'Maybe I better stop coming,' I said. 'If I get on your nerves so much.'

'Oh yeah?'

'Yeah,' I said, and my throat was like sandpaper. 'I mean, I could get a job somewhere else, couldn't I?'

'Right little smart arse tonight aren't you eh?' he said, and I saw that I could never win. That whatever I said, or didn't say, would be taken as defiance when he was in this kind of mood. 'Got a lot to say for yourself eh? That right? When I thought I told you not to speak unless I asked you to.' I didn't answer him. I stared back at the water and waited. 'Right little mummy's boy you been all week,' he drawled on. 'Know exactly what you're doing, you know.'

'What?'

'Being all sweetness and light, mummy's little golden boy, when we all know what a crock of shit that is! She doesn't know the half of it eh? She doesn't even know what a fuck up her precious son is, does she?'

I kept my eyes on the water. I could feel something rising within my chest, something I had not felt for a long, long time.

'I'm confused,' I shrugged at him. 'I thought you wanted me to go to school to get the truants people off her back. I did what you said, remember? I didn't tell them about your drug dealing friend and I went to school all week.' I flicked my glance up to meet his again, and I could almost see the blood pooling in anger behind his eyes. The thing in my chest though, I knew what it was now and I knew that I had every fucking right to feel it, anger and pure cold hate. 'I thought that's what you wanted me to do,' I said again, staring at him.

'I don't give a shit what you do!' he retorted, spit spraying from his lips.

'Well you obviously do!' I cried back at him. I immediately bit my lip and bit it hard. I stared into his bloodshot eyes. I shook my head at him and resisted the urge to smile in bitter amusement. 'I can't win. You were angry with me for skipping school and getting Mum in a mess, now you're angry at me for *going* to school, because she's pleased with me? So I can't ever win can I?' I tore my eyes from his and looked back into the sink. It was full to the brim, so I turned off the taps and began to lower the glasses into the water. I pressed my teeth down upon my lower lip. I'd said too much, and I knew it. Howard was frighteningly silent beside me, and I could hear his angry breath wheezing in and out between his teeth as he stared at me.

I froze when the hand fell onto my neck. There was the automatic urge to shake it off, to recoil away from something which stained and possessed me. But my body reacted by turning to stone, my hands frozen claws beneath the water, my feet planted to the sticky floor tiles. The hand rested on my neck like a dead thing. And then when it moved, it moved sluggishly, exploring my muscles as they trembled, intensifying the pressure slowly. The thumb dug into the front of my throat, nestling in viciously, like a worm trying to burrow into a hole, while the thick fingers crept around to the back, making their mark, constricting the air flow. My eyes watered and my vision blurred on the rims of the pint glasses as they bobbed in the water.

'That hurts,' I whispered and to this Howard chuckled very gently.

'Good. Anything to shut you up.'

The Boy With The Thorn In His Side-Part 2

'Why don't you leave me alone?' I winced under the pressure.

'Because I don't want to. Because you piss me off. You get on my nerves. You make me angry.'

'How the fuck do you think I feel about you?'

His grip tightened like a bracelet of cold steel. I felt the air flow stop and my hands flew out from the water, gripping and grasping at the vice that held me. The pain was immense, shooting agony through my nerves. I tried to duck down, pull away, anything to escape as he crushed down on my windpipe. The grip relaxed as suddenly as it had tightened and he was shaking with uncontrollable laughter next to me. My eyes ran with water and the hand remained on my neck, holding me in place. This time the hand moved against my hot skin, pressing into it, his fingers pushing up my neck and underneath my hair, before sliding back down again, spreading out across my shoulder blades. I couldn't take it. I couldn't live with it. I wanted to die and I wanted to kill him, and I never wanted to breathe the same air as him again, so I made a sound of pure disgust and tried to pull away from him. The hand gripped my hair, closed like a claw around my entire skull, and then suddenly the basin of water was flying up towards my face.

As I went down into the water, I felt the glasses trying to make room for me, rolling and bumping against each other, and my forehead cracked straight into one, and another smashed into my nose and cheek. Hot water flooded my nostrils as I struggled wildly, my hands scraping and tearing at the hand that kept me there. He held me under the water long enough for me to start to think he was serious, for me to start to fear this was it, this was how he did it, this was how he finished me off. Not by beating me, not by cutting me up, but by drowning me in a sink full of pint glasses. Pure and utter terror filled my brain and my soul and every fibre of my physical body, and then he yanked me backwards by my hair and hurled me away, down onto the kitchen floor.

My back hit the wall and I threw up violently between my legs, coughing and gasping for air, my belly heaving and tossing up soapy water. I was amazed and horrified, and yet again reminded of how small and helpless I always was, and how there was never any way out. He stood over me, his legs spread and his eyes dancing with laughter. I pushed back my soaked hair and glared up at him.

'You're fucking insane!'

'Hey, maybe,' he replied with a shrug. He appeared calmer already, his stance relaxed, his smile smug. The red had seeped away from his face. 'You just remember to keep a polite tongue in your head, you just remember who the boss is around here. Or every now and then I will have to remind you.'

'Just you remember to look over your shoulder!' I hissed back at him, wiping my face with my hands. Howard raised his eyebrows at me and squatted down.

'Oh yeah? What is that supposed to mean little man?'

'One day,' I panted, as hatred hurtled through me, cold and sharp. 'One day I'll be big enough. That's all you sick son-of-a-bitch...one day I'll surprise you with a knife in the eye, how would you like that?' I stared into his eyes and I meant it, I meant every word. I even looked around the kitchen for a knife. I wanted one and I wanted one badly.

His face remained calm, and mildly amused. He clicked his tongue and shook his head at me sadly.

'I do sometimes wonder, what exactly it will take to get that smart tongue out your head? And that fucking arrogant look off your face? Eh? I do wonder that sometimes, you know. When I think I've finally got you all in line, and you're being a good boy like you're supposed to be, you go and show me that look in your eye again! Like right now! Makes me want to stamp on your face.'

'Go on then,' I challenged him, refusing to flinch. 'Do it! Do whatever you like. Then maybe I'll go straight to the police and tell them who did it!'

Howard simply laughed at me. He dropped his head back a little way, closed his eyes briefly and let steady laughter roll from him. Then his eyes snapped open and were back on mine and he lashed out, striking me across the face and knocking me back into the wall. I didn't even try to get away. I just covered my head with my arms as he continued to land blows on me, one after the another, thump, thump, thump slowly and methodically.

The Boy With The Thorn In His Side-Part 2

'Drive you mental yet?' he asked me in a weary tone. 'Just tell me when it's driving you mental.'

'*Fuck you*!' I screamed back at him, kicking out with my foot and grazing his knee. He laughed again and stood up suddenly. I was shaking with rage. I felt like a volcano starting to tremble awake. Howard cracked his knuckles and shook out his arms. 'I'll tell Mum,' I said then, pushing my way up from the wall. He grinned. 'I will. That's it. I'm gonna' tell her everything, tonight. I won't leave her alone until she believes me.'

He yawned at me. 'You'll have a good job waking her up,' he smirked. 'She's out all night on those pills. I like her that way you know. Good and quiet. See, she's a good girl for me. I don't have to remind her who's in charge. But you.' The smile was a snarl as he pointed one finger down into my face. 'You. You must like it. That's what I think. You fucking ask for it, little man.'

'I'll tell her in the morning,' I said, my back pressed flat against the wall. His smile merely stretched upwards.

'Try it,' he said, as he turned calmly towards the closed door. 'And I'll kill her.' His smile slipped down, receding into a straight, hard line, his lips almost transparent. 'Right in front of you,' he went on. 'Just try it.' With that he opened the door, slipped through it and closed it softly behind him.

I shook my head at the closed door. I wondered if he expected me to carry on with the glasses and I just knew he fucking did. I stayed where I was, just breathing, feeling the slime of soapy water and dregs of beer sliding down my back and chest beneath my t-shirt. The corner of my forehead was stinging, so I put my hand there and brought them down to examine. There it was, blood and mess strung out between my fingers. My t-shirt was soaked through, my hair dripping all over the floor. What I wanted to do then was take my own head by the hair and ram it again and again and again into the hard, tiled floor. I wanted to smash it until it fell apart in my own hands. I felt this climbing roaring agony inside my chest, a hysteria that aimed to reach the top and break through and explode. I rubbed at my cold arms and decided I was never coming back there again. I also decided that if I ever got the chance, if I ever found a way, if there was no way I would get caught, then I would do it, I would fucking kill that bastard before he killed me first.

I forced myself towards the door and tugged it open. My head was already spinning and pulsing with pain. I peered out. The hallway was narrowed by the lines of cardboard boxes containing crisps and nuts. I slid out through the door and hurried down to the end of the corridor, and emerged blinking, back out into the hot, dark club. I pushed urgently through the crowds, the doors in sight, desperate to get out. As I neared the entrance, manned by two men who resembled bulldogs in leather jackets, I felt a hand snatching at the back of my t-shirt and I rounded in fear, my fist pulled back. Behind me was the surprised face of Jaime Lawler, holding up his hands to me.

'Whoa sorry mate, didn't mean to scare you!'

'Fuck off,' I said, and walked away. I shoved my way outside, and felt the cold shock of the night air upon my wet clothes. Jaime Lawler was at my side.

'What the fuck happened to you? You're all wet!'

I reached out and shoved him. 'I said fuck off!'

He held up his hands again, but kept walking. 'Sorry! Hey, relax, it's just me, I'm on your side mate!' I shook my head, shoved my hands deep inside my pockets and marched on. He laughed a little. 'Come on, what happened? Someone shove your head down the toilet or what?'

'Just get lost!'

'All right, all right, keep your hair on, I'm just joking mate.' He walked briskly beside me, a faint smile upon his long, pale face. 'I just wanted to check if you needed anything, that's all mate. You know, for the weekend? Got a good deal for you this time.'

'What?'

'Whatever you want. What do you fancy?'

'How much?'

'I can do you a wrap of whizz for a fiver this time.'

I kept walking. I kept my eyes on the black pavement as it rolled beneath my stamping feet. Jamie Lawler kept up with me easily.

'I can do you some downers too,' he was saying. 'Take the edge off the next morning. Try it for free.'

'I haven't got any money on me.'

The Boy With The Thorn In His Side-Part 2

'Ah that's okay, I'll get it off you next time I see you.' He shrugged his thin shoulders at me and stopped walking. I did too. 'I trust you man,' he grinned, and nodded to an alley running between two shops.

We lowered our heads and slunk over to it, wandering half way down until the walls grew so dark we could barely see our faces. The streets beyond were full of the noise of the drunk, yelling and screeching their way back home. I hovered in an alley way with Jaime Lawler, my hair wet and my head leaking blood, my body shivering violently from head to toe, and I absorbed misery to take the place of the fading anger.

'Do you know a place called Chaos?' I asked him, as we made our deal.

He nodded instantly. 'Yeah, in Belfield Park.'

'What's it like?'

'It's like a rock, or indie place, it's all right. Cheap beer. Place is a dive. Why, you thinking of going?'

'Maybe.'

'Well let me know, I can get hold of some blinding fake I.D's for a tenner.'

I nodded okay and walked back out of the alley alone, my unpaid for purchases stuffed deep inside my back pocket.

9

    I let myself in the back of the house and crept silently up the stairs. As I crossed the landing I could hear my mother snoring deeply in her room. I paused outside my own room; breathing fast, my brain pounding in my skull, my jaw tight, not allowing me to speak even if I had wanted to. I gave up anyway; I gave up before I even let myself consider waking her. I went into my room and closed the door behind me. I stood where I was, peeled off my wet, sick splashed t-shirt and threw it to the floor. I kicked off my boots, removed the drugs from my back pocket and threw them on the bed. I pulled off my jeans and kicked them away. I climbed under my duvet in just my boxers, dragging out my little tin from under the mattress as I did. I knocked my notebook out and watched as it thumped down to the floor, revealing the pen still tucked inside the last page I had written on. I snarled impatiently, reached down and punched it right under the bed. There was no point in any of that now. All I needed now was sleep and to get that I would need a little help.

    I rolled myself a joint, and sat with my back to the wall and my arm slung loosely around my middle. I sat and smoked and replayed what had just happened in my head. It made me sick. Nothing was ever going to be good enough for that man. I gritted my teeth against the bad taste in my mouth. Go to school and be a good boy, then get your head shoved under water anyway. Being good would get me nowhere, because Howard would still give me a good kicking any time he felt like it. Why hadn't I realised that before? Why had I been such a fucking idiot for so long? Scuttling around, living under his thumb and his rules, avoiding my friends just to avoid a beating. There were no rules, because the guy was insane, and insanity does not follow rules. Howard didn't follow rules, did he? No, he fucking didn't. He didn't keep to his word, did he? No. He just enjoyed violence.

    All his talk about keeping me on the right path, that was bullshit, all of it was. When I thought back over what had happened in the kitchen at the club, it became obvious to me, and I didn't know why I had not grasped it before. He liked violence. He got off on it. It was like me and the music. Music calmed me down, made me feel

The Boy With The Thorn In His Side-Part 2

better, lifted me up and chilled me out. I trembled on the outside and on the inside there was a roar of rage thudding to get out. The man was a total lunatic and nothing was going to change that, nothing.

I sat there and smoked, thinking up ways to kill him. I felt detached from reality and the rules it expected us to follow. Thou shalt not kill. Well how about if someone is doing their best to kill you? Would it all right then? I thought about poisoning him. There had to be a way. Maybe I would ask Anthony what he thought. We could come up with a plan, couldn't we? Then I started to think about waiting until he had fallen asleep. Creeping into their room with a massive knife in my hands. Pulling back the covers and plunging it right into his twisted black heart. I closed my eyes and then opened them again. The pot was loosening my limbs and sending them to sleep, one by one. Drowsiness was creeping in and my head wanted to loll forward and my eyes wanted to shut down. I felt it all gradually growing numb within me and didn't feel anything anymore, not fear, or anger, or anything.

I stubbed it out, pumped the vanilla scented air freshener around the room and snuggled down under my duvet to sleep. I was just floating into oblivion when I heard him come in downstairs. He was still worked up by the sound of it. Slamming doors. Crashing into things. I closed my eyes, yanked the duvet up over my head and held my breath in the darkness. Would he come for me? Knowing Mum was out cold, would he want to start again? It seemed I was not on his agenda however, as he stormed right past my door and into his own room. I let my breath back out, slow and ragged, thinking thank God he didn't come for more. I briefly considered sneaking downstairs and fetching a knife to keep under my pillow, just in case.

I could hear him talking. He threw something against the wall, maybe his shoes, or something that was in his way. I heard my mum murmuring back in a thick, sleepy voice. I curled into a ball, encased in darkness. He was still talking and she was talking back, protesting, her voice sounding high and thin, as the bed springs began to creak over the top of it. Howard started swearing at her. He sounded angry. I pressed my hands to my ears and tried to locate the entrance to sleep I had been so close to before he came home. It was then that the noises begun, and there was nothing I could do to block it out, nothing I could do to stop them entering my ears and my mind. She was moaning, he was groaning, and the thump of the headboard, the screams of the bed springs told their own story. It didn't sound like anything nice, or fun. It sounded like an animal taking what it needed to survive.

I threw back my cover, reached out blindly for my Walkman and yanked it into bed with me. I pulled on the headphones and pressed play. I ducked under the duvet, closed my eyes and tried to push it out. I concentrated on the music. It was the very song that had got me into trouble earlier. I nodded along with it, squeezing my eyes shut, pushing out everything else, what was happening next door, what had happened earlier, all of it. It was just The Roses, just Ian Brown's voice inside my head, and a magnificent spiralling wall of guitars and drums that went on forever, as long as I kept on rewinding it back to the start...

The next morning, I woke up with one thing and one thing only on my mind. It was the most important thing. It propelled me from my bed and sent me scrabbling around the room for clothes to throw on. It was the most vital thing in the world. It had slammed me in the head the second my eyes had opened. The club that played the good music. We had to go. I knew it. I knew it would be all right, because everything is always all right when you have good music! Everything else, soapy water and pint glasses and drugs in alley ways and mothers crying, all of that would fade away, I knew it would, it would cease to exist in a place like that. We were going to find that club, the one that played the good music, and we were all going to go and get off our heads, and have the best night of our lives ever. We were going to remember it forever. I dressed and flew out of the house while my mother and Howard still lay snoring.

I rushed around to Mike's and pounded on his door. He answered it, yawning widely and tugging his tatty dressing gown around himself. I flew inside and he stopped yawning then, and his expression became tense and sober. His nostrils worked, and his lips clamped shut and he shook his head at me as he closed the door.

'You've got to be joking,' I heard him say.

I had no idea what he meant. I didn't care. I jumped up and down like a kid in a sweet shop.

The Boy With The Thorn In His Side-Part 2

'Hi Mike! Morning Mike! Listen to this, I've got the best night ever planned! You're gonna' love it!'

He stared at me as if I were crazy. 'You know your head is cut, right? What the hell happened?'

I had totally forgotten. I shrugged at him and lifted my hand, raising my fingers and running them gently along the length of the cut. I grimaced at the red smear on my fingers and shrugged at him.

'I forgot about that. I'm not working at the club anymore Mike. That's what that is.'

'So, you're not gonna' try and tell me you fell off your bike then?' he crossed his arms and sighed at me.

I smiled a little. 'No mate. It seems me going to school all week to please my mother got Howard a little wound up.' I turned and headed into the kitchen. Michael followed, shaking his head angrily, grabbing the kettle from the side and shoving it under the tap to refill it.

'Bastard,' he growled.

I sat down at the table. I felt okay. I felt good. It was partly being back in his house, like the old days, relaxing with the knowledge that there were no parents about to show up and look over your shoulder. And it was partly thinking about tonight, thinking about the club and good times.

'Forget about it,' I told him. 'Have you got any passport sized photos? We might need some.'

'What for?'

'Fake I.D,' I replied with a grin. Michael got two mugs down from the cupboard and sloshed milk into each one. 'I've got some photos somewhere, we just need to get some done for you, then this friend of mine can sort them out for us.'

'Why'd we need them?'

'To go to a club!' I cried, the excitement flooding me again, making me feel giddy with it, making it impossible to sit still. I gripped the edge of the table with my hands and grinned like a lunatic at Michael.

He stared back at me with wary eyes. 'What club? Are you okay mate? Really?'

'Yes! Definitely okay! I'm just really excited! There's this club you see, over in Belfield Park, and it plays the music we like Michael! It plays good music!' I bit my lip and stared at him, still fidgeting and squirming while he took the information in. 'It's called Chaos,' I burst out, when he refused to join in. 'Ever heard of it? We can go tonight Mike, if we get the I.D sorted! How cool right? A place for us? A place that plays our kind of music!'

Michael nodded in interest and then turned his back to make the teas. 'Okay. Sounds like a plan. We can do that.' He placed the mugs on the table and sat down opposite me. 'Sounds cool. Billy and Jake too?'

'Yes!' I cried, clapping my hands together. 'Call them! Can I borrow the phone while I'm here? I'll call this guy to sort out the I.D.'

'Who's the guy?'

'Oh, that Lawler bloke. He's okay.' I picked up my tea and blew across the surface of it. I wanted to laugh out loud. I didn't want to think about anything bad ever again, just fun, just good times and good friends and good music. That was how it should be, I reasoned, that was how it should always be!

'So excited,' I told him. 'I can't wait to see what they play. I am never going back to K's again in my life. It's diabolical the shit they play there, and what's even more depressing are the pretentious sheep who try to dance to it! They haven't got a clue!'

Michael nodded in vague agreement with me. 'So, tell me what happened with Howard,' he said.

I made a noise that let him know it was a subject I did not want to be dragged back into. I glanced down the hallway, wondering where Anthony was.

'The usual, I told you. But I'm not going back there, not ever. That's it. I can just stay out of his way now.'

'But you go to school all week and he still lays into you?' Michael shook his head in disgust and rubbed a hand against his face. 'Danny, please, let's just tell the police. Or a teacher. Someone. I'm begging you mate.'

'Can't,' I shook my head and sipped my tea.

His fist thumped onto the table top. 'Why the hell not? You're just gonna' keep letting him get away with it? He won't stop, no

The Boy With The Thorn In His Side-Part 2

matter what you think. And do you know what I'm really scared about?' I met his eyes and shook my head slowly. 'That he'll go too far and kill you one day...you only have to look at the size of him, the size of you...That's what scares me mate. Do you think I want to go to your fucking funeral knowing I could have done something to stop it?' He was looking at me in this terribly pained way that was almost more than I could stand. I wanted to tell him again about the music. I wanted to start a list of songs I was hoping to hear there. I was already wondering if their D.J took requests.

'Mike,' I put my tea down and sighed at him. 'It's not that simple and you know it.'

Michael shook his head at me, and leaned across the table. He looked pale, I thought, like he hadn't been sleeping well recently.

'Tell your mum then,' he pleaded. 'I'll come with you. We'll wait until he goes out and we'll go and tell her together. Tell her everything.'

I scratched my head and tried to think of a way to explain to him what my mother had been like lately.

'She's not herself,' I told him slowly. 'Something's wrong with her. And Mike, I did tell her once. I told her what he'd done and she didn't believe me. I don't see why she would believe me now, all this time later.'

'The police,' Michael said again, pleadingly now.

I sighed in frustration. 'Mike, we can't trust them. Look what happened to Anthony, and we still don't know exactly who was involved in that. You have no idea what he's capable of...I mean...' I trailed off for a moment, my mind momentarily dragging me back to the sink full of murky glasses and bubbles, the rush of water up my nostrils. 'If anything else happens to you or Anthony, I would never forgive myself Michael. And I'd end up in care or something, because my mum's in no fit state to take care of us both. Worse things happen there Mike. They really do.'

Michael's lips trembled slightly as he pressed them together. 'Stay with us,' he said.

I felt a little annoyed with him, as the last of my excitement plummeted to the floor.

'Not safe,' I told him adamantly. 'And if he goes to prison I'd be dead anyway. He's got people everywhere, he said. They'd get me, or he would when he got out. No. I've got a better plan.' Michael's eyes widened and he waited for me to explain. I licked my lips and considered telling him the thoughts that had consumed me last night. Thoughts of poison and knives, and blows to the back of the head. 'Wait 'til I'm sixteen and just move out. They won't stop me and if they do I'll just run away.' I grinned at him, hoping to raise his spirits. 'Me and you could get like a bed-sit together or something! And jobs.'

To my relief Michael grinned back at me and his shoulders relaxed slightly. 'That would be so cool.'

'Course it would.' I slurped down the rest of my tea and got up from the table. 'Come on, we need to sort out the I.D. and talk to Billy and Jake. Tonight is going to be the best night ever Michael. I am telling you.'

By the afternoon, they were all on board and as excited as I was. We would all do the usual; tell our parents we were sleeping at Billy's and Billy would tell his he was staying at Michael's. We would sleep at Michael's afterwards, to dissect what I hoped would be the best night of our lives so far.

I got ready up in my room, taking painstaking care over my choice of clothes. I desperately wanted to wear one of my Nirvana t-shirts, but I also wanted to wear the Oasis one I had bought recently. God, then there was my Clash one and my Jim Morrison one. I wanted to look like me, like I hadn't tried too hard, but I also wanted to make a statement about who I was and what I lived for. In the end I went for Nirvana, tipping Kurt a wink as I pulled it down over my head. I had this fluttering restless sensation in my gut, which I supposed was excitement, although it was hard to tell when it was accompanied with the usual knot of dread I carried around with me. I dragged out my tin and plucked out the wrap of speed from Jaime. I stared at it for a while, trying to decide whether to take some now or later. Offer some to Michael again, or keep it to myself? Unable to make my mind up, I stuffed it into my back pocket along with the pills I planned on taking towards the end of the night.

The Boy With The Thorn In His Side-Part 2

I left my room and crept lightly down the stairs. I was in the hallway, tying up my boot laces when I heard the creak of the leather sofa and the grunt that was unmistakably Howard's.

'Oi, where d'you think you're going?' his voice called out. I glanced nervously up the stairs. I knew Mum was in bed with yet another migraine. Why the hell wasn't he at the club? That knot of fear was coming to life again, clenching and unclenching painfully inside my stomach and I knew why. 'Hey!' his voice boomed out, making me jump. 'I'm talking to you!'

I had my laces tied. I reached for the door handle but he was already behind me, his shadow darkening the door, his bulk filling the space behind me, and as I fumbled with the catch and opened the door a crack, his hand shot out, slamming it shut again. His large, sneering face loomed over my shoulder, his mouth rasping whisky breath into my ear. I kept my eyes on the door and my hand on the catch.

'Don't you fucking try and walk out when I'm talking to you.'

'I'm going to Billy's,' I said stiffly. 'Mum said I could.' I attempted to open the door again but he kept his hand there, holding it shut.

'I don't think so. I think you can stay here and keep me company. You've given me a bad headache you know. I've taken the night off work because of you. I've had to pay the bar staff extra to collect the glasses. You've dumped me right in it!'

I blinked and shook my head, incredulous at the audacity of the man. 'What do you expect? I'm not working for you after what you did last night! I don't wanna' be anywhere near you.'

'You're staying in,' he replied, his hot breath coating my cheek. 'You'll do as I tell you.'

'No.' I shook my head, my eyes still fixed on the door. 'You got no right. You can't stop me.'

'We'll see about that,' he said, and plunged a fist into my side.

I doubled up instantly, choking on the pain. It was sickening, rocketing throughout my body from the point of impact. I shook my head, desperately. Please don't, I thought, please don't try and stop me going there. I needed to go there, I had to go there, because what else was there? What else?

'Stop it,' I tried to tell him, forcing the words up with a cough. He grabbed my arm, turned me around and held me back against the door. 'What have I ever done to you?' I looked into his eyes and asked him. I tried to find the answer there, I tried to search his eyes for pity, or remorse, for anything remotely human, but all I could see was the burning glint in his eyes. And I could feel it pulsing from him again, the waves of violent intent, the urge he was compelled to satisfy.

'You exist for one thing,' he informed me. 'And you're getting out of line again. This is my house and my rules, and if I say you're not going out, then you're not fucking going out!'

I stared back at him, breathless with pain, tight-lipped with anger. It was stirring again within me, the blood pumping faster and harder through my veins, and I liked it and I wanted it. I wanted to kick him in the balls again and then stamp on them for good measure. I wanted to be able to do something to him that would make him stop and pause the next time he wanted to take a shot at me. Something that would rein him in, make him think twice. There was no way he was stopping me going out. No way. If we had to fight to the death in the hallway, then so be it.

'You are pure fucking evil,' I told him then, my mouth moving upwards into a parody of a smile. 'You know that? I don't know how you even sleep at night. I hate you more than you will ever know, and if I ever got the chance, I would fucking kill you in a second!'

He rocked back on his heels, his small eyes just gleaming slits in his vast and leering face. He moved them slowly up and down my sagging body, and then he struck again, his fist shooting into the pit of my belly. I crumpled in half, gasping and grunting. He laughed, and I went down onto my knees, my stomach exploding inside of me.

'You won't ever get the chance you little shit stain, it'll be me killing you and don't you ever forget it!' My head was hanging down, my hair all over my face, my body crippled with the blows, when his foot lashed out, catching me in the face and sending me back into the door with a dull thud.

'*Mum*!' I screamed out and glancing through my hair, I saw the sudden panic in his eyes and opened my mouth again. 'Mum! Mum, help, *help*!'

I had bought myself time, so I turned to the door, clawing at it and clinging to it. There was the unmistakable sound of the bedsprings creaking in their room. Howard looked uncertain, licking his lips rapidly and staring from me, up to the landing, and back to me. His nostrils were twitching, his big chest jerking up and down as his breath whooshed in and out. I hung onto the door handle and used it to pull myself back up. My back now turned to him, I didn't waste any more time. I didn't look back at him, I just scrambled desperately with the catch, got it open, made a gap big enough for me to squeeze through, and I was out. The cold night air slapped my face, taking my breath from me once again. I opened my mouth, sucked it in and stumbled forward.

Sharp spikes of pain made me wince and cry out, but I was laughing as I ran, as I forced my feet to move one after the other. I ran to Michael's house and hammered on it like a madman. I looked over my shoulder just once, half expecting to see Howard's raging face behind mine, but he was not there. Anthony wrenched the door open in a panic and I nearly fell in over the doorstep. I bundled myself in and he closed the door and examined me in shock.

'Danny? What the hell?'

Michael appeared in the kitchen doorway, holding an open can of lager and frowning in surprise and concern.

'Oh my God!' he cried when he saw me. I could feel the wetness on my top lip, so I pressed a hand to it and stared blankly at the blood on my fingers. 'What now?'

I couldn't speak for a moment. My gut was twisted and writhing in pain, so I leaned against the closed door and just breathed and grinned at them. Pain was okay, I kept telling myself, it's just data, it's just information being sent to your brain, it won't kill me.

'I'm okay,' I told them when I had the breath to.

'You're not fucking okay!' Anthony exploded, stepping towards me and lifting my chin. 'Did that bastard just do this? Mike get some tissues or something! Did that bastard do this Danny? Jesus Christ!'

I moved my face from his hand. 'He tried to stop me coming out,' I explained. 'But it's okay, I made it look! We can go!' They looked at each other darkly. Michael came up the hall, ducked into the downstairs toilet and came back out with a clutch of toilet paper in his hand. He passed it to me and I held it to my nose and lip.

'Last night as well,' Michael said then, his dark eyes moving from me to Anthony. 'He laid into him at the club, cut his head.' Anthony's face was creased in concern. He reached out and pushed my hair to one side, wincing when he saw the size of the cut to my forehead.

'Well that's it!' he cried then, turning around and kicking the nearest thing to him, which happened to be the door I was leaning against. He plunged his hands back through his short dark hair. 'Fucking bastard! Fuck!'

I rubbed the tissues into my nose until the blood was all mopped up. 'He's off on one,' I remarked. 'Dunno why. He's been drinking too. Maybe things are going tits up for him, I dunno.'

Anthony shook his head at me, his eyes wide and black with anger. 'I'm going over there,' he said flatly. 'I'm going over there to teach him a lesson. See if he'd like to pick a fight with me!'

I put my hand to his chest. 'No. Don't. Not now. Not tonight.'

'This can't go on Danny,' he told me seriously. 'We have to do something mate. I'm serious.'

'Just not tonight,' I begged him, looking to Michael for help. 'Please not tonight. We're going out remember? To the club that plays the good music?'

'You can still go,' Anthony replied. 'I'll rip his head off while you're gone.'

'Not tonight,' I said again, firmer this time. I nodded at Michael and put my hand over the door knob. 'We've got to go Mike yeah? Meet the others? It's important, right?'

Michael came to the door and pushed his unfinished lager into Anthony's hands. 'Don't do anything stupid,' he said to him, anxiously. 'Promise me you won't go over there, while we're gone? Promise me. I don't want you back in jail again.'

I watched Anthony's shoulders falling slowly in defeat. He sighed and rolled his eyes and shook his head all at once, as we pulled open to the door to leave.

The Boy With The Thorn In His Side-Part 2

'All right,' he agreed, but then he put his hand out and caught my shoulder. 'But we talk about this seriously in the morning, agreed? We can't let this go on any longer, all right?'

'All right,' I grinned and told him. 'See you later, okay?'

We slipped out of the door and escaped into the night. Into *our* night. We ran side by side, and we did not look back. We ran to where we would meet Billy and Jake out on Somerley road, to where we would hop onto the next bus that would take us into Belfield Park. I screwed up the bloodied tissue I still held in my hand and hurled it into the nearest bush, while examining my friends with wide-eyed anticipation.

'This is gonna' be the best night ever!' I promised their doubtful, shadowy faces.

10

The night that followed at Chaos was everything I had dreamed and hoped it would be. We jumped off the bus in Belfield Park and hurried down the high street before taking the second left as Jaime had instructed me to do. There was a kebab place on the corner and when I saw this I whooped loudly and declared we were close. We followed the road down to its dead end and then took a right which led down a narrow lane, already bustling and crowded with people. At the end of the lane stood a three-storey, grubbily white-washed Victorian building. It loomed up out of the darkness before us, almost church like in its height and grace and mystery. Break On Through by The Doors was pumping out onto the street. I turned to my friends and jumped up and down on the pavement.

'This is it!' I declared excitedly, emotionally, gripping a wide-eyed Billy by the lapels of his shirt and spinning him around in a circle. 'This is the place!'

We merged into the flock, we grinned and slapped hands and hugged each other, and we didn't even need the fake I.D. We shoved our money into the hands on the doors that reached for it, and there was no real queue, just a disorderly crowd of revellers who surged towards the opening. We found ourselves swept up among them, piling down some stairs to the lower floor, where there was no natural light and the walls were painted a dark and disturbing yellow. We paused at the bottom of the stairs while people flowed past us on either side. The bar curved around to the left, the floors were wooden and scarred, and battered red and black sofas were stuffed into the corners. Mismatched tables and chairs and stools were arranged around the edge of a large dance floor, complete with stage at one end. The floor was already full. I wanted to run onto it and jump up and down and throw my hair about. The crowd looked young and wild and hungry.

'Everyone looks like us!' Billy said beside me, his hand curling around my arm. I looked into his face and beamed.

'I know,' I said, looking at each of them in turn, at their flushed cheeks and their smiles of recognition. 'I told you, didn't I?' Just then the music changed and I immediately started leaping about, wrapping my arms around Billy's neck and taking him with me. 'Up In The Sky!' We bounced around like that, all four of us, until we were on the dance floor, going mental, screaming the lyrics into each other's ears, and when I looked at Billy's face, it made me so happy, because I could see how happy he was, *because* of the music! And we jumped and hugged and laughed and sang it out loud, and I was singing and wondering how the hell these songs seemed to know all about our lives?

'Our music!' I kept shouting at them. 'They play our music!'

I gave Jake the money to get the drinks in. He was the tallest by far and looked older than he was. We bounced around until the song ended and then flung ourselves at the nearest table when Jake came back with the drinks. He placed four whisky and cokes on the table and we hovered around the edges as there were no spare chairs. Sonic Youth's Sugar Cane had just come on. I picked up my drink and had a hard time getting it down me, my grin was so huge. Billy came to my side. His eyes were big and solemn and he touched my arm and looked like he was in shock.

'Danny,' he said. 'This is the best fucking place in the Universe. I never want to go home ever. But we have to drink up quick and dance and do it all quick, 'cause they'll take it away from us when they realise we're under-age! I swear to God they will!' He looked desperately panicked at the very thought. I laughed at him, nodding along to the music.

'Don't be stupid Bill, they can't kick us out now we're in and we've paid. Look around mate, does it look like anyone gives a shit? Relax!'

We drank the whiskys, so Jake went back and got bottles of beer next. 'That's it,' he said, handing me the change. 'Out of money.'

'Doesn't matter,' I shrugged. 'Who needs booze when the music is this good?'

With the drink and the music setting my brain on fire, a short while later I nudged Michael and told him to come to the toilets with me. He nodded without question and followed me across the dance floor, both of us gaping in wonder at the rock chicks and indie girls who swayed as we passed them, pint glasses in hand. Michael patted me on the back as we pushed into the toilets. They were painted black and the strip light on the ceiling flickered ominously as we walked in. They were crowded too; I had never seen so many interesting hairstyles and tattoos on display in one place.

'Amazing,' he kept saying to me, over and over. 'Amazing Danny, so amazing, best place ever!'

I was laughing helplessly as I shoved Michael into a cubicle and piled in behind him. I had a quick piss, throwing my head back and hooting when Blur's For Tomorrow started to play. I moved back so Michael could take his turn, and while he was at it, I took out the wrap of speed Jaime had given me. I had cigarette papers in my other pockets and made us both a speed bomb. I held one out to Michael when he had done up his flies and turned around. 'You want to?'

He stared at it, his mouth falling open in surprise and then closing again slowly. He made a sort of awkward face and shrugged his shoulders at me. I was about to withdraw my hand and leave him out of it after all, when he suddenly snorted laughter through his nose and snatched it from my hand.

'Oh why the hell not? You crazy bastard!'

We didn't need any more drinks after that. We bounced back out onto the dance floor, and when Supersonic kicked off, we dragged Jake and Billy out with us, and that was it. We sang at the top of our lungs, slinging our arms around each other, roaring out the words. And all that followed after was endless dancing and the worship of the music we loved. The music jumped from one genre to the next, playing Nirvana's Come As You Are, behind Suede's Animal Nitrate, and followed by The Clash, Should I Stay Or Should I Go? Of course I thought I was going to die with happiness when they played I Am The Resurrection. As soon as that long drum intro started, I just stood still, my eyes bulging from my face, my skin and hair slick with sweat, and then they all grabbed me and threw me about, knowing how much I loved it, how much it meant to me, and fuck, did I scream out those lyrics! I thought the music couldn't get any better, but I was wrong again and again and when Smells Like Teen Spirit started, it was like a bomb had gone off inside of us! It wasn't just us either. It was the whole place! The dance floor was like this unified thing, an animal, twisting, leaping, shoving, moving, and the floor was being pounded, and the vibrations shook up and down my body.

The Boy With The Thorn In His Side-Part 2

After that Billy and Jake seemed to be fading fast. They scraped enough money off the floor to buy themselves a coke to share and slunk back to the table with it. Michael and I continued to go off like rockets. We thought of Anthony when Primal Scream's Movin' On Up started, and Michael bellowed into my ear that he would drag him along next time.

I soon worked out that although the DJ had been well and truly in control at the beginning of the night, he was now operating a request system. I watched the line of people winding slowly up the black spiral staircase to reach him. I dragged Michael with me, gripping the thrumming hand rail with sweat slicked hands, damp hair in my eyes, and my blood hurtling through my veins at breakneck speed. The DJ was a tall guy in his late twenties with long black hair and he grinned and nodded when I reeled off my list of requests. By the time we had descended the stairs again, Panic by The Smiths was already playing, and I started laughing and just couldn't stop.

I knew I was as high as a kite, as happy as it was possible to get, as full of life and love as I would probably ever be. I felt on top of the world, bigger and stronger than ever, in control and I didn't want it to ever end. That was the only bad thing, the only thing that caused my mood and spirit to flag; the thought of it all coming to an end. I grabbed Michael and sang into his shining face, screaming about burning down the disco, hanging the blessed DJ, and he was pulling away and laughing at me, and he tripped over his feet and landed in a heap with me on top of him still screaming it, still desperate for him to listen, to know, to understand, to understand what?

Song after song, after song. 'Not one bad one! Not one shitty song! Not one single one!' I repeated it like a broken record all the way home. I couldn't keep still on the bus, I wanted to be dancing and jumping, with the music vibrating all over me. I wanted my head to be permanently full of it. I didn't want it to ever be turned down or turned off. 'Not one bad song,' I said it again and again. 'Not even one!'

Back at Michael's, we entertained a sceptical looking Anthony with our run down of the most amazing night we had ever experienced, while Billy and Jake sunk onto either end of the sofa, asleep before their heads hit the cushions. I could remember every single song that had been played, a fact which astonished Michael. I babbled on for a few more hours, talking so fast that Anthony had to keep holding his hand up and telling me to slow down, to calm down. He listened, but regarded me with a sombre and suspicious eye. Eventually he declared he was off to bed and dropped a load of blankets on top of where we lay on the lounge floor. When he was gone I took out the pills from Jaime and passed one under the blankets to Michael.

'What's this?' he whispered, his face pale and clammy, his pupils like specks of dust in his massive brown eyes.

'It's so you don't feel crappy tomorrow,' I told him, still smiling endlessly with the warm and fuzzy feeling that had captured me. 'So Anthony won't notice anything.' He looked impressed and took the pill. We lay on our bellies beside each other, kicking our legs up and down under the blankets.

'Such a good night,' Michael said softly, turning his face to the side to grin at me. 'The best ever.'

I smiled back, this huge dopey smile, and I felt like the love and the light and all of everything that was pure and good, was alive and living inside my brain, shining out at him from behind my eyes. I was sure of it. I believed in it totally and utterly.

'You deserve it,' he told me then. 'You deserve a good time.'

'There's a lot of joy...in a lot of things, isn't there?' I said to him, before the pills took hold. I think it was the last thing I said to him, but I'm not sure. In my dreams I carried on talking all night long. Listing the songs, clinging on to the feeling.

The Boy With The Thorn In His Side-Part 2

11

Michael and I slept through Billy and Jake waking up to hangovers that sent them scuttling home. We slept right through the morning, wrapped tight in delicious dreams. The music rang on inside my head. Anthony tried all morning to coax us from our slumbers, but we were too far gone, too deep down, not coming back for anyone. He just had to wait.

When I started to wake up properly, I remembered that my body was battered and that pain was a constant companion. I pushed this knowledge aside however. I listened to the music inside my head and my feet danced at the ends of my legs. I was not in a hurry to move, or speak, or live. I just wanted to stay there, wrapped in blankets on the floor of the darkened lounge, while Sunday morning life kicked into action outside the window.

Anthony stomped in and out, waving a wooden spoon about and talking about breakfast, and then lunch. Eventually he sat down and turned the TV on, keeping a watchful eye on us as we stirred slowly and reluctantly into life. After a while, he picked up a cushion and threw it at us. We laughed under our blankets, but this was not the effect he wanted. He got up, stood next to us and poked at Michael with his shoe.

'Wakey wakey,' he said gruffly. I opened my eyes and saw his grim expression bearing down on us. He started poking at my shoulder with his shoe. I had the sudden urge to punch his foot away. My smile faded. He looked pissed off and about to explode. 'Rise and shine,' he said. 'You *fucking* little bastards.'

Michael merely giggled, not understanding the look upon his brother's face. I understood it and it made me wary. I sat up slowly and rubbed with both hands at my sleepy face. I tested my lip with my tongue. It felt crusty and swollen. Anthony had not finished with us. He squatted down, his eyebrows raised, his face expectant and waiting. I offered him a pointless shrug.

'Was a good night,' Michael was murmuring beside me. 'Was an amazing night.'

I wanted to agree with him, and drag back the memories and the good feeling I had woken up with, but I was caught in the glare of Anthony's dark eyes, and I felt the accusation lying behind them.

'I ought to kick both your arses,' he told us then, his eyes flicking angrily between us.

Michael sat up, frowned and yawned. 'What's the matter with you?'

'Don't treat me like an idiot,' he snapped, shaking his head. 'I know what you two did. I saw your eyes when you got in. I sat and listened to you babbling away for hours, not making any sense.' He nodded when Michael's cheeks burned red, and then his eyes turned on me. 'And as for *you* sunshine, aren't you supposed to be meeting someone down the beach? I've been trying to wake you up all morning, so don't blame me if she's pissed off home by now.'

I stared back at him blankly. It took a few minutes for the information and the reality to sink in, and as I stared, Anthony stared back, his mouth a tight straight line, his dark eyes full of disappointment and anger. When the realisation hit me fully, it sent me lunging up from the floor, slapping a hand against my own cheek as I mumbled; 'oh fuckinghell Lucy.'

There was nothing for it. I was bone tired and heavy headed, but I had to go. I pulled on my jacket and stumbled out of the front door, straight into the dazzling cruelty of the afternoon sun. I couldn't run. My body was like wet lead and I ached all over. I felt like I'd gone twenty rounds in a boxing ring. I felt a rising rage and disgust within me. I loped and trotted and plodded mechanically towards the beach, and every now and again I would pass a wall and feel the urge to drag the back of my hand along it. Don't ask me why. Just that I was starting to feel the hurt again, on the inside, and maybe some hurt on the outside would take my mind off it. I wanted to be in bed, and that was pissing me off, but I had to find her, I had to explain.

She was not there. I trudged along the beach front to check the shop and the café, but they were deserted. She had gone. I lowered my shoulders in recognition of defeat, in surrender to misery, turned around and started to trudge slowly back the way I had come. The music was still pumping through my brain in a strange and distorted way. Jumbled up lyrics and melodies that tried to out run each other. I

The Boy With The Thorn In His Side-Part 2

clung to it though. I played the night back over in my head, and it was either remember that, or remember the foot to my face and the blood spray, and the things that were to come.

I walked slowly and clumsily towards her house. I staggered along the road she lived on, recalling with bitter memory how Michael and I had gone up there to cut people's lawns. How naïve we had been, I thought then, as I slipped past like a ghost. Thinking we could impress these kinds of people, with their huge houses, and their gardens the size of football pitches. I planted one foot in front of the other, slowly and deliberately. People like that, I was thinking, people like that act like they want to help you and like you, but in truth, they don't want you anywhere fucking near them. Under the pretence of niceness, they were always searching for the cracks. The proof they needed to know they were right to distrust you in the first place. I knew it was going to be like that when I knocked upon the Chapman's front door.

Her house had an unobstructed view of the sea and an epic, sweeping drive. I felt small and rat like as I slunk towards her front door. The door was heavy and thick, and would have looked at home on a castle, or on a country manor. I lifted the brass knocker with pathetically weak hands and let it fall again. I had to lean with one arm against the wall, my legs giving up the effort, my body feeling fluid, like the sea I could hear washing in and out behind me. As I waited for a response, I glanced around. I looked at the crawling creeping flowers and plants that grew up the sides of the house and around the windows. There were window planters and borders, and shrubs, and millions of things I didn't know the names of. I gazed around at the lawn, and at the gardener who stood watching me from the other end, gloves on, cap low, and eyes blinking in the sunshine. I sighed and sensed inevitability and failure all around me, all inside me. I gave myself up to it.

Her father answered the door, dressed in casual weekend trousers and a polite short sleeved shirt. He wore these soft white shoes upon his feet, and I imagined that he had a game of golf planned for later in the day, or something. I opened my mouth and asked for Lucy, and I watched his forehead crease and crinkle into about a million little lines of despair and worry. His lips twitched and his body visibly stiffened.

'I really need to see her,' I added, not even convincing myself. His mouth tightened, and he straightened his back and shoulders and looked as if he were trying to distinguish a way to speak the truth politely.

'Well she's very upset Daniel,' he said, with this little shake of his head, when probably what he felt like doing was giving my dishevelled body a good shake.

'I was supposed to meet her,' I tried to explain sorrowfully. 'I was late, because I slept in, because I was feeling ill...but that's why, I mean, can I explain that to her please?'

He looked me up and down very quickly, and I knew what he was thinking and seeing behind his neat little spectacles. 'I'll tell her you're here,' he said, his face nothing less than an awkward, blustering mess.

I nodded and smiled and waited patiently, eyeing up the roses, as they were the only plant I knew the name of. When she came to the door moments later, she stepped neatly outside and pulled it shut behind her. I could see right away that she had been crying, as the rims of her eyes were all red. I felt like shit because of it, but I could also see that she was angry, and I had never seen her angry before. She crossed her arms tightly over her chest. She looked like she had made an effort for some reason. She was wearing a dress, for one thing. And make-up. I wanted to groan, which would have been cruel, but I wanted to tell her that she should know I didn't give a shit about those stupid things.

'I waited for you,' she said, her voice wavering slightly on the last word. She took a breath and glanced away to compose herself before going on. 'I waited for three hours on that beach for you. Where were you?'

'At Mike's,' I told her, hoping the desperate look in my blue eyes would do the trick. 'I was just asleep! Didn't mean to sleep that long, but we all went out to this crazy, amazing club last night Lucy! I just slept in, and as soon as I woke up, I ran down to the beach and then came straight here.'

'It's gone one o'clock,' she told me icily.

I nodded. 'I know. Well, I know now. We had a really late night.' I offered an apologetic smile and a slight shrug of the shoulders but she was having none of it. She was silent as she ran her brown eyes up and down my shabby appearance, just as her father had done.

'You look awful.'

'Thanks.'

'What happened to your face?'

I smiled slightly. She was pissing me off, to be honest. Looking me up and down like I was a piece of dog shit on the precious green lawn. I touched a finger to my cut lip and rolled my eyes. I felt like whipping up my t-shirt and flashing her a glimpse of my black bruises, laughing in her screwed up little face and asking if she had a better reason than that to be pissed off?

'Nothing,' I told her. 'I fell over.'

'Where did you go?'

'This club called Chaos,' I said, starting to get excited again. 'This amazing place in Belfield Park! Plays all the music we like! None of this mainstream pop shit, just decent, proper music! You *have* to come next time Luce, I'm serious. They didn't play one bad song, not one.'

She was just frowning and not caring. 'How did you get in? You're not old enough.'

'Fake I.D,' I said. 'But we didn't even need them in the end. It was brilliant Lucy, we had the best time ever, just the most amazing night ever!'

She regarded me with still, cool eyes. 'Yeah, you look like you did. Did you take that stuff again?'

The question caught me off guard. I opened my mouth, and had no idea whether to lie about it or tell the truth. My hesitation and flustering was enough of an answer for her though. She nodded once, answering her own question and I just smiled a helpless smile.

'I just wanted to have fun,' I said defensively. 'Just wanted to have a really, really good night. I needed to.'

'So, you can't have fun without it? You can't have a good time without taking that stuff? Even though it made you so ill last time? Have you completely forgotten about that Danny?'

'Course not,' I shrugged. 'Listen, Lucy I just needed a good time, I'm serious, you have no idea how crap things have been lately.'

'And did you?'

'What?'

'Did you enjoy your night at this club, on speed, or whatever else it was this time!' She was getting angrier by the second and I sighed and glanced over my shoulders in a bored kind of way. I felt like backing off and leaving her to her little tantrum. Her arms tightened over her chest and her lower lip shook at me. 'And how was the morning after?' she went on. 'I'm assuming it wasn't as terrible as last time, seeing as how you can walk by yourself and you're not crying all over me!'

My mouth fell open in surprise and hurt. I was genuinely shocked she had hit me with that. My weak smile evaporated to nothing.

'That's not fair,' I said rigidly. 'You have no idea the crap I've had to deal with lately, you have no fucking idea! All right for you, isn't it? Up here with your perfect house and your perfect family! It's not like that for everyone you know! You have no idea!' I was getting angry with her now, and it was an ugly thing. Jealously and resentment directed at the last person who deserved it. Her expression was indignant, and I felt small and judged.

'No!' she shouted right back at me. 'Because you never tell me! You don't tell me anything at all Danny, you keep it all to yourself, whatever it is, you just want me there for company or whatever! You just expect me to there to comfort you, without ever telling me why you need it!'

I took a deep breath and looked away from her. I could see the gardener out of the corner of my eye. He had his gloved hands resting on the end of his rake. A curtain twitched in one of the front rooms. I didn't need this shit. I was going to have worse shit than this to deal with pretty soon, and I wanted to get some sleep somewhere first. I was close to telling her to piss off, close to telling her a lot of things, but I tried to calm down, I tried to gain control of things before they spiralled out of control.

'Look, I'm sorry I was late, but I did go, I was just late Lucy, and I'm here now! Ran all the way I did.'

The Boy With The Thorn In His Side-Part 2

'Late,' she snapped. 'Because you were too busy coming down, or whatever the hell you call it. I don't even want to know. I think it's pathetic if you want the truth. I think you look a total mess, and you're screwing up your life, and it's not worth it, not for one night of fun! And because taking it is so important to you, you missed our date.'

'Date?' I asked, not understanding. I saw the instant flash of hostility in her eyes, the anger which slipped quickly into hurt, and I took a reproachful step towards her, reaching out for her arm. She pulled away from me. Tears had sprung into her eyes.

'Well I thought it was a date,' she said, and her whole face seemed to tremble with the effort it was taking her not to cry. 'But obviously I was wrong, obviously I was wrong about a lot of things, and obviously I've been wasting my time and making a complete idiot of myself, and you would much rather be getting off your head and lying in bed all day than being with me so....' She left the statement hanging in the air and gazed down at her shoeless feet, her teeth raking back over her quivering bottom lip.

'I wouldn't rather do that,' I told her, sinking my hands into my pockets. 'You're not being very fair Luce. It's only happened once...'

'Yeah, and it will happen again,' she declared with a sudden and definitive toss of her head, as she spun around and pushed open the door. 'Until you sort yourself out.'

I stepped forward desperately. 'I can't do that without you!'

'Danny, I'm not going to be your counsellor or something,' she said this softly, now safely returned to the warmth of the hallway. 'I just wanted to be your girlfriend, that's all. But I don't think that's what you want right now.' She sniffed up her tears and closed the door on me. I found myself facing the wood again. I let out a growl and kicked it, again and again, with a rush of anger that shook through me without warning.

'Lucy! Come back and talk to me! Lucy!'

The door reopened and Mr Chapman stared down at me unhappily. His face was even more concerned and twitchy now, and I felt his middle-aged eyes running up and down me again, making me want to snarl and lash out like a cornered dog.

'I just wanna' talk to her!'

'She doesn't want to talk to you,' he explained this calmly and firmly. 'Now, I don't know yet exactly what you've done to upset her so much, but I strongly suggest you go away now and don't come back.' He gave me a long, warning stare, and then closed the door again. I felt the rage boil over again, and kicked and punched at the door in my face.

'Well fuck you!' I heard my voice screeching back at him. 'Fuck you mate! Think you're better than me! Fuck you, you stuck up bastard!' I would have gone on longer, kicking and shouting at the door, but the gardener was already on his way over, marching in olive green boots across the lawn, with his rake still in one hand. I gave him the finger and stormed away.

I walked back to the estate in a whirlwind of fury and self-pity. My mind was a muddle of guilt, rage and self-loathing, and my feet wanted to kick something, my hands wanted to punch something, and if someone had stepped into my way I probably would have knocked them out. I'm turning into him now, I thought in growing horror as I walked on, he's infected me with it, and that's what will happen, that's what I will become. A monster. It was almost like I could feel it happening inside of me, like my soul was curling and peeling away from me, blackened and rotting, revealing something primitive and ugly beneath.

I was storming blindly past Michael's front door, when it flung open suddenly, and Anthony appeared before me, practically jumping right into my path. He stopped me with a finger held in the air, and a dark look in his eyes.

'A word,' he said, and so I stopped and stared right back at him, waiting and dreading and hating.

'What?'

Anthony breathed noisily down through his nose, and as he kept the finger pointed at my face, one of his eyebrows rose on its own.

'You *ever* give my brother that nasty dangerous shit again, and I'll kick your fucking arse, right?'

I recoiled from him in miserable anger and shock. I swung my body around his, but paused long enough to snarl up into his face; 'Oh

The Boy With The Thorn In His Side-Part 2

yeah? Like to see you fucking try! You're just like everyone else!' I stuffed my hands deep into my pockets and rushed away from him.

I couldn't bear it. I didn't think I could bear it, not ever. I walked in a circle, not thinking, just breathing too fast, feeling like I was about to explode one way or the other. I didn't know what to do or where to go. I couldn't go home. I couldn't go anywhere. Pity overloaded me then. Grief, and guilt and regret, it wrenched itself through me, dragging me down, crushing me slowly. I'll just go home and find Howard, I thought then. Let him kill me. Let him do it. They'd all be happy then, wouldn't they?

Instead, I ended up at the park, sat on a bench, and shivering in my Nirvana t-shirt. I swung my feet back and forth, scuffing the soles of my boots against the tarmac. The swings shifted restlessly just in front of me. I watched a massive seagull land on the top of the slide, where it sat for ages, just laughing at me. I stared at the ground, and watched the rubbish roll by, and I felt nothing less than wretched and pathetic and hated by everyone. I wanted a drink. I wanted a hundred drinks. I wanted a smoke. I wanted to smoke until my eyes bled and my vision failed. I wanted a pill to put me out of my misery. I wanted to learn how not to give a shit about anything, how not to care, and I wondered if it would ever become possible.

I could feel a lump in my back pocket. I searched there, and pulled it out, and it was my knife, and I didn't even remember putting it there, but it made me smile just for a second. I passed it from one hand to the other. Then I laid the blade down onto one palm, and I felt my body begin to loosen, and relax. I took deep breaths, staring at the knife, before running one curious finger down the sharp edge of the blade. I held it by the handle and started to try to carve my name into the bench. I had carved Dan in jagged, spidery letters when I stopped suddenly, and gave in to a crazy impulse, slashing the blade across my own arm instead. I took a sharp intake of breath and heard the knife clatter to the ground. I held my wrist up to my face and stared in morbid curiosity at the cut I had made. Thick dark blood welled to life along the slash, and so I pressed a finger into it, and watched the blood dripping faster, trailing a ruby zigzag down towards my elbow. I stared at the mess of it all in complete detached wonder and felt a strange and numb calm wash over me.

A short while later I picked up the knife, slipped it back into my pocket and walked away from the park. The cut was stinging, but the blood had stopped. As I walked I focused my mind on the stinging, and I felt satisfied by it. Don't ask me why. How can you explain these things? I suppose, if I look back now, I was trying to take some control, by inflicting the pain on myself instead of waiting for someone else to do it. I don't know. Who knows? Who cares? It was him or me. I knew that all along. I knew that from the beginning. It was always going to come down to that.

Half an hour later I was letting myself into Jack's flat. He grunted from his favourite sofa where he was sprawled out in white vest and loose grey trousers. The smell of stale sweat and cold curry permeated my nostrils. The flat was warm though. The TV was on. He made me a whisky and coke without saying a word and passed it to me when I sat down. My body lolled into the sofa, too heavy and broken to ever move again. I stared at the TV screen.

'Don't tell him I'm here,' I said after a while.

Jack lit his cigar and laughed. 'You on the run?'

'Just don't tell him,' I repeated. 'He's evil you know. He's gonna' kill me one of these days. One of these days, he's gonna' kill me.'

'Well I don't expect to see his lordship tonight,' Jack told me with a sigh. 'So, you can stop getting your knickers in a twist. Oh, that reminds me though. Someone else is looking for you.'

I looked at him sharply. 'Who?'

'Jaime Lawler,' he replied, eyes firmly on me. 'Came round earlier. Says you owe him money.'

'Oh yeah. I do.'

'Lee says you're not working at the club anymore? That right?'

I nodded at him. 'I'm never stepping foot in that place again in my life. Not with that evil bastard.'

Jack smoked his cigar and drummed the podgy fingers of one hand against the armrest of the sofa.

'Well then, seems to me you better start thinking of other ways to earn money kiddo. Or you're gonna' be finding yourself in all kinds of trouble.'

The Boy With The Thorn In His Side-Part 2

12

The most important thing was making sure I did not feel anything. I'd wondered if it was possible, that day on the bench. I discovered it was pretty easy with a little bit of help. That became my main purpose every single day. There were moments where the last drink wore off, when a new day began without my permission, when the cold fingers of reality would arrive to tap me on the shoulder. I never looked reality in the face. I turned away and picked up another drink. Nothing panicked me more than the sensation of the veil beginning to lift. I would catch a glimpse of my own mind ticking back into action, starting to form thoughts again, and that was never a good thing, because thinking too much led to pain, one way or another. Thinking too much made it all come back, and it was too much for me to stand. In moments of sad clarity such as these, I would feel as if I had awoken briefly from a confusing dream, and I would look down at myself, usually slumped like a rag doll on Jack's grotty sofa. I would ask stupid, hollow questions while tears filled my eyes.

'Why is he like that?' Jack would only shake his head and sigh. 'Why does he want to destroy me? You must know. I'll save him the trouble today. I'll go and jump off the cliff.' I meant it when I said it, but I never did it.

My questions would simply echo, unanswered around the darkened flat, which had become my refuge and my prison. Then Jack would do his best to cheer me up, and there was always something on offer, and he was always generous with his offerings. I would never say no, and then I would drift away again, and there would be no pain, no sorrow, no nothing.

I listened to music. Sometimes it drowned out the pain, sometimes it intensified it. Bobby Gillespie singing Cry Myself Blind; it was like he was talking to me and I'd sit and nod and tell him yes, I have had a broken heart, yes I have lost my mind, yes I have woken up screaming because I'm so lonely I want to die... That was a tough one. I'd blow out my breath, stare at nothing and see Lucy in my head, her hair falling over her face, her smile telling me everything was gonna' be okay...except it wasn't, was it? She was gone, I was so lonely, I was gonna' cry myself blind...It hurt so much without her I couldn't think straight.

Nothingness was always welcome. I tried to fight back with it when the self-loathing crept in. It haunted me when I was alone, when Jack was out. I would sit and rip myself to shreds, peeling back the layers until I became a nothing person, an empty shell who simply lived and breathed. My aim was to reach a point where I would not be able to experience fear anymore, because I wouldn't be able to feel anything. Waking up sober was a terrible torture. Instantly my mind was sickened and I felt disgusted with myself, for what I had taken, for what I had done to myself, for everything, and I would think, I am dying slowly inside, this is a slow death, and he will win. I found that I did not really care, so long as all of this was over.

Rebirth seemed a nice option, if only such a thing existed. I daydreamed about it sometimes when I was spaced out in the flat. Being born again as someone else, someone new. Someone better than I was; someone who was innocent and pure, and good and strong. Sometimes I would lay and stare at the skin that covered my bones, and I would have the strongest urge to start scratching away at it, to scrape back the layers in case there was someone better hidden underneath.

When I slept, Howard was there, infesting my dreams. I sought to drink and smoke as much as I could to find a level of unconsciousness that would hold the dreams at bay. But it never worked for long, because he was always there, looming over me, with doom in his eye and he was twisting a knife around in my belly, laughing and laughing as he turned it, curling my guts slowly up the blade. Nights were full of horror. I twisted and turned among wretched dreams, sometimes waking myself up with my own screams.

The day after Lucy closed the door on me, and Anthony threatened me, I pushed them all away inside my mind. I decided I didn't want or need any of them. I hid out at Jack's flat until Howard hunted me down there. He came through the door like a tornado, spewing out eye bulging rage, his teeth shining and gnashing, his hands reaching for me. I knew it was coming and I did nothing to avoid the storm.

The Boy With The Thorn In His Side-Part 2

'Your mother has gone to Leeds to see John,' he stood before me and said, planting his hands on his wide hips, staring down at me while he huffed and puffed. 'What do you think about that eh?'

I shrugged and told him what I really thought. 'I don't give a shit.'

He laughed. It was high pitched and manic. He told me that it was about time I learnt my lesson again. That he would make me give a shit. I wondered if he had been drinking, because he had a crazed look in his eyes, and he was sweating like a pig, and I just sat there and stared up at him, a look of dull defiance on my face.

'I'll get you back in line,' he started ranting, before he grabbed me and threw me to the floor. He was in a state, wrestling with the waist band of his jeans. 'Get you right back in fucking line!' He realised he was not wearing a belt and went completely insane, kicking over Jack's glass coffee table and sending it shattering to the floor. He then started pacing around the flat, and I looked up from the floor and saw the door, but I couldn't even be bothered to try to get to it. I just didn't care. He came back from the kitchen, brandishing the cord from the kettle, and he put his foot on me and started lashing out with it.

'All right,' I heard Jack saying in the background. 'That's enough, Lee…come on now…That's enough!'

'Just kill me then, just kill me,' I tried to tell him and when he was done he lowered himself down on top of me, twisted my hair into his hands and pressed his face against mine. 'Do it, just kill me,' I dared him, breathless with pain.

'Your mum should have aborted you when she had the chance,' he breathed into my ear. 'That's what she wanted to do to you…She doesn't give a shit Danny, do you get that now? She doesn't give a shit!'

I knew what Howard was doing, putting me right back to square one, and I didn't care, in fact I was glad. It was easier that way.

He left, and I found myself existing in a fire of agony that would not cease, and I started to cry, even though I didn't want to and Jack got me onto the sofa, and the pain was electric, the kind of pain you cannot even breathe through, the kind of pain that makes you want to die, the kind of pain that ties your mind up in a cage. I writhed

101

and panted on the sofa, and it was Jack that rolled me a joint and held it to my lips.

'He doesn't know any other way,' I heard him murmuring softly. 'It's all he knows. You shouldn't antagonise him like that...You shouldn't do it! Best you just stay on the right side of him, with your mum gone again.'

The joint did nothing to help the pain, and I lay there and whimpered until he fetched me a shot of whisky, followed by another. Eventually I guess he got annoyed with my crying, because he came and pushed a pill inside my mouth, and I swallowed it and I was so glad, so relieved, because whatever it was worked quickly, and I felt my body being lifted by gentle hands that carried me away and for ages after that I felt like I was floating, just floating on the ocean.

When I woke up in the night, he was sat beside me with his hand resting on my head. I rolled away from him, shivering as I felt his fingers unwind one by one from my hair. I wanted to cry again, because I knew he did that sometimes, and I didn't understand why, or what it meant, only that in a strange kind of way it was almost nice, comforting. I would just bury myself in the blankets and the thick deep sleep would arrive to claim me and I would forget about it all in the morning. I would wake up searching for escape, and everything that existed inside my head was pushed away, stamped down, wiped out.

There was nothing to do, nowhere to turn to except oblivion, and Jack let me have whatever I wanted. If it was there I could have it. If it wasn't there, then we would call Jaime Lawler over.

'Give us a smile,' he would tease sometimes, before handing it over. 'Give me the eyes.' He pushed food in front of me but it turned my stomach. I didn't want to do anything that would prolong my existence, but I didn't have the courage to end it suddenly either. 'Try this,' he would say to me. 'Just try this...c'mon, it'll cheer you up...'

The only thing that made me move was music. The only thing that made my heart beat was music. The only reason I left the flat was music. I had to leave the flat to find the music, and when I was in The Record Shop, though Terry viewed me with a perturbed and disdainful expression, he never turned me away.

The Boy With The Thorn In His Side-Part 2

He let me stay in there for hours if I wanted to. I didn't talk to him much. He laughed about this, saying that at one point he could never shut me up. He made me cups of tea and he started offering me money to sort out the shelves, or to answer the phone. Sometimes he tried to pull conversations out of me, asking my opinion on new releases, offering me singles and albums to take home and try for free.

'Your opinion is worth more than mine,' he would explain. 'The kids that come in here don't take my word for it these days!'

The shop was busier than it had ever been. It was the same kinds of kids that came in, day after day. Terry called them Indie kids, and they all had hair like the Gallagher's, or hair like Jarvis Cocker. They wore parka coats and flared jeans, and devoured music by the likes of Pulp, Suede, Blur, Elastica and Supergrass. Terry had a fair amount of sarcasm for the lot of them. Members of a scene, he explained. Followers of a rule book.

'Not like you,' he told me once. 'You're cool, because you like everything.'

It seemed like word got out quickly about the fat man letting me hang around in the shop, letting me work for money. Michael came through the door one day after school. He shook his head slowly and sadly when he saw me crouched on the floor, dusting off cassettes before I put them in order. Just the desperate look in his eye made me want to sever an artery. I looked away from him. I wondered what the hell he wanted. He picked up a CD and squatted down next to me, while Terry went back to his magazine behind the counter.

'You're never at school,' he started, and he was right. I had given up on that again. I hadn't been for weeks. My mother was still up in Leeds with John. I was starting to wonder if she would ever come back at all. I rolled my eyes and ignored him. 'I've been talking to Lucy,' he went on regardless, speaking in low tones, with his eyes on my face. 'I took her to the café yesterday Danny. I explained everything to her. Are you listening? I know you don't want people to know stuff, but I had to explain it to her, I had to make her see why you didn't turn up that day.'

I didn't look at him. I didn't allow the words or the information to infiltrate my mind. I picked up another cassette. The best of Dusty Springfield. I started to wipe it clean with the yellow duster Terry had given me. Michael sighed beside me.

'Listen,' he said. 'She understands. The reason she was mad at you, is she went back the next week, in case you went back...she said she really thought you would, you know, because you'd been going every Sunday for like months. She went back Danny, the next few Sundays in a row to see you there. To sort things out.'

I rolled my eyes again and shrugged loosely. I placed the cassette on the shelf under D and picked up the next one. Guns 'N' Roses, Appetite For Destruction. The casing was split, so I put it in another pile, knowing Terry would want it in the discount bin next to the counter. Michael clicked his tongue angrily.

'Danny, can you speak? For fucks sake mate! I'm just gonna' keep coming in here until you do! Did you hear what I said? About Lucy? She's gonna' come and see you in here mate, I don't know when, but she said she would because she wants you two to make up, you know?'

'Going to Chaos this Friday,' I told him then, frowning down at the next tape in the pile. More Bob Dylan Greatest Hits. 'If you wanna' come. I'll meet you there. Or whatever.'

He nodded instantly. 'Okay then. I will. I'll see you there. We'll talk then, right? We'll catch up.' I nodded and he got up and walked out.

I had another visitor not long after. Jaime Lawler, at first just hovering outside of the door, finishing off his cigarette. I watched him from inside. He was tall and thin, and hunched up against the cold, with his cap pulled low and his tracksuit jacket zipped right up to his chin. He nodded at me when he saw me looking. Terry was on his stool, his wide berth dripping down either side of it. His nose buried in the NME. He didn't even look up when Jaime walked in through the door. He played it cool at first, well about as cool as he was capable of. He picked up a CD, and then put it back too quickly. Walked along and picked up another, and then came right up to me with it. Not exactly subtle. I was starting to think the guy was a bit simple, to be honest. He could have had DRUG DEALER tattooed across his forehead and it still would have been more discreet than his behaviour

The Boy With The Thorn In His Side-Part 2

at times. He loped up to the side of me with this lop-sided grin on his thin face.

'All right mate? You working in here now or what?'

'Sort of,' I shrugged.

He looked pleased and stared around at the shelves full of music. 'Wow, pretty cool ain't it? Must be your idea of heaven eh?' He nudged me with one spiky elbow and I flinched. He looked sorry and tried a grin instead. 'Still waiting for my money mate,' he said then, leaning towards me and dropping his voice to a whisper. I nodded at him. I dug around in my back pocket and brought out a crumpled ten-pound note and a handful of change. He took it and examined it before slipping it into his own pocket. 'That don't even really touch what you owe me mate,' he said, with a regretful shrug.

'I know. I'll get you some more.' I nodded at Terry. 'He's started paying me a bit. I might get a proper job here when I'm sixteen.'

Jaime looked hopeful. 'Oh yeah? When's that?'

'August.'

He made a face. 'Fuckinghell I can't wait that long mate! Look we'll talk later yeah, I got to go and meet this mate of yours now. You know he's working in The Ship?'

I was totally confused. 'Who is?'

'Anthony. Me old mate from school.'

'He's working in The Ship?'

'Yeah, out the back, cheffing. I'm gonna' go and get me a pie and chips, warm me right up.' Jaime patted my back and headed for the door.

I stepped behind him. 'What do you mean you're meeting him? What for?'

Jaime pulled open the door and a rush of cold air swirled around our ankles. He looked down at me, and there was for once an almost human look in his restless grey eyes, and it looked like he was trying to decide what to say to me, and how to say it. He grimaced a little and scratched at his scrawny neck, and then pushed his cap back so that he could rake his short nails through the front of his wispy blonde hair. He tugged the cap back into place and clapped me on the back instead. I really wished he hadn't. It hurt so much I was almost sick.

'Well you know me,' he said. 'Keep everyone's secrets don't I eh? Ask him yourself if you wanna' know. Seeya' later mate. You at Chaos on Friday or what?' I nodded that I was. He snorted as he left. 'I'll be expecting a begging call from you then. Seeya' mate.'

I went back to my work, dazed and wondering and swallowing pain. Part of me wanted to chase down the road after him. But the other part of me wanted to know nothing about anything and went back to sleep instead. There was nothing I could do anyway, I reasoned. I hadn't seen Anthony since he had laid into me for giving Michael speed that night. I imagined he hated me, and that was that. Truth was, I was too ashamed of myself to go anywhere near him.

'Dodgy as fuck, that one,' Terry remarked wearily from his stool. I couldn't have agreed with him more. I went back to the tapes, taking my time over each one, cleaning them and checking them for wear and damage. The Stone Roses were playing Shoot You Down on the record player. 'All this new indie Britpop stuff,' Terry started saying. 'It's all influenced by The Stone Roses, I mean, it started with them and Inspirals and all that right?' I looked up and shrugged, not sure if I could be bothered to get into a debate with him right then. 'And they were influenced by The Smiths. It all comes back to The Smiths you see.'

'Bullshit,' I told him. 'Who were they influenced by then? Sixties guitar bands?'

'No, punk you idiot!' he roared back at me. 'It's a well-known fact that Morrissey was a fan of The New York Dolls. I'm putting them on next to educate you.'

I just sighed and let him get on with it. The man had an unhealthy obsession with The Smiths. According to him, anything good about music today could be attributed to them. He slipped off his stool after a while and went out the back to put the kettle on. While he was gone, the door opened again and Lucy walked in. She looked awkward and nervous in her smart school uniform, her bag on her shoulder, and two thick text books clutched to her chest. Her face brightened when she saw me kneeling on the floor.

The Boy With The Thorn In His Side-Part 2

'There you are!'

'Yeah,' I said, and stood up.

She hugged her books and smiled sheepishly. 'How are you?'

I shrugged at her. 'Good.'

Her smile faltered, and then returned stronger. 'Want to try and sell me some music? You normally can't shut up about it.'

I shook my head at her. I was tired. I didn't need this, whatever this was. I felt like cringing under her pitying glare. I couldn't stand the thought of what Michael had told her. I imagined them sat in the café together, their heads lowered over their coffees or their milkshakes, while Michael filled her in on the full story of my pathetic little life. I felt a cold anger shaking through me. It was directed right at her, and yet again, I thought, here he is, here is the monster right on cue, seeping through me, taking me over. I wanted her away from me. I was no good for her. I would only drag her down and destroy her. Couldn't she see that?

'I just wanted to see you,' she tried to explain, her smile gone now, her eyes heavy with sadness. 'Michael...I mean, he spoke to me...He explained so much to me Danny...and I had to see you, I just had to come and see you.'

I gave her a hard look. 'Well now you've seen me,' I said, and turned away from her.

13

    I stayed as invisible as I could for the rest of the school term. I was rarely seen anywhere and I liked it that way. It was safer for everyone. I felt I had well and truly burned my bridges with Lucy, and on the rare occasions that I did make it into school, I ducked my head and looked the other way if I saw her coming.
    'You're being an idiot,' Michael told me angrily whenever I was around him long enough to listen. 'She just wants to talk to you! Why are you pushing us all away?'
    'She's better off without me,' I replied coldly, and walked away from him. The only thing that kept me going, the only glint of light on the horizon was going to Chaos on a Friday night. If music was my religion, then Chaos became my church. I went every week without fail. I went with the others and I went on my own. It didn't matter to me either way. I went high and I went straight. As long as I went, as long as I made it to Friday, then there was some joy and some pleasure, and the adrenalin from a happiness that eluded me the rest of the time. I felt like a different person when I was on the dance floor, or when I was sat in the corner, just listening to the music thumping through the walls and up from the floorboards.
    I was always looking for music that made me shiver. You ever felt that? You know, when the words, or the chords, or the arrangement, something, at some point in a song makes you shiver, makes a tingle run down your spine, makes your hairs stand on end. I fucking lived for that. I hunted it down. When it came it took my breath away and it felt like I was falling...I felt the music beating in my veins and I remembered that I was alive, and that this was a life. Friday was my day, my only day. I would meet with Jaime first, if I had the money. Sometimes he would come to Jack's flat; sometimes he would meet me in the alley behind The Record Shop. I never offered speed or anything else to Michael again and he never asked me for any.
    Anthony strolled into the record shop one day, wearing what looked like chef's whites under his big winter coat. I felt the childish urge to laugh at him, and right away he was smiling at me with this mischievous sparkle in his dark eyes. We looked at each other and it

The Boy With The Thorn In His Side-Part 2

was like we both wanted to giggle though I had no idea why. He gestured to himself and did a little bow.

'What d'you think of the threads? Pretty cool eh?' I just nodded and grinned, and he came up to me and patted my shoulder. For some reason the gesture, and the weight of his hand on me, made me want to cry.

'Jaime said you had a job,' I said instead.

'Oh yes. Working man of the house I am these days mate. Mum's done a runner. I'm the proud father of a sixteen-year-old boy!'

We both laughed, and he patted my shoulder once more and then took his hand away and stuffed it into the pocket of his coat.

'I'm sorry Danny,' he said then, and I could see it, the awful regret behind his eyes. I shook my head at him. 'No really,' he insisted. 'I didn't mean what I said to you that day. I would never do that, you know that right? We're mates. More than mates. You're family. Yeah?' He was staring right into my eyes, millions of unsaid things passing easily between us, and so I smiled at him and nodded, and watched the relief fill his face as his shoulders sagged with it. 'I mean it,' he told me. 'You're family.'

'Hey, I deserved it,' I told him. 'I'm sorry too, yeah? I wouldn't, you know, ever do that again. I haven't.'

'I know that stupid,' he grinned and winked at me. 'But hey, I'm working on things, just so you know. To help you out, I mean. I haven't forgotten. It's just taking longer than I thought that's all.' I nodded and waited for him to say more, but he didn't. 'You're all right though?' he asked me. 'You're doing okay?'

'I'm okay,' I told him, and he looked relieved.

I worried about it afterwards though. What did he mean? What was going on between him and Jaime? Did Anthony trust Jaime? Was that a good idea, or an incredibly dangerous one? So long as Howard thought I had nothing to do with Mike or his brother, he would leave them both alone. But how long would it stay like that? If Howard got a sniff of anything, if he even got an inkling that people were up to something behind his back...It didn't bear thinking about. What would happen to Michael if Anthony was sent back to prison? They had no idea where their mother was. So, when I saw them coming, I did my best to avoid them. And when they showed up at Chaos, it was fine, because it was our world, and we were safe from view, and we were all united and full of hope and life, but then when it was over, I would go home alone.

Things were steady between Howard and me while my mother was away. I sensed his calmness, his sense of control over me restored. He had me right back where he wanted me, and he knew it and he fucking loved it. He made me go about with him, as if I were his little pet. In the company of other people, he would sling a fatherly arm around my shoulders and tell them how I had got myself a job in the record shop. He liked to keep up these false pretences and it made me wonder what his motives were underneath. Did he hate me or love me? Did he loathe me, or did he want me as his son? There were times he appeared so reasonable. Times he would join Jack and I in the flat, laughing at the TV, engaging in conversations, trying to coax me out of myself, trying to let me know how far we had come. And then there were times he would grind his lit fags into my skin just for the hell of it, just because it made him feel good, and there were times he would stare deep into my eyes and say; 'how much pain can you take eh? Tough little fucker. How much can you take?'

'This is all wrong,' I would tell him. But he didn't understand. I didn't know what he understood, or what motivated him and I didn't think I ever would. There were times I lay awake for hours dreaming up intricate ways to murder him, and there were times I just wanted him to be nice to me.

Things changed again as soon as my mother returned from Leeds. Work that out. He gets his precious Barbie doll wife back and goes all aggressive again. He went back to complaining about me quitting the club to work in the record shop instead. He seemed constantly on edge and he seemed to direct it all at my mother, as if my failings were all her fault. He was quick to temper and his expectations grew increasingly unrealistic. Was he trying to push her away? Would she finally get to see the real him, the monster he had kept under wraps for her for so long? Or did she already know? I would lie on my bed, staring at the cracks in the ceiling and listening to them arguing downstairs.

The Boy With The Thorn In His Side-Part 2

I wondered how long before she felt the force of his feet, or his fists. I felt like it was coming, or something was. It felt like things were unravelling faster and I didn't know whether I ought to welcome it or fear it. I did everything I could to avoid the man. Disappearing out of the back door if I heard him come through the front. Leaving Jack's flat if there was any hint of Howard coming over. I did whatever it took to remain off his radar, to not get on his nerves with my existence. But when Howard became fixated on something that irritated him, he was like a rabid dog attacking a bone with no meat on it. He wouldn't let it go.

With my mother back, I started going to school again. She was in a constant nervous state about my attendance. If I didn't go, the school would phone her, threatening all sorts, winding her up into meltdown about my future. She would cling all teary-eyed to Howard, as if he had all the answers, although she obviously had no idea what his answers usually involved. So, I would go back to school. Trail my way through days of misery and boredom just to please her, and she would go overboard with the praise and the encouragement at home. Making me special dinners. Buying me CD's she thought I would like. It was as if she had suddenly remembered my shadowy existence, and thought she ought to be nurturing it in some way. She would be oblivious to the darkening rage on her husband's face. She did not see the massive fists clenching and unclenching as she babbled on about how proud of me she was. It was a no-win situation. Didn't matter what I did. Either way I would be pissing one of them off.

But the answer hit me right between the eyes one afternoon when I was at school, sat slumped at my desk, while the children around me scribbled frantic notes in the margins of Hamlet. I glanced around at them all; as usual unable to concentrate on anything for very long, the remains of last night's highs giving me an ear bashing of a headache and a dull, sick feeling in my belly. Being close to my peers just reminded me of the distance between us, how I was not one of them, and never had been. I sat there, feeling the urge to escape building stronger and stronger inside of me. I was trapped on a never-ending roundabout of despair, unable to ever please anyone, least of all myself. I suddenly started thinking about what Mr James had said to me once; about having a hard job keeping me in this school if my behaviour continued. It was so easy and simple, it was almost beautiful. There would be repercussions, but it would be worth it, just to be free of this place, this chain around my neck. I smiled to myself and started to kick the chair in front of me, the chair occupied by Edward Higgs.

He turned to glare at me and I stared back, my expression blank. I noticed how grown up Higgs looked. He was so much taller and broader, and when I looked down at myself in comparison I felt stunted and fragile, and a surge of hatred rushed up from my guts. I kicked his chair harder and harder, knocking him forward and into his desk.

'Idiot!' he hissed at me, before flinging his arm into the air. 'Mrs Baker! Danny Bryans is kicking my chair on purpose!'

I felt the eyes of the class turn upon me in wonder. Mrs Baker rose slowly from her desk, a fidgety look on her face. She peered over her spectacles at me.

'Danny, what on earth are you doing? Stop that please, there is no need to be disruptive.' But disruptive was exactly what I planned on being. I kicked the chair harder and harder, until Higgs gave up and got to his feet, holding up his hands for the teacher. 'Danny!' she barked at me. She left her desk rather reluctantly and approached mine, fat hands fluttering around her hips as her long floral skirt swished around her ankles. 'Danny, that's enough, what *are* you playing at? That's enough I said!'

I stopped kicking and stared up at her, narrowing my eyes. 'Fuck you.'

A collective gasp of horror arose from the class, followed closely by an expectant silence as they all stared at Mrs Baker, wondering what the hell she would do now. I thought she looked confused. Hurt even. She shook her greying perm at me.

'What did you just say?'

'I said fuck you,' I told her with a shrug. 'What are you deaf?'

'Get out of my classroom right now!' She spoke through her teeth, and pointed a slightly shaking hand at the door. 'Go to Mr James's office!'

I got up and said nothing as I walked casually to the door, enjoying the stunned silence that followed me. I closed the door behind me and traipsed down the corridor, trailing one hand lightly along the wall as I walked. As I went, I inhaled all the usual school smells for what I hoped would be the last time. Blackboard dust, disinfectant floor cleaner, and canteen chips. I arrived at the heads office and opened the door without knocking. This was going to be fun.

Mr James was on the phone, and stared at me in surprise as I sauntered on in. 'Let me call you back,' he said, and hung up on them. He was frowning at me as he nodded at the chair opposite his. I slumped into it and stared back at him. 'To what do I owe the pleasure?' he asked me. 'First you grace us with your presence at school, and now I'm honoured with a personal visit!'

'Just came to tell you what I told Mrs Baker,' I said to him, and as I said it, I lifted my feet and planted them down on the edge of his desk. He stared at me in total horror. His hands spread out slowly across the desk and his lips pursed tightly together, allowing no sound to come out. 'Go fuck yourself,' I added with a shrug. 'Both of you.'

'I beg your pardon!' he roared at me then. 'And get your damn feet off my desk!'

I yawned. 'Are you gonna' make me?'

He looked like he was for a second. He shoved back his chair and got violently to his feet, and pointed his finger at me.

'Get your feet off my desk right now young man, or I'm phoning your mother to come and get you!'

'Do it. I don't care. Call the bitch.'

He shook his head. He looked dazed and baffled and saddened and furious all at once and I really wanted to laugh at him.

'You don't care? What the hell is wrong with you boy? You're never at school, failing nearly every subject, and when you are here you are disruptive and rude! I told you before young man, I do not have to tolerate this kind of behaviour in my school!'

'Good, cool, throw me out then.' I got to my feet and walked around the chair.

Mr James shook his head at me. 'What is this about? You want to be expelled? I don't understand you Daniel.'

I walked around the edge of his office slowly, taking it all in, the filing cabinets, and the pot plants, and the framed pictures of his family that he kept upon his desk.

'You warned me once, if I kept it up, you'd throw me out.'

'I did Daniel, but there's no need for this. I don't want to see you expelled. I don't want to see you ruin your life.'

'Too late for that,' I muttered in reply. I was bored. This was taking too long. I picked up a large spider plant from one of the filing cabinets and held it in my hands.

'Too late? What does that mean? Why don't you put that down and talk to me properly Daniel? Tell me what's bothering you. Whatever it is, we can sort it out, you know. We can help you.'

'Help me?' I said, with a laugh. 'Throw me out. That would help me a lot right now.'

'Well I won't do it,' he told me adamantly. 'This is ridiculous and childish. You have everything ahead of you, and you are a smart young man Daniel. I don't understand what this is all about. What is wrong with you?'

'Dunno,' I said, and let the plant slip through my fingers. It crashed to the floor, the terracotta plant pot cracking open to spill the black soil out across his carpet. 'Oops.'

'Oh, get out!' he yelled at me then, pointing at the door. 'Go on get out! Get out of my school right now!'

I was relieved. I smiled and slouched over to the door. I opened it and looked back over my shoulder at him.

'Call my mum and tell her I'm out, or I'll come back and burn the whole fucking place down, and I mean it.' I walked out, leaving him in his stupefied silence.

I walked home slowly, hoping he would get right on the phone to my mum and Howard. I could almost imagine how the phone call would go. He would tell my mum I couldn't come back. He would tell her how strange and threatening I'd been. He would suggest I still had a problem with drugs. He would say the school were not equipped to deal with such things. He would tell her I needed help, and she would believe it all, she would suck it all up like she always did, and I knew this was true, and I saw it all over her tear streaked face when I

The Boy With The Thorn In His Side-Part 2

walked in through the back door. Here I was. Her druggy drop-out son. Hurray!

She was at the sink, peeling potatoes. When she saw me shuffle in, she dropped the peeler and turned to face me, hugging her arms around her thin body as if to comfort herself. I viewed her coldly and turned my eyes on Howard. He was sat at the table with a newspaper spread out before him, but he rose to his feet as I walked in, and all at once his body and his being consumed all the air, and I felt like I was going to choke. He stepped behind her, took hold of her shoulders and kept her standing, while his eyes shot icy daggers at me.

'Why did you do it?' she started saying, shaking her head and sending fresh tears flying all over the room. 'Are you insane? Have you gone crazy? Why would you do such a thing? Why? What are you going to do now Danny? Don't you even care about your future?'

I shrugged with my hands in my pockets and my eyes on hers. 'Not really no. Couldn't give a shit if you want the truth.'

She pressed a hand over her gaping mouth and wailed thinly behind it. 'Why are you doing this to me? Why do you want to hurt me so much? *Why* Danny?'

'Because he's a selfish little bastard, who doesn't care about anyone except himself,' came the slow, cold words from Howard's mouth as he rubbed her shoulders from behind.

'Are you on drugs again?' She asked me. 'That's what Mr James thinks! He said we should get you some help...take you to the doctor...Lee,' she looked up into his face. 'That's what we need to do, the school said!'

'It's up to you,' he shrugged back at her. 'But I don't know how we'd make him go. And what will they do anyway? What can they do about it? But it's up to you, call them if you want to baby.'

I wanted to leave them to it, so I balled my fists at my sides and walked towards the hallway.

'He just doesn't want to go to school,' Howard snarled over her head then. 'That's what it is. Wants to spend all his time in that record shop. Thinks that's where his future lies!' He laughed out loud at the very idea. I stared back and felt nothing but numb hatred for the pair of them.

'You won't have them bothering you anymore,' I said. 'And if it makes you happy I'll go and sit the exams in the summer.'

'Ha!' Howard cried in triumph. 'See honey? He gets to do what he wants! You can see exactly what he's playing at!'

I laughed over my shoulder as I trudged down the hallway. 'Oh, you're so funny Lee,' I said to him. 'If only Mum knew the truth eh? If only she knew.'

It made me chuckle as I walked up the stairs. The whole thing was ridiculous. They had followed me out to the hallway, and were staring up at me with their matching expressions of disgust and outrage glowering on their stupid faces. In that moment, I saw them as one person, as one enemy, one monster. My mother looked and sounded like she had been devoured completely by Howard, like she had been absorbed into him and even the eyes that stared out from her face were his, like he had crawled right inside her soul. That's never happening to me, I thought, staring back at her, I would rather die first. She was clinging to his shirt like a small tearful child and he was staring at me with stone like eyes, and a flicker of a smile upon his face.

'You really are the most selfish, unpleasant piece of work I've ever had to deal with,' he said, which was ironic really, if you thought about it. So, I laughed. I knew I would pay for it as soon as she passed out, but in that moment, I didn't care. It was playtime. I could let him know what I really thought about him.

'You sound like you're talking about yourself Lee,' I told him with a smirk. 'Although I could add a few things to the list that Mum doesn't know about.' I raised my eyebrows, daring him to disagree.

'Danny go to your room,' my mother said then, pulling her wet face away from his shirt. 'It's best if we all calm down, then we can talk about this tomorrow and see what to do.'

'Do?' I cried back at her, incredulous. 'We're not going to *do* anything mother, so don't stand there trying to make out you give a shit about me. We all know you don't and you never have!' I stomped up the stairs, but she called out to me.

'Danny!' I paused and looked back at her, and I wondered what she really saw when she looked at me; something evil? Something damaged and broken, something she had never really loved? *She should have aborted you when she had the chance.* I searched her eyes with my own, begging her to see the truth, pleading with her, but then I saw her hands rising to find Howard's again, and I saw the way it was always going to be. I nodded at her.

'Just leave me alone. Before you know it, I'll be out of your hair for good.' I turned and ran swiftly up the stairs. I closed my door, sat on my bed and pressed my hands together between my knees. I squeezed my eyes shut and let the waiting begin.

I waited in my room for hours. The knot of dread and fear inside my stomach increased in size like a bad-tempered tumour. I moved restlessly around my room to shift it, but it clung to me wherever I went. I thought I would vomit if it went on much longer, so I took a deep breath and pulled the chair out from where I had wedged it under the door handle. It was close to midnight and I was desperate for a piss. I had considered aiming it out of the window, but what was the point in delaying the inevitable? Might as well let him get it out of his system now, before it built up any longer. I reminded myself that once it was over, it was over, and another day would begin. I swallowed dry air, opened the door and dashed to the bathroom.

He pounced on my way back. I heard the single creak on the stairs that gave away what would happen next, and then he loomed up like a horrific shadow out of the dark chasm of the stairs. I tried to run, but he pinned my arms to my sides and when I opened my mouth to scream, he slapped his hand over my lips before any sound could be made and hauled me back into my room. He kicked the door shut behind us and hissed into my ear.

'Don't try pulling that stunt again shit stain! She won't hear you anyway! She's out cold!' He pushed me down on the bed, twisted my right arm up behind me and planted his knee into the small of my back. I grunted in pain and there was no escape. 'I've just about had enough of you,' he was snarling over me. 'You still don't learn do you? You're still not doing what I say in my own fucking house! Thought you were clever eh? Getting kicked out of school so you can hang about in that shop all day! What's it gonna' take eh? What's it gonna' take to get you in line and keep you there?' He pulled back his knee and looped a hard fist into my kidneys. 'More of that?' he asked breathlessly, pressing his cold thin lips to my ear every time he spoke. Another fist thundered in, hitting the same spot and opening up the pain again, making my body want to weep and bleed. Break me, I thought to myself, with my face pressed into the duvet, my eyes closed tightly as another fist smashed into my ribs. Break me all apart, do it, do it, break me all up, do it, just fucking do it!

He stopped punching then and leaned down into my ear. 'You think your mum can hear anything?' his voice rasped and licked against my skin. 'She can't hear a thing. She's fucking comatose on sleeping pills.' He put his hand around my neck then, holding me down, while his other hand was wrestling with something. 'So, don't bother calling for her this time little man, because she won't fucking come, and she wouldn't fucking come even if she could hear you, do you know that? She wishes she had aborted you. She's told me a thousand times little man. She even went to the clinic, that's how close she came, that's how much she never wanted you! So, call her if you like and see if she cares! Because no one cares Danny! No one cares about you, except me, so I don't know why you keep fucking me off all the time and making me angry! I don't get why you keep messing with me, you little fuckbag, why do you do it? Why do you want to wind me up all the time? You're still not the good boy I told you to be, are you? You're a scruffy little fucked up dope head, that's what you are! So, what're we gonna' do about that then eh?'

He was tugging at something and when he got it free he held it down in front of my face, and I opened my eyes to see his belt doubled over.

'You asked for this yet again,' he told me in a hoarse, choked voice. 'Yet again you pushed me to it. You never fucking learn. When will you fucking learn you won't win Danny? You won't ever win!'

The first strike sliced into my skin and I wanted to scream, so I wriggled enough to get one of my hands up to my mouth, and I pushed it right in, crammed my fist right back against my teeth so that I wouldn't. Because I didn't want to give him the satisfaction. I crushed the pain down with my teeth and waited for it to be over.

The Boy With The Thorn In His Side-Part 2

14

I awoke the next day calm and refreshed. I spent some time just watching Kay as she slept beside me. I knew she would sleep for hours yet and that was just fine by me. I liked watching her sleep, and I also liked the time to myself I would get when I slipped out of bed to go downstairs. I had already heard the newspaper boy shoving the paper through the letterbox. I glanced back at Kay and thought how tiny she looked, how delicate. She looked serene, sleeping so peacefully, but I sighed as I flipped back the duvet and swung my legs out of the bed because I knew that as soon as her eyes opened, they would fill with dread and anxiety. She would remember what happened yesterday and the despair would consume her.

As much as she liked to try to gloss it over with her fluttering eye lashes and candy smiles, she couldn't hide it from me. That boy tormented her. She was obsessed with him. She was overdoing it with attention one moment because she assumed he was heading in the right direction. Showering him with praise, going back to her old soft ways with him, showing no spine. He did it on purpose, I was pretty sure of that after all this time. Wound her up with false hopes, viewing her with scorn and disdain the entire time, before he dashed them all, right on cue, fucking up in spectacular fashion. Liked to think he was a bad boy, didn't he? Telling his teachers to fuck themselves and threatening to burn the school down. Very funny. Very fucking funny.

It had reached the point when I dreaded her speaking his name. My skin would prickle with barely contained rage. You wanted him dead, I wanted to scream into her pitiful little face, you told me yourself! You were going to get rid of him and he's haunted your very existence ever since! Fuck, sometimes I felt like the only sane one in the family, the only one who could see things the way they really were.

I paused outside his bedroom, tying my dressing gown neatly around my middle. I felt good. Better than good, I felt fucking amazing. I might have been approaching middle age but I was in the best shape of my life. Hadn't let myself go, not like Jack. I rocked back on my heels, sniffing the air, before I shuddered involuntarily, thinking about what was happening to him, what he was turning into. It was laughable really. He was becoming on the outside what he had been on the inside for a very long time.

I turned my head to the bedroom door, located the sound of muffled, laboured snoring, and nodded to myself in satisfaction. The boy was on his last warning and he had his instructions to remain put. Fuck his friends, fuck his job, fuck all of it, unless I said otherwise. I smiled a delicate smile when I remembered the last thing I had said, before leaving him alone in the dark; 'One wrong move, and I bring your mother in here and introduce her to this.' I'd slapped the belt against my hand and he'd flinched on the bed, although only half conscious. He knew I meant it though. And I did mean it. To be honest, I was starting to think she needed a wake-up call. It was like one step forward, three steps back with that boy, and most of the time it was her undoing all my hard work.

I cracked my knuckles outside his door and then padded softly down the stairs in my slippers. I picked the paper up from the mat and carried it into the kitchen with me. I was half way through filling the kettle when I heard the banging on the front door. Not knocking, but banging, hammering. I slammed the kettle down and marched towards the front door. I rolled my head on my neck and cracked my knuckles again. This was no time in the morning for visitors, and I was reminded of my growing disgust towards the place. This estate was not for the likes of Kay and me. I had been scanning the property pages for homes for sale up on the hill. That was where we belonged, in one of those houses.

When I wrenched open the door, my irritation spun into anger, in fact it was enough to ruin my entire day; the sight of that little black-haired freak on my doorstep, glowering at me in his school uniform. I jutted towards him in a fast, snapping motion, watched him jerk back in surprise and sneered into his face; 'get the *fuck* away from my house!'

The boy composed himself quickly and scowled back at me with pure hatred in his glittering eyes. He glared back at me like he had every right to be stood on my doorstep first thing in the morning.

'I want to see Danny,' he said to me.

The Boy With The Thorn In His Side-Part 2

I cocked my head to one side and frowned at him as if he were stupid. 'I'll repeat it for you,' I said. 'In case you are deaf, or just stupid...get the *fuck* away from my house!'

'What have you done to him now?' the boy demanded, his fists shaking at his sides, his voice rising quickly. I looked at his chest, puffing upwards with anger, and I wanted to laugh. I smiled instead. 'They say he's not coming back to school. What have you done to him now?'

I had an idea then. A bit of crazy one, but fuck it. I pulled my neck in, took a breath and scanned the street for sound and movement. Satisfied that we were alone, I reached out suddenly and took the Anderson boy by surprise, gripping him by the lapels of his school blazer and wrenching him right through the front door. There was this amazing, this *satisfying* expression of utter horror upon his face, and I imagined for a moment what he was feeling, being dragged in like that, knowing what he knew, fearing whatever he feared.

He was too shocked, too stunned by my sudden actions to make a single sound, or noise. The only noise that came from him was the grunt he emitted when I slammed his body back into the hallway wall. I kicked the door shut and held him in place, with my nose pressed right into his. Right away, I felt better already. The irritation and anger was all gone, replaced only by the urges that pulsed behind my eyes. His eyes were dark and wild, terrified and full of outrage. His mouth hung open, soundless and afraid.

'You know,' I said to him, pinning his head to the wall by pressing my forehead into his. 'I think I've just about run out of patience with you and your interfering brother. Sticking your nose in where it's not wanted. I thought I warned you both before...I thought your brother said he had learnt his lesson? Maybe it's time I taught him another one eh? Is that what you want you miserable little fuck up?' His body squirmed under my touch, but there was fire in those eyes, so I narrowed my own. 'You want to know where Danny is eh?' I asked him softly, purring my words into his slack mouth. He moved his head in a nod. I crushed it still with mine. 'He's in his room. In a *world* of pain. Which, by the way, he fucking asked for like he always does...You can go and see him if you want, you can fucking join him if you want, if you want to find out how much you can take...You fancy that fuck-up? You want that? I'll take you up there right now if you want. I'll take you apart. I'll break every bone in your body if you like. And then, while you're thinking about that, I'll get on the phone and let the cops know there's still stuff to be sniffed out in your house...Because there is you know...Not anywhere you'll ever be able to find it mind. But sniffer dogs, you know? Fuck me, they're good at their job! They'll find what's still there, and what'll happen to the big boy then eh? Back to prison where he belongs? And how about you?'

I moved my head back just enough to stare deep into his eyes. I laughed softly, remembering what Jack had said about him once. Eyes like pools of melted chocolate. Christ's sake man, I had said to him, write him a fucking valentines card why don't you? I shrugged my shoulders at him and gave him a pitying look.

'Oh, dear me, what will happen to you then eh? No parents about. No older brother. Be carted off to care in a shot, and then we'd see what a tough guy you really are eh?' I sneered laughter, opened the door and hauled him roughly towards it. 'Now of you go boy, off you go to school, go and think about that for a while. Go and think about how quickly I can fuck up your life with one phone call.' I shoved him through the open door and he sprawled down onto his knees. 'Have a nice day!' I called, and slammed the door.

I picked the phone up and stalked into the lounge with it. I twitched the curtain and watched the little shit picking himself up from the front lawn. He looked confused. He looked mad but scared, and he looked like he didn't have a clue what to do. Little boys, I thought then, punching in a number, little boys playing games they won't win.

The phone picked up. 'Mate?'

'Morning Jack. Listen. You're going to like this. I just had an early morning visit from that little Anderson shit you're such a fan of.'

Jack made a noise at the back of his throat that was either a snort of laughter or a choke of embarrassment. 'Really?' he asked. 'Must have a death wish.'

'Yeah seems like it. Him and his interfering brother. Don't trust either of them. We need to put the shits up them again mate. Seriously. Can I leave it with you?'

He laughed. 'I'll put my thinking cap on then Lee.'

The Boy With The Thorn In His Side-Part 2

'Good.' I hung up the phone and glared back out of the window. I could see the dark-haired boy walking away quickly, shifting his school bag to the other shoulder. He marched around the corner. I stood there for a while, keeping an eye on the street. I had totally forgotten about my newspaper and my breakfast. I slipped into a kind of trance, I suppose, my hands held slackly in the pockets of my jeans, my eyes fixed on the world outside. I found myself thinking about Jack, contemplating the way he asked how high when I told him to jump. It was a never ending and stable thing, his loyalty to me. He was a strange man, and ultimately harmless, no bother to anyone. But it didn't pay to forget what he really was underneath.

We are all animals beneath the surface; we layer up with clothes and jobs and respectability but underneath it all, an animal lurks. Jack Freeman was nothing more than a dog on a lead, and it was me who held the other end of that lead. He presented an image to the world, one that everyone fell for and one that was mostly the truth. He was a shabby, shambling figure of a man. His hair needed a cut and he rarely washed it. His clothes reeked of stale sweat, whisky and last night's curry. When people complained that time went too fast, that life was too short, Jack would disagree with them. He didn't see it that way. He saw time as an awkward lumbering beast that always moved too slowly. Life, he said, it ambled on blindly, promising nothing and meaning even less.

I turned slowly from the window and walked into the hallway. Jack said that days all jumbled into one. He never knew what day, or time it was, and he cared little. He lived a simple life and always had done. For a long time now, he had followed my rules and adhered to my expectations. I trusted him. I had saved his scraggy arse on more than one occasion, and he remembered this as well as I did. I knew everything there was to know about the man. I knew what lay beneath his human skin. I knew about each dirty layer that piled upon his soul, and believe me, if you peeled them back, each one would reveal something more distasteful than the last.

I heard the whine in his voice at times though, of course I did. I heard the whine of a spoilt child who has been told he is not allowed to touch the cake, let alone taste it. His eyes sometimes, they were like something out of a cartoon; bulging and popping from the sunken, hollowed out sockets. I watched him shifting and fidgeting in his sagging grey chair and it amused me.

'It's good for you,' I told him once when we were alone. He had groaned and rubbed his greasy head into both curled palms. I had merely laughed at him. 'Exercising control. It's good for all of us. You don't want to be an addict, do you Jack? Someone with no self-control? Like all the pathetic little fuckers who call you up begging for their next hit. They'd do anything, wouldn't they Jack? Weak. It's good for you to practice control.'

He was mostly happy, I reasoned. He liked his flat and he liked his work, and he liked coming to the club, and he was never one to feel guilt when he saw the lives he touched run to ruin. People will always need something, he liked to say. People will always need something, be it booze, or drugs, or sex, or whatever. They all have their needs. All we do is supply, all we do is fulfil their needs. He didn't force anyone, did he? Oh no, not good old Jack. You could hardly even call the old git a pusher, a dealer. He sat on his backside most days, his fat spreading out onto the sofa that held his imprint whenever he hauled his ageing arse out of it. He had people like Lawler doing the hard work.

I started to climb the stairs, one at a time, slowly sweeping my hand up the wall as I went. I passed the photos Kay kept nailed up. Old photos of John and Danny as children. First day at school. Missing teeth. Cheeky smiles. They made me wince. Sometimes I had the strongest urge to knock them all off and send them shattering down to the hallway. Jack was drinking more, I knew that. Drink was only one of his weaknesses. It walked hand in hand with the other one. Sometimes I presented the rules to him when I sensed him wavering, when I inhaled his mewling self-pity. I arrived on the landing and pulled my hands out of my pockets. It was simple, I had told him. Let him come to your flat, let any of them come. Let them get high and let them drink, and let them do whatever the fuck they want to do. Let him trust you, let him become your friend, shelter him, provide comfort, a safe place to go, but do not go anywhere near him. Do not touch him. You're enjoying it, he told me miserably one night, his eyes drawn across the darkened room to the huddle that snored softly under a heap of his blankets. I had wanted to laugh out

The Boy With The Thorn In His Side-Part 2

loud and slap his saggy wrinkled cheek. Rules are rules, I told him, and the rules are simple, and if you break the rules my friend, I'll kick you back out on the shit heap and that will be the end of that.

I stood outside the boy's room and strained my ears. The house was still and silent, rocked only by the snores of two semi-conscious people. I walked into the bathroom, found a flannel and ran it under the cold water. Jack was relying more and more on the whisky. It was him and his good old friend Jack D. They walked this life hand in hand, and one was not the same without the other. He lived a simple life and he liked the small things. Countdown and Ready Steady Cook, Eastenders and The Bill. Spicy meat feast pizzas, and the first warm slosh of a Jack Daniels and coke. Dirty magazines and filthy books. Being alone. He had always been alone. People like Jack have to. They have to keep a distance, you see, surround themselves in a muggy kind of fog, a barrier between them and everyone else. Normal people would be repelled, you see, normal people would turn and run. I took the wet flannel and went back to the boy's door, and turned the handle.

You still can't control that fucking boy. Jack's words one night. My father's words every time I spoke to him on the phone. Words, followed by amused laughter. They were laughing at me. Jack knew it, and I knew it. You're obsessed, he told me, you're either in a bad mood or a good mood, and the reason is always the same. It was twisting up inside of me. It was making me restless all the time. I walked into the room and breathed him in. It was dark, but a mop of blonde hair showed at the top of the duvet, the rest of him hidden from view.

Jack didn't like it when I lost my temper with the boy. He flinched and winced and asked me to stop. You'll kill him one day, he tried to tell me afterwards; we'll end up driving his body all the way out to the fucking woods to bury him. Maybe he was starting to think they were on the same side? Jack and the boy. Maybe he was beginning to see me as the problem, as the common enemy? It's not fair, he said to me once, what you do to him is not fair. But I'll win, I replied and to this he looked sad, and gazed down at his knees and he said no more after that.

I lifted the duvet slowly away. I had slapped his face at some point last night and he had been bleeding all over his pillow. I grimaced. I looked down at his pale face, eyes closed but twitching, and I thought about all the things he did not know about Jack Freeman.

Then I woke him up by rubbing his face with the wet flannel. His eyes shot open, and he spluttered and coughed and tried to pull away, but I held him fast and scrubbed all the blood from his face. Then I yanked the pillow away, ripped off the cover and slung it to the floor behind me. I kneeled down next to him and pushed his hair back away from his eyes. I tried to determine what I could see in them. Caution, or something more?

Fear...fear maybe, but it wasn't enough. It was less than it had been...like it was fading, like his emotions were becoming numb to everything. I felt a swell of frustration rising inside me. I cocked my head to one side.

'I'll tell you what I told your little pal Michael just now,' I said to him, and then I saw it, oh yes, then I saw the fear! Flashed through his eyes like fucking lightning, it did! I smiled at him. 'Yeah that's right, I just had a little visit from him. Very nice. Gave him a few things to think about though. I think he's gone home to look for the rest of the drugs I had hidden in his house. Not the kind of place anyone would think to look of course, but you know those sniffer dogs they have these days? Wow, they're amazing!' I chuckled warmly while he stared on. 'Don't let that angry look get in your eyes,' I warned him then, holding up a finger. 'Try not to. Try not to let it come. I don't want to see it, because if I see it, I will have to make a phone call to the cops. Send them round to the Anderson's house, you know? See what they find. One phone call, you see, just one phone call and it's all over.'

I nodded at him and got to my feet. I was smiling as I considered his small body and all the times I had beaten it. It still wasn't broken, and neither was he. I would go after his friends if I had to. If that was the way to get through to him, then so be it. I smiled down at him and thought about the lead around Jack's neck.

The Boy With The Thorn In His Side-Part 2

'You have no idea,' I told him softly. 'You have no idea how much worse I can make things, with just a click of my fingers. No idea.'

He did a strange thing. An unexpected thing. He sat up slowly, eyes closing briefly against the pain. He moved back towards the wall, brought up his knees and folded his arms on top of them.

'I'm sorry," he said then, and his voice was small, barely audible, but I heard it, I wouldn't have missed it. Sorry. I frowned at him and I wanted to laugh out loud.

'You what?'

He coughed into his hand. 'I said I'm sorry.'

'And what are you saying sorry for, Danny?'

'Everything,' he replied with a limp shrug. 'Walking out of school. All of that.'

I wasn't sure I believed him, but it was still nice to hear it. I wanted to believe him of course, and that was the thing that frustrated me the most. How I couldn't get it through to him. How he only ever saw me as the enemy. I wondered then if he had an ulterior motive. Something he wanted.

'And where does that leave us?' I asked him.

He looked up at me. His eyes, deep blue and deadened. They fixed on mine.

'Whatever you want.'

'You'll keep away from those boys.'

'I do anyway. I don't go near anyone.'

'You won't give your mother anything else to fret about.'

'Course not,' he whispered. I moved towards him. I found the edge of the bed in the dull room and sat down on it. He stiffened as I reached out to him, brushing his hair back again. I searched his eyes, hunting him down. 'I'm sorry,' he said again, the words hushed and private. 'I won't make you angry anymore Lee. I really won't.'

'Yeah, well we'll see.' I took his face gently in my hand and turned it to mine. I wanted him to be telling the truth. I wanted him to be a good boy. *All* the time. And not just because he wanted something, and not just because he was afraid of me. I wanted him to want to be good, to want to please me, just as I had wanted to please my father. 'But I'm telling you now Danny, I am promising you, that this is the last chance I give you. The *very*, *very* last chance. Next time I lose it with you, next time you push me that far, I'll send the sniffer dogs round to their house, fuck their lives up forever. And I will drag your mother in front of you and beat her to within an inch of her life, and then me and you will take a special ride somewhere. Just me and you. And then it will be over Danny. I swear to God. I fucking promise you. It will all be over.'

The Boy With The Thorn In His Side-Part 2

15

July 1995

'We're like rats in a cage,' Michael told me nervously when he came into The Record Shop.

He was as jittery as hell. Scratching at his bare wrists and looking over his shoulder and peering constantly through the dusty windows. I felt his constant fear and it was a guilt that weighed me down. Despite me keeping my distance and keeping my promise to Howard, Michael and Anthony had been targeted for months. It was stupid stuff mostly. Broken windows in the middle of the night. Phone calls from people who would not speak. Unknown cars with blacked out windows that rolled slowly behind them if they walked the streets. They were too scared to breathe, let alone skin up. Anthony had paid for new locks on all the doors and windows and they were religious about checking them and double checking them. It made me sad. I knew what it was and there was little I could do. Howard and his minions, turning the screws, keeping them scared, holed up and helpless. One wrong move and you're slaughtered. Bad luck. They were in line too, just like me. I couldn't tell them what I longed to tell them. That I had a plan, building slowly and surely at the back of my head, amidst the fog and the rubble and the despair.

Michael still came to the flat sometimes, and Jack always promised not to tell Howard. He kept to his word as far as I knew. Jack told me that I was looking too small for my age; that maybe things cannot grow properly without love and care. He was drunk most of the time; a shadow hanging over him. Sometimes, very late at night, he would sniffle tears in the darkness. I still wanted desperately to believe that he was on my side. Michael did not trust him at all. We would sit side by side on one of the sofas, our arms touching, our eyes restless. If Jack was not there, Michael would hold my attention and talk fast.

'Anthony's onto it,' he would tell me. 'You have to keep going. Don't do anything stupid. Don't annoy Howard or raise his suspicions. Just keep your head down. Honestly Danny, honestly, honestly he's onto it. He's gonna' help you, I promise.'

School was over. The exams had been and gone. I had gone in for some of them, much to everyone's surprise. I sat the English exams and struggled through the maths and the science. That was it. That was all I had, and it wasn't much. The looks on their faces though; that had made it worth it! I'd walked in, head held high, eyes fixed ahead, pencils clutched in one hand. Michael had shaken his head and covered his mouth to laugh behind it. Jake and Billy had just stared and stared. Better than that, I finished first in the English exams. They were a piece of piss. I handed them in, walked out, and felt for one fleeting moment as if I were as free as a bird. It tickled me no end, surprising them all like that, as if I had given them a glimpse of my true master plan, of the real me that lay hidden under my wrecked and strange existence.

My friendship with Michael was continued in snatched moments, at the shop, at the flat and at Chaos. Leaping up and down on the dance floor, screaming along to the music, alive. Just alive. You had to remind yourself of it sometimes. He loved the fact Terry had given me a proper job in the record shop. He loved to tell me how insanely pissed off and jealous Billy and Jake were.

'You're down, but not out!' he liked to tell me, with a ridiculous grin upon his face. I supposed he was right.

I was surviving day by day, with my eyes fixed ahead, with my plans and my dreams rolling along inside my head to keep me company. During that time, I was exactly what Howard wanted me to be. In his presence, I was a boy beaten and pulped into shape and into place. I was all, yes sir, no sir. I kept my eyes dull and empty. I pushed feelings down, pushed emotions away, kept myself numb and obedient and safe. He loved it, and he revelled in it, but let me tell you now, he sure as hell didn't believe in it. He didn't believe in it any more than I did. But I had to string it out, I had to bide my time, keep the façade up, keep the fire out of my eyes.

The day that Michael came skidding into the shop with a wild panic in his eyes, was a day like any other day. The shop was sweltering, so we kept the door propped open and instead of tea, Terry and I took turns making each other milkshakes. I remember I had put Radiohead's The Bends on the record player, even though it always made Terry groan.

'At least put something joyous on,' he would complain. 'At least some uplifting lyrics that will give us all hope!'

The Boy With The Thorn In His Side-Part 2

You can't help how you feel though. And on that day, I was feeling down. I was feeling like there was a constant layer of dirt upon my skin, and I was feeling like I wanted to run into the ocean to scrub myself clean but that if I did, it would never work, or it would never last. I was putting records away in the soul section, nodding along to the music, wanting to sing along but not owning the energy to hold my head up properly let alone open my mouth and speak.

'Danny!' It was Michael, bursting breathlessly through the open door, sweat pooling on his wrinkled forehead, his hair whipped back over his head as if he had been riding his bike very fast. He ignored the look of alarm on Terry's face and gripped me by the arm. 'When do you finish? I need to speak to you!'

I pulled my arm free and glanced at the clock on the wall. 'Ten minutes.' I watched his shoulders drop in relief. He put one hand out and rested it against the wall, catching his breath.

'Good. You're coming with me. I just had the weirdest phone call ever from Anthony, and he told me to come and get you.'

I considered his statement for a moment and then I scratched my head and yawned. I was tired. I wanted to sleep and all my stuff was at Jack's flat.

'I dunno,' I told him. 'I kind of had something else to do Mike.'

'No, you can't,' he hissed at me, his eyes shooting from mine to Terry's, and then back again. 'Seriously Danny. He just called me at home from the pub. He sounded really upset! He scared me. He said he has something to tell us about Freeman, and we have to go back to mine and wait for him to finish work.'

Now I was really confused. I felt weary, my shoulders hanging, my head too big and heavy for my body. I didn't want to tell him what my plan had been before he came rushing in, because it was shameful really, because everything about my life had become shameful. I'd been thinking about it all day though; doing a few lines of coke with Jack and seeing if it felt as amazing as last time. Now I had this wide-eyed Michael all frantic before me, I could see that it wasn't going to happen.

'Okay,' I told him, not seeing that I had any other choice. 'I'll come with you to see Anthony, but I have to go to the flat first to get my stuff.'

'Oh God,' Michael moaned, looking up at the ceiling. I shook my head at him, not understanding. He rubbed at his eyes and nodded back at me. 'Okay, okay if you really have to, but the thing is Danny, Anthony told me not to go anywhere near Jack. I mean, he practically begged me.'

'He won't even be there,' I lied to him. 'So chill out. We'll be really quick.'

Michael smoked a cigarette outside while I finished up and collected my cash from Terry. Outside the shop, Michael grabbed his bike and started to push it along the pavement, and I fell into step beside him. I narrowed my eyes at him.

'What is wrong with you?' I asked. 'You look like you're gonna' shit yourself!'

''Cause I am,' he admitted, sucking the last few drags from his cigarette before chucking the butt over his shoulder. 'Anthony just phoned me at home and told me to stay the hell away from Jack Freeman, and now we're on the way to his bloody flat! If I don't shit myself I know I'm gonna' bloody piss myself!'

'What do you think it is Mike? Why does he want us to keep away from him?'

'I don't know, that's the point! He couldn't say over the phone. He'd just seen Jaime though. You know he's been getting him to spy and that, find stuff out?'

I didn't know, so I shook my head, baffled and astounded. 'Why?'

'I dunno. They're mates. They meet up. But the point is, he was very specific just now. Do *not* go to the flat, he said.' Michael blew his breath out slowly and looked up, shaking his hair from his face as the old council flats loomed up ahead of us on the other side of the railway tracks. We crossed the bridge in solemn silence, keeping our eyes ahead. 'I feel like a total prick coming here after what he just said,' Michael muttered, the nearer we got.

I offered him a brief and nervy smile. 'I'll be like two seconds. I'll just grab my stuff and we'll go.'

The Boy With The Thorn In His Side-Part 2

'Oh man,' Michael moaned, wiping his mouth on the back of his hand. 'What do you think it is? What do you think Anthony's worried about?'

'I don't know.'

'Oh Jesus.'

'Are you scared?' I asked, looking his way.

He nodded at me instantly. 'Are you?'

I tucked my hair behind my ears and grimaced. 'I'm always fucking scared.'

When we reached his block, the main door was propped open with a brick. I stepped into the dimly lit hallway while Michael leaned his bike against the wall outside.

Jack's flat was on the second floor. We climbed the stairs briskly, keeping close to the mustard coloured wall, keeping silent. Michael seemed to grow increasingly agitated the nearer we got to the flat. As we trailed along the corridor towards Jack's door, he whispered to me;

'Have you got your knife on you?'

I looked at him, rolling my eyes. 'What are you gonna' need a knife for Mike? He's a fat slug, he's not gonna' do anything.' We reached the door so I fished my key out of my back pocket.

'That's obviously not what Anthony thinks,' Michael reminded me miserably, his eyes shooting around nervously as I unlocked the door. The smell of curry hit our nostrils and we could hear the TV chattering. My stomach took a massive nose dive and I imagined Michael's did as well. He looked like he was going to be sick, and I wondered for a moment what had happened to the boy I used to know, the tough talking Michael Anderson, the boy who was not afraid of anything. We were like mice, cautious and scuttling as we entered the flat side by side. Michael pulled at the back of my t-shirt as I went ahead of him. 'Just get your stuff quick and go,' he hissed.

We emerged from the hallway and stepped into the lounge. Jack was right there, sprawled like a bearded whale on his favourite leather sofa, his jaws moving around and around, a lump of bright orange curry poised on the end of a fork close to his mouth. He hiccupped and burped and waved the greasy fork at us.

'Hello boys,' he said. We ignored him. Michael stayed put, and I crossed the room quickly, snatching up one of my jumpers from the back of the tatty grey sofa and slinging it under one arm. I picked up my tin from one of the coffee tables and stuffed it into a back pocket. Then I walked behind the sofa and started to pile my arms up with records and cassettes. 'What's up, you not staying?' Jack questioned, talking through his mouthful of food. I looked at Michael and he nodded at me. 'Lost your tongue?' Jack went on, sounding nervous. 'Gone all shy on me? Thought we had plans kiddo? You know? Your mate is welcome too, you know, you always know that.'

'Gotta' go,' I told him, heading back to Michael, and the door.

'Why you taking all that with you?'

'It's mine.'

'Oh, all right, all right then. Off you go. Back later then are you?'

'Maybe,' I said, just to keep him happy. 'See you later.'

We left the lounge and hurried back to the front door. 'Don't worry I'll save you some!' he yelled after me. 'I know you won't wanna' miss out!'

I slammed the door behind me. 'What's he on about?' Michael asked, his eyes wide with fear. I shrugged.

'Come on.' We grabbed at each other in mounting uneasiness and started to run.

We were sat in the kitchen, nibbling nervously at Marmite toast, when Anthony came sighing through the front door. We looked at each other, knowing the wait was over, knowing this was it, as he slung down his keys and kicked off his boots in the hallway. We sat hunched over the table and I pushed my half-eaten toast away. Anthony came into the kitchen, stopped, and just looked at us, and I swear to God, for one awful, terrible moment I was utterly convinced that he was going to cry. He just stared at us, mostly at me, and he looked wretched and gutted, and I thought; has someone died? That's one of those faces, that's a face like someone has died, or something really terrible has happened, and spikes of terror broke out across my skin and I felt freezing cold.

Instead of crying, Anthony coughed, cleared his throat and ran a hand quickly back through his short, dark hair. He looked troubled and was frowning, and then it was like he was unable to meet our eyes properly, and the more we stared at him, waiting, the more he couldn't look at us, until finally he turned and wrenched open the fridge.

'Okay then,' he said, turning back with beer in hand and eyes to the floor. He didn't say anything though, he just kept us waiting even longer and started to pace back and forth with his beer.

'Come on then!' Michael snapped at him suddenly, his outburst making me jump so badly I knocked half of my cup of tea all over the table. Michael swore and rubbed irritably at his eyes. 'Come *on* then,' he pleaded. 'Tell us what the hell's going on.'

'All right, all right, give me a chance, hang on, I got so much to explain. Shift up Mike.' Michael moved along the bench and Anthony slipped in beside him. He held his beer in one hand and his head in the other. He looked like he was in some kind of terrible pain and my hands were growing slick and greasy with sweat. 'My head is killing me,' he complained. Michael thumped the table.

'Anthony! For fucks sake!'

He looked up. 'Right, okay, I know, okay, give me a chance. This isn't easy you know.' He closed his eyes for a moment and rubbed two fingers against the middle of his forehead. 'I don't even know if it's definitely true, I mean, I've gone and scared you all, and me and I've only really got Jaime's word for it.'

'What's Jaime got to do with it?' I asked in a small voice. 'What's been going on between you two?'

Anthony lowered his hand and looked at me with a sigh. 'Well that's the thing,' he said. 'I mean, that's why this is hard to explain. Look, you know I said to you a while back that I was onto things? To help you?' I nodded yes. He scratched his neck. 'Okay, well, that all started way back, when I came out of prison again and bumped into Jaime. Mike told you we went to school together right?' I nodded again. 'Yeah, well, anyway. I started meeting up with him every now and then, just buying some grass off him to start with. Started grilling him when I could get away with it, you know, about Howard and Freeman. Just finding out anything I could about them, but to be honest, he didn't know much. Not really. Only that it's true Freeman used to be a cop.'

My eyes widened and Michael's did too. 'That's true?' I asked. My heart was beating hard inside my chest. I picked up my half cup of tea and sipped it.

Anthony nodded at us. 'Well to begin with Jaime wasn't totally sure, but he reckoned only a cop or a criminal would know the stuff Freeman knows. He dug around a bit when he could, you see. To help me. Because I asked him to.'

'Why the hell would he do that for you?' Michael demanded. 'He works for them.'

'Hmm,' said Anthony, making a face that told us otherwise. 'He sort of works for me too.'

My jaw dropped. 'What?'

Anthony laughed a little nervously. 'This is the bit even Mike doesn't know. I've been paying Jaime for a while now. Well, from the start really. I've been paying him to spy for me, to find stuff out, whatever.'

Michael held up a hand, shaking his head in bemusement. 'Hang on, hang on, let me get this straight. You've been paying Jaime Lawler to dig dirt on Freeman and Howard?'

Anthony smiled slightly, shrugged and nodded. 'Basically, yes. I wanted to know anything. Anything he could find out, anything he heard, like if Freeman was a cop once, and how he knew Howard in the first place, and as it happens, Freeman really was a cop, a detective even, until about three or four years ago.'

'No way,' breathed Michael, looking at me. 'That fat sack of shit, a cop? I never would have believed it.'

'How did Jaime get anything out of him?' I asked then, shifting forward slightly. 'He never told me that.'

'Just questions,' Anthony shrugged. 'Waiting 'til he was drunk, that kind of thing. But we needed more than that, we needed confirmation, so we came up with a plan. Last night, Jaime came into The Ship and kicked off big time, reeling around the place, smashing stuff and starting on people until he got himself arrested.'

My mind was spinning. I didn't understand a thing. 'Why?' Michael asked.

'To get arrested on purpose,' Anthony went on very patiently. 'Cost me a bit, I can tell you, but you should have seen him guys! You would've thought he was blind crazy drunk, but he hadn't touched a drop. Anyway, to cut the long story short, he ended up in a cell and demanded to see Officer Heaton and no one else.'

'Why him?' I asked. Anthony sat back a little and drank some beer.

'They went to school together,' he told us, while our jaws dropped yet again. He nodded at our shocked faces. 'Same year. Few older than me. Heaton agreed to speak to Jaime to shut him up. He was causing mayhem in the cells. Anyway, Heaton spoke to him and Jaime offered him a deal no copper worth his salt would ever refuse.'

'What?' Michael demanded, his hands planted and splayed against the table top, his eyes bulging from his pale face. I knew exactly how he felt. I didn't think I could cope with this much longer. The suspense and the building fear were killing me. I wanted to get up and run out and never have to hear any of it. Every time I looked into Anthony's eyes I had the most awful feeling of dread, heavy and dragging in my belly, pulling me down slowly.

'He offered to give him the location of some big-time crack dealer over in Belfield Park, in return for Heaton running a quick background check on our pal Jack Freeman. So Heaton took him up on it of course. Ran the check, gave him the information that came up and Jaime gave him the number. One less lowlife crack dealer operating in Belfield Park by the looks of it.' Anthony grimaced again and rubbed his eyes with one hand.

'Dangerous for Jaime,' I whispered, my eyes on the table. Anthony was silent for a moment or two and then he sat forward.

'Okay, so anyway, this is where it gets interesting. And when I say interesting, I really mean disturbing.' His eyes found mine and I really wanted him to stop talking and I wanted him to stop looking at me, and I wanted him to stop looking so damn scared and anxious. He rolled his shoulders back and rubbed vigorously at the back of his neck with one hand. 'You're not gonna' like this much,' he said, his voice gruff and small, and again, his eyes on me. 'But you need to know, so here goes. Okay. Well it's true that Freeman and Howard have known each other for years. And for a lot of that time Freeman was a cop, who made it all the way up to D.I. But then a few years back, he was pushed into early retirement because he was being investigated. Someone made an accusation against him and it was taken seriously enough for him to be suspended. It didn't get very far though, the investigation, before the witness backed out and changed his mind. The accusation was dropped and he pretty much got away with it. But his career was over. Then he turns up here. Called over no doubt by Howard who was getting his knickers in a twist about me and my mates threatening him that time. All falls into place when you think about it, eh?' His voice had dried up to almost nothing. He lifted his beer and guzzled about half of it before banging it back onto the table.

There was a long silence between all three of us then. I think none of us wanted to be the first to speak, the first to ask the question that hung like ice in the air, strangling us all. My eyes travelled to meet Michael's, and he just looked confused and pale and sad, and then I looked at Anthony, and oh Jesus Christ, he was just staring right back at me in this awful, this terrible knowing way, like he knew I knew exactly what he was going to say, and I felt something slipping inside of me then, and this livid terror clawing up my throat. It was my question to ask, so I asked it.

'What was he accused of?'

Anthony swallowed and glanced down at the table. He was rubbing his thumb nail back and forth against the cloth. 'He had a rent boy as an informer, you know what that is? You know what that means?' Michael and I shrugged and nodded at the same time. My mouth felt coated with something vile, something I wanted to retch up and spit out. 'This kid, he was fourteen, anyway, it was him that made the complaint, and it's all on file, and Heaton told Jaime what came up on the check, so I guess we have to assume it's all the truth...but anyway, he accused Freeman of molesting him, you know...' He trailed off and I was just blinking in shock and horror, and the whole room was spinning like crazy around my head, all of it suddenly fuzzy and unreal. I shook my head hard, trying to shake it all away and when I felt Anthony's hand on my forearm, I wrenched my arm away, and I heard Michael saying, shittinghell, shittinghell!

'Danny?'

The Boy With The Thorn In His Side-Part 2

I opened my mouth to speak. But I felt sick. I was going to be sick. I lunged away from the table and ran to the kitchen sink, where the Marmite toast lurched up violently from my belly, sending splats of twisted brown and black gunge across the worktops. It was followed by another lurch, and this time my tea flew up after it, splattering the draining board. I gripped onto the edge of the sink with my hands. I felt the whole world dancing around me. I wanted to get off. I wanted to die. I didn't want to have to turn around and look at them, not ever, not ever. I thought he was my friend. I was breathless and panting, and my stomach kept heaving and trying to breathe for me.

'Danny?' I heard Anthony from behind me. He sounded desperate and panicked. 'Danny? Has anything ever happened...like that?'

I did not want to turn and face them. I did not want to face myself. I wanted to scratch my face off. I wanted to scratch all my skin off. I wanted to scratch *him* off. I thought about walking to the door and leaving. I thought about finding a dark hole somewhere and shredding my skin off, layer by layer, until I found whatever was left of me hidden underneath. Instead, I shook my head slowly from side to side and said. 'No.'

Anthony breathed a sigh of relief, and I turned around to see his eyes focused firmly on Michael, who had turned as white as a sheet. 'Anything Mike? Anything weird?'

'No! God no!' Michael reached for his cup of tea, his hand shaking visibly as it snaked across the table.

'Okay that's good,' said Anthony, but then his eyes were back on me. It was the way he looked at me that did it. My knees felt like jelly and I wanted to sink to the floor, but somehow I had to keep it together. Somehow, I thought, some fucking how there has to be some hope somewhere. So, I sat back down and kept looking at him. My eyes filled with frightened tears and so did his.

'Sometimes,' I mumbled, my lips trembling. I wiped my eyes with my hands. 'Sometimes he sat next to me at night. He stroked my hair and stuff. I thought I was dreaming.' I nodded, remembering how I would wake in the morning with fuzzy memories in my mind, memories that I ignored, shoved away, and recoiled from...Sometimes he would just be sat there. Just staring at me. Looking like he was going to cry. I dragged a hand across my eyes again.

'What else?' Anthony urged me.

'Nothing, just…' I shrugged my shoulders, wondering how the hell I could ever explain to them that I really hadn't minded Jack doing that. Because it hadn't seemed like anything weird, or wrong, and because it was nearly always after Howard had hurt me. He'd been on my side, hadn't he? I'd heard him telling Howard to stop…I shook my head at their waiting faces. 'Nothing, that's it.'

'Anything else?' Anthony asked, his voice tight, his face taut and still. I shook my head miserably, but at the back of my mind, I was crawling up the walls and trembling with fear and confusion. I pressed my face into the palms of my hands and just held it there, just rubbing and rubbing at my eyes and my head, trying to make it all just go away. I shook my head.

'Fucking dirty son-of-a-bitch!' Michael burst out suddenly, hissing through his teeth, as he rose abruptly from the table, with his hands raking through his unruly black hair. He was shaking his head at us.

'That's all though?' Anthony turned his attention back to me. I swallowed and rubbed at my arms. I was trying like hell to pull myself back together, to not disintegrate in front of them. I lowered my head back into my waiting hands.

'Yeah, that's all,' I told him.

'It's okay,' Anthony was telling me urgently. 'It's okay because we know now, so that's fucking it right? You guys never go near the slimy pervert ever again, right? And I'm gonna' find a way to fuck him up, you can believe that. *Both* of them.'

'You think Howard knows all this?' asked Michael, standing close to the back door with his arms folded across his chest. He blew his hair up and out of his glaring dark eyes. 'I bet he does, dirty evil bastard! Both of them Anthony! I knew it, I *knew* there was something dodgy about that guy didn't I Danny? Filthy shitting pervert!' He shuddered and shook his head and his lips were all curled back in revulsion. He was looking at me and I wanted to shrink away in shame, remembering the countless times he had told me how uncomfortable Jack made him, and all the times I had ignored him and

The Boy With The Thorn In His Side-Part 2

encouraged him to come to the flat. 'I said, didn't I? Why the hell would Howard's friend let us go to his flat and drink and stuff? Why would he? I knew there was something dodgy going on, I knew it! Oh fuckinghell, this is horrible!' He unfolded his arms and covered his mouth with one hand, just shaking his head from side to side.

Anthony took control of things. He picked up a pack of cigarettes and passed them out to us, lighting each one in turn. 'You're right,' he nodded at his brother. 'This is all to do with Howard. Right from the very start.' His eyes met mine, and I could only stare back at him, trapped within a grim and frightened silence. I heard the truth of it all come crashing in on me, and the truth was deafening. 'He brought the guy here,' Anthony said to us. 'We know that. Called him up and got him here because I threw my weight around at that party. Calls in his old perverted buddy and sets him up in his old flat. Gets him dealing with the likes of Lawler, and letting you kids use the flat to score and get drunk.' Anthony was nodding as he puffed nervously away on his cigarette, his eyes on me. 'Jesus,' he said, with a brief smile. 'I thought I was scared of that guy when he got me sent down again, but I think I'm even more scared of him now.' He shook his head, and in between drags his teeth were nibbling restlessly at his lip. I had never seen him look like that before; like he was shitting himself. 'This is heavy, serious shit. I didn't really have a clue. I'm guessing you did though, hey?'

I glanced down at my hands, clasped together on the table to stop them shaking. About a million memories of pain and fear rushed through my mind and all I could do was nod silently, and think, you're right Anthony, you don't have a clue, you really don't...

'What now?' Michael croaked from the back door where he stood huddled against it. Anthony shrugged at him.

'I don't know yet.'

'I've got a plan,' I said then, lifting my eyes to meet theirs. I breathed in, wondering if it were possible to inhale their courage and their strength. 'I'm sixteen next month. Terry can hire me properly. That's one thing. The other thing is I can leave home without the cops bothering to look for me. So, I lay low until then. Carry on as normal and pretend I don't know all this. We find a place to live. We don't tell anyone. We go. All three of us. They won't know anything about it. We find a place together.'

I looked from Michael, to Anthony, licking my lips as they took it in. I could hardly stand to look at them, hoping as much as I was. Hope was such a painful thing, I remembered. God, it hurt. Michael looked at his brother, who lowered his cigarette and stared at me wonderingly.

'Are you serious?'

'It's been my plan for ages,' I shrugged at them. 'I've even got money saved up. Been buying way less music.' I smiled a little. 'Anyway, Terry will increase my hours when I'm sixteen, so I'll have to keep my job there, but we'll move somewhere else, and they won't know, we'll just go. We can afford a place if it's all three of us.'

Anthony was smiling now. 'So where are you thinking?' he asked me.

'Belfield Park,' I said, smiling back. 'So we're close to Chaos.' I watched the smile spreading up Anthony's face, lighting up his eyes, taking over his face. Michael came forward, looking at me as if he did not understand me. 'Plenty of bed-sits and flats,' I explained. 'Cheap as chips. We can all bus into work. If they find us, or bother us, we'll go further.'

'Anthony?' Michael arrived at his brother's side and nudged him. 'What d'you reckon? You're always saying we can't afford this place now Mum's gone. And I just got that Saturday job in McDonalds, that'll help, right?'

Anthony stared at him before laughing out loud. 'You boys don't need to convince me for God's sake!' He stubbed out his cigarette, reached across the table and ruffled up my hair. 'Jesus Christ mate, you've got more balls than anyone I've ever met! Come on, I'm serious, Mike? Grab the paper! There's places to rent in the back of it. We need to start looking now!'

Michael dashed out of the kitchen, excitement lighting up his face, while Anthony just looked at me, shaking his head and clapping his hands, and we just grinned at each other helplessly. I felt something stirring softly inside of me then. A nervous and heady kind of excitement that made me feel a little woozy, a little foggy in the mind. Anthony's eyes burned back into mine, unflinching.

'This is it,' he told me. 'Listen to me, I promise you, this is it. It's all gonna' be okay now.' I wanted to believe him. God, I wanted to believe him so fucking much.

16

 Hope was a dangerous thing. With only a matter of weeks to go before I turned sixteen, I was becoming hooked on it. It was more intoxicating, more addictive than any of the drugs I had been messing around with. It was also more fragile. It was a constant tease; easing me into calmer sleep at night, and awaking to hold my hand again when the morning arrived. As Anthony put in extra hours at the pub, and Michael started a weekend job at the McDonalds on Somerley road, I felt the soft fingers of hope caressing me at every turn. Still, I was holding back from it all the time, afraid to believe in it or let it carry me away. I stopped buying uppers and downers from Jaime and started shoving all my record shop money into a sock which I kept hidden at the back of my wardrobe. I made sure to take a deep breath of fresh hope every day, and I felt my mind getting clearer and my heart stronger. There was a chance, I told myself. A possibility. If we could get out, if we could get away without them knowing, then that would be it, wouldn't it? It would all be over.

 I sensed a new tension breeding at home. It seemed to seep from the very walls, permeating the air around us. I felt Howard watching me closely; a million dangerous promises paused behind his thin lips. He had a mobile phone. This sleek black brick he punched his demands into. I took deep breaths whenever I could; otherwise it felt like I would suffocate. I felt like all I had to do was make it to my birthday, survive that long, and I would be free. I started to sort out and pack up my belongings in private. Throwing what I didn't need into the rubbish when no one was at home. I packed records and tapes up in bags and scurried over to Michael's with them. They were packing up too. Slowly, but surely, peeling themselves away from their old lives.

 I was in a daze one day at the dinner table, headphones on, until Howard came to the table. Thom Yorke whined into my ears, while my eyes fixed on the knife and fork that lay on the table before me. My mother buzzed around the kitchen, with an oven glove on one hand and a cigarette in the other. She had just returned from the hairdressers; her stiffened waves now a startling shade of gold. I felt the barrier between us, and an immense sadness dropping on top of me as I sat there in my bubble of music. Howard stormed in, reaching automatically for my headphones, but I was faster, ducking away and pulling them off myself. He narrowed his eyes, grunted and slumped into the chair opposite me.

'He's up to something.' He picked up his fork and waved it menacingly from side to side. My mother placed the food on the table; sausage, chips and beans. She sighed softly and slipped into the third chair. I just looked down at my food and tried to be invisible.

'Okay honey,' she said, in the soothing voice she used for him when he was in a rotten mood. 'I know you've had a bad day, but please don't start this at the dinner table. Danny's been no trouble lately. You were saying it yourself the other day.'

Howard simply ignored her. His piggy eyes bore into me as I tried to eat. 'Just so you know,' he said, through a mouthful of sausage. 'I know you're up to something, all right? She may like to live on another planet these days, but I know all right?'

I continued to eat in silence, pushing my food around the plate so that it would look like I had eaten more than I had. I hated eating in Howard's presence. Every mouthful felt like I was chewing on glass, every lump of food slipping down my throat and threatening to stick.

'Can I go?' I asked. I couldn't bear to have to look at him any longer, knowing what I knew. I couldn't bear his eyes on me. I felt my body twitching to escape.

My mother nodded at me. 'Course you can love.'

'Have you done your jobs?' Howard barked.

I pushed back my chair and stood up. 'I've been at my job.'

'Job?' He rolled his eyes and laughed at me. 'That's not a job, you idiot. You don't get fucking paid yet do you?'

I breathed in, bit down on the words that filled my head, and forced a smile. 'What do you want me to do?'

Minutes later I was pushing the lawnmower up and down the back garden in the heavy August sun, while Howard sat on the doorstep watching me suffer. My mother had gone to answer the phone. His greedy eyes followed my every move. I kept my head down, watching the grass as the lawnmower devoured it in stripes. I could feel the small hand of hope slipping away from me then, to be replaced by the familiar chill of dread that clung to my spine, crawling up to my neck and flicking the hairs on end, one by one.

The oppressive heat burned down from a stark cloudless sky, yet the skin on my arms had broken out in goose pimples. I lifted my head when movement caught my eye. Howard had risen from the step. He looked over his shoulder, into the kitchen and then he came towards me. I pushed on, keeping my eyes down as I heaved the lawnmower forward. He fell into casual step behind me, still puffing lazily on his cigarette. I longed so badly for hope to return and take my hand again, but she had gone, she was hiding.

'Why are you giving Jack the cold shoulder?' Howard was walking close behind me, following my every step, sounding cocky and full of it like he always did, every word he spoke soaked in a snort of ridicule.

I leaned forward, pushing the mower and shrugged. 'What?'

'Don't just say 'what'! Turn the fuck around and look at me when I'm speaking to you!'

I stopped walking. I killed the mower and turned slowly to face him, pushing my sweaty hair out of my eyes with the back of one hand. The glare of the sun bounced into my eyes from behind him, so I had to raise a hand to see the face of the man who towered above me. A shark like smile gleamed upon his face.

'Why does it matter to you?' I asked him. 'What I do, or where I go?'

He puffed his smoke right into my face. 'Don't answer a question with a question shit for brains!'

'I've been busy, how about that?'

I watched him sucking up his breath, the great inhalation puffing up his chest and increasing his height.

'Sarcastic little mother-fucker,' he said softly. He cocked his head, and ran his eyes slowly up and down my body as if inspecting me closely for lies. He ran a sluggish tongue across his lower lip. 'See, that's how I know you're up to something. 'Cause you're not going round to Jack's. You're up to something. I can feel it. I *know* it. One minute you're all over Jack like a fucking rash, the next you're nowhere near the place.'

The Boy With The Thorn In His Side-Part 2

I shrugged at him, and glanced at the kitchen door, wondering how close Mum was to finishing her phone call. I was brimming over with defiance, if you want to know the truth. Oh, how much I longed to spit in his face, or stamp on his balls. It was all I could do to contain the sneer in my voice or the loathing in my eyes as I spoke to him.

'You really shouldn't worry so much,' I said, catching the shadow of my mother making her way briskly and urgently through the kitchen. 'I'm not doing anything wrong, just got bored of going there that's all.'

Howard had no time to respond. 'Lee!' my mother cried for him, as she appeared weakly in the doorway, stopping there and clinging to the wall. A steady flow of tears marched down her cheeks. Her whole face seemed twisted with grief, or shock, or something. Howard did not move.

'What is it baby?'

'My mum,' she whimpered in reply, covering her face with her hands, her big blue eyes staring out from between her fingers. 'My mum, she's died.' She turned suddenly and stumbled away from us, back into the house.

Howard turned his head and gazed down at me. A thin and malicious smile spread out across his face. We could hear her distressed sobbing coming from beyond the kitchen. I swallowed, looking away, and I felt like the only person in the world. I felt isolation swirling around me like a mist. And when I looked back up at him, he was grinning. His eyes were laughing at me as he reached out and circled his hand around my wrist. Right there, in the middle of the sun-baked lawn, he lowered the cigarette from his lips and pressed the glowing butt into the palm of my hand. I stiffened, hissing pain through my teeth, and then it was over. He walked away from me. He swaggered, strutted and whistled. He didn't look back because he did not need to. He went into the house and called out to her.

I stood in the middle of the garden for what seemed like a long time. I used my thumb to rub gently at the burn, hushing it, while my shoulders hung and my heart burned. I stood and I listened, my breathing fast and shallow. I listened to the crying and the wailing and the murmured words of comfort. I listened to Howard on the telephone. I listened to footsteps hurrying up and down the stairs. I imagined bags being packed and wished that they were mine. I made myself move then. I walked slowly around to the front of the house, and then as the howl of protest began to build up at the back of my throat, I picked up my pace and I ran. I found myself at Michael's front door, leaning into it as I banged upon it, looking back over my shoulder and doubting every shred of hope I had believed in before.

Anthony let me in and bopped me cheerily on the head with a rolled-up newspaper.

'Been phoning up about places,' he said, closing the door. 'Want to come and see a few with us tomorrow?' I nodded in silence, as the burn pulsed within my closed fist. Anthony frowned at me. 'You okay?'

Michael appeared in the lounge doorway, a piece of toast in one hand.

'This can't happen soon enough,' I told them both. 'Mum's going away again. Right now, she's packing. My Grandma just died.'

Michael made a face. 'Shit. Sorry mate.'

I shook my head at him. 'I'm scared guys. He knows something is up. He wants to know why I'm not round Jacks anymore. He's getting paranoid and worked up, and now she's not gonna' be around again...and....' My voice had faded down to nothing, my throat tight and dry. Anthony was looking at me gently.

'Hey. It's all right mate, don't panic. Soon enough he won't even know where we are. You've just got to hang on a bit longer, yeah? We're moving as fast as we can.'

I looked down at my hand. I uncurled my fingers and held out my palm. 'It's gotta' be faster,' I told them as they gasped. 'Or I'm fucked.'

The Boy With The Thorn In His Side-Part 2

17

I struggled with my impatience, watching Kay pack. She was irritating me the entire time, and as she talked, and wept and snotted all over the place, I kept getting these intense visions of violence in my head. She would pack a few things and then collapse all over me in tears again. It was on the tip of my tongue to tell her to get her fucking act together. Instead, I held her close and patted her shoulder and let her cry it out. I felt like reminding her that she had never liked the old bitch anyway, and every time she sniffed the snot back up her nose, I felt like grabbing a tissue and ramming it into her face. That would give her something worthwhile to cry about, I thought. But I didn't. I did everything the way I was supposed to. I helped her pack; made sure she had money, and checked her car for oil, water and fuel. She lolled against me in the driveway after I had packed the boot for her.

'Our last words were harsh ones,' she was moaning into my shirt. 'Do you know what the last thing I ever said to her was? Mind your own business and leave me alone!' She pulled back, gazing up at me with her streaming red eyes. 'How awful Lee! How awful is that!'

I agreed with her; it was awful, it was fucking disgusting to be honest. But I didn't tell her that obviously. I soothed her, and rubbed her back, and kissed her sweet little face, tasting her salty tears before she pulled away and ducked down into the car.

'We all say things like that,' I told her, as she pulled across her seat belt. 'That's life honey. We can't possibly know what's around the corner.'

She sniffed and nodded and turned the key in the engine. 'I'll be back by the end of the week. Trust her to want to get buried in the middle of bloody nowhere in Cornwall. You make sure Danny helps you with the packing and everything.'

'Oh, he'll be helping me all right,' I smiled at her brightly. 'Don't you worry about that. Call me when you get there okay?'

When she had gone, I had work. My mind was busy the entire time. My thoughts dominated by him and whatever it was he was up to. Jack came in late in the night. His brow was all creased and concerned, his rubbery lips jutting out like a petulant child. I sighed and rolled my eyes when he came to the bar. Why did I suddenly feel like his despair was my responsibility? I shoved a whisky at him and hoped that would be the end of it, but he hauled his fat carcass up onto a stool and beckoned me closer.

'No sign of him,' he told me, shaking his head, and reminding me of a shaggy, drooling dog. I scratched my forehead and winced at him. What did he expect me to say?

'Don't get all worked up,' I shrugged.

'Don't know what I did wrong,' he replied morosely. 'Did I do something wrong? I thought we were friends.'

'Well you thought wrong, didn't you?' I snapped at him in disgust. 'Isn't it obvious Jack? The little shit was using you all along. Maybe he's found another dealer, maybe he's given it up for lent, who knows? Who gives a shit?'

Jack viewed me darkly over the rim of his glass. 'You,' he said evenly. 'You do.'

'Oh, do I?'

'You've lost control,' he reminded me. 'It's all slipping away from you... You know what else is weird?'

I was losing my patience with him. The very sight of him appalled me. The man was turning into a joke. Sitting in his flat, mourning and moping over a teenage boy who wouldn't come near him with a fucking barge pole. The great fat bearded slug.

'I'm sure you're about to tell me Jack. What else is weird?'

'Lawler,' he said. 'He's jumpy as fuck... Whatever's going on, he's involved.'

I walked away from him then, pretended I had other people to serve. What was the point? Being too close to him was probably bad for my health. If the man was too stupid to realise the little shit had been using him the entire time, then I had little more to say to him.

I was going to drag it out of Danny that very night, when I returned home from work. I stood outside his room for a long time, just listening to his music beating softly through the closed door. I thought I recognised the song that was playing. I was pretty sure it was by The Rolling Stones. Something about losing your dreams, or your mind. It made me wonder what he was doing in there...what he was thinking and feeling.

Flashes of blood and gore slammed through my mind. I stepped back. My foot twitched and I could feel it kicking out, finding soft flesh and burying itself in it. My hands unclenched at my sides, and I could almost feel the hair falling through my fingers. I stepped back again, and I thought, no. No, let the little bastard stew on it a bit longer. Let him lie awake all night with his guts in a knot, wondering if I'm coming in. Let him think I'm coming for him at any moment. Let him dream about me and we'll compare notes in the morning. I went into my own room, peeled off my clothes and slipped gently into bed. I'm coming for you, I thought, as I drifted easily towards sleep, I'm coming for you, and then you'll be sorry...

He had something on his mind the next day; I could sense it right away. I listened from the kitchen, turned the radio off and stuck my head forward. I could hear him rushing around up there, scurrying from his room to the bathroom and back again, as if he had slept in, as if he was supposed to be somewhere by now. I walked slowly to the door and waited there, with my eyes narrowed and my hands trembling with the urges that rolled and thumped through my body. He was back in the bathroom again. Brushing his teeth. Not hanging around for breakfast then. The toilet flushed and the bathroom door opened again. He was coming down the stairs now, so I kept back. I could tell what he was doing. Stepping from one side to the other, avoiding the stairs that creaked the most.

I hung back until he came into sight, crouching down in the hallway to tie up his laces. He had his headphones around his neck as usual. The black cord wound down to the waistband of his jeans. He stood back up and I made my move; taking him out with a heavy blow to the back of the head that sent him crashing into the front door. I approached the fallen body, and I could feel the surge of power rocketing through me. It was like an electric current, it was like being on fire, it was like I was burning from the inside. I briefly considered the phone call I could make to Kay later. Just killed your precious little son, sorry about that baby, went too far, thought he'd bounce back like normal but he didn't! I'd be laughing at her, laughing at her dumb voice when it questioned me, laughing as I explained to her how I took him apart piece by piece, just because I felt like it...

I savoured every moment of delicious power, of knowing that he was down because I brought him down, that he would stay down until I let him up, that I was the boss and that was the way it was. I felt like I held the entire universe inside my own fist and could do with it whatever I wished. The boy was moving now, grunting as he tried to get his knees up under him, with one hand pressed to the back of his head, fingers splayed. I towered over him and then booted him in the ribs, laughing out loud at the breathless gasp he made as he slumped back down again.

'Don't move, don't even think of moving, don't even lift your fucking head unless I say you can, right?' He nodded, with his cheek against the carpet, his hair covering his face. 'Good. Going somewhere were you?' I asked him. 'Sneaking off again, were you? You're not going anywhere until you tell me the truth. So, we can do this the hard way, or the easy way.' I lifted my foot and placed it down on his neck, grinding my boot into the skin. He cried out, but kept still. Sensible. I leaned down over my knee. 'Where you going?' I could see one blue eye staring back up at me through a mass of tangled blonde hair. 'Where were you going?' I asked him again.

'Record shop...' he panted.

'Bullshit. I don't believe you. You're going to see them boys, aren't you? There's something going on between you and them, isn't there eh? I need to make that phone call to the cops, don't I eh?'

'No! No, you don't! I was going to work, swear to God I was...'

I increased the pressure on his neck and all he could do was squirm and take it. 'I want to know why you're not going around Jack's anymore. He's sad about it, did you know that?' He said something that was indistinguishable so I eased the pressure and leaned forward. 'What did you say?'

'He was giving me the creeps...'

'What kind of thing is that to say?' I roared down at him. 'What is that supposed to mean? Giving you the creeps? He wasn't giving you the creeps when he was handing dope and whizz out like fucking sweeties, was he eh?'

The Boy With The Thorn In His Side-Part 2

'I don't wanna' do all that anymore...'

'Really?' I sneered, pressing my boot down again. 'Is that so, you lying sack of shit? And you expect me to believe that, do you? You just woke up one day, and suddenly Jack was creepy and drugs are a no no? You know I could kill you right now, you pathetic little mother-fucker? Snap your neck in a heartbeat. Take you somewhere far from here and just dump you. I'd tell your mum you packed your stuff and ran away. Is that what you're planning is it eh? Running away again?'

'No,' he spluttered under my boot. 'No, I'm not.'

'You better not be lying to me,' I warned him, gazing down over my knee. I moved my boot around, feeling his neck with it. I felt like I was very close to slipping into some kind of trance. Everything seemed to have slowed down and blurred around the edges. I questioned dimly if I was actually just dreaming... 'I'll find out if you're lying to me. I'll find out if you go anywhere near those Anderson boys, and then I'll do exactly what I promised I would. I'll get those sniffer dogs sent round to their house, and I'll finish those little bastards for good. You'll never see either of them ever again. And as for you, well, I'll punish you and you'll realise then how easy I've gone on you up until now...' I straightened up and removed my foot. I heard the boy start to take deep, sucking breaths of air. He pushed his hair from his face with one hand, and then just lay still. 'Your mum's gone,' I told him, and he nodded. 'Gone to sort out the funeral and your Gran's stuff, and all that crap. While she's gone, you do not breathe unless I say so, got it?' I nudged his arm with my toe and he nodded again. 'You do not leave this house unless I say so, and you do not use the phone unless I say so, and you do not answer the door unless I say so. I want to know exactly where you are at all fucking times, you got that?'

'What about the record shop?'

I thought about this for a second. I knew it meant a lot to him, that place. He kept going on about how he would get a job there when he was sixteen.

'Hmm,' I said, scratching my chin. 'We'll see. Maybe if I drive you in and pick you up afterwards eh? When he's gonna' start paying you?'

'He pays me a bit. I'll give it you?'

I laughed, tickled by the hopeful, pleading tone to his voice. He moved his arms and crossed them in front of him, lifting his head slowly, his eyes on me, yet unsure whether they should be.

'Yeah, give it to me,' I told him blankly. I was bored now. There was a list of things to do lying on the kitchen table. I nudged him again with my foot. 'Right, up you get then. I'm writing a list. Got shit loads to sort out while your mum is away. Sale is going through on the new house, so we got to get this place packed up and cleaned up ready for tenants to start viewing. So, there's plenty to keep you busy okay?'

He was rubbing at his neck. 'What shall I do first?'

I smiled. I half wanted to tell him he was a good boy. But there was something too contrived about his question. It was like he was asking exactly what he knew I would like to hear. I watched him struggling up to his knees. I experienced a brief urge to boot him back down again, but it passed and I just felt tired. He turned to face me once he was back on his feet and scratched nervously at one arm.

'You can take everything out of the fridge and clean it from top to bottom. Then you can get started on the oven. Then you can go to the shop and get some things we've run out of.'

He nodded. 'Okay.'

I slipped an arm around his shoulders and led him towards the kitchen. 'Then you can pop over to Jack's and keep him company for a bit while I'm at the club. He misses you, you know. He told me that.' I felt his body freeze under my arm and I laughed, and hauled him along.

The Boy With The Thorn In His Side-Part 2

18

He broke my fucking headphones! Fuck! Fuck him! I just had to take it. I just had to get on my knees and clean the stupid fridge, with broken headphones dangling around my stupid, dirty neck. I could feel his imprint on my skin, I could feel the coating of dirt he had given me, and I longed to tear at it with my nails. Instead I cleaned the fridge, and then I cleaned the oven, while he sat at the table, drinking his tea, smoking his cigarettes and gloating. I bristled and shivered, and I had to find somewhere to put the anger, I had to push it down, contain it somehow. It was black and ugly and trembling to life within me.

When he said I could go to the shop, I took the money and ran. I did not feel my body start to shake until I had rounded the end house and pressed my back into the wall there. Then it came like an explosion; nerves rattling to life throughout my limbs, and as I looked up at the Andersons' house I couldn't help laughing at myself, picturing how I must look, all red faced and shaking like a leaf. I lifted a shuddering hand to my neck and brushed away the dirt I could still feel there, the dirt from his fucking boot. I laughed out loud because I had to. I felt like just curling up into a small ball and crying my eyes out, but what good would that do me?

I laughed at how insane and ridiculous it all was, but I was also laughing in fear, and the fear was escalating along with the physical reaction, my heart pounding so hard I could feel it vibrating in my eardrums. I fumbled clumsily for the cigarette in my back pocket, found it and promptly dropped it. I picked it up with useless shaking fingers and tried to light it. It suddenly seemed imperative, life and death even, that I light the cigarette and smoke it. Finally, I cupped my hands around my mouth long enough to get it lit, and pulled away from the wall. I made the best show I could of walking, no, *marching* across to Michael's house. I put my heart and soul into it, if you can believe that. Threw my shoulders back, held my head high and as I walked I smoked, and as I smoked I felt better, and a kind of vicious, energising anger railed violently through me. One day, I thought, I am going to get that son-of-a-bitch, I am going to make him pay, I am going to make him sorry.

'You'll have to go without me,' I told Michael when he answered the door to me. 'He's onto me. Won't even let me go to work and back on my own.'

I watched his face fill with dismay. 'No!' he argued, kicking at the door.

I shrugged and started to turn away from him. 'Can't risk it.'

'We'll meet you at the record shop,' he called after me urgently. 'The fat man will cover for you if he checks!'

I looked back at him, smiling as the relief washed over me. 'Okay. I'll meet you there.'

I had a plan then. A filthy little conniving plan. I got the things he was too lazy to get himself from the shop and carried them dutifully home. I found him settled in front of the TV, a cigarette on the go and the phone pressed to his ear. He lowered it to his chest when he saw me lingering in the doorway with the shopping bags.

'Talking to your mum,' he told me, flashing a friendly smile which at best just confused me, the way he could change like that. 'Just dump those in the kitchen.'

I took a breath and braved the question; 'Can I go to the record shop? He's expecting me.'

Howard made a face and checked his watch. 'Okay then,' he agreed. 'I'll pick you up from there later.'

Another breath. 'I can go to Jack's right after if you like. You know, see how he is.'

He nodded. 'All right then, I'll get you from there when I've finished at the club.'

He put the phone back to his ear and I legged it. Dumped the shopping on the kitchen table, flew out of the door and ran. It felt like I had air beneath my feet, lifting me up as I tore around the corner back to Michael's. It felt like I would be able to fly if I stretched my arms out far enough. The man had two personalities, I mused, as I went. There was the psychotic side, the side that gave me nightmares, the side that had me constantly believing I was about to die, and then there was that side, the almost normal one. I would never understand it. The way he could be standing on my neck and threatening to kill me one moment, and then smiling casually as if nothing had ever happened the next.

Michael and Anthony slipped silently out of the house after I knocked. I told them my plan, and we caught the bus into town and hopped off outside The Record Shop. I ducked my head around the door, and saw Terry in his usual position; head lowered into the pages of a magazine, while a mug of tea steamed on the counter. He looked up when he saw me.

'You're not due in,' he said.

'I know, can you do me a massive favour Terry?'

He looked instantly unimpressed. 'Depends what it is.'

'If my step-dad comes in here looking for me, can you tell him you sent me home with a bad stomach ache? I was like green and sweating and everything!'

He rolled his eyes at me and picked up his tea. 'Go on then.'

'Thanks Terry! You're a legend!'

Michael, Anthony and I spent the next few hours trailing around the dingy back streets of Belfield Park's least desirable quarters. We viewed bed-sits that turned our stomachs and put us off getting any lunch; each one more dirty, dark and depressing than the last. The final one on the list was situated at the very top of a four storey, red and white Victorian building. It jutted out from the corner of a road, almost opposite the lane that led down to Chaos. I couldn't stop smiling at this point, and Michael and Anthony smiled too, knowing why. I had to keep turning my head just to catch a glimpse of my Friday night heaven. The man from the letting agency was about Anthony's age, and dressed in a smart dark blue suit. He held a clipboard under one arm and smiled at us constantly. He unlocked the large metal door at the front of the building and gestured for us to go in first.

We swapped amused looks with each other as we began to climb the stairs. The walls were grey and peeling, covered in ancient spray-painted graffiti. The stench of fresh urine offended our nostrils. At the top of the stairs, we came onto a small landing, where we stood upon a threadbare red carpet and gazed at a large, red wooden door. The paint was flaking and patchy, and the glass window gone, boarded up with MDF. The young man used his key to open the door and ushered us through.

'It's very spacious inside,' he gushed excitedly. 'It has one of the largest living spaces,' he added, and as I walked in, I could see he was right. The main room was about three times the size of the other places we had looked at, and there were large sash windows going all the way around. The ceilings were very high and the walls had been recently painted with white emulsion.

I went up to one of the windows and pressed against it, feeling instantly how thin it was. I chuckled to myself as I gazed down on the rabbit warren of alleys and streets below us. It would feel like living at the top of the world, I thought, and I liked that. I could even see part of Chaos, poking around the corner, its dark eyes closed, its drumbeat silenced. I held a hand to the cold glass and willed it to wake up, to wake up and shine...

I turned around to see the agency man attempting to show Anthony how easily the double bed pulled down from the wall, and nearly crashing it into both their heads in the process. He blushed and lowered it to the floor, giving the sagging mattress an encouraging pat with his hand. He then stepped around it, pulled back the beige beaded curtain and demonstrated the tiny kitchen.

'Compact,' he quipped brightly. 'But meets all your needs. Oven and grill. Fridge with ice box. Storage.'

Anthony stepped briskly to the door on the right side of the bed. 'This must be the loo then?' he asked, pulling the door open. Michael and I both laughed when he hastily slammed it again. 'Compact,' he said. 'Meets all our needs.'

'You mean we can shit in it?' I laughed.

'The shower was just replaced,' the man from the agency piped up, offering us his brightest, most engaging smile. He looked to Anthony who had crossed his arms over his chest. 'So, what do you think?'

Anthony looked at us, and all three of us nodded and grinned in unison. Anthony strode towards the agency man, offering him a hand to shake. 'We can give you the deposit today,' he said.

We caught the bus back to Redchurch, our spirits high and a celebratory drink in mind. I sat next to the window on the way back, and I could not stop smiling, because I could feel that hope had crept

The Boy With The Thorn In His Side-Part 2

back in to hold my hand again. I could feel her there beside me as we hopped off the bus and stole around the back way to their house, and I wondered if hope was really a dangerous thing, as it seemed so transient, so fragile. One moment it was there and the next it was gone again. But with the deposit down, and the paperwork under way, there seemed genuine cause to breathe another sigh of relief.

'I'm going to call Lucy later,' I announced, when the three of us had been settled in the back garden for a few minutes with beers all round. Michael just laughed out loud and clapped his hands.

'About time!' he bellowed at me as I blushed.

'You'll be lucky if she gives you the time of day,' Anthony told me with a lazy grin.

'I'm gonna' tell her everything,' I went on, almost gritting my teeth as I talked, and staring down at the grass, as it pieced and pulled together inside my mind. 'All of it. And I'm going to say sorry to her. And then, I'm going to kiss her.' I nodded, and looked up at them as they exploded into laughter.

'You dozy bastard!' yelled Anthony, shaking his head.

Michael shielded his eyes from the sun with one hand. 'Well I better tell you mate, it was one of the things she complained about when I had that chat with her in the café!'

'Was it?'

'Yep, she was really pissed off. Said you never once tried to kiss her and you only think of her as a friend!'

'You moron,' Anthony groaned at me, while I grimaced in shame. He was lounging in a rickety deck chair, stripped down to just his jeans. Michael and I were sat on the doorstep. 'Well that's it now Danny my son,' he said to me. 'You've said it, we've both heard it, now you have to bloody well do it!'

I shook my head and laughed. 'No not yet! I need another drink first. I need the courage!'

One beer later, and they watched me, their cheeks puffed out with restrained laughter, as I got up and disappeared into the house to make the call. It was quick. Done and dusted, and when I returned I could feel my cheeks burning with warmth and my smile was starting to make my cheeks ache.

'She said yes,' I told their expectant, wide-eyed faces. 'She's coming over!'

Anthony was on his feet, spreading coals out on the rusty old barbecue he had dragged out of the shed earlier. He beamed at me. 'You jammy bastard!' I nodded in agreement. I sat back down on the step, just as the back gate creaked on its hinges. Billy and Jake appeared in the alley way, their hands wrapped around the handlebars of their bikes, their faces twitchy and unsure. 'All right boys?' Anthony called out to them, waving a set of tongs. 'Looks like we got ourselves a little party here!'

I watched as Billy rolled his eyes in relief, sighed and dumped his bike inside the gate. He headed straight for the bucket of cold water Anthony had filled with cheap bottles of beer.

'Thank God you called us!' he breathed out, helping himself to a beer and passing another one to Jake, who was hanging back slightly, his hands in his pockets and his expression wary. 'We were going out of our minds with boredom!'

'Well that's your own fault,' Michael retorted without sympathy. 'You know where we are.'

'So, what's going on?' Billy asked, flopping down onto the grass with his short legs stuck out in front of him. 'What's the occasion? Why you three looking so pleased with yourselves?'

I took out a cigarette and lit it up. I had a fluttery light feeling inside my belly; nerves and excitement and fear. I felt light headed with it. I watched them all from the step, feeling myself drift back from them slightly, to the outside. I was uncertain of what to say or how to say it. I tried to remember the last time I had spoken properly to either Billy or Jake, and I could not come up with anything. Even on the rare nights they had shown up at Chaos, I had been too out of my mind, too high on everything to really acknowledge them. In fact, I had avoided Jake like the plague, because his sombre eyes made me paranoid, and because he suddenly seemed so grown up, so mature and contained. He had even grown a little fluffy beard for God's sake. He seemed old before his time to me. I felt like there was a giant chasm between us. Maybe he had been thinking the same as me, as he made his way awkwardly towards the back door, hovering there with

The Boy With The Thorn In His Side-Part 2

beer in hand, drinking it in quick, nervous gulps. I looked up and smiled at him to break the silence.

'All right then Jake?'

He nodded, but remained unsmiling. 'I will be. Once the bloody exam results are in. Can't stand all this waiting around.'

I nodded, but I didn't understand. I hadn't thought twice about the handful of exams I had turned up to. I couldn't give a shit. They meant nothing to me and I had no idea why they meant to so much to him. 'Well you know you'll be fine,' I shrugged at him. 'So why worry?'

'I dunno,' he shrugged back. 'Born worrier I suppose. That's what my mum says anyway.'

'Sixth form then?' I asked him, struggling to think of ways to keep the conversation flowing. 'Like Lucy?'

'Yeah, that's the plan, if I get the right results.'

'You'll be fine,' I said, offering him a smile. 'Don't know what you're worried about.'

Jake returned the smile a little stiffly. 'So, what about you then?' he sighed, as he lowered himself down beside me on the step. 'You seem well. I mean, you seem better.'

'Not so bad today,' I corrected him with a wink. 'You never know with me. Next time you see me I'll probably be a total wreck!' I laughed, but Jake had trouble even smiling at my joke. He kept his eyes on me. They looked restless and troubled.

'Why?' he asked. I could only meet his gaze for a moment or two before I had to look away.

I shrugged and drank my beer. 'Complicated. Home stuff. Shit stuff. I dunno. Sometimes it's just easier to get wasted and forget about everything.'

'Well it's a shame,' he told me with some certainty, as if he had been thinking about it a lot. 'Because you're a nice guy, you know, you always have been. And you're clever. You probably don't realise it or whatever, but you are. You could be like a real writer or something one day.'

I laughed. 'I doubt it!'

Jake smiled tentatively. 'How about the record shop anyway? You're so lucky he gave you a job there like that!'

'I know, I know,' I grinned. 'Terry is a lazy arsed, opinionated rude fucker, but he don't half know a lot about music. We argue all the time. It's hilarious.'

Jake grinned at me and nodded. 'I bet it is. Well done. I mean, I'm glad for you. I hope it all works out. Good luck with it.'

I looked at him sideways, and thought that saying good luck was as close to saying goodbye as you could get without actually saying it. I didn't know why, but a kind of sadness washed over me then. I thought about the different paths our lives would take, and how it was inevitable that people would come in and out of your life, moving on when things changed. All those kids at school, I thought, most of them won't stay in touch, they won't stay friends. Some would go one way, and some would go the other. One day they would pass each other in the street and not even recognise each other's faces. Jake would get into the sixth form and then he would go away somewhere to a University, and he would meet serious, sombre faced people like himself, and he would do well, and he would have a good life, an honest life.

'And you,' I told him warmly. 'Good luck with everything. And hey, I'm sorry, yeah? About being a total prick most of the time lately. Hopefully things are looking up now anyway.'

'I'm sure they are,' he agreed, holding up his bottle to clink against mine. 'Definitely. Cheers mate.'

'Yeah. Cheers Jake.'

It was a different story when Lucy turned up. It was more like saying hello than goodbye. It was like seeing each other properly for the first time. How can I explain it? I felt this forceful and urgent desire, this need to be near her, when she arrived through the kitchen, bright eyed but hesitant. I did not hang around or hold back or hesitate. I did not hover in the background, or wait shyly for her to come to me. I got briskly to my feet and walked away from Billy in mid-conversation, to meet her in the house. Then we moved soundlessly back towards the hallway together, and through to the lounge. I took her hand into mine. Girl From Mars by Ash was playing on the radio, and I thought, if this goes well, I am going to remember this song forever...

The Boy With The Thorn In His Side-Part 2

'I'm a twat, and I'm sorry about everything,' I told her. I searched her eyes with my own. I looked into her face and all I could see was goodness, and all I could see was a future, a good future. Every part of my body seemed to tremble with longing and I felt like my entire heart, my entire life lay right there in her hands. Her fingers moved, entangling with mine and my heart lurched violently within my chest. She moved nearer to me. Her hair smelled like the beach.

'*I'm* a twat,' she said, with a teasing kind of smile that sparkled in her brown eyes. 'And I'm sorry about everything too.'

A raise of her eyebrows and her hand tightened on mine. I swallowed, leaned forward, and kissed her cheek. I heard her sharp intake of breath, so I stepped back and looked at her. I felt like everything was happening, everything was clashing together right in front of my eyes, and I felt like life was an amazing, wonderful thing, and then she reached up, her hand sliding slowly up to caress my neck, on the very spot Howard had placed his boot just hours earlier. I closed my eyes, leaned in and found her mouth with mine. Just the sensation of her lips, pressed against mine seemed to send my body into overdrive. I felt myself harden down below. I felt like a man, like someone who had finally grown. Her hands linked behind my neck, under my hair. I had never felt anything like it before and it was setting me on fire. She was kissing me back, and we kissed for a long, long time. I never wanted to let her go again. It had been such a long time coming, and now my body ached with a desire I never knew it possessed. My heart had flooded with joy. I kissed her and I held her tightly to me, and I wanted to tell her everything, I wanted her to know about it all, I wanted her to know me and see me totally, as I really was, and I wanted her to stand by my side forever, just radiating warmth into my life. I ran my hands back through her hair, and I could barely believe that I was almost sixteen years old and had never truly felt alive, until that moment.

19

Panic was not a feeling I was familiar with. I didn't think I had felt it since I was a child, hiding behind the sofa when I knew my father was after me. But I could feel it stirring now, niggling and needling at me. I felt it the night I called Jack to say I would be over soon to collect Danny.

'What you talkin' bout?' he had slurred back at me, his voice thick with drowsy inebriation. 'He ain't here!' I felt it again when I stuck my head around the door of the record shop, just as the fat whale that owned it was cashing up his paltry takings. He gave me a look of contempt that made me want to ram my fist into his nose.

'If you're looking for Danny, I sent him home,' he told me before I could even open my mouth. He folded over the top of a money bag and slapped it down onto the counter with a metallic bang. 'He's sick, not well, so I sent him back home.' I nodded and left, but it was wrong, it was all wrong. The way he said it; on cue, as if he had been drilled. The way he repeated what he had already said; he's sick, not well, so I sent him home. Like Jack's confusion, it struck a warning bell in my mind. It sent a shiver of panic coursing through my body.

And now the feeling was growing. And more than that, it was following me about, clinging to me petulantly. I couldn't shake it off. I was starting to forget how my stomach normally felt, without this strange and unwelcome feeling inside of it. I was slumped behind the desk in my office, a whisky in one hand and my head in the other. I had drunk too much, but there it was. That feeling. A hammering in my chest, a coldness to my skin, a sweat that seeped out across my forehead. The feeling that I was about to be found out. That there was nowhere left to hide, because my father would turn the sofa right over with one kick to get me out from under it. The feeling that I ought to be looking for a better hiding place, or be working out ways to cover my tracks. I took a deep breath before draining my glass and reaching for the bottle to refill it again. There was no denying it; the voice in my head chided smugly and there was no hiding from it. The feeling of something slipping slowly through my fingers, like an expensive wine glass that never really feels your grip before it slithers from your grasp and then shatters in slow motion into a million diamonds on the floor.

I lifted the glass of whisky up to my face and peered into it, as the brown liquid sloshed one way and then the other. You'll never find the answers at the bottom of a bottle, my dad was always fond of saying. He liked to say a lot of things, my dad. Got that boy in line yet? He was fond of that one too. Want me to come down and show you how? He always chuckled after that one. I studied the liquid in the glass and realised that it was a bit of peace I was looking for. I was looking for a way to make that queasy feeling in my belly go away. I was wallowing in self-pity and in the other thing. The other thing was lying under it all.

The other thing was a merciless and burning anger that roared within the very core of me. It had been building for a while now, ever since those kids stopped going to Jack's. That had been the start of it. I'd been struggling to control it, before it could control me. I had been trying to put it out even, but nothing worked. Drink just inflamed it and not drinking just prolonged the agony of it. Fucking my wife did not even touch it. Fucking my wife left me feeling unspent, unsatisfied and close to crawling up the walls with frustration. Getting hold of that kid and smashing his body until there was nothing left but dust and bones might just do it. But I couldn't do that. I couldn't lose control.

I told myself this every day. Kay was watching me. She had returned from her mother's funeral, thin and pale, her lips pressed together and her body stiffening when I laid my hands on her. I didn't understand. Shock, I presumed. Shock, and grief. I talked to her about the new house to take her mind off things. I told her how we were only days away from moving in, and she better start planning her colour schemes and styles. I told her how excited I was, how it would be a brand new, fresh start for all of us. I told her how well Danny and I had got on during her absence. I told her how I longed for the day he might accidentally call me Dad. What tormented me even further, was the distasteful knowing that there was an element of truth within the lies I fed to her. But that boy was mocking me at every turn, at every opportunity. Playing me for a fool. Taking the piss and laughing at me, just like my old man said he was. Plotting and planning something behind my back. I just knew it.

I took my chances to warn him when they came. It was like a drug, and I was not entirely sure when making that boy's life a misery had started to turn into some kind of addiction. It was a riddle to me, the way I longed to kick and punch him, yet at the same time, would have felt my heart brim over if he had called me Dad and meant it. I pondered it now. I wallowed in it. I swam in it, all the murky dingy depths of it. Maybe violence was an addiction like any other, I mused carelessly, sloshing the whisky down my throat and pouring another measure. Maybe that was it. It called to a weakness inside of you, just as booze and drugs did to other people. It harnessed that weakness and convinced you of your strengths instead. And then it had you where it wanted you, and it turned and twisted inside of you and became a constant urge that was impossible to satisfy. I wondered if that was what drove people to murder. That relentless urge to harm and maim, like an itch you could not scratch. When the opportunity to inflict damage arose, the adrenaline was on fire inside of me. And then afterwards, the wonderful magnificent calm would wash over me and I would feel clean and cleansed, and fresh and new. I could think clearly and breathe steadily. I sometimes felt like thanking him. There was no other way to satisfy it.

'What's going on?' I kept asking him.

'Nothing.'

I slapped his face. 'Wrong answer. Try again. What's going on?' I had him cornered in the kitchen. I could see the hatred in his eyes. And something else. Some knowledge, some secret knowing that he had. Something that steadied him and gave him hope.

'Nothing,' he kept saying, so I kept slapping him.

'I'm gonna' keep hitting you until you cry or bleed.'

In the end he did both, but he still wouldn't talk, so I took what I could, using my thumbs to rub the tears into the blood from his nose, working it all up into a paint which I smeared around his face while he stared back at me in silence.

'You're gonna' push me too far,' I tried to tell him. He shook violently, he breathed heavily, but he wouldn't say a word.

The Boy With The Thorn In His Side-Part 2

I thought about that boy and I longed to hurt him. I wanted to see his face all screwed up in pain. I wanted to hear the gasps and the grunts and the begging, and I wondered if my own father had felt like that about me? I supposed it was possible, but then it was different too, wasn't it? Because Danny was not my son. That made it different, so it wasn't really my fault, was it? My father loved me. I'd never doubted that, even when on the receiving end of his thickest belt. I'd seen it in his eyes. He was doing it for me. He was trying to set me on the right path, and I had always known this, and worked with it not against it. I had tried endlessly to please the man, to make him proud of me, and I truly felt that I had nearly achieved it. I had always put one hundred and ten per cent into everything, and look, now the rewards were rolling in! The new house, the cars, the club, the beautiful adoring wife. It was just that fucking boy. Just the boy putting on an act, pretending to be in line when I knew he wasn't, not really, not underneath where it mattered. The boy hated me, the boy had no respect for me, and this knowledge caused me pain somewhere deep and primal. It made me want to lash out. Because even when he was hurting and afraid, that boy still looked at me with loathing in his eyes. It tortured me to realise that I had still not won. That I did not have everything the way I wanted.

I had to do something. *Something.*

Sometimes I would stop and wonder, would it be any different if I were Danny's real dad? Sometimes I would stop on the stairs, with my eyes fixed on the childhood portraits Kay kept hung on the wall there. There was one picture that dragged my eyes towards it every time I passed. He looked about three years old. Chubby faced in blue dungarees, and with a shock of hair so blonde it looked almost white. Sometimes I stopped and looked at his shining blue eyes and felt this vicious tugging at my heart and I didn't know why. I didn't know what it was. I would lie awake at night. I simultaneously craved to inflict pain, to make myself understood for once, but then at the same time I would lie there and wonder about useless, pointless things; like would things have been different if I had met Kay when Danny was the boy in that picture? A child of that age would not have railed against me from the beginning, would he? A child of that age would have run to me. He would have accepted me and he would have called me daddy within time. A child like that would have done what he was told. He would have been a good boy. We would have had fun together. He would have looked up to me.

Useless thinking like that now, I told myself angrily. I had come along too late for that boy, that was the problem. The damage had already been done. Years and years of people letting him do whatever he liked, letting him walk around like a scruffy little tramp, smoking and drinking and skipping school. Everyone knew exactly how he was going to turn out now. No qualifications, no hope, no future. He'd be a drain on the system and on Kay and me forever, if I didn't do something about it soon. He was still a defiant little fuck up even if his mother refused to see it. Even if she was all over him like a rash since she got back from Cornwall and found he had a girlfriend. It made my stomach curl up, for fucks sake. A girlfriend, well whoopee doo! A girlfriend and that makes everything all right all of a sudden?

Kay was another thing that worried me. Her attitude and her demeanour since she returned added to my increasing paranoia. She seemed different, and I couldn't exactly pinpoint how, or why, and that made me feel like everything was slipping through my hands, without me even really knowing it. Was she planning something too? I thought back to the evening Danny had come through the door with that girl in tow. Stupid stuck up girl fancying herself a bad boy for a while, that's all it was, anyone could see that! And bloody Kay, fussing and fawning over the two of them.

I'd sneered in the background, treading a fine line between manners and hostility. It was Kay's excited gushing that really got to me. Showing a sudden interest in the precious son she knew nothing about! Laughable. Made me want to puke. Putting her arm around him, while her eyes glistened with tears, what was all that about? Telling him that she wanted things to change between them, that she hadn't been there for him, but now she was?

'Mum died not knowing that I loved her,' she'd told his stiff and unresponsive face. 'She died with bad blood between us, and there's nothing I can do to change that now. I'll regret that till the day I die, but I'm not going to let that happen with us.'

The Boy With The Thorn In His Side-Part 2

It was all 'us' all of a sudden, wasn't it? I felt shelved and sidelined. What was I good for then eh? Making the money and paying the bills evidently. I was just the dumb fucker who slaved his arse off every night so she could have new clothes and fancy nails. Why was she so interested in him now? Where had she been when Danny really needed her eh? When he was coming down on Jack's shitty sofa, sweating and vomiting, and then doing the exact same thing to himself again the next fucking day?

  I drained another whisky and curled my lip up. Something was definitely going on. With all of them. Danny was doing his utmost to avoid me; that was one sign. He was avoiding me at all costs, and when he was home, he hid behind his mother, and his fucking eyes said it all, didn't they? Ha ha, fuck you, they said! Avoiding Jack. That was something else. He'd loved going there, so what had changed? Why wasn't he going there anymore to get high and listen to music? Where was he going instead, and why? I had liked knowing where he was; in the palm of my hand and going nowhere. Now I felt like I had lost knowledge, and with that, control. Knowledge was power and without it you were blind.

  Jaime Lawler was jittery these days. That was another sign, wasn't it? He had no idea why Danny wasn't scoring anymore. Maybe he got clean, or got bored eh? Happens sometimes. Some kids are smarter than others, that was it. I knew different. I knew it couldn't possibly be that simple, because I had the unnerving sense of something unfolding all around me, something in motion, something just below our radars. I hated this. I loathed the feeling of losing control to a bunch of dopey kids.

  I snatched up the list I had placed next to the phone and glared at it in anger. It was a list of people I was meant to call. Removal firms, now that the sale had gone through. The letting agency to let them know when they could start sending prospective tenants around to the house. The list went on. Shit loads to do. Instead of making the calls, I had opened the bottle instead. And now here I was. Fuck it. I had not been this drunk in years. I needed to sleep it off before I drove home, that was for sure. I didn't normally believe in getting smashed. It was losing control, wasn't it? Oh well then, I thought, I've lost it, and so what? I picked up the phone and dialled a number.

'Yeah?' came the stumbling, drooping reply from the other end. I felt my last dregs of patience dripping steadily away.

'Jack?'

'Yeah, what?' Jack sounded angry, I thought, hostile and aggrieved, like I had done something to him personally. Maybe he was losing control too, I thought. Maybe he was missing his boys. I ran a spiteful tongue slowly across my lips.

'I'm fucking sick of this shit,' I told him. 'Something is going on, and we both know it. You want to do something for me? Something you'll enjoy?'

'What?' he shouted back at me aggressively.

'Go round to my place. Kay will be out. That little runt will be there alone. Teach him a lesson. Did you hear me? I want you to teach him a lesson he'll never forget.'

There was just silence, for a long time, on the other end. I could hear his breath rasping in my ear as he absorbed the information. Then; 'But you said...'

'Forget what I said. I've run out of options. They're up to something, I know they are, all of them, and it's me and you in the firing line Jack, if we don't put a stop to it one way or another. Do you understand that? If they're onto us, if they've got their heads together, all those little shits, it's me and you that will be fucked Jack. We'll lose everything!'

'But Lee...you don't know what you're saying...' His voice had dropped to nothing more than a whisper, husky with lust and wonder.

'I know what I'm fucking saying Jack. Just do it. Do whatever the fuck you want and I can guarantee he won't talk. Just teach him a lesson, do you understand? Teach him a lesson so bad, that by the time I get home tonight he'll be begging me to let him be my good boy again and come and live in my nice, new house. Do you get it Jack? *Do* you?'

'I get it. I understand.'

'Good.' I slammed the phone down. I tossed another shot of whisky down my throat and savoured the reckless swirl of adrenaline that was pumping through me again. I dialled a second number, and Kay answered it on the third ring. She sounded breathless with excitement.

'Honey?'

'Yeah, it's me baby, what's up?'

'I was just about to call you!' she gushed. 'The keys for the house are in the office! We can go and get them right now if we want to!'

'Oh wow,' I replied, trying hard to keep the extent of my intoxication out of my voice. 'That's amazing news baby! You better go and get them then!'

She squealed in excitement and I pictured her jumping up and down next to the phone. She had been strange and distant lately, but that didn't stop her eyes widening every time the big house on Cedar View was mentioned, oh no.

'Oh, thank you! This is so exciting! Danny's here, I'll get him to go with me.'

'Oh no, don't do that,' I said quickly. 'You go on your own baby, tell him to get on with the packing. I don't want you lugging heavy stuff around, do I?'

'Oh okay,' she agreed easily. 'Well I'll leave him to it, and shoot on over there and fetch the keys. I'll call you again later shall I?'

'You do that baby. I love you. You enjoy it. Go and take a look at that view again hey?'

When she had gone I lowered the phone slowly back down into the cradle and picked up my glass. I didn't know if I ought to feel proud, or sickened with my work. But it had done the trick, I can tell you that. I was calm again. Calm, and in control, with just a couple of phone calls. A couple of strings pulled.

171

20

  I was sat on my bed, killing time by making a mix tape for Lucy. I had tapes spread out all over my duvet, a notepad and pen, and a list of songs to tick off. It took me ages to decide on the first track of side one, but in the end, I had gone for The Stone Roses Breaking Into Heaven. I mean, you can't go wrong with a start like that can you? The second song had come to me in a shot; The Only One I Know by The Charlatans, and then continuing in a similar vein, the third song was Girl From Mars by Ash. It got trickier after that, and I was chewing on the end of my pen, scrutinising lyrics, trying to decide what it was I wanted to tell her. I wanted to put some Bob Dylan on there for her, but I couldn't decide which one. That was annoying me no end. I was really into The Bends, but I wondered if it would be too depressing for her? Billy for instance, sneered every time I mentioned Radiohead. Kill yourself music, he called it. I tapped my pen against my knee, and reached out to press stop on the stereo, and then paused again, not wanting to. I had to admit, the lyrics were spot on, and that was what I liked. Yeah, the melody, and the voice, and the guitars and the drums or whatever, they all made a good song great, or a great song genius, but I liked plenty of run of the mill songs if they had amazing lyrics, if they reached out to me somehow, if they meant something. Bulletproof...I mean, fuck!

  In the end I went for it. I mean, if I was trying to tell her something, then I should be honest, right? I knew she'd get it. I knew she would lie on her stomach on her bed and listen to the tape with her chin resting on her folded arms. And I knew she would think about each song, and she would listen to them properly, and she would ask me about them later. After that I went for Neil Young's Only Love Can Break Your Heart. Kind of on the soppy side, but hey. I had shit loads of soppy going on, and I loved it.

  It was the day before my sixteenth birthday. My room was bare and empty; all my belongings either already at the bed-sit, or packed up neatly in bags and boxes around me. I hadn't had to worry about it too much in the end, not with Mum and Howard buying their fancy house on Cedar View. The entire house was being packed up. I set up Slide Away to record for Lucy and stared at the bags and the

The Boy With The Thorn In His Side-Part 2

boxes, in hope and in fear. Everything is going to plan, I told myself, when the fingers of fear awoke to scrabble around inside my belly. I sat on the bed with my hands dangling loosely between my knees, while the stereo transferred music from one tape to the other. The door was slightly open and my mother poked her head around it.

'What you doing?' she asked me, hanging onto the door.

I yawned and shrugged. 'Making Lucy a tape.'

Her face lit up with a smile and she stepped inside, just a little bit. 'Oh, that is so sweet! Good boy. I knew she'd be good for you. I'm just going to pick the keys up for the new house. Would you mind staying here and doing a bit more packing for me?' I shook my head at her. I had no intention of moving yet anyway. There was still another side of meaningful music to create for Lucy. 'Thanks,' she breathed in relief. 'I'll go over to the new house for a bit so I won't be back for a while. You'll be okay?'

I just nodded. I didn't have much to say to her. She was confusing the hell out of me, to tell you the truth. There had been nothing between us since Howard came along, I mean, nothing but anger and disappointment. I didn't even look at her as my mother anymore; more like someone I used to know, someone who was little more than a ghost to me. I'd had too many other things to worry about, like trying to stay alive, to pay her much attention. But lately it seemed like she had changed. There was something different about her, something I could not really put my finger on. She didn't say or do anything differently. Of course, she was over the moon about me and Lucy, which was amusing to say the least. But it wasn't anything to do with that; the change in her. It was something else. It was something in her eyes when she looked at me. Some kind of unspoken fear, mixed with a steeliness I had forgotten she owned. That's the only way I can explain it. Sometimes she looked at me for too long, and although she did not speak, it was like she was trying to tell me something with her eyes. What, I had no idea, and I had too much to think about to care.

I looked at her then and wondered if now was the time to tell her I was not coming with them to their stupid new house. I chickened out though. Leaving her a note was what I was going to do. She looked at me a little too long, her nostrils working and her smile fading in and out, before she sighed softly, turned and left. I swallowed and faced the room again. One more night and that was it. I shivered a little as the enormity of it all spun through me yet again. One more night in this place and I would be gone. Anthony and Michael had already taken whatever they needed or wanted from their childhood home, to the bedsit in Belfield Park. They were spending tonight in the house and then in the morning I would take my stuff and creep out of the house before anyone woke up. The taxi would be waiting. It was all planned. It was going to happen.

I tugged the note I had written from my pocket and read it through once more. I planned on leaving it inside her favourite coffee cup. I knew that at some point, she would reach for her cup and come across the note, and hopefully by then I would be long gone.

Dear Mum, I am not coming to the new house with you, I am leaving home now that I am sixteen as I think this is best for everyone. I know you don't believe me, but I've tried to tell you the truth about Lee, and I can't live with him anymore. He makes my life a misery in ways you could not even imagine, and if I stay any longer I am going to kill him or kill myself. You can believe what you want, but I am leaving home, and I can't tell you where I am going because I don't want him to find me. I will call you when I am settled and let you know I am ok. Your son, Danny.

I had written and rewritten it about ten times, and each new version ended up shorter and sharper than the last. There was so much I wanted to say to her but it seemed pointless to even try. Sometimes I looked at her and wondered about her life. I knew as little about hers as she did about mine. She seemed jumpy around her husband lately, stiff and tense. Did she have her own fears that I knew nothing about? The move still seemed to excite her though, and I didn't understand why. Did she really think that things would be different in a new house? I put the note back in my pocket and pushed it roughly from my mind. Too late now, I told myself. I was going. Time to look forward, Anthony kept telling me. And he was right about that.

Slide Away finished, so I pressed pause on Lucy's tape and consulted my list again. Hmm. It was tricky. I quite fancied sticking a bit of Massive Attack on there for her. I'd got into them through Chaos, and through Anthony. Anthony was way more into the dance stuff. Primal Scream, Massive Attack, Leftfield. As always, I remained open to everything. Some of that stuff sounded amazing on the dance floor at Chaos. Really got everyone moving. I went for Safe From Harm and looked back at my list for the next choice. Just thinking about Lucy made me smile constantly. We'd been inseparable since that day at Michael's. In return for the mix tapes I made her, she wrote me love letters telling me how much she liked them. On the very first tape I'd put The Stone Roses Ten Storey Love Song as the first song on side one, and I'd known she'd love it. She handed me a note with all the lyrics carefully written out on one side, and she'd drawn a red heart around one paragraph to highlight it; the bit about when your heart is black and broken and you need a helping hand. She was spot on. It was perfect.

'That will always be our song, for me,' she told me shyly.

I kept every note and letter she wrote for me. I kept them inside my old notebook, and to me they were like buried treasure; precious, sacred things I could dig out and gaze on whenever I felt alone or afraid. They were proof that she cared about me. That I was worth caring about.

I'd told her everything. In slow and painful detail, I filled her in on the whole story. I watched the colour drain from her face, and at one point she couldn't stop the tears and just sat there and sobbed. I told her the latest information about Jack, and she had propped herself up on one elbow to stare down at me with her moist, brown eyes. Her fingers entwined tightly with mine.

'Thank God for Anthony,' she had breathed out when I had finally finished retelling the entire nightmare from start to finish. 'If he hadn't got Jaime to dig around...' she broke off, finishing the thought off inside her own head. She curled back into me then, lifting the edge of my t-shirt to place her hands on the last colours Howard had stamped on me. 'I don't know how your mother can live with herself,' she murmured, before pushing her hair back behind her ears and lowering her lips down to my skin. I felt her kissing me, slowly, gently, as the sobs hitched up in the back of her throat, and I closed my eyes and wanted to drift away with it. And as she kissed the bruises it felt like she was kissing them away, cancelling them out.

Tell the police, she had urged me at first, so I'd had to tell her all the frightening things that Anthony and Michael had endured lately, all the eyes watching, all the threats.

'Jack was in the police,' I reminded her. 'It's not worth it. We can't risk it. We just have to go. We just have to get away, leave, stay away, and then it will be over.' It was a mantra I was repeating to myself. I hoped if I repeated it enough, it would begin to feel possible.

Lucy was appalled with my mother. I sensed she feared Howard and all the things I had told her, but she felt something even uglier for my mother. Mum didn't seem to notice the dark and disgusted looks Lucy gave her, when she was clapping her hands and exclaiming joyously what a couple of lovebirds we were. She seemed pleased with me, I thought, as if getting a girlfriend was what I had needed all along, as if I'd be all right now. She didn't notice Howard glowering and darkening in the background, of course, but I did. And more than that, I sensed a dangerous change in him. He was losing his grip more and more as the weeks slid by.

Tell me what's going on, he hissed at me whenever he could and I could see the madness in his eyes. I'd had enough time to think about it to know that what motivated him most was control and power. He sought the gratification from both, in everything he did. He had power and control over everybody at the club, over Jack and over Jaime, over his wife, and until tomorrow, over me too. Who knew what dangers trembled under the surface of a man like that? Who knew what losing any amount of control would do to him? He kept telling me, over and over, whenever he got the chance; I know you're up to something, I can see it all over your face, I know it, I can feel it.

He took petty shots at me whenever he could. I had no choice but to endure it in silence and bide my time. I longed to lash out, I dreamt about returning the pain and the fear, but with escape so close around the corner, I would have been a fool to wreck it now. He sneered endlessly about my union with Lucy.

'She must need fucking glasses!' he would hiss at me. 'Nice girl like that going out with a piece of shit like you! I ought to call her dad up and let him know about your dirty little habits! Does he even know you're together? Bet he doesn't! I better give him a call and

The Boy With The Thorn In His Side-Part 2

warn him eh? We'll practically be neighbours soon.' I refused to take the bait. I said nothing. But I didn't stop Lucy from sliding her arms around me in the kitchen, while his face distorted with rage at the table. When she had gone, he would sidle up behind me, breathing his vile air into my ear. 'You fucked her yet? You fucked her yet, eh? Have you?' Jabbing me in the back. I closed my eyes. Envisioned sharp knives. 'Bet you don't even know how!' Just fuck off and die, you disgusting excuse for a human, I wanted to say to him, but I didn't. I said nothing.

I jolted out of my daydreams then, hearing a noise downstairs. It was like something had clattered to the floor in the kitchen. My heart leapt into full panic mode, battering violently against my chest. I was starting to think I had gained a genuine sixth sense about when things were about to kick off. My body was determined to protect itself by letting me know when something was up. The fingers of fear would jerk and spasm into life in the pit of my stomach, and the muscles would cramp and claw around them. They reached out, spreading their fear and this would kick start a physical chain reaction throughout the rest of my body; jangling through my nerves, putting everything on high alert. A second noise in the kitchen pulled me up onto my feet. I pressed pause on the stereo, halting Lucy's tape. I crept towards my open door and peered out. I stopped and listened.

Then I called out; 'Mum?' There was no answer. My breathing quickened and I tried to tell myself to calm down, that it was probably just some of the boxes falling over in the kitchen. They were stacked up everywhere, full of pots and pans and cutlery. I inched forward, taking pains not to step on any of the boards that creaked. Still nothing but silence.

I nodded to myself, but I needed to check for peace of mind, so I trotted briskly down the stairs and found that the kitchen door was slightly open. I gave it a push and it screamed on its hinges. When it swung back, I could see nothing but stacked boxes and empty surfaces. My shoulders relaxed, I stepped through the door and nearly squealed in fright when the slug like form of Jack Freeman appeared from behind the other side of the door.

'Shit!' I cried out, my skin prickling, my heart racing. He stepped forward very casually, dressed in his usual dark overcoat and suspicious brown suit. He used one tatty shoe to kick a chair out of his way. He was trying to light a roll up, but his lighter was low on fuel. His heavily wrinkled brow seemed to sag loosely over his eyes as he shook it out, tried to flick the flame and then shook it again. He was swaying slightly from side to side, and the smell that emanated from him was of the unwashed and the drunk. Finally, as I stared on in horror, he got his roll up lit and stuffed the lighter into the breast pocket of his overcoat, as his filmy eyes peered at me.

'What do you want?' I demanded, trying to keep the panic out of my voice.

He laughed at me, and his face was a shabby mess of wrinkles and folds of flesh that could not fight gravity. His big round shoulders shook with his apparent amusement.

'Just came to say hello, didn't I? Ain't seen you in so long, I thought you might be needing something, eh?'

I shook my head fiercely. I wondered why I was not more afraid, knowing what I knew about him, but when I looked him up and down in his filthy coat, I saw a man at his lowest ebb, a man just days away from sinking down into his own sick and piss and staying there for good. 'No, thanks. I don't want anything.'

He frowned, and then took an unsteady, lurching step towards me, before banging into another chair and reaching out to touch the wall to steady himself. 'Ahh that's not friendly, is it?' he moaned, looking genuinely upset. 'After all the times I was so friendly to you! All those times I let you come to my flat and help yourself? I thought we were friends Danny! We're friends, aren't we?'

'Sure,' I told him, with a shrug. 'But I'm ok thanks, I don't need anything.'

Jack sucked at his roll up and shrugged at me. 'That's a shame,' he told me, one shaggy grey eyebrow shooting up. 'I sort of miss having you around.'

'Been busy,' I said, through gritted teeth. 'Work, and that.'

He nodded slowly. 'Work? You mean the record shop? I thought he didn't pay you yet?'

'No, not yet, I mean…'

The Boy With The Thorn In His Side-Part 2

'Because if he's paying you, you can start paying me, eh?'
I frowned. 'What?'
'For the drugs, Danny,' he said, with a grin. 'They cost money, you know. Money I assumed you'd be getting me at some point. So, if he's paying you, you can pay me, right?'
I didn't know what to say so I said nothing. He chuckled and took a long drag on his rolled cigarette, his rubbery lips closing around it so tightly I thought he would inhale it if he wasn't careful. He looked at me with narrowed eyes.
'So, is he paying you or not?'
'Not yet, but when he does, I'll give it you, course I will.'
He nodded. 'Good, because that's a lot of money I've been spending on you.'
'You didn't have to. I didn't ask you to.'
'Well I felt sorry for you. I wanted to help you feel better. He treats you like crap, you know. And you know what else? He asked me to come over now, to check on you. He's pretty fucking wound up right now. Thinks you're up to something.'
I laughed softly. 'He's always wound up. You know him. There's nothing going on, Jack.'
He licked his lips slowly. 'He's a very twisted man, you know.'
I nodded, waiting. 'I know.'
'You know why I'm here then?'
I shook my head at him. 'No.'
'He's my boss, you know that?' Jack leaned forward, his eyes widening as if to make his point better understood. I nodded. He sniffed and leaned back again. 'He's my friend, but he's my boss. He gets people where he wants them, you know that. He has to be in control. He has to have all the power.'
I swallowed, wondering what the hell he was trying to tell me. I just wanted him to get out of there. 'He has something pretty big on you,' I said, and he nodded instantly, and I thought about what Anthony had found out and nearly puked right there and then. I gazed at the door, wondering if I ought to just leg it.
'Yeah,' he said, with regret. 'You could say that.'
'Well, whatever it is, it's nothing to do with me. I got stuff to do Jack. Okay?' I was nodding at him, urging him. I was giving him

the chance to turn around and go, forget whatever he had come for and just go.

Jack shuffled forward another step. 'I can't go, Danny.'

'Why not?'

'Because I can't, because I got to do what I'm told just like you do. And because, we're friends, right?' He was looking at me pleadingly. 'We get on, don't we? Behind his back, we have a laugh. We've had good times. I've looked out for you, haven't I?'

I was kind of stunned to tell the truth. I was stunned and speechless and running out of patience. I didn't have time for this bullshit!

'Looked out for me?' I laughed. 'Yeah, if you call handing out drugs like sweeties, you've looked out for me. Jack, I'm busy okay? You need to go.'

His expression darkened. 'Danny, you don't understand. I'm trying to tell you I care about you. More than he does!'

'Whatever. I'm still busy. You need to go!'

'Or what?'

This was ridiculous. I sucked in my breath and glared at him. 'Or I'll call the cops. I don't want you here, Jack. I don't want your drugs. I'm not your friend! So get the hell out right now, or I call the cops.'

'But I am the cops,' he said brightly, smiling enough to reveal his grey, mottled teeth. 'Didn't you know that Danny?'

'You used to be,' I said. 'Till you got chucked out.' I watched the curiosity swirling in his eyes, so I nodded at him triumphantly. 'Oh yeah, I know all about that. I know why you got thrown out. I know what you did. *That's* why I stopped coming to your shit-hole flat!'

He frowned, lifted a chubby nicotine stained finger and scratched at his head with it. 'Oh,' he said. 'Is that right? Who's been talking then, eh?'

'Doesn't matter,' I told him, nodding at the back door. 'Just get out.'

He looked at the door and then he looked back at me. His head thrust forward suddenly and his crumpled face grinned at me fiendishly. 'Oh yeah?' he said playfully. 'You gonna' make me then, are ya'? You fancy your chances eh?' I didn't answer. He threw his

The Boy With The Thorn In His Side-Part 2

half smoked roll up to the floor and lifted his hands, curling them as he beckoned to me. A dripping smile hung on his jowls. 'Come on then,' he said then softly, and my skin crawled with every word. 'Come on then, show me what you got.'

I took a sliding step towards the hallway. I wondered if my knife was still in my back pocket. Anthony had given me another one just recently. Just in case. My breath seemed frozen in my throat; my heart felt like it had stuck, and needed a blow to get it going again. 'Just get out!' I said again. 'Get the hell out of here!'

It would have been nice if he had taken my advice and trudged his gloomy way out of there. But I suppose he had his orders. He stared at me for a moment, his plump lips hanging away from his teeth, saliva trailing from one side to the other, his tongue protruding from the corner of his mouth. His shoulders lifted slowly, hunching up around his neck and he suddenly seemed controlled and menacing in a way he had never appeared before, with his fists up and his head low.

'Come on then,' the words fell softly from his wet lips, as he stepped towards me again. I swallowed. 'What you waiting for? Come on then, eh?'

I threw myself towards the door, and he came at me, spittle flying from his grimacing lips. I reached for the kitchen door to get through it, but he kicked it out of my grip and the two of us collided against it. His rough hands encircled my wrists and I struggled and for a moment or two we did this strange jerky little dance around the kitchen, as I lurched and thrashed my body towards the back door instead. His mood had shifted again, his face sort of crumpling, that pleading look returning to his eyes.

'Ah damn it, come on,' he grunted. 'We're friends, Danny, we're friends!'

I thought I was getting away from him, I thought his sweaty hands were slipping on my wrists, but then I felt the edge of the table slamming into my spine, and the pain crashed sharply through my body, all the way up to my neck, and he had hold of my t-shirt then, bunching it up in his hands, as his big reddening face loomed over me.

'Calm down! Calm the fuck down, we're friends!'

I fought with the floor for a grip on the lino, my trainers slipping and sliding. I kicked out at his shins and his legs and then I was free, so I lunged for the door, but his hands grabbed the back of my t-shirt and down I went, hitting the floor with my knees.

'Danny, calm down, come on, just fucking listen to me a minute!'

I spun around to face him, holding up my hands. 'You don't have to do what he tells you to do Jack!...Tell the police Jack, you can help us, we can get rid of him together, we can get him locked up!' They were desperate words and a waste of my time.

He stared back down at me, his greasy grey flecked hair hanging limply over one eye. He was breathing very fast, his nostrils stretched wide open, his lips curled back and his chest rising up and down dramatically. His face was a mess; anger mixed with regret and sorrow. He stared down at me and lifted up both his hands.

'I just want to be friends with you,' he grunted. 'He sent me here to hurt you! But that's not what I want. I don't want to hurt you, Danny, I want to care for you, do you understand?'

I nodded slowly, my hand searching my back pocket for my knife.

'You could turn him in,' I started speaking really fast, buying time, while my fingers scrabbled with the knife. 'Think about it Jack! You could fuck him right up! Get your own back! You won't be under his thumb anymore Jack! You'd be free! We all would be!'

'You're not listening,' Jack shook his head and stepped closer. 'You still don't understand. You can't go against him, not ever. You have to do what he tells you.'

I showed him my knife. 'Jack, I'm warning you.'

He frowned at me. 'There's no need to be silly. We can just talk. Come on, come back to mine, we'll put a film on, smoke some weed, whatever you want, you can have it.'

'I want you to get the hell away from me. Last chance, Jack.'

He either wasn't listening, or he didn't take me seriously. So I gave it to him. I tightened my hand around the handle and plunged it into one of his feet. He threw back his head and screeched in pain. I put both hands around the knife, got onto my knees and wrenched it back out of his foot, sending a vivid spray of red across the kitchen

The Boy With The Thorn In His Side-Part 2

lino. He threw his head back again, his hands flailing up to his whitened face, as he howled in agony. I moved back, away from him, holding the knife so tightly in my hands that it hurt. His blood dripped down the blade and onto my hands, greasing them against the handle, and I kept it pointed at him, and I kept my eyes on him, and slowly, slowly, I pressed my back into the wall and eased myself up it. His head lolled forward. His eyes looked pale and deranged with pain and shock and he gaped down in slack jawed horror at the blood pumping from his foot.

'Look what you done!' he gasped, pointing. 'Look what you done!'

I waved the knife at him. 'Do you want any more?' I asked him. 'I'll give you some more you sick son-of-a-bitch you ever come near me again! I'll fucking kill you! Both of you!' I held the knife still, pointed at his white washed and pinched up face. 'Get out, get the fuck out of here now, you fat sack of shit, or I'll stab you again! I mean it!'

Jack lowered his head and moaned into his shaking hands.

'You don't know what you're doing...' he muttered, taking a step towards the door. A huge red puddle remained on the floor where he had stood. 'You're gonna' regret this...you don't know what you're doin'...you shouldn't mess with him...You don't know what he's capable of!'

Oh, that was funny. That was so funny I could have laughed my fucking head off! My head was black with rage. I felt sickened and on fire. 'I fucking know!' I screamed back at him, keeping the knife up, suddenly flooded by the desire to lash out at him again with it. God, I wanted to. I wanted to see it slash through his grotty overcoat. I wanted to see his face twist up in pain and disbelief. I wanted Howard to come stumbling blindly through the door, right into my fucking knife. 'I'll kill him!' I said then. 'Tell him! Go and tell him *right* now! Crawl back to your master little piggy! Go on! Tell him I stabbed you and I'll stab him too! Tell him I mean it! I'll never be his errand boy, not like you, I will *never* be like you!'

Jack sighed in pained misery and shuffled his bloody way towards the door. 'You don't know what you're doing,' he said again, shaking his head at me. 'You silly little boy...'

183

'Get out! Just get out! You disgusting *fuck*!'

'All right, all right, I'm going, I'm going.' With his shoulders sagging in defeat, Jack opened the back door and whimpered in pain as he lifted his foot. Fresh blood spilled with every movement he made. His lips were pulled back in pain. He lifted the bloody foot out first, onto the doorstep, and the rest of his shapeless form followed, and he went and he said nothing else, and I watched, not even breathing, until he was gone. And then I sprang forward and slammed the door on him. I spun around. I was breathing incredibly fast now. I was close to total panic. My mind wanted to call time and shut down on me for a while. My body was reacting suddenly and violently, shaking as I ran to the sink and held the blade under the running water. I washed my hands frantically, rubbing and scratching at my skin until all his blood was gone from me. I wanted to be sick. My stomach lurched and heaved inside of me. I grimaced in revolt as his blood circled around and around in the sink, and then I turned around and gazed dumbly down at the floor. It was covered in blood and grotesque red footsteps. I didn't know what to do. My brain suddenly filled with mush.

The Boy With The Thorn In His Side-Part 2

21

I was lost. I was drowning. Stranded within a deep and immobilising trance. All I could do was stare at the dark red puddle that was slowly spreading across the kitchen floor. I stared at it and my eyes filled with water, and all I could think was how could that much blood come from one foot? Jack had walked out of there, grunting and groaning, leaving half of his blood behind. Maybe later I would find him collapsed on the driveway, having bled to death.

The phone rang suddenly in the hallway, cutting me from the silence and yanking me from my trance. I backed slowly out of the kitchen, still clutching the wet knife between both my hands, keeping my eyes on the blood, until I backed into the front door and reached out blindly for the phone. I fumbled for it, knocked it from the cradle, reached down to the floor and made a desperate panicky grab for it.

'Hello?' I did not recognise my own voice. It sounded so small and tight and seemed to come from another place entirely.

'Danny! It's Mike. We just took another load over to the bed-sit. Christ, we're spending a fortune on bloody taxis, you doing okay?'

'Mike?' I sank back against the door in sheer relief. I closed my eyes tightly and pressed the heel of my other hand into them, swathing myself in a brief and comforting darkness. The knife was still clutched between my fingers. 'Shit Mike, oh shit, *shit!*'

'What?' Michael sounded immediately alarmed. 'What is it?'

I swallowed and tried to find the words, but my throat felt tight and raw. 'Shit Mike,' I said again, and gave up.

'Shit, what is it?' he cried. 'What's wrong?'

'Can you come over here quick?'

'We're there, hang on,' he slammed down the phone and I was alone again. My hand started to shake. It shook so bad that the receiver fell through my fingers and thumped down to the floor. I kept thinking, any minute my mum or Howard is going to come through that back door and see that blood...any minute, any minute, any minute. I stayed where I was with my back pressed into the door. I told myself I had to move, had to get out of there, but it was like my body had gone into shock or something. It was useless. Nothing more than jelly and sagging bones. I was drained and empty. There was too much in my head. Too much fear, too much everything. I needed help, so I remained where I was, kept my eyes closed and took deep slow breaths.

Less than two or three minutes passed before I heard their footsteps running urgently up the driveway. Then they banged their way through the back door and just stopped.

'Danny?' I heard Michael call out. His voice sounded high and frightened. '*Danny!*'

'Here,' I called out weakly, suddenly feeling horribly sick as Michael stepped cautiously into the hallway followed by Anthony.

'Shittinghell are you okay?'

'Whose blood is that?' Anthony rushed to my side. He took my arm gently and pulled me away from the door, as if checking for wounds. I gulped air and shook my head. My eyes felt huge and staring and I was trembling all over.

'Jack's,' I whispered to them. They looked at each other in wonder, and then their eyes tracked slowly down to the knife in my hands.

'Shit,' said Anthony. 'Where is he?'

'He left.'

Michael's dark eyes remained fixed on the knife. 'Did you stab him with that?'

I nodded. 'His foot.'

Anthony pulled his shoulders back, and faced me squarely with his hands on his hips and nodded. 'I'm guessing he did something to deserve it?'

I nodded. I thought I was going to cry then. I was trying like hell not to think about any of it, why Jack had rolled up like that drunk and angry, what he had wanted. I felt overwhelmed with a horrible swamping kind of sadness.

'He was drunk,' I managed to tell Anthony, as the tears started to roll. 'Howard sent him.'

Anthony's face twitched. He was swallowing rapidly and just nodding his head, and his hand reached out for me and then stopped and returned to his hip.

'Right,' he said.

The Boy With The Thorn In His Side-Part 2

Michael tugged at his arm. 'Are we gonna' clean that all up?' he asked in a small voice. 'Before someone comes?'

'Yeah, I'll do it.' Anthony gave his brother a push towards the stairs. 'Get up there and get Danny's stuff. We're going. I'll clean up the kitchen and then we're out of here, okay Danny? We're gone.' He placed a hand softly on my shoulder. 'To the bed-sit right?'

I managed a nod and Michael shot up the stairs without a single word. Anthony turned and hurried back into the kitchen. I stayed against the door, numb and growing number. I could hear Anthony opening and closing doors. Water running into the sink. A bottle being sprayed. Michael came hurrying back down the stairs, clutching my ruck sack in one hand, and a bunch of full carrier bags in the other. He dumped it all at my feet and dashed back up for more. I continued to hold the knife so tightly it made my fingers throb. I could hear Anthony spraying and mopping in the kitchen. My feet were glued to the floor, my muscles all locked and refusing to move.

Michael ran back down the stairs and dumped another load of bags. He held out a bundle of hastily rolled up posters.

'Got these down for you,' he said gently. 'We can decorate the bed-sit yeah? And all the tapes on your bed, and that, I put them in the ruck sack okay? That's everything. You okay to get going?' He touched my arm briefly. 'I don't like the thought of hanging around here much longer.' I nodded at him and Anthony came back into the hall, a bulging carrier bag in one hand. He held it slightly behind his legs as if the contents were unsafe.

'Done,' he said grimly. 'You wouldn't know anything had happened.' He looked at me for a moment and then cleared his throat. 'Did the bastard do anything Danny? Are you okay?'

'I'm okay.'

'Good. Why don't you let me have that for a bit?' His eyes were on the knife. I eyed it suspiciously. Anthony stepped closer and prised it carefully from my frozen fingers, and slid it into the back pocket of his tracksuit trousers. He stooped down and grabbed some of the bags Michael had packed. Michael followed suit, holding my stereo under one arm for me. 'Let's go boys.'

I moved from the door. I had just remembered the note in my pocket. It seemed somehow the only clear and obvious thing inside my head. I had to leave it for my mum. I told them to hold on and walked shakily back into the kitchen.

'What you doing?' Michael called after me in exasperation. The kitchen floor was sparkling clean and the room reeked of lemons. I saw her coffee mug on the draining board, upside down. I picked it up, slid the note inside and put the mug back in the cupboard.

'Danny?' Anthony was calling from the hallway. 'What are you doing mate? Come on, we need to call a taxi quick.'

'Coming.'

I traipsed back down the hall. Anthony opened the front door and held it open while we scurried out under his arm, all instinctively scanning the street for trouble. Anthony nodded to the corner of the road, and we headed there, heads low, eyes moving everywhere. We got to their house and Anthony unlocked the door, told us to stay put and disappeared inside. Michael and I waited in silent shaking shock on the doorstep. The day was muggy. Everything seemed still, and waiting. I could hear a TV chattering in the lounge next door. Small children squealed from a back garden. I looked up at the sky and it was solid blue and cloudless. Sweat pooled under my arms and across my forehead and I wondered if I had ever felt so utterly wretched, so immensely exhausted and weak before. I didn't think my legs could hold me up much longer. Michael just stared around constantly, jittery and chewing at his thumb nail. Anthony reappeared and we looked to him instantly for reassurance and instruction.

'Taxi in ten minutes,' he told us.

Michael grimaced and spat out a chunk of nail. 'What if the police come?' he asked.

'They won't come,' Anthony told him.

'But how do you know?'

'Mike, that fat slug is not gonna' call the police, don't worry about it. The only person we need to worry about is Howard, and getting out of here without anyone seeing where we're going.'

'He's at the club,' I spoke up. 'He called Mum and told her to go and get the keys to the new house.'

Anthony leaned in the doorway, arms crossed and eyebrows raised. 'Then Freeman just shows up at yours uninvited?'

The Boy With The Thorn In His Side-Part 2

'Yeah,' I said, meeting his eyes.

'Howard sent him to hurt you,' Anthony said darkly, spitting suddenly out onto the parched front lawn. 'Sick *fucking* bastard...one last attempt to get control, eh? What a fucking...' He just shook his head, as his words dried up. I knew what he meant anyway. There weren't any words to describe what it was, what Howard was, what any of it was. Anthony sighed. 'That's what bullies live off, you see,' he told me. 'Fear and control. He thinks he's losing it so he sends his little sidekick over to help him out again...fuckinghell mate, I am so glad I gave you that knife.'

'Why'd you stab his foot?' Michael asked me then, still chewing relentlessly at his nail as his eyes shot anxiously up and down the street.

'I was on the floor,' I remembered. 'His foot was just there so I stabbed it.' I shook the images from my head, as the gruesome scene replayed itself over again. The drops of saliva as they flew from his rubbery lips when he threw back his head and howled. Anthony touched my arm, bringing me back.

'You did the right thing, you had no choice mate. He's lucky you didn't stab him somewhere worse! Oh hey, look boys.' He nodded and there it was at last, a big shiny black taxi cab pulling slowly into the close. Anthony slapped our backs and leaned past us to grab the bags. 'Here we go then boys,' he said as cheerily as he could manage. 'Say goodbye to your shitty little lives!'

It took less than ten minutes to load up the waiting taxi with what we had salvaged from our old lives. I took a window seat, my skin clammy and hot as I pressed my face up against it and watched the houses getting smaller and smaller. We sped away from it all and I wanted to feel better about it. I wanted to feel the weight lifting from me. I longed for a rush of pure relief. Instead I felt cold and numb and totally removed from everything, as the enormity of it all began to hit me. There was no hope, no relief, no sense of freedom. Just cold, hard fear.

22

On the morning of my sixteenth birthday, I awoke to the smell of bacon frying and to the sound of someone vomiting in the bed-sit below ours. Anthony had pinned old sheets and blankets to the large sash windows, but the morning sun burst through them with ease. I was so confused for a moment. I could hear Oasis playing Up In The Sky, but I had no idea where it was coming from or what was going on. I was on the left side of the pull-down bed, the side closest to the kitchen. I was face down, and because the springs were knackered it felt like I had been lying on rubble all night and I groaned as I rolled slowly over to my side. I could feel Michael sprawled out beside me, flat on his back with his arms and legs stuck out to the sides. I felt reality juddering to life within me. It was like my heart didn't want to get going, to be honest. I kind of felt the urge to punch myself in the chest, just to give it a kick up the arse. I didn't want to move but I made myself. I peeled myself slowly away from the thin and sagging mattress and swung my legs out of the bed. I lowered my feet dubiously down to the threadbare carpet and immediately pulled them back up again. It felt sticky to the touch, so I got my feet back on the bed and wrapped my arms around my legs.

Michael snored on behind me, and Anthony whistled softly to the music in the kitchen, scraping bacon around in the pan. I yawned, scratched at my neck and tried to work out exactly why I felt so crap. I found myself wondering if I could still remember Jaime Lawler's number by heart. I thought back to the stresses of yesterday. It was all a bit of a blur. We had arrived at the bed-sit in a flurry of adrenalin and fear. Terror buried under the surface of excitement. We were bordering on the hysterical the whole time. Collapsing in fits of tear streaming laughter when Michael pulled open a drawer in the kitchen and the knob came off in his hand. Anthony falling over backwards onto his arse when we carried up the TV he had liberated from his mother's lounge. I'd laughed and felt myself growing weaker with every step. I couldn't concentrate on anything. I was lost inside a shadow, and when we finally fell in front of the TV with cans of beer and cold toast, it was drink and drugs my mind felt drawn to. I watched Michael trying to cover up his own fear, licking his lips and jumping

The Boy With The Thorn In His Side-Part 2

at every single tiny little noise. Anthony was just Anthony. I didn't know how he did it, but I admired him even more. He remained calm and composed, offering us lazy, confident grins around the cigarette that dangled permanently from the side of his mouth.

'I'll go shopping tomorrow,' he told our silent, sombre faces. 'Get some proper food in.' He had then spent a good half hour trying to tune the telly in, cursing and making us smile faintly in a stupor behind him. After that, we sat and watched the TV in silence.

I had no idea what time I finally fell into an uneasy form of sleep, but I did know that it was hours after Michael and Anthony had both began to snore, and another few hours after the guy downstairs had turned his awful techno music off. I lay on my back beside Michael with my arms folded behind my head, not even remotely sleepy. All I could think about was the knife in my hands, my fingers curled tightly around the handle, and the strange bounce of leather versus steel, as the blade pierced right through the top of his shoe...I closed my eyes to wish it away, but it wouldn't go. The blood filled my mind. It pooled and swam and ran like a ruby river, gushing behind my eyelids. My hands began to shake as they relived the fleshy wrench of the knife as it ripped back out of the foot. My feet jerked and twitched at the end of the bed, as I fought the urge to release the nervous energy inside of me. My teeth found my lower lip and gnawed at it savagely. I shook my head back and forth and rubbed at my eyes, but I was unable to rid of my mind of Jack's face, saggy and flabby as it stretched the folds of skin into an almighty scream. I felt like punching my eyes in. They would not close. They would not rest. I felt this sad, sick twisting inside of me and wondered if it would be gone by the morning, if any of it would truly ever go away.

Despite the tantalising smell of frying bacon, and the relative safety of the fourth floor bed-sit and double locked door, I had realised miserably upon waking that it had not. If anything, the feeling had intensified, and as I sat shivering on the edge of the bed, all I could think about was my mother back at home, reading my note and wondering where I was. I can't explain the pain inside of me right then. I felt angry with myself for it. I should have been happy. Things were going to be so cool. We'd made it; we were safe and the good times could flow....but the fears and the sadness were ballooning helplessly inside of me. I felt panic close to the surface. What would she do with the note when she found it? Would she show Howard? How soon would he be after us? What if we'd been seen getting into the taxi? What if his people, whoever they were, had seen us in Belfield Park?

I gulped. My throat was dry and I had to open my mouth to breathe. I couldn't stop staring at the closed door. What if he was out there now? Lurking in the shadows, under the stairs or in the hallway? I hugged myself tighter. What if he was waiting out there somewhere, just waiting for the chance to get me alone? Oh my God, I thought then, as the goosebumps marched out across my skin, he would be insane with anger by now, he would kill me. I'd defied him in the worst way possible. I'd connived and planned behind his back. I started chewing at my nails desperately. What if he had Jack with him, hunting me down? Jack and his bloody foot? They would want to kill me, I knew it. I rocked myself back and forth. I was close to tears. Close to outright panic. Close to shut down, or something.

Anthony swished brashly through the beaded curtain, carrying a large plate of bacon and toast. He paused and frowned when he saw me rocking on the bed. He held the plate hesitantly out towards me.

'Morning mate, you all right? You don't look well.' I shook my head at the plate, so he withdrew it and crouched down in front of me. 'Come on, you sure? You must be hungry. You've got to eat. Got to get some meat back on them bones, yeah? What's the matter eh?'

'Feel sick,' I managed to tell him through my chattering teeth. 'Sorry.'

'Well okay, maybe later then yeah?' He placed the food on the floor and examined me quizzically. 'You're shaking like a leaf mate, are you cold?' I shrugged. I wasn't cold, not in the slightest. I was just shaking like a wreck. 'I went out like a light,' he said then, grinning at me. 'Must have been the stress of it all! I was whacked. You didn't sleep well then?'

I shook my head. 'Not much.'

'Should've rolled you a smoke,' he said, rolling his eyes. 'I bought a tiny bit of grass off Jaime. You want one now? Might help you chill out a bit.' He didn't wait for my reply. He picked his ruck

The Boy With The Thorn In His Side-Part 2

sack up from the floor, beside the rickety sofa-bed he had slept on last night. He perched on the edge of it and opened his little tin. He rolled the joint in silence, but every now and again I felt his eyes upon me. 'You're freaking me out, I have to say it,' he sighed eventually. 'What's with the rocking? Hey, happy birthday by the way!'

I tried to smile, but it didn't work. 'Thought I'd feel better...'

'But you don't?'

I shook my head. 'They're gonna' come after me Anthony.'

'They'd have to get through me first,' he reminded me sharply. He finished the joint, lit it up, dragged on it twice and then got up and came and sat next to me on the bed. He passed it to me and I took it between my trembling fingers. 'There you are mate, have a bit of that and chill out. They're not gonna' come after you. They don't know where you are, and why would they bother?'

I inhaled and passed the smoke back to him. 'You don't know them like I do,' I said to him. I was thinking about that night in the caravan, when Howard had followed me there after I'd tried to run away. Great black waves of fear shook through me as I recalled his words and his gleaming, vindictive eyes. I'd done it again. I'd broken the rules. Stepped out of line. He wouldn't just let it go, I knew it. 'We won't be that hard to find,' I murmured. 'He'll track us down. Easily.'

'They might just leave you the fuck alone,' Anthony shrugged, his tone hopeful and bright. I knew it was what he and Michael were counting on; escape and freedom with the nightmare behind us and only good times ahead. He was clinging onto it and I didn't blame him for one second. 'Have you thought of that? It might just be over.'

'It's not over,' I said, shaking my head firmly. 'I can feel it Anthony, that's why I couldn't get to sleep. My body wouldn't let me. That's why I just woke up in this stupid state. It's 'cause my body's telling me not to relax, it's telling me!'

Anthony laughed rather nervously, as Michael started to stir and turn in the bed behind us. 'Don't talk shit Danny, you're gonna' scare yourself like that.'

'It's true Anthony. I can feel it.'

'Well then we'll call the police. If they do a single thing, if either of them bother you even once, we'll call the police. Fuck it, we'll tell them everything. You're not alone now, you know. You remember that. You've got me and Mike here now.'

Michael yawned as he struggled up into a sitting position. 'What's wrong?'

'Nothing,' Anthony told him. 'Just Danny freaking out a bit. It's no wonder really.'

'You can't be with me twenty-four seven,' I pointed out. 'And we've all got jobs we need to go to.'

'Hey, can I have some of that?' asked Michael, nodding at the joint we were passing back and forth. Anthony held it out to him, and then scooped the plate of bacon and toast up from the floor. He placed it on the bed between us and helped himself to half a slice of slightly burnt toast.

'Just relax mate,' he said to me again. 'Just have a smoke, have a drink, do whatever you need to do. It's all bound to be a head fuck for you today. It would've been all right probably if that perverted shit-bag hadn't turned up yesterday. Christ, if I ever got my hands on that filthy, disgusting old fuck...'

'Yeah, it's not like you stab someone in the foot every day, is it?' Michael piped up sleepily, helping himself to a slice of toast with bacon. Anthony rolled his eyes at him and shook his head at me. Michael shrugged. 'Well it's not, is it? I didn't sleep so well myself actually. Had really weird dreams.'

Anthony patted my shoulder reassuringly. 'It's all gonna' take some getting used to, that's all. Give it time. You've been through more shit than most people deal with in a lifetime, and as I have to remind you again, it's your sixteenth fucking birthday!' He grinned at me and got to his feet, clapping his hands together as he did. 'Right, you two finish that off. I'm gonna' try the shower out, and then go and get us some decent food.'

'You're going out?' I questioned, staring up at him. He sighed very gently.

'Yep. Too right I am. In fact, we all are later. We'll have a walk down to the beach or something, yeah? Just to show you that nothing is gonna' happen!' He gave us a flash of his brilliant,

The Boy With The Thorn In His Side-Part 2

confident smile and walked around the bed and into the tiny bathroom. I stayed on the bed, pulling the sleeping bag back over me, and shivering still.

Michael was munching on bacon in between drags on the joint. 'You have to believe him, you know,' he said to me. 'He won't let anything happen to us.'

'He might not be able to do anything about it,' I told him unhappily.

'You need to call Lucy mate. Get her over here. You can't be all down and depressed on your bloody birthday!'

I nodded at him. I didn't for one moment believe that she could make me feel any safer, after what I had done, but I liked the thought of curling up with her and blocking the rest of the world right out. I could kiss her neck and play with her hair, and show her the mix tape I was working on for her. Maybe if I felt relaxed enough by then, I could just fall asleep beside her, I thought. That would be all right.

Anthony endured a very brief shower. We sat on the bed giggling behind our hands every time he screeched out that it was too fucking cold, and then it was too fucking hot. When he came out, he threw on some fresh clothes and made a very brash and cocky show of getting ready to leave our little hole. Michael got up when he had gone and double locked the door behind him. I watched him traipse over to the windows and press his forehead gently against the glass. The monotonous techno music had begun thumping again downstairs. Michael sighed, came away from the window and joined me back in the bed. We watched TV for a while, and then he made us both a cup of tea and we sat in the bed drinking it. He tried to say helpful and encouraging things to me, suggesting we have a house party at some point, or got out later to celebrate my birthday. I didn't say much. I just sat and smoked a chain of cigarettes until Anthony returned.

When he got back, he banged on the door and shouted at us to let him in. I watched from the bed as Michael unlocked the door and his brother bustled back inside, lugging four bulging plastic bags with him. He promptly dropped one, and two tins of beans rolled out across the floor. Michael pounced on the food, snatching up a selection pack of crisps and a packet of cheap ham.

'Get out of it!' Anthony yelled at him, trying to haul it all into the tiny kitchen. 'It's got to last!'

'You sound like Mum,' Michael smirked after him, picking up the beans and passing them to him through the beaded curtain. Anthony laughed out loud and started opening and closing the cupboard doors with exuberant bangs. Then he appeared in the doorway, shoving the curtain to one side and lighting a cigarette.

'Guess I'm Mum and Dad now!' he joked, winking at me. 'Fancy that eh? My age with two bloody kids!' he laughed and nodded at me questioningly. 'What about it then Danny-boy? What's the plan? You're sixteen mate!'

I smiled. I wanted to snap out of it, I wanted to please them and be brave for them, and I wanted to stop craving the things I knew I shouldn't touch again. 'Think I'm gonna' call Lucy,' I told him, and he grinned back at me wildly. 'Get her over.'

'And Billy and Jake,' said Michael. 'Party time!'

'That's more like it,' agreed Anthony, 'now you're talking. Let's get them all round and give that guy downstairs something to complain about! We're free boys! Let's enjoy this!'

Later that day, Jake and Billy and Lucy arrived together. They had caught the bus over and from the looks on their faces had been checking over their shoulders the entire time. Billy strode into the bed-sit, wide-eyed and impressed and carrying a bag full of tapes he wanted us to listen to, and Jake swung a heavy bag onto the side in the kitchen and plucked two nice looking bottles of wine from it.

'No one asks me for I.D anymore,' he shrugged in response to our astonished expressions. I watched them all from the safety of the bed I had barely moved from all day. I sat there and wondered dully if the house party included me telling them I had stabbed a man yesterday. I listened dutifully while Billy dissected The Stone Roses Second Coming album, as it played in the background. I nodded in all the right places, but my tongue was this useless lump of meat inside my mouth, and my mind, a tangled, bewildered mush. I saw Jake eyeing me warily from across the room, his eyes narrowed and uncertain. I knew what he was thinking. He was thinking I was messed up on drugs again, and that's why he was keeping his distance

The Boy With The Thorn In His Side-Part 2

from me. Well I wished I was. I would have done anything right then to escape it all.

But then Lucy accepted a glass of wine and dropped down onto the bed beside me, and there was no awkwardness, no hesitation between us and I found myself reaching out for her instantly. I needed something to hold onto and I held onto her. I wrapped my arms tightly around her neck and buried my face into her neck. The rest of them became nothing more than a background noise to me, as I clung to her, and she waited patiently, stroking back my hair, her body loose and sinking into mine.

'Something bad happened yesterday,' I told her when the others had started shouting at each other over the music. She curled her legs up with mine, and it was like there was this physical barrier between us and them. I could hear the talking and the laughing, and the music, but it all sounded far away from us. Her face was just millimetres from my own.

'What is it?' she asked me. I leant forward and pressed my lips onto hers suddenly, before pulling back and dropping my head down onto the pillow.

'Don't hate me.'

'Why would I hate you? I could never hate you, silly. Tell me what happened.'

'I stabbed Jack in the foot,' I whispered it to her, holding her face down next to mine, our hair covering us, shielding us from the outside world. She tightened her arms around my shoulders.

'Oh my God. Why did you?'

'He attacked me. Howard sent him. I had to do it.' I closed my eyes then. I thought, you know Jesus Christ, I just can't stand this, I just can't do this. I don't know how to put one foot in front of the other anymore. I don't think I will ever have the will or the energy or the courage to leave this bed. Images of pumping blood and red footprints and his screaming face had filled my head again, invading my sanity. 'He walked out okay...Mike and Anthony cleaned up...we came here.'

Lucy shushed me. She used her hand to smooth my hair back over my forehead and she kissed my nose. 'Shh,' she said. 'It's okay then. It's over. You had to do it. You got away. I'm proud of you.'

I opened my eyes. 'How can you be?'

'Because you're still here.'

She curled up with me. We felt like one. 'Everything is gonna' be okay,' she told me. She kept telling me it. 'Go to sleep. You're exhausted. I'll look after you. I'll love you forever, do you know that? Danny...you're my Danny-boy...do you know that?' Our bodies were tightly entwined and in that moment, somehow, I was able to believe her. I let her stroke my hair and she spoke to me softly the whole time, and I guess at some point, it worked and I fell asleep.

When I woke up, the lights were on and it was dark outside. The bed-sit smelled of pot and spilled beer. Jake was lying on the floor laughing hard with his hands clutching at his belly. Anthony was cutting up pizza in a massive box on the carpet. Lucy held onto me, and we sat up together, blinking. I didn't know what to say, or do, so I just watched them all. I watched them laughing and singing and shouting and I loved them. My soul trembled and swayed with it all. I wanted things to be good.

Just then, Anthony saw I was awake and leapt up to his feet, shoving the knife at Michael to cut the pizza. 'Birthday boy, birthday boy,' he sung in a drunken voice as he turned off the light and shoved through the curtain into the kitchen. There was a strange, hysterical silence. He came back through, carrying a small chocolate cake covered in candles. I laughed. Lucy squeezed my hand. It was brilliant. Happy birthday to you, they sang at the top of their lungs. They danced and clapped, and everyone was happy, everything was okay. Billy came to the bed when I had blown out the candles. He was drunk and stoned and smiling like a lunatic. He leaned towards me and he pressed a white envelope into my hands.

'Happy birthday from the happy fat man!' he garbled at me, before stepping backwards, tripping on someone's discarded shoe and falling onto his arse. They all roared with laughter and Michael jumped on top of him, ruffling his thick red hair. I looked at Lucy and she was smiling this serene and beautiful smile for me.

'Been looking forward to this,' she said, her arm through mine. They were all staring at me again. 'Open it!' she urged, giggling. 'Come on!'

'It's from Terry?' I asked, ripping it open.

The Boy With The Thorn In His Side-Part 2

'Yep,' said Lucy.

I opened the envelope and pulled out two tickets. My mouth fell open. My breath froze in my throat. My heart stopped. Oasis. October. Live. Bournemouth. I blinked again and again and again, my mouth hanging open, my hands holding the tickets and just shaking, shaking like crazy. They all started laughing at me.

'His face!' Billy screeched, rolling around under Michael. 'Oh his face!'

'Danny!' Michael was yelling at me, his dark eyes intense with excitement. 'We're all going!'

Anthony put the cake on the bed and shoved a glass of wine into my other hand. 'Cheers mate!' he yelled over the music. 'Happy birthday!'

I couldn't speak, or anything. All I could do was stare at the tickets in my hand. The room became a dark and spinning tunnel of lights and colours and noises around my head. I felt like I was standing on top of the world and it was spinning recklessly and violently beneath my feet, and I was looking up, I was looking upwards, my eyes on the sky, my head in the stars. If you could take moments like that and capture them completely, into some perfect essence that you could bring out again and again, whenever you needed to, whenever you needed help, whenever you needed a lift, or some hope, some light, then do you know what? I think we would all live forever.

23

I spent the next few days moving house and trying to control my ever spiralling rage and confusion. In between barking orders and screaming at the removal men, I punched vicious messages into my mobile phone and called Jack repeatedly. There were no replies to either. The flat was empty, and Jack gone. I'd stalked around the flat like a madman, like someone possessed, my hands clawing at my head, my eyes bulging and refusing to believe what they saw. It was the not knowing that was doing me in. Danny and the Anderson boys had vanished into thin air. That was one thing. But Jack shooting through and refusing to answer my calls was just about enough to send me over the edge. My mind was playing tricks on me, convincing me of endless ridiculous scenarios. I almost had myself believing that Danny and the other boys had killed Jack off, got rid of him somehow and cleaned up the evidence. I mean, why the hell wouldn't the man answer his phone? What the hell had gone on and why wasn't he talking?

I had become a very nervous man and I did not like it, not one little bit. Kay told me it was because of the stress. Moving house is as stressful as death and divorce you know, she kept saying this stupid useless thing every time she saw me looking aggrieved, or angry. I could only look back at her blankly, fold my fingers into a fist that had nowhere to go and wonder how close I was to punching her lights out.

I avoided her where I could. I had to. Such was my constant and burning desire to grab her by her skinny neck every time she opened her stupid mouth. She was driving me insane with her endless inane chatter about colour schemes and furniture, seemingly determined to pick airy fairy girlish styles that made me want to throw up. She wasn't going to get her way over any of it, but she didn't know that yet. I'd see what she was really made of when it all kicked off. I had already instructed the painters and decorators, and the colour schemes had been picked weeks ago. You're a grown woman, I wanted to scream at her when she got excited about pictures in home improvement magazines, and you don't even care where your own son is! The only times I could bear to converse with her, was if the talk concerned his whereabouts.

The Boy With The Thorn In His Side-Part 2

'Have you heard from him?' I'd ask her whenever I came home. 'Have you called John? He could be there you know.'

'He's not there honey, he was the first person I called, remember?'

'He's probably lying, hiding him.'

'Honey, why would he do that? He knows how worried we are!'

'I'm going round to those other boys' houses again. Speak to their parents this time. Maybe they don't even know we're looking for him! You know what those bloody kids are like.'

She wouldn't answer me half of the time. She wasn't making any effort to look for him herself. Knowing this increased my paranoia daily. Maybe she was in on it too. Maybe she knew where he was. It was becoming harder and harder to look at her face without slapping it hard. I lay awake at night, my fists clenched tightly at my sides, and I pictured her face whipping from side to side as I lashed at it. I thought about how her eyes would look, like blue marbles rolling around inside her skull. I imagined the look upon her face, the horror and the knowing clouding her eyes.

I showed my face in The Record Shop every day, hoping to catch him. Surely, he'd return there at some point? The fat bastard behind the till regarded me with increasing frustration and disgust.

'Has he called you? Has he given you notice?' I asked him every time. 'His mother is going off her head you know! If any of you are hiding him!'

'Why would we need to hide him?' The fat man spat back at me churlishly from over the top of his magazine. 'What is your problem anyway? Why the constant red face and anger?'

'He's missing,' I took deep breaths and stayed near the door. I feared getting too close to that fat sack of shit. He had the kind of soggy flabby face that would have made a great noise slapping down onto the counter. 'We need to know where he is...If you have *any* idea, or if you hear from him at all...' I was trying my hardest to be reasonable with the man. But he made a face that told me exactly what he thought of my request. He snorted.

'I wouldn't tell you!' he blurted out aggressively. 'Because I get the funny feeling it's *you* that boy is hiding from, now go on, get out of my bloody shop!'

I had to back slowly out before I found his face with my fists and reshaped it into a squashed and bloody pulp. It was all so unfair and so frustrating and I was becoming more and more convinced that they were all in on it. All of them. Kay, and John, and the fucking fat pig in the shop, and Lawler the shifty little scumbag, the fucking lot of them! I longed to put the frighteners on all of them, but with Jack gone, I felt naked and exposed.

'I think you helped him leave,' I said to Kay when I returned home from the club one night, exhausted by the weight of it all on my shoulders alone. She was sat out on the balcony with a glass of wine and a pile of home improvement magazines set out on the little bistro table I had let her order. She was wearing a new silk gown and her feet were bare. She frowned at me and decided to ignore my accusation. Instead she tried showing me a picture of the kind of bathroom she longed for. 'Too old fashioned,' I snapped, shoving it away from me. 'Why do you want to make the house look like it belongs in the nineteen bloody thirties? This is a modern house Kay! For Christ's sake! What's wrong with modern things eh? Nice things!' I turned away from her and gripped hold of the railings. The security lights bathed the front lawn in a yellow glow which lit up the flower beds she had been digging around the edges. Flower beds, for fucks sake.

'I didn't help him leave,' she spoke in a small and tight voice from behind me. 'Why on earth would you think that? I had no idea Lee. I thought he was okay...I thought he'd settled down, with Lucy and everything.'

'Well that was all an act, wasn't it?' I turned around and shouted at her. 'And I bloody knew it was, and I bloody told you he was up to something, but you wouldn't have it would you!'

She stared back at me, a thick magazine held rigidly on her lap. 'You're exhausted,' she told me stiffly. 'You need to go to bed.'

'Don't tell me what I need to do.'

'Lee,' she breathed out slowly, her eyes fixing on the magazine, instead of on me. She uncrossed her legs and sat forward on

The Boy With The Thorn In His Side-Part 2

the chair. 'We have to accept what he wrote in that letter. He doesn't want to live with us. He'll be in contact when he's ready. We just have to wait for that, and then we will get some answers.' She looked up at me, and her expression was cautious, her position frozen. I had to get away from her. I had to. I couldn't even open my mouth and give her what for. I stalked past her, through the bedroom, down the stairs and out of the house.

Finally, on the fourth day, just as I was getting increasingly anxious about my own sanity, I punched in Jack's number and he answered.

'What do you want?' his washed out voice asked me. He sounded exactly as I had expected him to; as if he had been lost inside a bottle of Jack Daniels for the past few days. I was gripping my phone so hard my knuckles began to ache. I strode briskly out of the house, shoving my way through the French doors and stalking my way down the garden, away from listening ears. The house was full of people all the fucking time. Painters and decorators, and neighbours Kay seemed intent on impressing. She was swishing around the house with this lost and pained look on her face, just because I wouldn't allow her to paint our bedroom dusky fucking pink.

'What do I want?' I hissed through my teeth as I stormed down the long green lawn, away from the house. 'What do I fucking want? Why haven't you been answering your phone? I've been going out of my fucking mind these last few days! Where the hell have you been?'

'Been busy,' he replied, haughtily like a sulky child. 'Had stuff to sort out.'

'Yeah, you've been busy getting the fuck out of town!' I roared at him incredulously. He sniffed in response. 'Yeah I've been to the flat, you disgusting waste of space, what the hell is going on?'

He sniffed again. 'You've seen the boy?'

'No, I haven't seen the fucking boy!' I had to stop walking, I was so apoplectic with rage. I was at the end of the garden, shielded by thick summer shrubs and a six-foot wood panelled fence. 'Why do you think I've been going out of my mind you stupid useless bastard? What the hell went on? You fucked up, didn't you? Because he's fucking vanished! Gone!'

'It's your own fault,' his groggy, alcohol soaked voice informed me smugly.

'Just tell me what happened Jack, I am not dicking around here.' I looked at the fence, and remembered that another garden stretched down to meet it from the other side. I lowered my tone and edged slowly away from it. 'Where are you anyway?'

'Essex,' came the dull reply.

'Why did you leave?'

'It's your fault, you know,' he told me yet again. 'You had to push things, didn't you? You couldn't just let things lie. You couldn't be satisfied, could you? You had to have complete control of everybody!'

'You're talking crap.'

'It's true Lee, and you know it, and you've always been the same. You're just ten times worse now you've got money behind you. You've turned into a monster.'

I could feel the black rage creeping up on me again, colouring my mind a vivid shade of fury and threatening to overspill and consume me. Heat was snaking around my neck and the electricity was flying through me, setting me on fire. 'Just tell me what the fuck happened you useless shitting pervert!'

Jack sighed heavily and dramatically on the other side of the phone. He cleared his throat, gurgling on thick smokers' phlegm and I closed my eyes and moved my ear from the phone in repulsion.

'You shouldn't have done any of it,' he said. 'You shouldn't have set me up in the flat like that, with boys coming over. You knew exactly what you were doing.'

'Why not? You liked it, didn't you? Thought we were on the same page!'

'Does the word torture mean anything to you Lee? Does it?' He sounded angrier now, I thought, and I almost wanted to laugh at him. I was starting to wonder why I had ever called on him in the first place, why I ever thought I could rely on him. He was weak.

'What's the matter with you Jack?' I questioned him brashly. 'I thought you were hard! Turns out you're all soft and squishy like the rest of them. You didn't have to take me up on the offer you fat fuck. You can say no, can't you?'

The Boy With The Thorn In His Side-Part 2

'It's not easy to say no to someone who can destroy your whole life in a second Lee,' Jack replied hoarsely. 'It's not easy to say no to someone when they hold all the strings. When they dangle temptations in front of you like fucking smack!'

'What are you whining on about?'

'You know what I'm on about Lee. I couldn't say no to you, not when you know everything about me. Not when you've always made it perfectly clear that you could destroy me in a heartbeat.'

I was getting tired. I shook my head and gritted my teeth. 'Jack, I think you're forgetting it's always me who helps you out. It was me who sorted that little rat out for you back home wasn't it eh? You would have done time otherwise mate. *Time.*'

'Exactly what I'm saying Lee. You know everything.'

'Well if you don't like it Jack, maybe you ought to do a better job of controlling yourself! Don't try and blame me for your shitty little perversions.'

'But you got me here Lee,' Jack replied, his voice a growl of indignation. 'You obviously have your own perversions, ever thought about that?'

I rolled my eyes impatiently. How I longed to have him right in front of me then. How I longed to grab him by his grubby shirt collar and ram my mobile phone right into his eye socket. 'Just shut up whining,' I snapped. 'Just tell me what the hell happened when you went to the house. That's all I'm asking you. Then you can go to your own sick hell for all I care!'

'You're the sick one,' he rasped at me spitefully. 'At least I try to control myself. You! You fucking love it don't you eh? You seek it out, and you always have done! Weaker people you can scare and control and hurt. Like your own brother!'

I laughed coldly. 'Don't mention that pointless sack of piss to me,' I told him. 'Just tell me what happened. Just tell me how badly you fucked up the job I gave you.'

'He stabbed me all right!' Jack barked suddenly down the phone. 'The little shit stabbed me with his knife, which, by the way, you neglected to tell me he had! The little shit knew everything about me Lee, he knew about what happened in Essex, somehow he knew, and that's why they stopped coming to the flat! Then he stabbed me, right in my fucking foot! You happy now! *Are you?*'

I laughed. Oh, how I laughed. I laughed until my belly ached and my eyes watered, and the whole time, I could hear him roaring his anger down the phone at me, and I could see him in my mind, fat and grey and washed up and nursing a mammoth hangover as well as a mammoth hard on.

'Your *foot?*' I managed to utter in response. 'Your *foot?* How the hell did that happen? You were drunk Jack. Drunk and weak and pathetic. I bet you tried romancing him, eh? Was that it? Did you ask him out on a date?' I creased up again, my hands on my knees and the phone jammed between my neck and my shoulder.

'He said you've got the same coming to you,' he muttered at me. 'If you don't leave him alone. So, there you go. Now you know.'

'You think he'd try that on me? Oh, you are funny Jack. You really are. Did he say where he was going? Did you get any clues?'

'Course he didn't bloody tell me where he was going! You know, if you've got any sense you'll forget about it Lee. It's over. He's gone. Why don't you forget about it and leave him alone eh? Everyone will be better off if you do.'

I chuckled and straightened up. 'Don't think so Jack.'

'What's the point? What's the point in it now eh?'

'Point is Jack,' I replied, standing completely still while a righteous picture formed neatly in my mind. 'I didn't give him permission to fucking go.' I removed the phone from my ear and hung up on him.

For a few still and calm moments, I just stood there, in the middle of my lush green lawn, and my tongue flicked back and forth across my lower lip. Then I got myself moving, shoving the phone into my back pocket and swinging my arms as I marched past the house.

I saw Kay frowning at the French doors.

'Got to go to work baby!' I called out to her, waving one hand. 'Problems!'

She nodded back and pulled the doors shut. I walked around to the front of the house, down the drive and turned left towards the Chapmans' house. Of course, Kay had already spoken to them a

The Boy With The Thorn In His Side-Part 2

couple of times about Danny's whereabouts, but asking again wouldn't hurt anyone, would it? It was three doors down. I could already see Mr Chapman's modest Renault parked neatly on their drive. I felt a welcome calm take hold of me now that I didn't have to worry about Jack anymore, and I approached their door brashly, lifted the heavy knocker and let it drop again. I stepped back, jamming my hands into my jeans pockets and when the bespectacled Mr Chapman opened the door to me, I cocked my head in a friendly, chirpy manner and offered him my most sociable smile. Instantly, a worried line appeared on his forehead, and his eyes flicked left and right behind the lenses of his glasses, as if looking out for someone or something.

'I'm sorry to bother you Mr Chapman,' I told him amiably. 'I was wondering if I could have a quick word?' I could see his expression was troubled and nervous.

He cleared his throat. 'What can I do for you?'

I took my hands from my pockets, planted one on my hip and the other on his door frame as I leaned into it. 'Look,' I said, 'I don't know how much your daughter has told you, but it's been four whole days now since we saw Danny, and we still have no idea where he is, or who he's with, which as you can imagine is very worrying for us.'

'What do the police say?'

I rolled my eyes. 'Oh, you know what they're like, Mr Chapman, they're sympathetic but they haven't got the time or the resources to go round chasing teenage runaways. They've said all they can do is keep checking in with his friends to see if any of them have heard from him. I mean, Lucy, she must have heard from Danny, mustn't she?'

'Listen to me Mr Howard,' Mr Chapman spoke very softly, but firmly, and as he spoke he pulled his front door close behind him, as if shielding his home from me. He peered at me over the rims of his glasses and his eyes were like steel. 'Look, I'm afraid I know all about you. My daughter has filled me in on every distressing detail, and all I can say to you sir, is even if I *did* know where Danny is, I would *not* be passing that information on to you. From what my daughter tells me, the boy ran away from you for his own safety, and I think it's probably best if it stays that way.' He nodded very curtly, indicating that the conversation was over, and he stepped back, preparing to close the door. My lip curled back in anger. I tossed my head and glared at him.

'Kids?' I spat. 'Delinquent kids? And you believe them over me? That's intelligent!'

'I believe my own daughter, Mr Howard.'

'You're mistaken,' I said, jabbing a finger at him. 'About everything. And that's a dangerous mistake to make Mr Chapman, because that boy your precious daughter is so fond of, is a drug addict who stabbed a good friend of mine in the foot the other day because he refused to give him money to buy more drugs! Is that the kind of boy you want your daughter hanging around with, is it?' I shook my head in dismay at his blank face. 'Well it's up to you I suppose, she's your child. But don't say I didn't try to warn you.' I turned on my heel and marched away from him, back towards my own house and the car. I could feel the desperation spreading through me, jerking through my muscles, the urge for violence, tightening me up, taking me over like a disease. I got into the car, turned on the engine and screeched off down the road.

I drove into town and parked in a space along the high street. I sat there for five minutes with the radio on low, just telling myself to calm down, to think clearly, to be clever and careful. I will find that little son-of-a-bitch, I said to myself, just nodding and breathing, as I tried to loosen my fingers on the steering wheel. I will find him, I nodded, I will, but I must be patient. I pulled my hands away from the steering wheel. They ached and were greased with sweat. I shook them out, and rested my head back for a moment, forcing myself to breathe in and out slowly and purposefully. That little shit would destroy me if I let him. He would destroy everything I had worked so hard for. People wouldn't want to come in the club anymore if the word got out about Jack and his past indiscretions. The police would start sniffing around. They would have no choice. It would all be ruined. I tried to stay calm, but the anger swirled like a tornado inside my gut and my chest. It wanted to come out. It was battering me from the inside. My head felt thick and heavy with it and my eyes hurt. Mr Chapman had not helped me. Stuck up, condescending prick. I looked to the right then, a movement outside the café catching my eye.

The Boy With The Thorn In His Side-Part 2

A young woman with a bright red dress on, was bumping her baby's pushchair down the step, and waving goodbye to some people still inside. I narrowed my eyes and watched, and drummed my fingers against the wheel. Two figures came towards the door. One was another young girl, blonde haired and fiddling with something inside her oversized handbag. She was chatting and laughing to the young man who came out with her, and then he waved her off and stooped down to pick up the sign from the pavement. It was Danny's friend. The tall thin one with the floppy hair.

I lit a cigarette and turned the engine back on. The tall kid carried the sign back into the café and closed the door behind him. One of the café lights went out and the shutters started to come down. I signalled and pulled out of the parking space. I drove slowly away and turned down the next road to the right. I parked up again, got out, and sauntered casually down the long and narrow alley that ran behind the row of shops. I leaned against the wall there and smoked my cigarette down to the butt. I looked up when there was a noise from the back of the café. The back door was shoved open with a metallic groan, and the tall kid stepped out, shook back his floppy long hair, and walked off in the opposite direction. I had a huge smile on my face, watching him go. The thought of a little dose of genuine fear was enough to send tingles down my spine. I scratched my balls, flicked my cigarette butt away and moved after him.

I stalked him down the alley. I felt like a big cat hunting its prey. There was nothing like it. I watched his thin legs, moving stick like within loose blue jeans. I watched the way his spiky elbows jutted out as he marched along. I watched him shaking and tossing back his hair and thought why the fuck don't you just get it cut you miserable girl's blouse? When I was ready, I scrunched my boots into the gravel and the kid whirled around suddenly in surprise. I moved fast and was on him in seconds, snatching up the front of his t-shirt and ramming him back into the nearest wall, enjoying the satisfying sound of his bony spine cracking against the concrete.

The boy doubled up, winded and wordless. His face hung down low so I brought my knee up to say hello to it. With a loud grunt of pain and a spray of blood, the tall kid fell forward into the dirt, and I towered above his crumpled body, smiling grimly.

'Tell me where Danny is,' I said to the boy, as he pushed himself up onto his hands and knees and coughed up blood and dirt. I glanced quickly up and down the alley to ensure we were still alone, and then I squatted down next to him. I took his hair and wrenched his head back so that we could see each other properly. I greeted his terrified face with a sunny smile. 'Tell me where he is.'

The boy coughed up another spray of gravel and gore, and shook his head in my grip. 'Don't know, don't know! I really don't!'

I cocked my head to one side and clicked my tongue at him. 'I don't believe you prick.'

He shook his head again, straining against my hold. 'I don't! I really don't! I have no idea, I swear I don't! We're not friends! Haven't been for ages!"

'Still not sure I believe you,' I mused, rising to my feet and dragging him up with me. I used my body to back him up against the wall. I looked him up and down with a sneer. He was bigger than Danny, but he was still no match for me. He was a skinny, wiry, floppy haired little cunt. I took my old Swiss army knife out from the front pocket of my jeans and showed it to him. His eyes grew even bigger and rounder. I laughed, and then whipped the knife upwards, using it to hack at a handful of his stupid long hair. Then I presented a handful of mousy brown fluff to his terrified face.

'Give this to him when you see him,' I said. 'Tell him it's just the start. Tell him if he doesn't come back home right now, I'm going to hunt down all of his friends, including that pretty little girlfriend of his, and I'm going to cut bits off all of them, okay?' I stuffed the knife back into my jeans, pressed the hair into his hand and let him go. 'You tell him that when you see him okay? Tell him it's not over until I say it is.' He nodded at me silently, dumbly, his face a mess, his eyes watering. I felt much better. I felt refreshed and new again. I left him where he was and headed back down to where I had parked the car.

The Boy With The Thorn In His Side-Part 2

24

It was Anthony who opened the door to a strained looking Billy, five days after we moved into the bed-sit. He shuffled through the door, checking back over his shoulder as he did, his hands jammed so deep into his pockets that his shoulders appeared hunched right up to his ears. Anthony looked him over with a quizzical frown.

'All right there, Billy? You look like you've seen a ghost!'

Billy shrunk past him. 'More like a monster,' he mumbled unhappily.

'You what?'

Billy released a weary sigh and looked at Michael and I, sprawled out lazily on the bed. Anthony locked the door and turned to face him, folding his arms over his chest. 'I've got bad news,' Billy told us remorsefully. I sat up then, my eyes narrowing and my mouth closing. He was looking right at me, so I guessed it was my bad news. Billy sighed again and grimaced back at me. 'Howard attacked Jake last night.'

There was an audible gasp from all of us. Michael jerked up beside me, his mouth gaping at Billy. 'You are fucking kidding me!' he cried. I just stared. Billy shook his head in misery.

'After he finished work,' he told us. 'Out the back of the café. Just crept up behind and attacked him.'

I got up from the bed, shaking my head and pressing my hands to each side of my face. I was wearing my old Nirvana t-shirt and a pair of boxer shorts. We had been enjoying a lazy morning, our favourite kind. Crappy TV on low, music on loud, a bit of a smoke, and Anthony's cooking. Billy looked like he was about to say more, but wasn't sure how to. I nodded at him and he blew his breath out unhappily.

'He told Jake to give you a message Danny.' We all stared back at him in silence, our breath held, our hearts thumping. Billy swallowed. 'He had a knife and he cut off a chunk of Jake's hair and told him to give it to you, and to tell you that if you don't go home, he'll start cutting bits off all of us.'

'Oh my God,' breathed Michael in horror, stumbling up from the bed. '*Shittinghell!*'

I looked at Anthony and saw that he was still and calm, his dark eyes focused solely on Billy. 'And then what happened Bill?' he asked him. Billy took a deep breath before going on.

'Jake came to my house and my mum opened the door to him, and he said who did it and she called the police.'

Anthony nodded, eyebrows raised. 'Seriously?'

'Yep. They came and took a statement off him, and said they'd go and find Howard, and they asked if we knew where Danny was, and we said no.' Billy took another breath, licked his lips and eyed us nervously. 'And Jake didn't tell Howard either. He didn't tell him where you lot are. You think he's been arrested by now Anthony?'

'Who knows?' shrugged Anthony, pushing his hand back through his hair. He looked at me then, wonderingly. 'Well mate, sounds like the prick has lost it big time. I don't know whether we should be pleased or scared, eh?'

I found the edge of the bed and sat back down. 'Is Jake okay Billy?'

'He's fine, yeah,' Billy nodded. 'Just a bit shook up, you know. He said to tell you sorry, by the way.'

I frowned. 'What the hell for?'

Billy shrugged awkwardly. 'Dunno, I guess for not sticking by you when things were tough, you know, when you were skipping school and high and stuff. He thinks he was harsh on you. He didn't know, you know?' Billy scratched his head and stuck his hands back into his pockets. 'We didn't know,' he said, sounding confused. 'We had no idea.'

'Don't worry about it,' I told him softly.

'Did we do the right thing?' he asked then, his tone slightly desperate as he looked back at Anthony for the reassurance he so often gave us. 'Telling the police and that? My mum, she just took over!'

'Serves him right,' was Anthony's reply.

'It's fine,' I agreed. 'Maybe they'll catch up with him, hey? God. Poor Jake though. Tell him I'm sorry, will you?'

'Sorry?' Anthony looked at me sharply. 'What have you got to be sorry for, you twat?'

'He's after me,' I sighed. 'I'm not gonna' let him go through you guys to get to me.'

The Boy With The Thorn In His Side-Part 2

'What does that mean?'

'He won't get us anyway!' Michael blurted out then, staring from me to Anthony, to Billy, his brow creased and his eyes fearful. 'He'll be arrested by now, won't he? He can't just attack Jake in broad daylight like that and get away with it! He can't do anything to us, now that's on record, he just can't! Isn't that right Anthony?'

Anthony nodded sombrely. 'He'd be nuts if he did. Danny?' I looked up. 'What are you thinking?'

I bit down on my lip and slid from the bed again. I felt their eyes on me curiously as I found my jeans on the floor and pulled them on. 'I'm thinking about going back to work,' I said quietly.

Billy gasped. 'Are you insane?' he yelled. 'After what just happened to Jake?'

I sat back down to pull on my socks. 'I've got no choice Bill. The fat man won't keep my job open forever, and I haven't even thanked him for those tickets yet, for Christ's sake. I've messed him about enough. I need to be there.'

Billy turned helplessly to Anthony. 'Are you gonna' let him do this?'

'What?' he shrugged in reply, a sparkle in his eyes and a grin on his face. 'He can't spend the rest of his life in this room, can he Bill? He's got no choice.'

'You going now?' asked Michael. 'I'll come with you.' He started searching the floor for signs of his own clothes. We hadn't exactly shown ourselves to be house proud so far in our new surroundings. The floor was so covered with discarded clothes and dirty dishes and cups, that the carpet was barely visible. He set about tossing and kicking things aside until he found his black jeans and started to yank them on. 'I'll go with you to work, then I'll go and see Jake. Come back and meet you when you're done, yeah?' He looked at me hopefully, shaking his hair from his eyes.

'Cool,' I nodded. Billy groaned loudly and raked both his hands violently back through his stiff auburn hair.

'Oh, for God's sake,' he complained. 'I'll come too. Jesus Christ.'

As for Anthony, he made me smile. He dropped down onto his sofa bed, crossed his legs at the ankles and picked up his little tin from the arm of the chair. He was grinning like a fool, this long, lazy smile lighting up his eyes, as he pulled the lid from his tin and set about rolling himself a little smoke.

'Proud of you all,' he announced cheerily, as we began to troop solemnly from the room. 'Get on out there and take no shit! Fight back!'

The three of us emerged cautiously from the darkness of the hall downstairs, blinking and feeling the urge to shield our eyes from the bright August sunshine. No one spoke as we rounded the corner and waited at the bus stop together. And we were silent when we boarded the bus, paid our fares and took our seats. It was only a fifteen-minute bus ride back into Redchurch, and I felt the tension building in me with every second that passed. I couldn't shake the feeling of being a criminal, returning to the scene of his crime. I looked at my friends, at their sick and frightened expressions, and I felt another layer of guilt settle over the first one. I gazed out of the window and thought; I owe it to them to not be scared anymore. When we got to the stop closest to The Record Shop, we got up and jumped off the bus. The sunlight was dazzling in that area of town, bouncing and rebounding from every available surface, shop front and car. I closed my eyes briefly, breathed in and then faced them with a smile. I owed it to them to stand up, and I was going to show them we had no reason to hide.

'Could be an interesting day,' I joked, as they walked me towards the shop.

Billy was fiddling anxiously with the leather bracelets around his wrist. 'What'll you do if the cops come here to see you?' he asked me and I shrugged.

'I dunno. Hey, say hi to Jake for me, won't you? Tell him I said sorry, won't you, that he got caught up in all of this.'

'Well maybe he'll be more on your side from now on,' Michael muttered somewhat darkly, as his eyes flitted restlessly up and down the street. He patted me on the shoulder and attempted a smile. 'I'll be back around three, yeah? After I've seen Jake I'm gonna' pop into work and see if they've got me some more shifts yet. Some girl quit last week, so I should get offered some.'

The Boy With The Thorn In His Side-Part 2

'No problem,' I nodded, and watched them go. I turned around and pushed gratefully into the shop. I was met with the warmth and the smell that was instantly and indescribably comforting. I could have bathed in it. I wanted to breathe it in, and let it settle through me and on me. The smell of old things, coated in dust, smeared in finger prints, and aged by love. Radiohead's Bones was playing and I paused to hear the lyrics. I inhaled it all and approached the counter, where Terry looked up at me from his stool, a brief and surprised smile filling his face.

'Oh, look who it is!' he boomed. 'All better now I see?'

'Was the funniest thing,' I grinned back at him, resting my arms wearily on the counter top. 'Couldn't stop puking for days. You wouldn't have wanted to catch it Terry.'

'Got a delivery out the back,' he told me, jerking his head in that direction. 'Some old bird just dropped it off in the alley. Four bloody boxes of records. I can't go near 'em mate. Makes me sneeze.'

'I'll put the kettle on first shall I?' I laughed, and he looked pleased and handed me his empty mug.

'Oh, just to warn you,' he said then, 'you've had a pretty constant visitor these last few days.'

I paused in the doorway and forced another smile. 'Let me guess. Massive angry bloke? Wanting to know where I am?'

'That's the one,' Terry nodded and made a little grimace of disgust. 'Bloody thick necked twat. Been getting right on my wick, he has. You know I like my peace and quiet in here. Bit mental, is he?' He sort of winced as he asked the question, as if the very thought of it offended him.

'Yeah. That's him.'

Terry rolled his eyes, made a little grumbling noise in his throat and swivelled on his stool to face me properly. 'Fucking beefed up, testosterone fuelled, monkey brained psychopath.'

I laughed out loud. I wanted to hug him. 'Yes! That's him! Brilliant Terry!'

Terry grunted. 'He the one that runs that club down the road now?'

'Yep. He owns it. Doesn't like music though. Nothing.'

Terry's eyebrows shot up towards his receding hairline. 'Christ,' he snarled. 'I could really get to hate some people, couldn't you?'

'I've left home,' I told him then, lowering my voice slightly but keeping the smile upon my lips to let him know that all was good. 'Just so you know. Moved in with Mike and Anthony. That's what he's pissed about.'

'Well who could bloody blame you?' Terry roared at me, making me laugh again. 'I'll call the bloody cops if he comes in here again, shouting the odds.' He shook his head and clicked his tongue and looked back down at his copy of NME.

'You do that Terry,' I told him. 'And hey?' He looked back up, wonderingly. I felt a little embarrassed then, but I stepped forward and held my hand out to him. I didn't know how else to thank him for the Oasis tickets. I wanted to let him know how amazing and beautiful it was, how it meant the world to me, and made me smile from morning until night, just thinking about October. He frowned and raised his lip up and took my hand in a confused manner. 'Thanks,' I said, and shook it before dropping it and stepping back again. Terry looked completely baffled. 'For the tickets,' I nodded. 'Just amazing. Best present ever. Can't even....' I shrugged and shook my head and sighed. It was useless. There were no words in the world to describe what those tickets meant to me. 'Just...thanks Terry. I owe you. I mean, you've been bloody brilliant.'

Terry rolled his eyes, and waved his magazine at me irritably. 'Oh *that*! Jesus Christ I got them to shut you the hell up! Forget about it.'

'Amazing though Terry...I can't even...'

'Oh, go and put the kettle on and stop embarrassing us both,' he sort of grinned at me, and there was a pinkness creeping into his soft round cheeks. 'I did it for the shop, yeah? Can't have staff working for me if they've never even been to a live gig for Christ's sake! Can't call yourself a music fan if you don't go and see it live! Go on now. Tea.'

It was coming up to one o'clock and I had just brought out another round of tea and biscuits for me and Terry. I had spent all morning sorting through the boxes the old lady had left for him in the

The Boy With The Thorn In His Side-Part 2

alley. I found a copy of Marvin Gaye's What's Going On, and Terry insisted I keep it.

'Beautiful songs, bloody good singer,' was all he would tell me. I put the tea and biscuits on the counter and turned to the record player. Blonde On Blonde had just finished, so I took it off and slid it carefully back inside its sleeve. I flicked through the pile Terry had chosen. He had a couple of Neil Young records in the pile, and Sandinista by The Clash. I fancied something a bit livelier, so put that on while he was farting away in the toilet out the back. I stuck my tongue out, urggh, he sounded like he was having a hard time in there, and I put the record on, closed the lid with care and turned around, just in time to see a maniacal face pressed up against the shop window. Howard.

All at once the rest of the shop just fell away from me, even the music seemed to fade into nothing. There was just me and his wild, leering face. He seemed to materialise inside the shop without even opening the door or walking in. He was just suddenly right there, filling the space as always, dominating the atmosphere and stealing all the air. An icy coldness flooded my veins.

'Well look who it is!' he declared in delight, the words rolling from his hanging tongue, dripping with glee, as he closed the space between us and slammed both his hands down upon the counter. I jumped, moved back. Felt the memory of fists against skin jarring through my body. I watched his tongue flicking rapidly around the edges of his gaping mouth. 'The original whizz kid eh! Finally crawled out from his hiding place! I ought to grab hold of you and drag you down the police station for what you did to Jack!'

I forced myself to breathe. It was like I had forgotten how to, but I opened my mouth, felt the air tickle the back of my throat and sucked it in, sending it swirling through to my lungs. I ran my eyes over the monstrous man who stood before me, and then it occurred to me that I had never seen him appear so dishevelled before. He was unshaven and his hair and beard looked like they needed a trim. His eyes were all wrong; like they had been forced open for too long, and now were too big and round and staring to close properly.

'And I'll tell them what you sent him for, you sick motherfucker,' I said to him, speaking my words slowly and softly, and as I spoke, I remembered the fire of defiance that had lived in me such a long time ago, the constant urge to fight everyone, to rail against everything, to be heard. I searched for it now. I dug deep down inside of myself to bring it back to the surface, and clung to it as I stared into the eyes of a man who looked scarily close to the edge.

His top lip lifted like a hungry dog. 'Oh yeah? You little shit!'

'Yeah,' I said. 'I hear they're looking for you anyway, after you attacked Jake for no reason!'

His face loomed closer to mine and I moved back instinctively. 'Oh yeah? Well smart arse I think you'll find they've already spoken to me about that, and they were perfectly happy with my alibi! I was with my bar manager Mark at that *exact* time, and he was only too happy to verify that for them!'

'You mean you paid him, or threatened him to give you an alibi?'

Howard snorted violently through his nose. 'Whatever. I told the cops how your drug addled friends have always had it in for me. They were very keen to know where you were, you know. Maybe Jack's made a complaint, eh? Could find yourself in all sorts of shit now.'

I shook my head and bit down on the retorts that sprung to mind. I didn't want him here, infecting the air, wrecking my space and my peace. I sighed, and I was tired of it all, of this never-ending game of trading insults. 'Look I'm busy,' I told him. 'Was there something you wanted? A record you're after?' I heard Terry flushing the toilet out the back.

'Don't give me that you fucking little piss bag!' Howard spoke viciously, his nostrils flaring wide as spittle flew from his lips and sprayed the counter. I watched the droplets land and spread on Terry's magazine. 'You know why I'm here. To take you home. To give you another chance.'

'I don't think so,' I told him, looking him right in the eye. I stared at him, I stared right into him and I willed him to see how much I meant it. '*Never* gonna' happen.'

Just then Terry came shuffling around the corner, hoisting up his gut to buckle his belt under it. His eyes clouded with rage when he spotted Howard in his shop, and he headed for his stool on his puny

The Boy With The Thorn In His Side-Part 2

legs. 'You again!' he bellowed instantly. 'I thought I told you to sling your hook bully boy! Go on! Out you go!'

Howard straightened up and stiffened, his hands falling away from the counter. I regarded him curiously and saw his face changing. I saw fear there, I knew I did, fear, and panic and uncertainty. It fascinated me because I didn't think I had ever seen him like that before.

'I hope you know the kind of scum you've got working for you,' he snarled at Terry. Terry climbed onto his stool and waved an impatient hand at him. Howard pointed at me. 'This kid is a drug addict! He has a police record as long as my arm, did you know that? You ought to check your till and your stock carefully fat man!'

'Go on,' Terry repeated in absolute disdain, waving a podgy hand as if swatting at a fly that was irritating him. 'I don't want you in here causing trouble! I'll call the law!'

'Oh really?' Howard fixed his manic stare back on me. 'Well then, little man, aren't you the popular one these days eh? Yeah. Ooh everyone loves Danny so much! Danny has so many people sticking up for him! Don't know why everyone thinks you're so great when you've been nothing but a little fuck up from day one!'

I just stared back at him, steady and unflinching. I felt almost drowsy with the strength that was building up inside of me. It made me want to smile, and laugh, and sit down and let it all through spin through my head. Lee Howard, I thought, look at you, falling apart before my very eyes. I didn't have to say or do a thing. Behind me Terry had picked up the phone and was dialling.

'Calling the cops!' he said to Howard. 'Come in here, insulting my staff!'

He was starting to retreat. Backing slowly towards the door. He had come for something and he was being forced to leave without it. He looked like he was panting slightly as he raised a finger again to point at me. He nodded his head and reached out for the door behind him.

'This isn't over,' he told me. 'I'll be coming for you! I'll be coming for you, you little cunt when you least fucking expect it! You can count on that little man. I'll be coming for you. You still got a lot of lessons to learn off me!'

'Get out!' Terry yelled, and he went. The door eased itself shut behind him. I said nothing. I closed my eyes and released a massive, shaky sigh. I could hear Terry muttering away indignantly beside me. I opened my eyes and rubbed at my face and gave him a thankful, withering smile.

The Boy With The Thorn In His Side-Part 2

25

  I returned home, but I could not remember the journey. There were no thoughts inside my head, only black smoking rage. I found myself sat in the car in the driveway, breathing heavily through my nostrils, as the windscreen steamed up before my eyes. The next minute I was at the front door, shouldering my way roughly through it, slamming my body against the wood until it yielded to me, and I couldn't remember climbing out of the car, or if I had locked it behind me. I was in the hallway then. *That little shit, that little shit, that fucking little shit!* They had painted it an off white. Antique Cream, they called it. The new carpet was a dusky yellow. A huge mirror hung on the wall next to the lounge and I stared back at my reflection, and saw a hulk, a brute, steaming, sweating, my insides burning, my brain frying, and I wanted to smash my skull into the mirror. I looked down and to my right. We had bought a new table for the hall, solid dark mahogany, with two deep drawers to store notepaper and telephone directories. The phone sat in its cradle on the top. Next to it, a sparkling crystal vase stuffed full of lemon and white flowers. The phone went first. Dragged from the socket and hurled against the far wall. Then the vase went. I threw it into the kitchen. *Little fuck up, little scruffy skinny arrogant up his own arse never learning his lessons little smarmy smiling little shit stain!*

  I heard a noise of fear and surprise and whirled into the room. It shone back at me, hurting my eyes. The new floor we'd had laid, black and white tiles, sunlight streaming from the window and bouncing back from them into my face. Kay was stood there, mopping in her dressing gown, her face frozen, her eyes wide. The vase lay shattered across the floor, the flowers limp in a puddle of water. I was at her then. I had to, before she opened her mouth and spoke. *Fuck him, fuck him! Gonna fucking kill him gotta' stop him, gotta' stop this. Gotta' get that fucking look out his eyes!* I was at her, slipping both my hands around her throat, and the mop banged to the floor and there was a horrible, dreamlike silence as she stared up into my eyes, not seeing me, not knowing me.

  It was over before it began. I released her and walked out. I ran up the stairs and shut myself in the bedroom. I found the bed and crawled onto it and lay on my stomach with my arms right over my head. My brain pulsed like a heartbeat. Pain shot spikes around my temples and into my eyes. *Fucking shit, little shit, fucking shit!*

I heard her out on the balcony that afternoon. I must have slept for a long time. I woke up groggy, rubbing at my forehead, greeting the last traces of my headache. I sat up on the bed and could see her out there. Still in that bloody silk dressing gown. Did she think she was on a permanent holiday or something? I stretched out my limbs, yawned, and blinked rapidly. My head felt like I had been in a car crash. She was sat out there at the little table, a mug of coffee in one hand and a cigarette in the other. I could see a paperback book on the table. She was smoking her cigarette, and sipping her coffee, and gazing out at the sea, as it shimmered on the horizon. I found myself wondering what she was thinking about. I wondered if I had left marks on her neck. I wondered why she was still here, yet somehow I had known that she would be.

Her head jerked to look at me when I rose slowly from the bed, stretching out my limbs yet again, shaking them out, flexing the tight muscles. I was hungry. Must have slept through lunch. My stomach was a dark pit of desires and needs. I walked to the doors and eased them gently aside. Her eyes took me in and the hand holding the cigarette drooped slightly towards her lap. She didn't say anything. I stared into her eyes and tried to read them. I couldn't quite tell what I saw there. I moved forward and kneeled before her. She looked a little surprised then. She tapped her cigarette against the ash tray and put her coffee mug down.

I put my big head into her lap and let the tears come. My face, hot and hurting, rubbed into the delicate silk of her gown, and my hands moved up to reach around her waist, to clutch her there, and I sobbed. I sobbed and her lap grew wet.

'I'm sorry,' I gulped, when I finally felt one of her hands landing lightly upon my head. I rubbed my eyes into her gown, the tears balling up and rolling like beads across the material. 'I'm sorry...I'm so sorry baby...so sorry, oh baby....'

After a while, she cleared her throat. 'What is it?' she asked. I lifted my head and looked at her still face. She looked pained and

The Boy With The Thorn In His Side-Part 2

wary, weak and haughty. I had no idea what she was thinking about me. Tears spilled rapidly from my stinging eyes.

'Oh, I've messed up, I've messed everything up!' I moaned, finding her hands with my own and holding them tight. I felt her thin fingers like sticks inside my palms. 'My head...oh it was hurting so much, and I've took it out on you, I've taken everything out on you, and oh I am so sorry baby, so sorry...it's all got too much! All of it! I can't think straight!'

She smiled, slightly. It came and went. She pushed my head back down into her lap, and tugged one hand free of mine. It came back to my head, pausing, before rifling gently through my hair. 'Calm down,' I heard her say to me. 'You just need to calm down. It's okay.'

'I went to the shop,' I mumbled from her lap. 'He was there. I spoke to him.'

Her hand froze on my scalp. 'Danny?'

'Yes...yes baby, he's okay, he's back working there.'

'Well see, I told you, didn't I?' She sounded nervous I thought. She swallowed and coughed. 'I told you he would be okay. We have to respect his decision Lee. He doesn't have to live with us if he doesn't want to. Give him some time.'

'I know, I know, I see that now,' I told her, squeezing her one hand between mine. 'I know you were right baby, you were right about it all...I think it just all got to me, all the moving house, and stress at work and him running off, because I didn't want you to be hurt and upset baby. I didn't want that.'

Her body felt stiff under my head. I nestled my cheek into her thigh. 'He was okay though?'

'Oh yes, yes, full of it as always. His boss threatened to call the cops on me if I didn't leave.'

'Well just don't go there again,' she told me, her tone a little brittle I thought, a little annoyed. 'Just leave him alone, let him have his space. He'll be fine as he is. Perhaps he'll call me or come and see me when he's ready. But I'm just going to wait Lee. I just want to wait. All right?'

I felt tight with resentment and spite, but I reeled it in and closed my eyes in her lap. I took deep breaths and spoke softly to her.

'I know, you're right. I keep trying to be a dad to him, and it's not what he wants, is it? I just thought, you know, eventually...And work, God it's a nightmare honey...so much to do, so much going on...oh I know it will all iron itself out eventually, but oh God, I've got to relax, I've got to stop taking on so much and taking it all out on you. It just pains me you know? Do you know?' I gave her a moment to reply and when she didn't, I sighed against her legs. 'Honey, I never thought I wanted kids until I met you, and then I realised I had just never met the person I wanted to have kids with...and now it's too late. I thought I could be a dad to Danny but he never wanted to let me, did he? That's why it mattered so much to me, you know? That's why I've been trying so hard to find him. It's not good baby, the way his life is gonna' go, holed up in some shitty Godforsaken place with druggies and criminals! Throwing his life away...He could have worked for me, you know? I was hoping he would. I could have shown him the ropes at the club.'

'Well he's not like you,' she said then, and her voice came like an icy wind, slicing into my brain, bristling under my skin. 'He's not into flash cars, and sharp suits, and fancy clubs Lee. He just likes his music and his friends, so that was never going to happen.'

I forced the words out before I could think about it too much. 'I know, I know, I was wrong. I know that now. I'll leave him alone.'

'For now,' she added, her tone softening just a little bit and her hand returning to stroke hesitantly at my skull. 'It's best for now. We can concentrate on us, hey? Being on our own.'

'Yes, I know, yes, you're right. You're right honey.'

The right words, I thought. Chosen carefully.

Leave him alone.

All right then.

Give it time. For now.

The Boy With The Thorn In His Side-Part 2

26

After kicking off in the record shop that day, Howard retreated. I waited for something else to happen but nothing did. We looked around, we held our breath, we waited, and when still nothing happened, we all began to relax into our lives. At first, it was hesitant and cautious, like the careful peeling of a plaster from damaged skin. Slowly does it, bit by bit, to minimise the pain and the shock. Life had a pattern of its own, I found. There was day to day living to be done, simple things, but it all bowled me over to tell you the truth; it was strange being able to just live. A few weeks after Howard had stood raging in the middle of his shop, Terry asked me to work for him full time. He even drew up a proper contract and everything. It was weird. I felt grown up and trusted. I felt like I was dreaming most of the time. Floating on air above all the shit I had escaped from.

Michael had picked up some extra shifts at McDonalds, and Anthony was working every hour they offered him at The Ship. Between the three of us we were easily able to cover the rent on the bed-sit, pay the bills, and start to eat some decent food. All three of us boarded the bus and made the journey back into our old territory faithfully every day. It wasn't pleasant, and it made our stomachs sink and our words dry up in our mouths, but it had to be done. There was courage, but also terror. It felt like we were stepping over an invisible line every time we climbed from the bus. It felt like we were exposed, and anything could happen. But nothing ever did. I'm not proud to admit that sometimes I still contacted Jaime Lawler, and arranged to meet him in the alley behind the record shop.

Jaime looked even thinner these days. Haggard, and with a haunted look in his eyes that made me feel uncomfortable to be near him.

'Just can't get to sleep some nights,' I explained, although God knows why I felt the need to justify my drug use to him. 'Lie awake for hours, and then I can't get up in the morning.' Jaime smiled thinly in the dark of the alley where we made our exchanges. His grey eyes, hooded by a frown, moved in a constant panicked state, up and down the alley, over his shoulder, everywhere. He was light on his feet, looked prepared to run at any given moment. 'You still work for him?' I asked, and in response he laughed a hollow, cold laugh.

'You could call it that,' he replied, shifting restlessly from one foot to the other. He looked at me and looked me right in the eyes for a change. 'That bastard scares the shit out of me. Not many people I'd say about that.'

'I know what you mean,' I said, moving away from him, not wanting to hear any more of what I considered to be the past. 'Thanks Jaime, see you at Chaos some time?' He nodded, lit up a cigarette and walked away. I thought about him as I watched him go. It was a strange thing, a relationship of mutual dependence and trust, but I was yet to think of him as a friend.

Lucy called me one Sunday to make sure I was at home. 'Course I'm at home,' I laughed down the phone at her. 'It's Sunday! Day of rest and all that.'

'Right, well stay put,' she told me, and I started to smile at the undeniable excitement in her voice. 'I've got a late birthday present for you, and I'll be over in half an hour. Don't go anywhere!'

When she hung up, I relayed her message to Michael and Anthony, who were instantly intrigued and started trying to guess what it could mean. True to her word, she was tapping energetically at our door half an hour later. I leapt from the bed to open it and there she was, grinning fiendishly back at me, with this squirming, wriggling, white and tan Jack Russell puppy in her arms. I immediately grabbed it from her, as Anthony groaned out loudly from behind me; 'What the hell is that?'

Lucy stepped in and closed the door behind her. I was giggling like a madman, with the puppy covering my face in exuberant wet kisses. 'Late birthday present,' she shrugged. 'What do you think guys?'

'I'm not cleaning up after it!' Anthony retorted with a roll of his eyes and a lazy grin. I sat down on the floor with the tiny pup. I felt like a child on Christmas day. The little pup's tail was wagging so fast it was a blur. He couldn't wash my face fast enough. It seemed to be all he lived for, slathering my grinning face with warm puppy kisses. I hugged him to me, shivering with delight at the feel of his soft warm body, and he put his front paws up on my chest and just wagged that tail faster and faster. I looked up at Lucy and shook my head and laughed.

'Are you mental? I can't believe you got me a dog! Best present ever!'

'Zoe's uncle had one left over,' she explained, crouching down beside me. 'I just had this crazy idea when she showed it to me. I remembered what you said to me that day down at the beach. Well you can have one now, can't you?' She glanced quickly at Michael and Anthony. 'If it's okay with you guys, that is? Zoe said she'll take it back if it's a problem.'

'It's a 'he',' I said, as the pup fell off my lap, landed on his back and started wriggling from side to side while I rubbed at his fat round belly. Michael arrived next to me, kneeling to stroke his silky little head.

'Fine by me,' he said. 'But he needs a name!'

'Oh, I got a name for him already,' I told them, lowering my face so that the puppy could shower me with more kisses. 'Kurt!'

'Kurt!' Anthony exploded scornfully. 'You can't call a puppy Kurt! That's not a dog name!'

'Not sure Cobain would approve mate,' Michael laughed beside me. He was tickling the pup's neck, and he was twisting and snapping at his fingers. Michael yelped and withdrew his hand and rubbed at it. 'Ouch! He's got teeth like needles! Call him Jaws!'

Lucy laughed at him. 'Kurt is a great name Danny. Call him Kurt. Look I think he likes it! Kurt? Kurt?'

'Oh God,' groaned Anthony, retreating into the kitchen to put the kettle on. 'Listen to you lot talking to it like a baby! It'll be like having a kid!'

'You sure it's okay?' I called after him.

He laughed in response. 'Course it's bloody okay. As long as you clean up after the little runt! I do *not* want to be stepping in dog shit first thing in the bloody morning.'

I turned the pup over and stood him on his little fat legs. 'Aw you wouldn't do that, would you Kurt? You're gonna' be so smart, I can just tell!' I picked him back up and he nuzzled his little face right into my neck. I took a breath then. Happiness was disorientating, head spinning. I reached out and found Lucy's hand with mine. 'Thanks Luce.'

'You're welcome,' she said, returning my smile. 'I just thought it would be sort of good for you. You know, they say dogs are really good for people.'

'He's the best present ever, the best present in the whole world,' I leaned forward then, pulling her to me and finding her face with my lips. Michael moaned instantly and jumped to his feet. 'You're the best girlfriend in the world,' I told her, and it was true.

She was a light. How can I explain it any better than that? That's what she was. That's what she'd always been to me. A light; warm and glowing and constant and good. You ever feel like you're in such a good mood, it's like you are walking around with a chunk of sunlight stuck in your eye? You want to blink and shield your eyes, because it dazzles and overwhelms, and you are too used to the darkness. But you can't get it out, it's lodged right in, and after a while you get used to it, and you walk around with it, and it's so bright and shines so hard, it bathes everything else in the entire world in gold. Well that's how I felt about Lucy. She was the sunlight in my eyes.

They returned to school that September; Billy, Jake and Lucy. They met at the end of Lucy's road every morning and walked in together, no doubt feeling older and wiser and a little bit jumpier. I was glad that Billy and Jake walked in with her. I didn't like the thought of her walking to school alone. I didn't like the thought of any of them being alone.

I picked up my old journal again the day after the Oasis gig. I couldn't not. There were too many words and emotions and images compacting inside of me, bursting to get out, and there had to be a release somewhere, somehow, so it came in writing. To say it was one of the best nights of my life would be an understatement and the words not enough to do justice to the experience. It was one of those nights when it felt like anything was possible. Anything in the world. We were together, we were united, we were all the same, and feeling the same things as we jumped and leapt and hugged and sang. Nights like that make you feel on top of the world, like you are

The Boy With The Thorn In His Side-Part 2

flying, like you are so high you can never come down, you can never be brought back down again. Nothing can touch it. Terry was right about that. You can't appreciate music properly until you go to see it live. Until you see and hear and feel it in its rawest form. It was electric. We were part of one organism, this surging, sweating, worshipping mass of people. All going crazy, bellowing the words to the songs that meant so much to us, the songs that made sense of our lives, Supersonic, and Cigarettes and Alcohol, Slide Away and Don't Look Back In Anger, and fucking Live Forever!

I wondered if I ought to dare feel free, finally. I soaked it all up, this thing called life. I sat on the bed the next day, buzzing with it all, restless with excitement, the songs thumping and roaring through my head as I lay my notebook on my lap, my pen flying endlessly across the pages. I wrote and wrote until my hand ached, and my neck cracked. I wrote about the gig, and I wrote about Lucy, and the dog, and then it was like pulling a plug out of my consciousness, letting it all stream out of me.

They were good times. The best of times. Lucy came over every Friday night without fail. We snuggled on the bed, when we could, enjoying the time we had alone before Anthony and Michael returned from work. Stopping and starting, moving forward and then retreating in shyness, under the covers, exploring each other's bodies. I felt a yearning for her all week long. Her parents would not allow her over on school nights. Mid-week she would drop into the record shop to say hi after school. I'd make her tea and she'd sit up at the counter with me and Terry, and we'd do all we could to influence her tastes in music, practically fighting over the record player to play her what we wanted her to fall in love with.

But Friday night was what we all lived for, what we all kept in sight. We travelled towards it from Monday, with our arms reaching out for it in hope and love. We got ready in the bed-sit, and Anthony would throw beers at us, and Jake and Billy and Lucy would arrive together. I seized these nights and I never wanted them to end. They were better than ever now that I was surrounded with my friends, and had no fear to accompany me back home afterwards. Those nights were filled with the music we sang along to, the people we saw ourselves in, and a short walk back to the bed-sit for tea and toast before it was all over until next week.

    I couldn't help but feel an almost desperate sadness roll over me every time an amazing Friday night came to an end. I didn't like good things ending. The only thing that made it bearable was the promise of another one. Lucy would go home. Another Monday would roll around. I would hop on the bus and make another sombre journey back into the past. With my face against the window, the closer we got the more my eyes scanned the streets and the alleys for any sign of him. My mind told me not to do it, not to torture myself, but my body told me I had to do it. The club was only a short distance down the street from the record shop, yet it didn't start to show any signs of life until around six o'clock, by which time I was always safely back in the bed-sit, curled up with Kurt and a nice cup of tea. Another day done, another day I had made it back home safe. Another day and still nothing had happened. I would sit still and listen out for the scrabbling fingers of fear within my belly, and they were still there all right, they were still a part of me and every breath I took. Sometimes I felt like I was walking a tightrope every day, balanced precariously between the normal world, and the world of pain and fear and hate I had left behind. Every time I placed a foot forward, I felt the potential to fall and just keep falling.

    Sometimes when alone, I would think about my mother. I didn't want to, but she invaded my thoughts. I would find myself wondering about her home on Cedar View, her life in her big new house. Lucy walked past her sometimes, when she was digging in flowers in her front garden. She told me that she looked thinner than ever, with dark circles hanging beneath her blue eyes. She told me that she asked after me but never asked where I was. I was relieved she had not tried to find me so far. What would I say to her now? How are you? How's the decorating going? How's the psychopathic husband? I wondered how he was dealing with the rage, and the desire to attack and cause pain. It was what he lived for, wasn't it?

    Thinking about the past did me no favours, and I realised this, but it was hard to give it up. It was hard to pretend I was someone new, unaffected by what had gone on before. They liked to think I was fresh and new, and brave and moving forward, but it wasn't as simple

The Boy With The Thorn In His Side-Part 2

as that. The scars remained. My body, peppered with reminders. I was still only sixteen years old, and at times I found this staggering and unbelievable, because I felt so much older, like a decrepit old man wearing the mask of a fresh-faced baby. Then other times, I felt it the other way around; I felt small and weak and young and in fear of the entire world, the entire future. I felt like I had been robbed of something I could not even explain to myself. There was an undeniable emptiness that filled me when the good times faded out. There was a hole, a space within me, that drugs and drink and music and friends kept at bay most of the time, but it was still there, it was always there, waiting for me to fall back in, and it crept back when I was alone, when the night was over. I shivered, and the only thing I could do was write about it and try to find words for it.

'Aren't you going to let anyone read what you've written?' Lucy would ask me sometimes. 'You know, show it to someone, or try to get it published or something?'

I would slam the book shut and smile at her. 'Not yet. Be like handing over a piece of my soul. And besides, no one would understand what the hell I'm on about.'

One by one, I sensed my friends relaxing around me. They stopped checking over their shoulders quite so much. They stopped peering and squinting into the distance and around corners, on the lookout for trouble. I didn't want to disappoint or scare them, by warning them not to relax too much. Anthony still met Jaime every once and again for a pint at The Ship. They were friends, I guessed.

'Course I see him about,' he told Anthony when questioned about the movements of Howard. 'But he don't know who buys what from me, he just holds the strings, takes his cut. I wouldn't ever wanna' mess with that bastard. I try and keep my distance much as I can.'

Sometimes when the three of us were lazing around in the bed-sit, spaced out on a bit of grass, and sprawled across the two beds that were never packed away, Anthony and Michael would broach the subject with me tentatively. They would suggest that it was over, that Howard had given up and let us go.

'He got what he wanted in the end anyway, didn't he?' Michael would shrug very hopefully. 'Your mum all to himself. You out the way. He should be bloody happy with that!'

I pulled my sleeping bag up to my chin, and laid my hands back down on Kurt, who was curled up on my lap inside it. 'Mmm,' I replied, knowing they wouldn't like to hear what I really thought. 'I don't think that was all he wanted though. I've thought about it a lot.'

'I bet you have,' Anthony nodded, his eyes solemn. 'I don't doubt it. But maybe now it's time to stop, yeah? Start forgetting about it and get on with your own life.'

'He would have done something by now, surely?' Michael asked, looking at his brother for support. Anthony nodded in agreement.

'I think he's a very patient man,' I told them. They looked at each other again.

'You have to stop it,' Anthony warned me. 'Things are good, yeah? We're all working, having fun and sticking together. You've got Lucy, and a cool job, and that little runt of a dog in there. And nothing has happened. He's had plenty of chances Danny. I really think it's all right. I really think it's over.'

I forced a smile, just for him. 'Yeah, you're probably right. Time to forget about it and relax.'

But it was easily said, I reflected later, when my stomach refused to let me sleep at night. I did not really want to listen to the hairs that stood themselves on end all over my body, when I climbed back on that bus at the end of the day. I did not want to believe my eyes when they urged me to stare into every shadow, on the way home from Chaos on a Friday night.

There were times I would be bouncing around on the dance floor, and I would become utterly convinced of a snarling face in among the crowd. It was there, and then it was gone, leaving only a dead weight of fear in my belly and a dryness to my mouth. But I was just drunk. Or I was just tired. I was just imagining things that were not there, and I was having trouble letting it all go. My stomach was so used to being all tied up in knots, that it was a painful, confusing process when it attempted to unwind.

The Boy With The Thorn In His Side-Part 2

I knew that more than anything, my friends wanted me to be happy. They wanted it to be over and so I tried to relax, for them. I felt like I would never be able to repay what I owed them, so I did my best to just be happy and carefree. But every couple of nights I would wake myself up screaming. I would hear their feet hitting the floor in alarm, and I would hear my own screams going on and on, even after they had clutched at my shoulders, and shouted in my face to convince me it was not real. I would flail out wildly with my arms, as I tried to fight Howard off, or my hands would be crawling around my own neck to ease his hands from choking me. My own voice would echo coldly around the bed-sit; 'It's not over! It's not over! It's not!' I knew that, just as much as Howard knew it.

27

February 1996

My notebook was never far from me. I sometimes took it to work stuffed inside the waist of my jeans. It made a nice change from having a blade stuffed down there. Those days were gone, or so we liked to keep telling ourselves. Writing was a therapy, like the music. The two were interwoven at times, one feeding the other. I'd hear a great song and I'd feel the need to jot down the lyrics, or to write about it in some other way. I could never just keep it all inside myself. It was too much, you see. Sometimes I found it hard to listen to what people were saying to me, because there were all these words and all this music inside my head. I wanted to be alone with it, or I wanted them to get it the way that I did. It meant so much, you see, and it made me feel so much, and why didn't other people get it like that?

I'd hear a song, and it would cause this utterly jolting and physical reaction inside of me. It would take me over, and it would take me somewhere else. Set all kinds of things off inside of me. Some songs, they drag you down with them, they take your hand very gently and ease you out of the sunshine. They want you to feel their pain, and they want the shivers to run through you as all your hairs stand on end. And then there are the songs that set your heart on fire, and I mean, they fill you up with indescribably joyous energy, the kind that makes you believe you will live forever. Primal Scream's Movin' On Up, was one of those for me, during that time. When I heard that, or sung along to that at Chaos, my heart was exploding with hope, let me tell you, my body felt like it had wings, my soul knew that nothing bad could ever happen to any of us, ever again. Music can do that you know.

So, you hang onto hope, once you've got it, and you take it forward, you hold it close. You wrap your arms around it and protect it from the dark. Maybe you don't totally believe in it yet, but you are trying to. And people smiled when they saw me. Terry did, he smiled and rolled his eyes and shook his head. I couldn't have asked for a better boss. He even let me take the dog to work with me. We put a little cardboard box down behind the counter and he slept in there,

The Boy With The Thorn In His Side-Part 2

good as gold. I think Kurt single-handedly helped increase Terry's takings, to be honest. The shop was doing better. People came in to see the little dog, and they came in because they knew I could find them what they were after, or failing that, I could turn them onto something they had never heard of before instead.

Lucy came in one Friday after school like she always did. I made her a cup of tea and started filling her arms with records we were taking home to listen to. She hopped up on one of the stools, drank her tea, and listened patiently to me while I wittered on about the day we'd had. As always, she had her overnight bag with her, her clothes and make-up all stored inside for the night at Chaos later. We had this little routine going. We'd catch the bus back to the bed-sit, then take Kurt for another walk around the block. We were like an old married couple then, walking arm in arm, and she would be smiling and telling me how glad she was about the dog.

'You treat him like a baby,' she teased me all the time. 'He's so spoilt!'

That day I was buzzing, full of it. I'd just taken Primal Scream off the player and replaced it with the Oasis Morning Glory record. 'Had the best day ever,' I started telling her right away. She smiled and listened. 'This old fella' calls us up, he's moving into a nursing home and can't take everything with him, so do we want to go through his record collection before the skip arrives to take it all to dump? Terry was out the door in a shot, right Terry?'

Terry barely glanced up from his magazine. 'Always worth a look,' he remarked.

'So anyway,' I went on, while Lucy shifted on her stool and sipped at her tea. 'We jump in his rust bucket and drive over, and it was totally worth it wasn't it Terry? Original Beatles and Stones records Luce, no joking, original Buddy Holly, Elvis,' I started counting them off on my fingers while her smile faded in and out. 'Billie Holiday, Etta James, Aretha Franklin, The Temptations, and...'

'Can't you see she's not interested?' Terry looked up and barked at me. 'You're boring the poor girl and you're boring me too. Nothing there that tickled my fancy much.'

'But they'll sell!' I laughed back at him, while he glowered back into his magazine. 'Sold half of them already!' I looked back at Lucy with a huge grin. 'I've got a list see, this little book? Rang a load of people in there I did.'

'Brilliant,' she nodded. I wondered if there was something up with her then. Her smile didn't seem to want to stay still. It was like it crept off every time I looked away, and then shot back into place when my eyes were back on her. I felt Kurt sniffing at my shoes so stooped down to pick him up.

'Oh, he's so bloody efficient,' Terry complained with a quick smirk. 'Boy wonder, or what? Go on then. Off you go. I'm letting you out early.'

I frowned at him. 'How come?'

''Cause your bloody eager ways are getting on my wick, go on off you go.'

Lucy finished her tea and put the mug down on the counter. She picked her bag up from the floor and slung it over one shoulder. I saw that look on her face again then, sort of pained and dreading. I grabbed my coat from out the back, picked up the records I was borrowing and slung them under one arm and clipped Kurt's lead to his collar.

'All right then,' I nodded at Terry. 'Me and Kurt will be off. We know when we're not wanted. Come on Lucy.'

'Morrissey.' Terry mumbled.

I looked back. 'You what?'

'The dog. His name is Morrissey.'

'No it fucking isn't!'

'It is if he wants to work in my shop. See you later kids.'

'For fucks sake,' I complained and pulled open the door. I slipped my arm through Lucy's once we were out on the pavement. The bus stop was just up and across the road and the bus was due in ten minutes. It was times like that I sometimes still got nervous. I'd try like hell not to scan the area, not to try and pick trouble out where it didn't exist, but it was hard.

We crossed the road and hovered under the shelter. I kept my arm linked through hers and my hands in my pockets. It was freezing stood there.

The Boy With The Thorn In His Side-Part 2

'You all right?' I asked her finally, as it was becoming more and more obvious that she wasn't. She looked at me and blew her breath out slowly. I felt something coming. Something I would probably rather avoid. I almost covered her mouth with my hand but I didn't. She leaned into me and sighed. 'Lucy?'

'No, not all right,' she said, her head on my chest so I couldn't see her face. I hugged her to me and waited. 'Got something to tell you, and it's not good, well, you might think it's good, I don't know yet, so...'

'What the hell?'

'You want me to tell you now or later?'

'Now!'

She pulled away from me. The bus was nowhere in sight. 'Right,' she said. 'Well this morning I walked past your mum's house on the way to school, and she opened the front door and called to me.'

My eyebrows shot up under my hair. 'Really?'

Lucy nodded, her expression grim. 'Yeah, so I went. Danny,' she paused again, looking away briefly, as if searching for the best words to use. Then she looked back at me, and shook her head while she exhaled again. 'I went right up to the door Danny, she was....well, *hurt*.'

I felt cold. I pulled my arm away and stared at her. I don't know why it came as a surprise, what I knew she was about to tell me, but somehow it did. It really did.

'Hurt? What d'you mean?'

'Beaten up. Black eyes. Cut lip. Bad.' She kept her eyes on me, searching for my reaction. I blew my breath out between my clenched teeth then nodded, and bit at my lower lip.

'Right,' I said.

She touched my arm. 'She wants to see you. She begged me to tell you.'

I looked at her sharply. 'Begged you to tell me what? That she's got beaten up or that she wants to see me?'

'That she wants to see you.'

'Right.' I looked over my shoulder. I could see the bus in the distance, making its way slowly up the road from the centre of town. Lucy's hand squeezed my arm so I looked back at her and forced a smile. 'Dunno why I'm surprised,' I shrugged. 'Makes sense he would start on her.'

Lucy sighed, moved closer to me and wrapped both of her hands over one of mine. 'You don't have to do anything,' she told me. 'She's a grown woman. It's up to her what she does. She married him after all!'

'Wonder what she wants...'

'I don't know,' Lucy shook her head. 'She didn't say. She just said she wants you to go see her. She said he is away for a few days.'

I nodded silently, trying to take the information in. She just stared at me, her hands around mine, her eyes wide and desperate. I guessed it couldn't have been much fun for her carrying that information around all day. So, I smiled at her and squeezed her hand in return.

'It's okay,' I told her. 'Don't look so worried Luce. Maybe she just wants to see me.' I shrugged a little. 'Maybe she wants to say sorry for not believing me.'

I watched Lucy gulp and frown. 'You think so?'

'I dunno.'

'Would you really want to hear that though?'

'Not sure,' I admitted. 'I suppose it's been on my mind.'

I could see this came as a surprise to her. Her mouth opened then closed again quickly. She looked as though she was trying hard not to let her disappointment show through.

'Oh,' she said. And then; 'But what if it's a trap? What if he's not really away? What if he comes back suddenly and she doesn't know? I don't think you should go Danny.'

The bus pulled up jerkily beside us and I nodded towards it. 'Let's go home and see what the others think.' She clung to my arm, and we got on the bus, and every time I looked at her after that, I could see the fear etched all over her face. I didn't have the heart to tell her how I really felt. That asking Michael and Anthony's opinions was not going to change my mind, because I had already decided I would go and see my mother.

When we walked into the bed-sit, we found both Michael and Anthony squeezed into the kitchen making cheese on toast. Lucy

The Boy With The Thorn In His Side-Part 2

dumped her bag on the bed and released a sigh. I said nothing. I left it to her to explain things to them. I had the strongest urge just to be alone with my gathering thoughts, so I dropped onto the bed, positioned my pillow behind my head and crossed my ankles. I didn't even look at her. I just immersed myself in silence, until eventually she yanked back the beaded curtain and let rip. I knew what she was doing, and I understood it, of course I did. She wanted them to be as appalled and outraged as she was. She wanted them to think seeing my mum was a terrible, stupid idea, and she wanted them to talk me out of it so that she wouldn't have to. I just stayed on the bed, stroking Kurt on my lap, and listening to them talking about me. Michael didn't say much, but I knew he would think the same as Lucy. He would think I was nuts.

Finally, Anthony pushed back the curtain and strode out of the kitchen, licking butter from the side of his thumb. He shot me one look which told me right away he was on my side. He picked up the phone, while Michael and Lucy looked on warily.

'We can find out if he's really out of town,' he said, and dialled a number. We all watched and waited. 'Hello, is that K's?' he asked, when the phone was picked up. 'Yeah, hi mate, I'm enquiring about work in the area and someone said you guys are hiring. Is Lee Howard there for me to speak to at all?' Anthony turned to look at our expectant faces. Lucy was biting her nails, with her other arm wrapped tightly around her middle. 'Oh, is he out of town? When do you expect him back? Oh okay, that's great, I'll call back in a few days...Thank you. Bye.' Anthony hung up and looked right at me. 'Gone to Essex to see his parents and won't be back until Monday.'

Lucy looked immediately at me. 'I still don't want you to go!' she said, blinking hard as her eyes threatened to fill with tears. 'She can't just click her fingers and have you back in her life Danny! She doesn't deserve you.'

'Too bloody right she doesn't,' Michael grumbled from beside her, his arms crossed rigidly over his chest, his eyes dark and angry.

'It's not safe,' Lucy went on, coming to the bed and standing next to me. 'You don't know he won't come back early and catch you there!'

I reached out and pulled her down onto the bed with me. 'Come with me then.'

'Good idea,' Anthony said with a nod.

'We could all go,' Michael shrugged, but I shook my head at him and looked at Lucy. She moved her head, resting her cheek upon my shoulder.

'Come with me,' I said again. 'Come with me in the morning. I think I need to hear what she has to say.'

I didn't expect any of them to understand. I didn't really understand myself. You'd have thought my first reaction to her request would have been to tell her to fuck off. But I was curious, and my imagination had gone into overdrive. Why did she want to see me while he was away? Did she want my help somehow? Did she want to tell me I was right along, and she was sorry now that she knew?

No one really embraced the night that followed at Chaos. Their hearts were not in it, and neither was my head. I kept catching sight of Michael and Anthony, huddled and talking. Whenever I looked at Lucy, she looked like she was fighting tears. She smiled bravely when I went to her, taking her face in my hands and tipping it up to look at me. She was perched on a stool at the corner table we always nabbed.

'You've got your worried face on,' I said to her, and she laughed at me gently.

'Sorry.'

'You don't have to be sorry. What you thinking?'

'If you want to know the truth, I was just sat here wishing I hadn't passed the message from your mum on to you. How bad is that?' She exhaled slowly and lifted her hands, pressing them on top of mine, on either side of her face. I was swaying slowly to the music. I'd only had one pint of beer and it had gone right to my head. Oasis were playing Champagne Supernova and my head was full of memories from that night, when we had all been together, all hugging and jumping up and down with the crowd. A smile took over my face, and

The Boy With The Thorn In His Side-Part 2

I sang along softly while she started to play with my hair at the back of my neck.

Lucy kissed my cheek and rested her head on my shoulder, and I wrapped my arms firmly around her as she leaned forward on the stool. I could feel the sadness and the fear seeping from her.

'Wish I hadn't told you,' she said again with a heavy sigh. 'Then you wouldn't be going to see her tomorrow.'

'I get why you feel like that,' I told her. 'But you know what? For some reason, it actually makes me feel better that she wants to see me.'

'Does it?' she asked, jerking back to stare at me. 'But why? Why should you feel glad she wants to see you? Is that what you've been hoping for? I didn't know you felt that way.'

'No neither did I, but I dunno...it's hard to explain. I always thought she hated me, you know, even before he came along. It was always a nightmare, me and her. I guess I just want to hear her side of things, maybe.'

Lucy looked outraged all over again and her hands fell into her lap. 'Side of things? How can she have a side of things? She stood back! I mean, how can any mother do that? Just stand back and let...' She sucked in her breath and shook her head. 'I don't understand it. I never will.'

I moved to the side of her and leaned back on the table. My eyes drifted out to the dance floor, where the people seemed to all blend into each other, their bodies heaving from side to side.

'She didn't really know,' I said, staring out at them all. 'I mean, there was one time I tried to tell her and she didn't believe me, but you know, I'd told her so many lies and been in so much trouble before then, that I guess now I can see why she wouldn't believe me...I've been thinking about it a lot. I was a total shit Lucy. I didn't listen to her, I did whatever the hell I wanted. She couldn't cope. So, the thing was, he came in, and she was relieved probably. She thought he was a father figure, you know, strict and that? She was all pleased 'cause you know, I listened to him and stuff. Stayed out of trouble.' I shook a hand at the air dismissively. 'Anyway. Just don't worry, that's all. We'll just show up and see what happens, hear her out, then leave. And if the bastard does show up, so what? What's he gonna do if you and Mum are there? She knows what he's like now Luce, that's the thing, she *knows* now.'

I felt her shudder beside me. Then her arm snaked around my middle and pulled me close. 'You're braver than me,' she said. 'I'll come with you, if you're sure. Whatever you want. I love you, you know?'

I grinned down at her worried little face. 'Love you too.'

The next morning I woke her with a kiss, and watched her flutter out of her dreams and into the cold reality of the freezing bed-sit and the uncertain day that lay ahead. Her eyes clouded over when she remembered what we were going to do, and she gave me a small, brave smile, and I ruffled her hair and made her laugh. I was already dressed, and passed her a cup of tea after she'd pulled one of my hooded sweatshirts over her head. She emerged from the other side of it, hair a mess and yawning.

'Want some toast?' She shook her head.

'When we get back.' She sipped her tea and shivered violently under the blankets, and gazed around the room while I started tying up my boots. Anthony had a shift at the pub and had already left. Michael was snuggled up on the sofa bed, only his shock of black hair showing from under his sleeping bag. Lucy finished her tea, and went to the bathroom to sort out her hair and brush her teeth. I checked my pockets for bus fare, cigarettes and keys. I was so nervous by the time we left that I could barely speak. Lucy slipped her arm through mine and asked me if we could go shopping when we got back. I smiled. Lucy loved the shopping in Belfield Park, and rummaging through the charity shops and market stalls had become a new hobby of hers.

We left Kurt behind and sneaked out before Michael woke up. We climbed on the bus when it came, and huddled together on the back seat, and any conversation we had tried to maintain had all but dried up by then. We just sat and watched the world roll by. We passed the record shop, and the club, and remained on the bus while it weaved its way down the high street, over the two bridges and on towards the estate. We jumped off when it pulled in along Somerley road opposite McDonalds and I reached automatically for her hand. We crossed the road and the silence grew in weight and strength. I realised we would have to walk past the old house and my stomach felt sick and weak. Lucy clung to my hand and we marched on, walking as fast as we could, and I felt as though I was trying to outrun the memories.

I didn't look at the house. I couldn't bear to. I felt like I was three different people rolled into one, and it was making my head spin thinking about it all. There was the old me, the messed up new kid, getting into fights to make myself heard, and there was the me from the dark times I'd had in that house, and I didn't like that boy one little bit. I thought he was weak and cowardly and drenched in shame, and I didn't want him inside me ever again. And then there was the new me, the one people said was wise beyond his years, an old head on young shoulders, they said, quiet, but happy. They were all inside me crashing into each other, and they all had voices demanding to be heard.

By the time we came out onto Cedar View, my guts were a twisted mess. We slowed our pace and Lucy looked at me as we approached the house. 'No offence Luce,' I smiled shakily. 'But it's even flasher than yours!'

Lucy clicked her tongue and rolled her eyes at the manicured rose bushes and perfect, lush green lawn. 'It's all pathetic,' she insisted. I stopped at the gates, which had been left open. There were stone lions roaring on either side of the drive. I shook my head at them and Lucy growled. 'Horrible,' she spat. 'He put them there.'

'What about the rest of it?' I asked, gazing around.

'Your mum does the garden. About the only thing he lets her do by the look of it. They had painters and workmen and everything in and out of here for months, changing it all. Come on,' she said then. 'It's all vulgar. It's all for show.'

'Okay,' I laughed. 'Calm down Luce.'

We walked down the driveway towards the huge front door. I seemed to feel myself shrinking, the closer we got. There was a flurry of movement at one of the windows to the right of the door, which made my stomach leap into my mouth, and Lucy tighten her hand even more on mine. She was practically clinging to me now. The door opened before we could even knock on it. I opened my mouth and gasped. Her face. What had he done to her beautiful face? Tears flowed from her swollen eyes. They filled mine too.

'Danny...' she croaked through her broken lips, 'thank God!'

The Boy With The Thorn In His Side-Part 2

28

  She pulled back the door, and her eyes ran with tears and her broken mouth tried desperately to smile, but that was impossible and all that emerged was a strained grimace. Six months, I thought, as Lucy and I stepped cautiously through the open door, can it really be six months since I left? She closed the heavy door behind us and just stood there staring at me. It was awkward to say the least, so I gazed around at the hall, thinking shit; here I am, in the bastard's new house. I could feel him there and I'm not joking. Everything was bright, white, clean and sparkling, but that didn't diminish the darkness that seeped through everything. It was all how I had expected it to be. Pristine and spotless. The carpet was thick, a creamy shade of lemon, the walls white and the ceiling high. I felt immediately uncomfortable, stifled and uneasy. I stood waiting, not saying anything because I had no idea what to say. My hand remained linked with Lucy's. I wondered if we ought to remove our shoes, or wash our hands or something. My mother clasped her hands together under her chin and looked me up and down. She was sobbing. Just a little bit at first, but they were getting louder and harder, racking her rail thin body, and all she could do was stare at me and look me up and down.

  In the end, it was me who moved towards her. It was a sort of sliding half step, my free arm lifting, as if reaching out. I don't even know why I did it. She went to me, sobbing harder, and throwing her skinny arms up and around my neck. I was taller than her now, I realised, as she cried against my collarbone.

  'You've grown,' she was murmuring. 'Had that growth spurt.' I felt myself stiffen under her touch, and while one hand remained with Lucy's, the other fluttered reluctantly down to the small of her back. She sighed, sniffed, and pulled back, taking my face in her cold shaking hands. 'Oh Danny,' she said, again attempting to smile through her split and swollen lips. 'You're really here...and you're okay, you're okay.' I wasn't sure if she was asking me or telling me, so I nodded and cleared my throat.

  'I'm okay.' She stood back from me then, her shoulders dropping as she exhaled loudly, and I looked her over and raised my eyebrows. 'He did this to you then?'

She nodded miserably and rubbed at her wet eyes with the sleeve of her cardigan. She gestured towards a door behind us.

'Please, go through. I'll put the kettle on.' With that she turned and walked into the kitchen. I got a glimpse of it before following Lucy into the lounge. It looked too bright and sparkly, black and white floor tiles beaming back at me, neat white blinds, and kitchen units so white they hurt my eyes. The lounge was no different. It had Howard's stamp all over it. It was huge, at least three times the size of the room we'd had in the old house. The walls were a dusky green colour, the carpets cream, and arranged around the biggest TV I had ever seen in my life sat three fat, black, leather sofas. I didn't want to sit on any of them, so I hovered around the edges, hands in pockets. Lucy sat in a slow, stiff manner, as if the sofa somehow offended her. She sat on the very edge of it, and her face was set hard, as my mother walked back in and placed a tray of tea and biscuits down on the large, glass coffee table. I looked at Lucy's face and knew exactly how she was feeling. She looked like she didn't want to touch anything in case she caught something unpleasant.

My mother lowered herself onto one of the other sofas and I could tell she was trying not to wince, or gasp or invite attention to her injuries. I scratched the back of my head, walked around the sofa and sat down next to Lucy. The sofa groaned beneath me, making my stomach turn over. I watched my mother restraining her pain and thought God I did that so many times back then. Keeping it all under wraps, under clothes, pretending even to myself that it wasn't there. She opened her mouth to speak and then closed it again. Her hands rested lightly on her tiny knees. She looked shrunken I thought. Like he had sucked the very soul out of her.

'So, when did it start?' I asked her. Lucy's hand landed on my knee and stayed there. My mother looked surprised and her eyes rose reluctantly to meet my stare.

'After we moved in,' she croaked through her battered lips. 'Although, if I'm honest, looking back, the signs were there for some time. Him being controlling and strict, flying off the handle over silly things. I always shrugged it off though, you see. Blamed it on the stress of his job and moving. After a while though, there were no more excuses to be found.' Her eyes travelled back to the carpet and stayed

The Boy With The Thorn In His Side-Part 2

there. 'I should have known better,' she said. 'I should have believed you when you tried to tell me what he was really like.'

'Hmm,' I said. 'So, what do you want?'

She looked taken back. Her eyes blinked rapidly. 'What? I don't want anything...I mean, I...' she lifted her shoulders in a weak shrug and gave up. I felt irritated then, looking at her.

'Why now?' I asked. 'It's been six months. Why now? You know where I work, you could have come there any time to see me.'

She met my stare. 'I thought it was safer for you if I didn't,' she said softly. 'He went very strange Danny, after you left...I thought he'd be pleased really, you know, to have you out of his hair, but he went wild, and it was like all he wanted to do was find you and he wouldn't let it go. He even accused me of helping you and of knowing where you were.' She looked down at her hands, now gripped together tightly on her knees. 'One day he came home and just grabbed me round the throat, for no reason...I mean, I was just stood there mopping the kitchen floor...That was the first time.' Her head dipped lower under the intensity of our eyes. Nobody had touched their tea.

I stared at her for a moment. I half thought about getting up and walking out. But then I realised she was offering me something I had never had before. A chance to speak, an opportunity to tell my side. Years had been filled with silences, dark nights wrapped in private pain, surreal days where I walked stiffly, cloaked in dirty shame, silent. I took a breath and opened my mouth.

'You want to know the first time he hurt me?'

She looked shocked and desperate, and shook her head in misery. 'Second time I met him,' I told her and right away, her head jerked up, her eyes clashing into mine. She frowned heavily, not understanding. I nodded calmly. 'Oh yeah, you remember he came to dinner that time, because John arranged it, because he was leaving and everything?' She nodded, her mouth hanging open, her hand rising to it. 'He stayed in the kitchen to help wash up. He came up to me and told me nothing I could do would scare him off and then he squeezed my neck. Had bruises the next day, but I didn't know what it was. I didn't want to believe what it was.'

Her hand caressed her broken mouth and she released a noisy, juddering moan behind it. 'I didn't know that...oh I didn't know that

247

Danny, is that what he did? All the way back then? ...Oh God...I am *so* sorry.'

'I tried to tell you,' I said to her. 'You and John both thought I was making up lies to split you up from him. Then you let him move in. You hardly knew him.' There was anger in my voice now, even I could hear it.

'I didn't know,' she said again, shaking her head. 'I thought you were being malicious, after the way things went with Frank. Why didn't you come right away and tell me?'

I shrugged. I felt reckless. Part of me was enjoying the haggard and bewildered look upon her face. 'Loads of reasons. I didn't understand it. I wasn't sure what it was, if he meant it, or what. I didn't know if I was imagining it, or making a big deal, and I knew you'd take his side over mine, I just knew you would! Then I was scared as time went on, when he got worse, and I was embarrassed and I didn't want anyone to know, and I bet you get that now, don't you?' I nodded at her swollen face, my eyes narrow. 'Or do you invite the neighbours round to have a look?' She shook her head at me because she had no choice, and because I was right and she knew it. I nodded and went on. 'He turned everything around, I bet you see that now too. It's never his fault, is it? He's always got his reasons, I mean number one being it's for your own good, obviously. Number two being he makes you think life will be worse if you tell. He told me constantly I'd end up in care if I talked. He threatened my friends, he fucked them over, Jesus, you don't even know the half of it Mum, what he did to Anthony?' She shook her head violently and I laughed. 'Well, long story, if you've ever got the time. But he got him sent back down, all because Anthony knew what was going on and stood up for me. So, after that, I stayed away from my own friends, so he'd leave them alone. Just went around on my own. Perfect for him.'

I stood up then, pulling away from Lucy's grasping hand and storming around the back of the sofa away from the both of them. The memories and the escalating anger were too much for me then and I wondered how to go forward, what to say, where it would end. Why was I even there? Talking to her? There was so much she didn't know, so much she had turned away from. I looked up and found her staring at me.

The Boy With The Thorn In His Side-Part 2

'I got arrested once,' I said then, planting my hands on the back of the sofa behind Lucy. 'For fighting down at the beach with some kids from school. You never knew about it, because he kept it from you, because we had a deal. He picked me up from the station because you were at work, and he took me home and taught me a lesson. I had no doubt after that day, Mum. He was fucking insane. '

Mum swallowed more tears and sat up a little straighter. 'What about that time I went away?' she asked. 'When your Gran was ill?'

I laughed and folded my arms. 'Oh, when I had my infamous bike accident?' She nodded stiffly from across the room. 'Well that was probably the first time I actually thought I was gonna' die. I mean, seriously. You had that yet? You been on the floor yet, with him kicking the shit out of you?' I closed my mouth, pressed my lips tightly together and shut my eyes briefly. When I opened them, she was still staring at me and waiting for more, silent tears running rapidly down her sunken cheeks. Tears were threatening, but then so was violence. I looked around at his palace and felt like whipping out my dick and pissing up the walls. 'He used his belt on you yet?' I asked her just for fun, and I watched her mouth gaping again, behind her hands. It was like I was torturing her for the hell of it, but what else did she expect? What did she even fucking want? It was all rising inside of me, and instead of feeling pity or empathy for her and the state she was in, all I could think about was the times I'd been on the floor, just taking it.

'Danny,' she started, barely able to form words behind her sobs. She reached out to me with one hand, but remained seated. 'I didn't know...*please*, I didn't know, I didn't know all that...'

'Does he stand on you?' I asked her. 'He likes doing that. Makes him feel really big, I reckon, keeping you down with his big fuck off boot. You see, that was an interesting time. Jack shows up out of nowhere, and next thing we know Anthony is arrested. Someone got in their house and hid drugs there, so he got busted and sent back to jail. That was your husband Mum, and Jack. They did it to get Anthony out of the way, because he was trying to help me! I thought I was gonna' die up in my room. It went on so long. He phoned the school, told them I'd had an accident. Everyone believed him, everyone except Michael. But I couldn't go near him after that, you know why?' She shook her head, sniffing and whimpering. 'He threatened to do something to him, like he did to Anthony. I believed him Mum. He said he'd kill you too. God, he said that a lot.'

I walked around the sofa, and started rubbing at my head with my hands. It was all getting too much and I could sense Lucy shifting uneasily on the sofa. There was too much. My head was full of it, and I'd tried so hard to crush it all down, to make it fade away. What did the bitch want to do to me? Dragging it all out again, and why? For what?

'So, I didn't tell anyone, 'cause I was scared of what he'd do. I hated myself for what happened to Anthony. So, you don't even know, if he's just started knocking you about, you don't even fucking know what he's capable of.' I dropped my hands and stared at her. 'He's evil Mum. He's *sick*. He's not just some violent thug, he's...I don't even know what he is. He's, he's beyond that, I'm telling you! Why else would I run away and not tell you where I was going?'

She got shakily to her feet and hugged herself with her arms, quivering from head to toe. 'I was blind,' she said, her voice strangled with tears. 'I just saw what I wanted to see. I know that now. You were being good, and he was so firm all the time, and sometimes...I know this sounds terrible, but I just felt relieved, to take a back seat, you know? I was wrong. I was a mess. I should have stood up for you more...That time he hit you, at Christmas?'

'Yeah that was me trying to show you,' I told her through my teeth. 'I tried to provoke him so you'd see the real him. And I told you once, and you accused me of telling lies. You believed him over me. You would have seen it if you'd cared mother. But you never cared about me, you never wanted me, so I suppose it was easy for you really?'

She came towards me then, this awful shivering whining mess of a woman, and I stood my ground and crossed my arms. I glared into that face and I thought of all the times I'd needed her. 'Not true, that's not true,' she was blubbing on. Her hands landed on my arms, gripping and clawing. 'He might have told you that, but it's not true Danny, I couldn't cope with you, I admit that, but I loved you!'

The Boy With The Thorn In His Side-Part 2

'Bullshit,' I laughed at her, tearing my arms from her grip. I looked her up and down in pure disgust, and the anger was winning now, and I knew that somewhere deep and ugly inside of me, I hated her, I really fucking hated her. 'If you'd cared you would have kept an eye on things. You never once asked me if I was happy. Never once asked me what I thought of him. If I'd thought for *one* second that you cared, I would have told you stuff. You'd be in one room, off your head on sleeping pills, and he'd be in my room attacking me! He didn't even care! You let him! That's the truth of it Mum! You *let* him!'

She reached for me again and I moved back. 'I didn't know, I thought he was talking to you, sorting you out...I thought...'

'I know what you fucking thought!' I roared at her then, my breath taking the hair from her face. 'You thought it was great the control he had over me! That's what you thought mother! You thought it was great how well behaved I suddenly was, and hey, what's wrong with the old-fashioned way anyway? Odd clip round the ear, the odd slap. Belt when you really deserve it. Kettle cord once at Jack's place. Probably did me good, eh? That's what he thinks, you know. It's all supposed to make me a *good boy*. Does he say that to you? Does he?' I stepped towards her, leaned down so that my face was close to hers. 'Is he trying to make you into a good girl Mum? Is that it eh? Are you tidy enough for him? Is the house too dirty? Do you look at him the wrong way?' I waved a warning finger right into her face. 'Be careful with that! Don't look at him wrong!'

She looked like she was sagging slowly down to the floor, her mouth hanging open in horror, her eyes a mess. 'I didn't know...' she kept saying it. Over and over again. 'I didn't know he went that far...I didn't know...he was so good at convincing me it was all you, it was all your fault, and all he was trying to do was help you, and have a bond with you.' She sniffed, sucking her snot and tears back up her nose, and she wiped her face and glanced down at the floor. 'He'd even cry sometimes...*cry* because you hated him, because you wouldn't let him be a dad to you. I fell for it...I was such a fool, such an idiot! I didn't know the truth until we moved here. Not really.' She looked up then and her eyes met mine. 'You remember once you said to me, we reap what we sow? Well this is it isn't it. I'm reaping what I sowed. What I caused.'

I snorted and moved back from her again. 'You don't expect me to feel sorry for you do you? 'Cause I don't! He hasn't even got started on you yet! This,' I gestured violently at her battered face. 'This is nothing! Wait until he really gets started!' I wrenched my coat up then, yanking my jumper and t-shirt up, turning just enough so that she could see. I heard her moan. 'Like *that*!' I yelled in triumph. 'Wait 'til you look like that! Then I might feel sorry for you!' I pulled my clothes down and faced her. I was shaking hard. I smiled at her viciously. Was a part of me enjoying this? Seeing her suffer, making her see the truth, finally? I'd waited so long, I thought, I'd waited so long for her to see me.

'I don't want or expect your pity...' she started to say to me.

'Well you never felt sorry for me, did you? Do you know how sick it used to make me, watching you two fawn all over each other? Kissing and cuddling on the sofa? When behind your back he was pure fucking evil? Oh, you thought it was great, didn't you Mum? Danny doing what he was told finally. Danny keeping his room tidy, so he could come and inspect it twice a fucking day! Oh, you *loved* it, don't tell me you didn't! Danny doing what he was told, whoo hoo! Yeah, I did what I was told because I was fucking terrified the whole time! Do you want to hear any more about how it was?' I asked her, bringing my face aggressively close to hers again. ''Cause I can tell you a horror story from beginning to end, if you like!' I pulled away, my face crumpling, pain crashing in, and I wanted to get out of there, I wanted to get far away from her and her beaten face. Lucy shot up from the sofa, came to me and wrapped her arms around me.

'Don't do this to yourself,' she said. 'Let's just go, you've had enough.'

'No, please don't go! Not yet!' My mother spread her legs and held out her hands, as if that would be enough to stop us getting past. Her hands were shaking as she looked at me pleadingly. 'Please don't go yet, I know you're angry, and you have every right to be! You can tell me, tell me anything, please, I need to know, I want to know...'

'Why?' Lucy turned and shot at her. Her voice was different, I thought. She didn't sound like my Lucy at all then. She kept one hand

The Boy With The Thorn In His Side-Part 2

on my arm and faced my mother. 'Why do you want to know? Why now? You have no idea do you?' Her voice was rising, becoming shrill and tight with anger. 'Danny is lucky to be alive! Did you know that? What about the drugs Mrs Howard? What about the big uproar from you and the school over that? You know who gave him the drugs, do you? Your husband and his sick little friend! They were in it together from the start.' Lucy's lips snarled back, and she looked at me, holding my hand, rubbing it with hers. 'Let's go,' she hissed.

'I don't understand,' my mother cried, her hands back over her mouth. 'What are you talking about? Lee doesn't do drugs! He doesn't....' She shook her head behind her hands and I guess the full truth was really hitting her then. You could practically see it, when you looked at her face. She reached out for the sofa, gripped the back of it with one hand. She looked like she was going to be sick, as her eyes moved from Lucy, to me. 'What about Jack?' she whispered. 'Why would he do that? Why would he sell you drugs?'

I had to sit down. My eyes were pissing me off, filling up with fucking tears, pain rushing in from every angle, memories, horrors, chasing away the anger, and I couldn't take it. I sat down and covered my face...don't go there...don't go there, for fucks sake, why did I come?

'They were in it together,' Lucy was saying behind me. 'Your husband brought Jack here on purpose, supplied Danny with drugs, to keep him quiet, to keep him out the way, and while you were swanning around with new haircuts and clothes, your son was practically having a nervous breakdown! And it gets worse...' Lucy came around the sofa, holding her hand out to me. 'We're not staying though, ask your precious husband if you want to know the truth, we're going, come on Danny.'

I didn't take her hand because I couldn't move. I was rigid, frozen, barely there. Tears were sliding slowly down my face behind my hands and I didn't want either of them to see. Lucy tugged my hand away from my face and pulled me until I got up.

'Please don't go,' Mum was sobbing again, still clinging to the sofa as if she was too weak to stand up alone. 'What are you talking about Lucy? Why does it get worse? What do you mean?'

'Ask your husband,' Lucy snarled at her, dragging me towards the door. 'Ask him about Jack's past, ask him why he was thrown out of the police, ask him why he sent him round to Danny on the day he ran away! Ask him why!' She was shouting now, really shouting, and I had never heard her raise her voice before. I shook my head; it was hurting it was hurting everywhere.

'Don't Lucy,' I uttered, glancing at Mum.

'We're not staying here to rake it up any more,' Lucy went on, her arm suddenly tightly around my waist. We were in the hallway and my mother followed us, her face aghast, her hands up under her chin. 'You've no idea how long it's taken Danny to get his life back together again, and I'm not gonna' let you ruin it all!' She was at the door, fumbling with the handle and lock. Her cheeks were bright red, her eyes wide and glazed with fury. I hung back, felt my mother's hand on my shoulder, tentative and light.

'Please come back another day,' she was begging me. 'Please come again, please tell me about Jack, tell me everything, *please*, I need to know, I need to make it up to you somehow, I need to...I am sorry, Danny? Danny?' I turned slowly, and her hand turned with me, moving to settle on my chest, just below my shoulder. Tears made her face look like a blurred reflection. 'I need to get away from him too Danny...He's going to kill me. I know it. I don't how to...I'm not as strong as you are...'

I looked at her, and my jaw tightened. I wondered what to tell her. I wondered if I owed her anything. 'I was lucky I had my friends,' I told her stiffly, my lips barely moving to allow the words to escape. She nodded vigorously. 'They helped me. They saved me. I'd be dead if it wasn't for them, one way or another. That's the truth. They stood by me, they put themselves at risk and everything is good now.' I breathed out slowly, turned and found Lucy's hand again.

'Good,' my mother babbled, smiling through her wet washed face. 'Good, good, I am so glad, I am so relieved. Please say you'll come again? If he's away? Or we could meet? Please say you will...I know I don't deserve it, I know I don't deserve anything from you, but please, we need to talk. There's so much more that needs to be said Danny. *Please*. I don't want to lose you again.'

The Boy With The Thorn In His Side-Part 2

I nodded and sighed. I glanced behind me and saw the hall table, neatly laid out with telephone, notepad, pen and vase of carefully arranged flowers. I went to it wonderingly, picked up a sheet of paper and scribbled on it. I folded it in half, and turned to my mother. She had a hopeful smile pulling up her busted lips. It made her look like she was snarling at me. I pressed the paper into her hand.

'Call that number,' I said to her, before heading out the door with Lucy.

'Thank you,' she gasped after us. 'Thank you!'

Outside, the February sun was a hammer upon my head, and the ice-cold air a slap across my face. I caught my breath, and started walking. Lucy quickened her pace to catch up with me, but suddenly I did not want her anywhere near me.

'What did you write?' she asked me, her breath puffing out in front of her like bursts of steam. 'What number did you give her?'

'999,' I replied, and walked on, head down, shoulders hunched.

29

I guess I retreated a bit after that. I pushed them all aside. I don't really know why, except I suppose I needed time to think. On the way back from Redchurch I shut Lucy out completely, pulling on my headphones and pressing play. I sat slumped against the window, pulling my hand away when she tried to reach for it. Pretty nasty of me, I know, but I couldn't help it. The memories were making me sad and angry, and I was scared I would start shouting at her or something. It just seemed impossible that I would be able to contain that much feeling. I kept my mouth shut and my eyes turned away, simply to avoid hurting her.

She sat there beside me, her hands entwined in her own lap, her teeth chewing at her lips, while I pressed my forehead to the glass of the window and nodded along to The Stone Roses. Never go anywhere without music, I'm telling you. You never know when you are going to need it. I can remember nearly every song from every moment, you know. I can tell you that one was Made of Stone, and the words pounded in my head as I pressed my face to the window and watched the town rolling past the window. I felt like they were asking me; was I all alone? Was I made of stone? And this deep and dark depression seemed to settle over me. I felt like I'd always felt back then. What's the point in anything? Really? There's no God, there's no heaven, there's no afterlife, only this, endless turning shit and stress, so what's the point?

Back at the bed-sit, I avoided their eyes and their questions, only shaking my head to indicate that I was not in the mood for talking. I changed the tape in my Walkman, clipped the lead onto Kurt and went back out again on my own to walk him. I left them behind; their puzzled faces and their weighted silence following me out the door. I walked Kurt down to the beach and let him off. It was freezing cold, the sea was rough and grey and violently throwing murky looking froth up onto the sand. Kurt ran about barking at seagulls. I lit a cigarette and sat on the steps to the promenade.

I didn't think about anything for a while. Just sat and watched Kurt chasing the birds, and listened to the music. That's the nice thing about having music constantly with you, you see, you can immerse

The Boy With The Thorn In His Side-Part 2

yourself in it, in the melody and in the lyrics, you can hold your own shit at bay for a while. I'd picked Radiohead, completely at random. The sea crashed silently, Kurt's barking was muted, and my head was full of tortured words about everything being broken...

I sat there and instead of thinking about my mother, and what to do about it all, I thought about calling Jaime up, buying some speed or some pills or some coke from him and getting high, getting really fucking high. I remembered how it used to feel; like I was untouchable, like nothing could get through. I remembered how I used to laugh and smile at nothing.

Do you want to know the other thing I was thinking? I was thinking about pain, and what it was and what it amounted to, and how easy it was to withstand if you knew how. I was wishing I still had my knife on me, but I didn't, I hadn't carried one about for months now. I pulled up my sleeve and traced a finger down the jagged scar I'd given myself that day on the bench at the park. I touched it, stroked it, and couldn't deny the incredible urge I had to get something sharp and just tear into myself with it. I don't know why. I'm not a shrink. I just felt the urge. I wanted to see blood and I wanted to feel that little hiss of pain that reminds you that you are still alive. I wanted to scratch at my own skin until it all fell away. I hated it. I hated the feel of it, weighing me down, coated in the shame of the past...how to get rid of it? How to get free?

I rested my elbow on my knee, dropped my head into my hand and tightened my fingers in my hair. I closed my eyes. I breathed in and out and it didn't seem enough. It didn't seem real. Tears were stinging under my eyelids, so I wouldn't open my eyes for a while, refusing to let the bastards out, the weak shitty little bastards. I kept them in, I squeezed them backwards, I shook with it all inside of me. Finally, I had to breathe. I opened my mouth up wide and sucked in salty sea air, and opened my eyes and the tears dried on them, and I stared out at the sea, at everything.

Weeks passed, and my friends watched me like a hawk. Lucy was more attentive than usual, walking on eggshells around me, the rigid smile she offered doing fuck all to soften the fear in her eyes. I was feeling suffocated. If they weren't offering to come with me every time I left the bed-sit, then I'd find them whispering in corners, or asking me if I was all right the whole time. I knew I was lucky to have people that cared, but I was biting my tongue the whole time for fear of snapping at them. I knew they meant well, but I didn't want to be that person anymore, that scared kid they all felt sorry for. I didn't want to be watched over or seen as a victim. I decided it was time that I stood tall and took matters into my own hands. It was time I had some control for once. It was time I addressed the past, so that I could move on into the future and leave it all behind.

I showed them my bravest face, whether they bought it or not. I got drunker than usual when we went to Chaos, just to let rip, just to not give a shit, and it worked. I told Lucy to stop worrying, that everything was fine, but she didn't believe me. I could see it all over her face.

'You're thinking of going back to see her again,' Michael said to me when we were alone in the bed-sit one evening sharing a bottle of cheap wine. Anthony was on a late shift at The Ship, so we had the place to ourselves. I frowned at him, wondering how long he had been thinking about asking me that question. I took a sip from the wine bottle and held it out to him. He took it from me, and I stuffed my arms back under my sleeping bag where I had Kurt all curled up asleep on my lap. It didn't matter what we did, the bed-sit was always freezing cold, winter or summer. Anthony had bought two electric heaters, pinned thick blankets up over the windows and stuffed towels under the doors, but it made no difference. You could always see your breath when you spoke. You had to wear three pairs of socks and we seemed to be permanently wrapped up in duvets or sleeping bags.

'You mean my mum?' I asked him patiently, and he nodded, guzzling from the bottle, his dark eyes watching me carefully. I rolled my eyes at him, shook my head and looked back at the TV. TFI Friday was on, one of our favourite new shows. I didn't want to have the conversation I could sense him gearing towards.

'It's just Lucy thinks you are,' Michael went on, when a few minutes had passed. 'Because,' he went on when I didn't answer. 'You keep changing the subject whenever anyone brings it up, and you're really quiet about it...not good quiet...She's really worried about you mate.'

The Boy With The Thorn In His Side-Part 2

He passed the bottle back and I eased one arm up from the sleeping bag to take it. I sighed and looked at him. 'I knew it. She put you up to this.'

'You can't blame her mate. You've been weird since you saw your mum. Might help if you told us about it, you know.'

'Nothing to tell,' I shook my head. 'Nothing that Lucy hasn't already told you.'

'But not what happened Danny, I mean how you *felt*, how you are now. Whether or not you're thinking of going back?'

I drank the wine, staring back at the TV. I felt dozy and sleepy. I wondered why everything always had to be so hard. I swallowed, wiped my mouth and passed it back.

'Let me ask you a question Mike,' I said to him. He nodded at me, waiting. 'What do you think about your own mum these days? I mean, she wasn't exactly mother of the year either, was she? Do you know where she is? Would you go and see her if she wanted you to?'

Michael smiled at me wearily. 'We've got her address,' he replied with a casual shrug. 'My Aunt sent it. Apparently, she's getting help for her drink problem. So fucking what? You think I care?'

'You wouldn't go and see her then?'

He shrugged again. 'Don't think so. No reason to. She left, didn't she? Her choice. I'm not chasing after her. If she wanted to see me, then fine, she can come here, see how it goes. I'm not running after her, not ever.' He passed the bottle back to me.

'What about your dad?' I asked. 'Do you ever think about him?'

'Nope,' he said, shaking his head quickly. 'Not once. Wouldn't waste my time mate. They screwed up, see? They don't get another chance.'

I looked back at the TV, drank some more wine. Michael lit up a cigarette beside me and tucked his legs up under his chin. We were quiet again for a while, just watching and chuckling at the antics on TFI Friday. During the ad break, we finished the wine and I lit up my own cigarette.

'Do you ever think about it though?' I asked Michael. 'I mean, *why* they screwed up so bad, or if they care about it now, if they regret it?'

Michael turned his incredulous eyes upon me. He looked about to ready to burst with indignation and contempt for my musings. 'Why would I waste my time mate? The way I see it, it's simple, right? They never wanted kids, 'cause they were both massive boozers, got pregnant twice by accident, had me and Anthony and then legged it the first chance they got. What more is there to understand?'

'But would you talk to them, if you could?' I persisted. 'If you got the chance? If either of them turned up here, knocking on the door? You'd have questions for them, wouldn't you? You'd want to try to understand it?'

He sighed. 'Look Danny, I get it, this is obviously how you're feeling since you saw your mum. I get it, you want to go and see her again, I don't like it, but I get it.'

'Do you?'

'Yeah,' he said. 'You must want to make her feel bad yeah? Rub her nose in it a bit, make her feel bad, 'cause you got away from it all, and now she's getting it, which is funny if you think about it, considering she didn't believe you.'

I frowned at him and shifted under my sleeping bag. 'That's not really it Mike. I mean, I do sort of want to tell her the stuff she doesn't know, to get it off my chest or whatever. But I don't think I want to make her feel any worse than she does.'

'Oh, you think she feels bad?' He shook his head and laughed. 'You think she feels guilty about what happened to you?' I shrugged at him. 'Yeah, right, well I don't. I think she feels scared and wants your help. And I think if you go back there, you're asking for serious trouble. Think about it. That bastard has left you alone for ages. You really want to give him a reason to start it all up again?'

'I know that,' I told him, dragging the ashtray across the bed to tap my cigarette against. 'But it didn't make me feel good Mike, seeing her all beaten up like that.'

'Yeah, she probably wants you back again so he can go back to hurting you and not her!' Michael was staring at me angrily. He tapped his cigarette and wiped at his mouth hard. 'For Christ's sake Danny. Why'd you write the 999 down for her then? That must have made her feel like shit, and rightly so! Why should you help her?'

The Boy With The Thorn In His Side-Part 2

'I regret that now,' I looked him in the eye and told him. 'I've felt bad about it ever since.'

'Oh, shittinghell Danny,' Michael sighed miserably and shook his face into both of his hands, before dropping them heavily and looking at me in pity. 'Mate. Please, *please* do not feel sorry for that woman! She's a grown woman mate! She can leave any time she wants, she can call the cops, tell the neighbours, get a divorce! What's stopping her? *You* were a kid, and you shouldn't forget that Danny. Why the hell do you feel bad?' He glared at me, expecting an answer that I just didn't have. 'What have you got to feel bad about? So, you were a pain in the arse as a kid? So fucking what? You should have been able to tell her the first time he did anything, and she should have believed you and that should have been the end of it! He should have been out! You know that don't you? You know she let you down? What about Freeman and all that shit?'

I got off the bed. Pushed my sleeping bag down in one quick motion, tipping unsuspecting Kurt out onto the floor. I ran my fingers through my hair, back and forth, stretching and yawning as I stepped out from the bag. 'Don't,' I told him, before walking into the kitchen to put the kettle on.

'Sorry,' he called out after me. 'But you *have* to remember all that shit Danny, so you don't make the mistake of going back to her! I don't wanna' remind you of all that shit, but you have to remember, you have to ask, where was she eh? Where was she the day you broke down on the beach? Where was she the day you had your famous bike crash? All the rest of it? Eh?'

I turned the kettle on and reappeared in the doorway. It was time for the conversation to end. And to do that I knew I would have to give in to him. 'All right,' I said. 'You're right. I'll leave it.'

He turned around on the bed to face me properly. I thought how much like Anthony he looked these days. If he grew much taller they would look like twins.

'Look,' he said to me. 'You don't owe her anything. She's done sod all for you. She let that bastard move in when she knew nothing about him, she didn't care if you liked him or not, she didn't believe you, she turned a blind eye and she's still fucking with him! And now he's beating her up, she wants to see you? You went and saw her, and you told her to call the cops. What else can you do? Nothing mate, nothing. Because if you go back there, if you try and help her or anything, that crazy bastard is gonna' catch wind of it and then we're right back to square one, aren't we? You don't want him back in your life, do you Danny?'

I looked at him and shook my head. My mouth felt dry, and my skin was crawling with goosebumps. 'Okay,' I told him, and in that moment, I meant it. 'Okay. You're right. I know it. Sorry.'

Michael laughed a little nervously. He got up to turn the channel over. 'Well hallelujah! Thank God!'

I made the tea and brought it in. We wrapped our hands around the warm mugs, with our sleeping bags pulled right up to our chins.

'This much coldness is insane,' he remarked, puffing his breath into the air to demonstrate. 'It would drive anyone mental. I can't cope with it much longer, I'm telling you. I keep expecting to wake up and find us all frozen stiff!'

'We should complain again.'

'Anthony has, millions of times! They don't give a shit, but hey, you know what?' he looked at me with a sparkle in his eye. 'Anthony reckons another month or so and we could afford another place, a bigger, better place. Like a flat, with bedrooms and heating!'

I grinned back at him. 'God, that would be amazing Mike.'

'I know. Everything will be amazing, just so long as you stay away from the past, yeah?'

I smiled, and nodded and looked back at the TV. I knew that would be enough to satisfy him, but inside my own head, I knew it was never going to be as simple as that.

So, in my head, I devised a plan. I didn't mean to. I want you to know that. It just kept happening. It got into my brain and refused to be kicked out. It formed slowly over several sleepless nights. I would lay awake, remembering how those cold fingers of fear had once lived inside my belly, scrabbling around in there at night. I wondered if it was the same for her. I imagined how she felt, hearing her husband return from work at night. I wondered how quickly he started laying into her, what little things he used as reasons and

The Boy With The Thorn In His Side-Part 2

justifications for hurting her. I wondered if there were house inspections, and interrogations about her whereabouts. She had no friends, I knew that. No one to turn to. I'd lie awake, knowing exactly how she felt if she broke a cup, or left a smear on the window when cleaning it. I knew that she probably found herself living with a constant gnawing terror in her gut that warded off sleep, and peace and sanity. I lay awake, night after night, denying to myself what I knew deep down inside; that I had to see her again. Maybe just once. I had to see her again and get some answers.

I knew what my friends would say, so I did not tell them. I asked Terry if I could work late one night.

'You don't have to pay me,' I was quick to point out when he looked ready to argue. 'I've got this list of people I've got to call about records they wanted. I'm too busy to do it in the day.'

'Well it's up to you then,' Terry told me with a shrug. 'I'll be upstairs getting my lips around a frozen meal for one. Let me know if you have any trouble closing up.'

I had no trouble closing up. I ran up the stairs and slid the keys under the door for him. 'Cheers!' I heard him call out, as I dashed back down the stairs. I grabbed my coat from the hook, pushed my arms through it, clipped Kurt's lead on and went out the back way, taking care to properly slam the heavy door behind me. It was dark. I paused to button my coat up to my chin, and pull my scarf out from my pocket to wrap around my neck and over my mouth. I put my hood up, shoved my hands into my pockets and set off down the alley as if I owned it, with Kurt yawning and trotting alongside me.

I tried to ignore the violent lurching of my heart, which felt like it had been asleep for some time, only to be rudely awakened by the memory of fear. It was remembering now all right, as I walked with my shoulders hunched against the cold, towards the back of Howard's club. They would just be starting to open up, I thought, and sure enough, there was Howard's flashy silver Merc, parked out the back. I breathed in and then out, looked straight ahead and kept walking. I walked down to the end of the alley and then turned right and came out onto the high street. I walked fast, because it was cold and I wanted to warm up my bones, and I walked fast because I wanted to outrun my fears. My mind was fighting a battle with my body the entire way there. My body was playing the old game, screaming at me to stop, to turn around and run, while my mind attempted to argue calmly back, and I took deep breaths and I walked on.

I listened to Oasis as I walked; they were telling me not to stand aside, not to be denied...It helped. I'm telling you. When I reached the house, I stopped on the driveway and pulled my headphones down. The security light flicked on, drenching the drive in cold yellow light. Immediately I saw a movement in the kitchen and as I approached the front door, it opened. She was surprised to see me. Tears filled her eyes again. Her face looked much better, not so swollen, and the bruises had faded. She looked like she was going to have a scar on her lip though. I slipped past her and into the hallway with Kurt, and began to unbutton my coat. She was wide eyed and nervous, but smiling.

'He's at work,' she told me, her voice coming out croaky, little more than a whisper. She closed the door and gazed down at the dog. 'So, who is this then?'

'This is Kurt,' I told her. 'And I know Lee is at work, because I checked.'

'What are you doing here?' she asked me, stepping forward and sort of reaching for me with her arms, before thinking better of it and wrapping them around herself. I shook a hand through my hair, flattened by my hood.

'Came to see if you called that number yet,' I said. She opened her mouth and then closed it again, her shame turning her cheeks pink.

She shook her head at me. 'I know I should...'

'Easier said than done?' I asked, a smile tugging at my lips.

She smiled back. 'I need to work out what to do. I'm not as strong as you Danny.'

'Plenty of times I should have called that number, but didn't,' I told her and shrugged. 'So are you gonna' make me a cup of tea or what? It's freezing out there.'

She turned into the kitchen. I unclipped Kurt, and he scampered around the hallway with his nose down, before hurrying quickly after me and sitting down on my feet. I didn't blame him. I felt the same. Everything about the house made me feel small. The kitchen was immense. The shininess made my eyes ache. At the far end were French doors that led out onto a patio. Two cream sofas were positioned there with a view of the garden. The ceiling was high, as were the cupboards. I could imagine my mother stretching up on tiptoes to try to reach them. The interior doors were huge, making me feel like a child. It was like the house had been designed for giants. Or monsters. I felt an overwhelming sense of relief that I had got away before they moved. I didn't fit in a house like that.

My mother looked tiny, I thought, as I watched her move jerkily around the room, making the tea. She was wearing a long blue top and tight jeans. She had lost weight where they had been none to lose. Her golden waves were twisted and pinned up at the back of her head. I leant back against the marble worktop and felt my mouth growing drier. My stomach was now in knots. I kept expecting Howard to walk back in at any moment.

'Can't say I like your house much,' I remarked to break the silence. She crossed her arms and waited for the kettle to boil. She offered me a wry and knowing look.

'Well not exactly your taste, is it?' she grinned, nodding her head at my scruffy attire and nearly shoulder length hair. 'I've missed you, you know,' she said. 'I was shocked when you ran away that day. Really shocked. I was that naïve; I really thought things would be better in this house, when we all moved into it together. Then I was sort of relieved, in a weird way. I don't know, it was like I always had this awful tension inside of me, and whenever I looked into your face, I would see it staring right back at me.'

'Yeah? What was it? The truth?'

'It was after my mum died,' she went on, gazing at the kettle as the steam began to pummel out of the spout. 'I realised what an awful relationship I'd always had with her and that I was doing the exact same thing with you. I started to see things about Lee, after she died, things I'd either not noticed before or made excuses for. I started to feel uneasy, but at the same time, I so wanted things to work out. Didn't want to be on my own again, I suppose.' She shrugged her small shoulders and turned to pour the water from the kettle. 'So, I was relieved for a while when you went, for you and for me. What I couldn't understand was Lee's reaction.' She was frowning as she set the kettle back down and picked up a teaspoon to swirl the teabags in their mugs.

'He hates to lose,' I said, my eyes shooting back to the front door. 'It would have been okay if he'd thrown me out, if it had been on his terms, not mine.'

'Maybe you're right,' she sighed, picking up one of the chrome canisters that lined the worktop like soldiers. 'Are you still one sugar?' I nodded and watched her spoon it in. 'He kept going on about it, especially the first few weeks. Storming around the house, furious all the time, accusing me of helping you go. He even accused me of not caring about you like he did! Said you were holed up with druggies and criminals. I couldn't understand why he cared so much, I mean, he was horrible to you most the time you were here. Why would he want you back? I didn't get it.'

'Control,' I said flatly, taking the tea when she handed it to me. 'There's probably a name for what he's got. He has to be completely in control of everything. He has to own you. That, and he's addicted to violence. Which explains why he attacked my friend Jake for no reason because he couldn't find me.'

Mum turned and rested her back beside mine. She wrapped one thin arm around her body and held her tea up to her lips. 'I think you're right,' she murmured. 'The first few times I made excuses...I was probably in shock. I couldn't think straight. I tried to understand why he did it, but all along I knew why really. Because he wasn't the man I thought he was. He was someone else entirely. And it all came out. And then it got worse.' She sipped her tea as her eyes filled up with tears. 'I'm terrified of him now,' she said softly. 'I don't know what to do.'

'He's pretty good at deceiving people,' I said to her. 'He's king of the castle and that's what he thrives on. Yeah, he fooled you, but not just you. He fooled the cops, the school, John. He took advantage of what he walked into, you know.'

'I do know,' she nodded firmly. 'Me and you at each other's throats, because you didn't like my boyfriends.' She laughed a little and pushed a strand of golden hair back behind one ear. 'Well you were right, weren't you? They were all bastards or idiots one way or

The Boy With The Thorn In His Side-Part 2

another. Jesus Christ, I should have listened to you. I should have known you were only trying to protect us all. I really don't deserve you, you know, not then, and certainly not now.'

'I was a little shit though,' I reminded her with a grin. 'I wasn't like John.'

'God no,' she laughed. 'You weren't, and I bet I bloody told you it a million times a day! But I didn't love you any less, you know that, right?' She turned her body to face me. 'You were hard work, oh yes, from day one, but that just scared me you know, as you got older. You were becoming more and more like me.'

'Really?'

She looked me right in the eye. 'Yep. I was just like you, with my mother. Didn't think about it until she'd died. But I was always arguing her, challenging her, fighting her. Now if you ever have kids, just don't make the same mistakes hey?'

She winked and smiled at me, but I felt unable to return it. I felt terribly worn down then, as if just being in his house was draining the life from me. 'I am never having kids,' I told her. 'Never. No way.'

'Well of course you'd say that at sixteen years old.'

'No, I mean it, I really do. No way I'm risking passing on that mother-fucker's parenting skills.'

She just stared at me in silence. I sighed and looked down at Kurt sat on my feet, and wondered what the hell I was doing there. I checked the door again, and I hated the feeling that was rising inside my chest, that old fluttery feeling of panic. I rubbed at my eyes with my hand.

'I don't even know why I came...'

'I don't deserve you to be here, I know that...'

'No one knows I'm here. Not even Lucy. They all think I'm nuts. They think I'll get all caught up in it again.' I shrugged and put down my cup. 'So, are you going to leave him or what? 'Cause I think that's the only way I can keep coming to see you. If you're not with him.' I found it hard to look at her then. Inside was this awful heaviness pulling me down, grabbing at my heart and squeezing all the joy out of it. Michael had been right, I thought, I should stay away from the past. She was thinking about it, holding her cup in both hands

267

under her chin, as he eyes scanned the room nervously and her teeth chewed at her lip.

'There's a part of me that still loves him,' she replied so softly I almost missed it. I felt like punching myself in the head when I realised what she had said. I pushed one hand through my hair and held onto my head, while my heart was yanked down to the floor.

'Don't say that,' I begged, turning away from her. 'I come all the way here, to help you and you go and say that! You can't say that Mum, if you knew him like I do, you wouldn't be able to say that!'

'A *part* of me, I said, a tiny part of me. There are obviously sides to my relationship with him that are different to yours.'

I just stared at her, enraged, unable to believe what I was hearing. 'What does that mean?'

'It means it's complicated, that's what it means. It's not as simple for me to just leave, Danny. I'm not young. I have no friends round here thanks to him, and the house is in his name, and I have no job!' She finished her tea, wiped her mouth with the back of one hand and carried the cup over to the sink. I felt the strongest urge to just laugh at her.

'You don't need money. You just go. You just leave. Go to John, or back to Southampton. Call the police. Get him arrested. There are plenty of choices Mum. Or you can carry on like you are, a prisoner living with a psychopath, and this will be the last time you ever see me.'

'I do want to leave him Danny, for goodness sake, I do!' She whirled around, tea towel clutched in one hand. 'I just need to work out what to do, financially and everything else. I know I can't go on like this, I know that, I know I can't...' She made a noise like a sob and covered her face with her hands. 'He'll kill me if this carries on...I know it.'

'He's dangerous,' I said, my eyes shooting back to the door again. She lowered her hands and traipsed slowly back towards me. 'I'm serious. If he's only just started hitting you, you've got no idea how bad it will get. He enjoys it Mum, haven't you noticed that yet? He gets a kick out of it, I swear to God, it's like a drug, it calms him down...' I had to break off, move back from her, my eyes held prisoner by the door. The memories were back again, dark images

The Boy With The Thorn In His Side-Part 2

crashing through my mind, trying to force their way through before I could push them back where I kept them.

She folded her arms and her eyes searched my face. 'That's why you came back today? To convince me to leave him?'

I sighed, my shoulders dropping under my heavy coat. 'I dunno. Don't know why I'm here, or what good it will do. Maybe I'm an idiot, hey? I ought to stay away. Let you get on with it.' I thought suddenly of Lucy, up in her room doing her homework, and a sharp pain pulled at me and made me want to run towards her. 'No one thinks I should be here.'

'Then why are you here?'

'I don't know,' I repeated again. But I did know. I knew there was still this little part of me that felt like a kid who just wanted to make his mother listen to him for once. 'Maybe I needed to hear something from you,' I exhaled loudly and glanced again at the front door. 'I don't know.'

She stepped towards me, her face so wrecked with emotion that I could hardly bear to look at her. She was slowly reaching out for me and I was torn in half, caught between wanting desperately to fall into her arms and running for the door and never returning.

'That I'm sorry?' she asked me. 'That I was a crap mother from start to finish, that I let you down so badly, that I will never forgive myself? I should have known better Danny.' She stopped right in front of me, and her hands rose hesitantly and jerkily up to my face. I froze, dreading her touch as much as I craved it. Then I watched her hands curl into fists and draw back under her own chin. 'I thought it was drugs,' she whispered, her eyes brimming with tears. 'And God, how much I want to ask Lee about what Lucy said, about the drugs, because I still don't understand Danny, I don't understand any of it. Was that true? Was it him and Jack all the time?' I nodded at her and her eyes fell shut, squeezing our fresh water. '*Bastards*. I can't say anything, I can't let him know I've seen you...'

I pushed my hands into my pockets and tried to swallow the lump that was forming in my throat. 'No,' I said. 'Don't let him know, don't say anything to him, whatever you do.' She moved forward suddenly then, catching me off guard and her arms were around me before I could react, or pull away. I stiffened against her and she just

269

held on. She buried her face in my clothes and the sobs shook both our bodies.

'I'm sorry, Danny,' she was mumbling into my chest. 'I'm so sorry....so sorry....'

'It's all right,' I told the top of her head. 'I'm okay, you know. I'm okay.'

'I *will* leave him,' she said, wiping her eyes on her sleeves and pulling back to look at me. 'There has to be a way. I'm going to speak to John. What do you think?'

I managed a tight smile. 'Think that's the best thing I've ever heard.'

She nodded firmly. 'The least I can do is get that man out of my life and then I can start to try to make it up to you.' She planted her hands on her hips and shook her hair out of her eyes, and I thought she looked stronger like that, almost like the old her. 'I've got to get myself out of this God awful mess.' She eyed the kettle and then looked back at me. 'How long can you stay?'

I shrugged. 'Another hour maybe. As long as it's safe.'

'We can see the road from here,' she said, nodding at the window. 'And the light goes on when a car pulls in the drive. If he does come back, you'll have plenty of time to run out the back way.'

I nodded. 'Okay then.'

I ended up staying another hour. I breathed in and out, slowly and methodically the entire time, nurturing a thin restraint on my pounding heart. Never again, I kept telling myself, my eyes narrowed as they moved constantly between the door and the window, never again will I get stomped on by that evil bastard...and if Mum leaves him...Relax, I told myself. My mind whirled with hope and fear. My mother chattered on. I took my turn when I was supposed to. I told her about the bed-sit, and my job, and my writing, and my dog. She sat up on a high kitchen stool, her hand wrapped around her cup, and her eyes moist as she listened to me talk about my life.

'You always were a strange kid,' she grinned at me, and I supposed I was meant to take that as a compliment.

'I'll write down my address,' I said to her, before I left. 'So you can pass it on to John.' She passed me a piece of notepaper and I scrawled the address on it and passed it back.

The Boy With The Thorn In His Side-Part 2

30

April 1996

    I'd felt myself teetering close to the edge of sanity many times since he left, but I'd pulled myself back. I'd held on. I forced myself to fall back on the things I knew and trusted; patience and composure. I had my eyes wide open. I suppose that was one good thing to have come out of it all. I knew I was surrounded by jealous back-stabbers who wanted to see me fail. They were everywhere, waiting to see if my empire was about to implode. Fuck you, I wanted to say to them, fuck you all. That greasy whale still gloating in his cesspit of a record shop. Those sneering, long haired kids still sneaking around town when they thought I wouldn't notice, thinking they had won. I allowed these things to grow and swell and burn inside of me.

    I went to work and I worked hard. The club was a ridiculous success. I had more money than I knew what to do with. I drank a little more than I used to and then I went home. Each day I woke up and wondered whether today would be the day I got my revenge. I thought about it constantly. Did I want revenge, and if so, what? I had to be careful. I sometimes felt like I was utterly detached and removed from the rest of society. I was lost at times, without Jack. We'd been the same, him and me. We saw what had to be done and we got on with it, no time for tears, no cause for regrets, or worries. I missed the understanding that had existed for so long between us; that we were above the rest of them, that whatever we wanted was ours for the taking. We'd had some good times, you know, me and Jack. I didn't have anyone I trusted anymore, and I missed just sharing a drink with him. I sometimes found myself gazing around, wondering if I ought to try to replace him, narrowing my eyes in search of another right-hand man. But there was no one. That Lawler kid was nothing but a waste of space junkie, no good to anyone. Jumped out of his skin if you so much as spoke to him. I didn't trust him. I watched his movements like a hawk.

    There were a few other guys in the ranks. Nick was one. He'd been a sort of bodyguard for a few years now. Personal assistant you might call him. He was reliable and as hard as nails. Never flinched

The Boy With The Thorn In His Side-Part 2

when I gave him orders, no matter how grim. But he wasn't Jack. He wasn't Danny either.

For months I'd trawled the streets after dark in my car. Part of me was looking for him, part of me was desperate to catch sight of him walking alone, and part of me was just killing time, just searching for ways to soothe my rage. In the end, I'd resorted to sorting Kay out when she needed it, and it was enough, almost. I'd let things drift so long with her and she'd been taking the piss for months. I knew there was more to his disappearance than she was letting on. I knew she'd been in on it somehow, she must have been. She never once sat and shed a tear for him, you know? That always struck me as very odd, for one thing. It was like she already knew he was safe and she didn't need to worry.

So, I'd known, I had always known she was involved. The night I returned home from work and found her curled up asleep on the sofa with a piece of paper clutched inside her palm, was the night I had my suspicions confirmed. It was back in February, and I had driven home from the club in the early hours of the morning, with a can of Carlsberg wedged between my thighs. My car prowled slowly through the back streets of town, my eyes as always scanning the streets and the alley ways, peering into crowds and clusters of youths, trying to pick him out.

When I arrived home, I'd reached for my Jack Daniels and a glass. Right away, I'd noticed the state of the kitchen. Two mugs and a plate turned upside down on the drainer. Why the fuck couldn't she follow the job through? Dry them, and put them back in the cupboards? I put my whisky down and did it myself, snatching a clean tea towel from the hook and rubbing aggressively at each mug, and the plate, before putting them where they were supposed to be. I wondered why there were two mugs. She didn't normally have visitors. I poured myself a whisky and downed it. I would have to speak to her again about the state of the house. I mean, it was a joke. What the fuck did she do all day anyway? Lounged around in her bloody dressing gown watching crappy American chat shows, no doubt. I didn't make her go out to work, did I? All I asked for in return was a nice clean house to return to. She should have known how I liked things by now. For fucks sake, even the fucking boy had done a better job than her. I peered around at the rest of the kitchen, feeling with my socks for any dirt or dust on the floor. I could feel something that felt like biscuit crumbs, and my body grew rigid with displeasure.

I stalked through to the lounge to discover the TV still on, flickering in the darkened room. 'Bloody woman,' I muttered, storming over and switching it off. I turned around, deciding to settle on the sofa to sink a few whiskys, and that's when I saw her there. She was fast asleep. Curled up sideways and covered in her silly pink fluffy throw. The phone was on the coffee table next to her and there was another plate down on the floor. For fucks sake. I walked over to her. Considered giving her a good slap to wake her up and send her to bed. It was then that I saw the curl of paper sticking out the end of her tightened fist. I stopped and mulled it over. I crouched slowly down next to her sleeping face, cocking my head over to one side and listening to her breathe. I wondered how far under she was. I put out my hand, closed my thumb and forefinger around the edge of the paper, and tugged. It slipped from her grasp easily and she did not stir. I stood up and moved back, grimacing as I uncurled it in my own hand. It was an address. An address in Belfield Park, written in that sneaky little shit's handwriting. I folded my hand over it and glared back down at her, considering my options as the heat flooded me violently.

I turned in a slow circle, letting it sink through me. Then I stopped, and stared back at her, shaking my head slowly from side to side. I curled a fist and considered smashing it quickly into her pretty little nose. That would wake her up. Then I would grab her by the hair and shove the piece of paper into her gaping mouth. I'd make her fucking eat it. I shook the fist at her as she slept on.

'You were meant to tell me when he got in touch,' I snarled at her in the darkness. I opened my hand and watched the paper float back down to land on her covered lap. 'You lying, sneaking, treacherous little *bitch*...' I narrowed my eyes. A satisfying realisation washed over me and I felt calm again. I nodded at her. 'Oh, you want your precious boy back now do you? Is that it? You miss him, do you? Well sweetie, you only had to say. If you want him back that much, I'll get him for you.' With a smile upon my lips, I left her alone and walked out.

The Boy With The Thorn In His Side-Part 2

    The next night I left the manager in charge of the club and drove over to Belfield Park. It was a stinking, filthy, rotting corpse of a town. It reeked of fish and chips, seagull shit and decaying seaweed. All the homeless people gravitated there. You saw them shuffling about everywhere. Sleeping on benches and downing cans of Special Brew with their toothless friends. Tough dogs on chain leads. Sleeping bags and newspapers scattered around their feet. The buildings were all collapsing, sagging within their own depression. They needed to take a fucking bulldozer to the entire area in my opinion. It was a waste of money, wasn't it? A seaside town in a state like that, full of dossers and scroungers, layabouts and criminals. I drove around the miserable back streets, with my window rolled down and my elbow hanging out. I caught a glimpse of people heading to Chaos. I drove smoothly past them, my eyes squinting as I took in the dirt and the squalor. Every street was mile high with rancid Victorian doss houses. Bed sit city, people called it. I felt above it all, as I passed them by, the Goths and the skinheads, the metal heads, the hippies, and the punks, all flowing, all pushing towards Chaos, like warped followers of some twisted religion, all flocking towards their church.

    I smoked as I drove, finally turning the car around and letting the engine idle lazily at the end of the road, with the club in sight. I recalled the address on the paper and counted the dwellings to the right. A smile pulled my lips across my face. That was it then. The tall red building. The shit-house on the corner. How nice. I smiled further when I thought about going in there, finding the little shit stain in the middle of the crowd and making a fool out of him. Dragging him back out by his scrawny neck. Dragging him back to his lying whore of a mother. The anger clenched painfully at my chest. I wondered what to do. I had been given the information I needed. Not just the address, but the evidence against Kay. She was a lying bitch, keeping things from me, planning things behind my back.

    I tapped my ash out of the window. I glanced up and to the right, as another bundle of scruffs made their way towards the club. I pressed myself instantly back into the seat, because it was them, it was fucking them! It was all of them. There was the dark-haired boy,

Michael, and his older brother. Christ, you could hardly tell them apart these days. The other two little idiots were there too. The ginger one and the one I'd given a talking to in the alley that day. And there was the precious boy himself. Her darling son. King fucking Danny, eh?

I felt the trembling start in my dry, pursed lips, and in my nostrils as they widened, and in my eyes as they rolled back to stare at my step-son. He was throwing his head back with laughter, one arm slung around his girlfriend's shoulders. My eyes glazed over, and I felt sick, and numb and raw. Tears moistened my eyes. I gave you so many chances, I was thinking, so many chances to be good, so many chances…and you couldn't do it, could you? Couldn't just be a good boy? My hands were frozen to the steering wheel, clawed and shaking and I hung onto it, using it to anchor my aching body to the car. I put the car into reverse suddenly. I took one more lingering look at the laughing boy, with his friends. I wanted something so badly then, and it angered me, what I wanted, it repulsed me and shamed me. I screeched off down the road with it banging and clattering noisily inside my head. I wanted to give him one more chance.

I kept away. I forced myself to. It was too soon. Too obvious. He would be nervous and jumpy, having passed his address over to her. It made me laugh sometimes when I was alone at work. I would sit behind my desk and chuckle. Why did he trust her eh? Why did he think she gave a shit? Big mistake, I would tell him when the time came. I let the weeks and the months slide by. I kept up the sunny pretence when I had to. I kept myself ticking over, I kept my mind on work and I tried not to let anything show. But I was watching, the whole time, I was watching her and watching for signs of him. I knew he came over sometimes. There were less biscuits in the tin, and she didn't eat the bloody things, did she? One day I found white dog hairs on my trousers. Another day I found the toilet seat up in the downstairs loo. I knew it was him. I bet he was feeling full of himself all right. I bet he thought he was untouchable.

I pretended I knew nothing. I let them think they had fooled me. I let them carry on their little game of pretence and lies. I didn't know exactly when I would put a stop to it; I just knew that I would feel it, when it was time, when it was right. You can't rush things, I reminded myself, as ever. Patience is the key. Patience is always the key.

31

May 1996

They were not happy about me seeing her. None of them were, except Anthony. He didn't say much about it, but I got the feeling that he was the only one who sort of understood it. He never gave me any grief about it anyway, never tried to talk me out of going.

'Shittinghell, not again,' Michael would roll his eyes and complain every time he found out I'd seen her. I didn't tell them when I was planning it, but they always knew by the time I returned. 'You're insane,' he would tell me, shaking his head. 'And why the hell do you have to be so secretive all the time? It's like when you were on drugs, only I think I preferred that!' I'd shrug my shoulders, keep my thoughts to myself and allow him the opportunity to do the same. 'How do you make sure it's safe?' he would ask me.

'I go when he's at work,' I told him. 'We sit by the window, so we can see if his car comes. I'd run out the back.'

'He's gonna' find out,' Michael gripped my arm, and his dark eyes searched mine, pleading with me. 'One way or another, sooner or later, this is gonna' backfire.'

'He's old enough to make his own decisions,' Anthony spoke up from across the room. Michael glared at him and Anthony returned his glare with a patient smile. 'It's his business if he wants to help her Mike.'

The very idea seemed to enrage him. He stood up from the bed, his feet hitting the floor with a thud. He looked between me and Anthony accusingly, as if we were in on this together, just to infuriate him.

'Why bother?' he demanded to know. 'What has she ever done for him? One day, that psycho maniac is gonna' catch on and then they'll both be dead meat!'

It was obviously an idea I had entertained myself. But nothing ever happened. Howard remained what he had been for almost a year now. A gruesome and somewhat ghostly figure from the past. We still hurried out of Redchurch after a certain time and life went on. I visited my mother when I could, which was usually once or twice a month and I said very little about it to anyone. I still didn't fully understand it myself, so what was the point in trying to explain it to the people who hated her? The thing was, every time I saw her, she seemed stronger, more like the old her. It made me remember some good times we had shared, in between annoying boyfriends. Her, John and I, muddling our way through together.

She would sit and stare at me with this shininess to her eyes, telling me about funny things I did and said when I was a little kid. She had the old spark back, maybe. That fire in her eyes, and instead of clashing, we were meeting somewhere in the middle, as friends. She had confided in John to a certain extent. Told him that she wanted to leave Lee and set up on her own. He had opened a bank account in his name and posted her the debit card and the pin number. She could put money in whenever she wanted, save up for her escape and Howard would not realise a thing. If she needed to call John or me, she went next door and used her neighbours phone. They were an old couple called Gladys and Stan, and they doted on her.

I would go and see Lucy after visiting Mum. I'd be a bit high on the adrenaline of it all. She would look at me the same way Michael did. Fear and reproach in her eyes, and every word she spoke, picked out cautiously, just in case.

'I feel better,' I tried to tell her. 'I can't explain it. It doesn't mean I've forgiven her, or we're all okay, it's just I feel better when I talk to her. It's helping me understand stuff. I can't explain it to you any better than that.' She would just slip her arms around me, rest her head down on my shoulder and hold me tight. She wouldn't say anything about it unless I pushed her.

'I'm just scared,' she would say, a flicker of a smile dancing on her lips before fading away again. 'Silly me. I'm sure you know what you're doing.'

They were more on edge than I was. One night we were mucking about at the back of the crowd that queued to get into Chaos, when Michael became utterly convinced he had seen Howard's car. One moment it had all been laughing and joking, pushing each other about and ruffling Billy's new haircut, and the next, it all changed. Michael, his face as white as a sheet, one hand reaching and clinging to his brother's arm, while the other pointed down the road, to the fast disappearing brake lights of a low, silver car. Anthony slapped him on the back and told him to get his act together.

'Millions of cars like that about,' he moaned, rolling his eyes at me. 'For Christ's sake Mikey, don't give us all the willies when we're here to have a good night.'

The atmosphere had changed completely. Before Michael got scared, it had been electric, pumped full of joyful apprehension and the sense of belonging.

'Sorry,' he started mumbling when we all looked on uneasily, shuffling closer together, our hairs on end, our good feeling dead inside of us. I didn't blame him. I couldn't count how many times I had felt my heart stop at the sight of a silver car. But I had learnt to live with it. What else could you do? I looked at my friends then and felt like a shit who didn't deserve them. They were all tense, forcing smiles, while their eyes flitted about nervously, and their imaginations worked over time. I felt a guilt so heavy it made it difficult to breathe.

A similar thing happened just a few weeks later. Enough time had passed to convince us to breathe again. We came out of Chaos at two in the morning, sweat shining on our foreheads, our eyes alive with the music that still pumped through our veins. As usual, I felt on top of the world. I was right up there, right up there in the sky, pounding my feet upon the earth, shaking it up. I had one arm around Lucy as we drifted down the road and towards the takeaway place on the corner. We were craving chips and kebabs, followed by a smoke and wind down music back at the bed-sit. They'd played my Smiths request just before we bustled out, and I was still singing it in a loud and drunken voice, as we bundled down the road together. Lucy clung to me and smiled as I sung the words to The Boy With The Thorn In His Side. I liked the last lines best, because they seemed sort of apt when I thought about our situation. Look them up.

'You're nuts,' she told me, wrapping both arms around my middle. I could feel the sweat on my back drying in the night air. 'But I like it when you're nuts,' she added. We had reached the shop and we piled noisily in through the double doors, leaving only Billy and Jake outside to finish their cigarettes. Anthony was ribbing Michael about some girl he had pulled.

The Boy With The Thorn In His Side-Part 2

'Old enough to be your fucking mother,' he was laughing as Michael viewed him with cool disdain.

'Just jealous,' he responded calmly. 'I saw you giving her the eye.'

We ordered our food, laughing and talking easily, with sleepy eyes and groaning bellies. We were heading back towards the doors, when Jake pushed them open and scuttled in, Billy at his elbow, both wide-eyed and alarmed. It was Anthony they went to. I saw Jake grab his elbow, pull him close, and all at once I felt like the floor of the kebab shop had turned to mush beneath my feet and I was sinking slowly down.

'What is it?' Anthony was saying, maintaining his cool exterior as always, holding the door open while we pushed cautiously back outside. 'What? What did you see?'

I hung back, my hands warming under the white polystyrene container that held the kebab I now did not have the stomach for. I felt Lucy slide her arm through mine. I saw Michael sidling anxiously to his brother's side, while Jake spoke to him in hushed and slightly panicked tones.

'Swear to God,' he was saying, leaning in to him, pointing with one hand out towards the narrow alleyway that ran between Boots and Woolworths opposite the kebab shop. 'Over there. Billy thought so too, didn't you Billy?'

'Stop panicking, everyone, stop panicking,' Anthony told us, shoving his kebab and chips at Jake. 'Hold this.' We all watched breathlessly as he crossed the street and sauntered over to the mouth of the alley. He was swallowed by the blackness for just a second, and then reappeared, holding up his hands and shrugging. 'Nothing there,' he said, running back to us. 'No one there. You sure you saw him?'

'Dunno,' Jake shrugged his shoulders and glanced sheepishly my way. 'It was dark. There was someone there, right Billy? We saw a face when he lit up a fag.'

'Was a big fella',' Billy nodded, swallowing nervously. 'Same kind of build. Not much hair.'

'Could've been anyone,' Anthony said, taking back his food and heading around the corner towards home. We scuttled after him, looking back over our shoulders. Jake was looking very confused and scratching at his neck.

'It was really dark,' he said, looking at me. 'Probably wasn't him...Sorry everyone.'

'You obviously thought it was him,' argued Michael, catching him up. 'Or you wouldn't have looked so panicked, and told Anthony. I thought I saw his car weeks ago.'

'Calm down, calm down,' Anthony was telling us all. He reminded me of a sheepdog, herding us all back home, munching sporadically on his chips while he lingered at the back, his eyes moving restlessly across the darkness. We scurried on and he held the door open while we piled into the foul-smelling hallway of our building. I watched him close the door slowly, sticking his head out for one last scout of the area before he let it slam behind him. He turned and exhaled in relief and saw me staring at him, as the others started up the stairs. 'It's all right,' he said. 'Take no notice. They're jumping at shadows. It was nothing mate.'

'Yeah, I know,' I told him. 'I'm not worried.'

'Good,' Anthony started up the stairs beside me. 'Let's not let it ruin our night.'

'I'm not worried,' I repeated, and he looked at me as if he did not believe me.

At the top of the stairs, they all waited for Anthony to unlock the door and let them in. They looked shaken up, scared and huddled together. I couldn't resist a look back over my shoulder as I came up behind him, my eyes staring into the darkness below, my ears straining for the sound of footsteps. Once we were inside the bed-sit, Anthony closed and double locked the door and then just stood with his back to it for a moment, just breathing, not looking at anyone. Lucy went into the kitchen and started to fill the kettle. Michael paced about from window to window, rubbing his arms and staring out at nothing. Billy and Jake collapsed onto the bed, murmuring to each other, their foreheads creased with frowns. I felt like a massive shit. They were seeing shadows, freaking out at the slightest thing, all because of me. All because I was seeing my mum, stirring up the past, making them feel unsafe again. I decided I would cancel our next meeting. I would

The Boy With The Thorn In His Side-Part 2

phone her in a few days and tell her what had happened. I felt Kurt's tiny paws on my legs and stooped down to pick him up.

'Better to be safe than sorry, eh,' I muttered, burying my face in the soft fur around his neck.

32

May 1996

'Why do you only ever listen to 'The Queen Is Dead'?' Terry was asking me, in what sounded like genuine puzzlement. I was crouched next to the door, with a tower of cassette tapes beside me. A middle-aged lady had just dropped off a box of old tapes. She'd spent a good twenty minutes telling Terry how her husband had been having an affair, so she had started dumping and selling his treasured possessions behind his back in revenge. She hadn't wanted any money for the tapes, which was fortunate, because most of them were shit. I was busy shelving them, and as most of them seemed to be by Abba, I was knelt by the door, in the A section, shoving them in one by one. My facial expressions were changing rapidly from dismay, to disgust, to outright horror.

'Because it's my favourite one obviously,' I replied to Terry's question. 'Why do you only ever listen to 'Blonde On Blonde'?'

'It's the best one,' Terry told me authoritatively.

'In your opinion,' I corrected him.

'But what you're forgetting,' he went on regardless, 'is that The Queen is lacking the best song the Smiths ever wrote.'

I rolled my eyes. The man was obsessed. ''Stop Me If You Think That You've Heard This One Before'?'

'Exactly. Best Smiths song ever and it's not on The Queen.'

'It's still a bloody good album Terry. What about 'There Is A Light That Never Goes Out'? I love that song.'

'Not as good as Stop Me.'

'Isn't it time we had a cup of tea?'

'I don't know Danny,' he sighed, rising slowly from his stool. 'Remind me who's the boss again eh?'

I looked up in time to see him smiling knowingly as he headed out the back. It was his way of killing arguments about music that would have no end, unless he reminded me who the boss was. I'm the boss, it's my shop, therefore I must be right about everything. He had asked me the same question this morning when I had turned up early for work. He'd shaken his head at me, pointed at the kitchen and told me to get the tea on.

The Boy With The Thorn In His Side-Part 2

I went back to my work, dusting off a Dolly Parton cassette and shoving it ungracefully into the D section. The Smiths were on the record player, so I started to hum along. I picked up the next tape, and rubbed it on my thigh to clean it off and that was when I saw a shadow fall over me. I looked up at the door quickly, but the sun blinded me, bouncing off the windows and the cars parked on the road, and whoever had stopped at the door to stare in had moved away. It took a second for my mind to catch up with my body, and then I took a steadying breath, got to my feet, opened the door and peered out down the street. I put up one hand to shield my eyes from the bright morning sun, and I can't deny I had the sudden strangling urge to close and lock the door. I pushed it down though, because I had to, because I had seen nothing, heard nothing. I went back to the tapes.

Moments later Terry waddled back in, holding mugs of tea and sloshing them over his belly as he walked. I slipped the last tape, an Elvis compilation, into a space in the E section, and approached the counter for my tea, wiping my dusty hands down the legs of my jeans. Terry eyed me curiously.

'What's the matter with you? Seen a ghost? You've gone all pale.'

I could have gone home at three, but I'd just discovered I liked Johnny Cash, after getting into an argument about country music with a bearded man who was a regular. He was one of the very few customers that Terry allowed to hang around the counter, drinking tea and talking about music. He'd finally got tired of my smirks and sneers about country music and had demanded Terry put some Cash on the record player. I'd folded my arms across the counter, slipped into my own little world, and listened. Moments in and my foot was tapping, my head was nodding and I had to admit that I liked it.

'The Man in Black,' the bearded man tipped his head at me and winked. 'You cannot be a music fan and not appreciate The Man In Black.'

'Cool,' I agreed with a smile. Terry merely groaned at me.

'See I've told you before not to be so narrow minded about music.'

I snorted in response. 'Says he that sneers at nearly everything that's been given the Brit Pop label!'

285

'I do not,' he argued back. 'I was the one who told you how big Oasis would be! And I like Blur, and I think Pulp are amazing, among others. It's all the other hanger-on's I can't stand, the bandwagon jumpers!'

'You're scathing about it as a genre,' I reminded him patiently.

'Because I hate genres, because if you give something a name, or a label, or pack it away in a fucking genre then it's far too easy to kill it or declare it dead. Look at your precious grunge sonny boy, what happened to that?'

I shook my head in despair. 'You know what happened to that Terry.'

'Excuse me, a type of music does not just *end* because one singer tops himself!'

'I never said it had ended,' I argued back. 'You're saying that! I still love grunge. I love all music.'

The bearded man laughed at us, patted me on the back and finished his tea. He picked up his purchases and slipped them under one arm. 'You do now kid,' he told me, and walked towards the door. I sighed and started to search the shelves for Cash records, while Terry sniggered at me from behind the counter.

'Here he goes again,' he chortled. 'Walk The Line is the best one, you know.'

'In your opinion,' I replied.

We closed at five, Terry shooing the last doe-eyed indie kid out of the door with a copy of Suede's Dog Man Star tucked under one arm. Terry had spent the last ten minutes trying not to laugh at the poor kid, who in his khaki duffel coat and John Lennon glasses, had tried and failed to engage Terry in a meaningful debate about the next big thing.

'Fucking Liam Gallagher wannabe,' Terry groaned when the door was locked. 'Can't anyone just be themselves these days? You don't see me walking around with a bloody Morrissey hair cut, do you?'

'You couldn't have one anyway,' I told him with a grin as I fetched Kurt's lead down from the hook out the back. 'Your hairline is receding. You could have a Phil Collins.' My shoulders were shaking with giggles as I clipped the lead onto the dog's collar.

'Don't *ever* mention that jumped up little bastard's name in my shop again young man!' came his petulant roar from behind the till where he was stood cashing up. 'I've warned you before smart arse! That name is not to be spoken in here unless you want the sack!'

I opened the back door. 'That, and Rod Stewart yeah?'

'Post The Faces, yes, that name is also banned!'

'I'll have to make a list,' I called out. 'See you tomorrow Terry!'

'See you tomorrow mate.'

I closed the door behind me and headed down the alley with Kurt trotting at my side. I stopped to locate my cigarettes and lit one up, thinking I would just about have time to smoke it before my bus arrived. As I cupped my hands around the cigarette, I heard a car purring softly up behind me, and without turning to look at it, I moved to the side to allow it to pass. It trundled past me as I puffed on my smoke and shoved the lighter into my back pocket. It was moving slowly, so I gave it a quick glance, then fell into step behind it. It crawled to a stop at the end of the alley and just sat there, the engine still running. It was then that I saw the number plate and stopped walking. I felt myself shrinking fast, mentally and physically. L-HOWARD. Howard's car, it was his car. My eyes flashed up and down the alley, seeking a way out as panic seized my heart, sending it beating into a wild frenzy that threatened to explode from my throat. I stood in the alley, staring, one hand shaking with the cigarette, Kurt's lead wound tightly around the other one.

Howard. I could feel it in every nerve and muscle in my body. The engine remained running, but the car stayed where it was, blocking my way out. I had to go that way. My bus stop was out on the main road. If I walked back the other way, I would have to go all the way around and would miss the bus. I looked down at Kurt and the little dog wagged his tail back at me. I sucked in a lungful of air and hoped it would unfreeze my blood and give me the strength to keep walking. I looked over my shoulder again, back at the shop. Terry would still be cashing up. I looked back at the car and it was still there, still waiting. Kurt shivered and whined on the end of his lead so I looked down at him again.

'We want to go home, don't we boy?' I said to him, and in response to my voice he wagged his tail so furiously that his entire body wagged with it. 'About the only time I've wished you were a Rottweiler,' I murmured, and looked back up, back at the car, still waiting. What did he want?

I sucked in another chest full of air and started to walk. It felt totally wrong to be walking towards that car. I kept telling myself that it was daylight, that there were people just around the corner, and that there was nothing the bastard could do to me that he hadn't already done. As I got closer, the driver's door flung open and he stepped out, leaving the engine on and flicking a cigarette butt to the ground. I stopped moving. I lifted my own cigarette to my lips, sucked on it hard, my eyes narrowing upon him, my other hand tightening on the dog lead. There was a silence between us that took my guts and scrunched them up so hard they began to ache. There was the hand, once more, inside my belly, clawing, sending warning signals all over my body. I lowered the smoke, breathed out slowly and waited to him to speak, waited for something to happen. He was looking at me with a very calm, pleasant expression on his big face, but there was no denying the gleam in his eyes because I had seen it a hundred times before. Finally, his little thin eyebrows moved up and down rapidly and he spoke; 'long time no see, eh little man?'

I realised that my feet were frozen to the ground. They felt like concrete, and this heavy, dragging feeling was spreading quickly through me. 'What do you want?' I heard myself asking him, my voice just above a mutter. He cocked his head at me. He rested one arm along the top of the open car door, and then his other hand tapped the roof of the car, in quick succession, *boom, boom*. His eyes drilled into mine.

'Saw you walking there,' he said. 'Thought I'd say hello. How are you?'

'Fine.'

'Your mum wonders how you are,' he said, dropping his arm from the door and stepping away from the car. I felt small as he approached me, his big arms swinging in short shirt sleeves. He

The Boy With The Thorn In His Side-Part 2

stopped just in front of me and his smile was radiant, and he seemed to inhale loudly, as if sucking up my fear through his flaring nostrils. I wondered if he had missed it. 'She's always asking about you, always wondering how you are. You look well. Off all those drugs now eh?'

I could not answer him. My throat had constricted, barely allowing me room to breathe, let alone speak. I just kept my eyes on his, trying to read them, trying to understand what this was, what this meant. He nodded his head at me calmly. 'Well you must be,' he concluded. 'You look so well. Feeling better these days, eh?'

'What do you want?' I asked him a second time. The alley around us had become nothing but a grey blur. It had ceased to exist. There was nothing in the world, except myself, and Howard and whatever was going to happen.

'So suspicious,' he mused, allowing himself a soft chuckle. 'I only wanted to say hello and see how you are. Your mum misses you, you know. It's been so long since she saw you. You could visit her, you know. She'd like that.'

I was finding it torture keeping my eyes on his, but I couldn't risk looking away. I was faintly aware of my chest rising and falling rapidly beneath my t-shirt, as my body tried again to kick start me into flight.

'I don't think so,' I said. 'Not while she's with you.' I pulled my feet up from the ground, and they felt like they were being sucked down into it, and I had just managed to put one foot in front of the other, when he took hold of my arm just above the elbow. The grip was loose, but I froze, and it was everything in that awful second, as his power encircled my arm, it was everything, holding onto me, not letting me go, everything. It all came back, in a horrendous flash of images and memories that slayed me, and made my legs turn to jelly. I stared at the ground, because I could not bring myself to look back into that face while a thousand brutal pictures raced through my mind.

'Whoa, slow down,' came his whispered reply. 'Why the hurry? Don't you want to come and see your mum? I can give you a lift, right now, if you want.'

I shook my head. 'No. She can come here, if she wants to see me.'

'Oh really? Okay, I'll pass that onto her,' and just like that, the hand fell away from me. I stumbled forward, nearly tripping over my own feet in surprise, and I forced my feet to keep moving on, not looking back. 'I'll give her the message,' the voice, thick with hunger, dripping with malice, followed me down the alley way, echoing from the walls. ''Cause she hasn't seen you in so long, has she? She misses you so much, you see. See you soon then, yeah? There's a good lad.'

I walked faster and faster, breaking into a run at the end of the alley, dragging poor Kurt with me, scurrying out onto the pavement, barely remembering to look both ways before I dashed out across the road towards the bus stop. Seconds later the bus pulled up and I ran onto it, throwing down my money, yanking off my ticket and finding a seat at the back, where I sat and huddled with Kurt, against the window. I was shuddering violently and felt extremely close to being sick.

I felt a little bit better when I stepped off the bus at the other end and took another deep breath to steady my nerves. I let Kurt do his business outside, before we opened the door and went into the building. By the time I had dashed up the stairs and reached the bed-sit, I was worked right up again, my heart a monster in my chest, my mind questioning whether Howard would have followed the bus here. I went inside and saw Michael lying on his belly on the bed, with a can of beer in one hand. I closed the door, locked it, then went to the window to peer out. Michael was watching me, already suspicious.

'You okay?' he asked me, and I flashed him a quick, brittle smile, thinking to myself that he probably knew me better than anyone.

'Yeah, fine,' I told him, and went into the kitchen to put the kettle on. I filled it with water, switched it on to boil, and leaned against the worktop with my arms wrapped tightly around my middle. I shook my head and swore at myself. Was I really going to do this again? Lie to him? Was I really going to pretend nothing had happened and everything was fine? Where had that got me last time? I licked my lips and stamped my foot and felt the frustration juddering through me. What the hell was I doing? Before I could think twice, I

The Boy With The Thorn In His Side-Part 2

stuck my head back through the curtains and looked at Michael, still on the bed. He looked up expectantly.

'Not okay actually,' I told him, and he was on his feet and in the kitchen, offering me his beer. I took it and his eyes focused in on my trembling hands.

'What's up?'

'Just saw Howard.'

'What?' Michael's mouth gaped in horror and he stepped closer to me, his eyes bulging as I nodded back at him and leaned back against the cupboard with the shivers twisting violently through me. I gulped the beer as he continued to stare. 'Oh my fucking God. When? Where? What happened?'

'Outside the back of the shop, in the alley. He drove past then stopped his car and got out.'

Michael covered his mouth with one hand and shook his head in misery. 'Oh no. What did he do?'

'Nothing. Acted all friendly. Wanted to know how I was.' I lifted my shoulders and dropped them, and passed Mike back his beer. 'Asked if I wanted a lift to go and see my mum.'

'Did he touch you? Did he do anything to you?'

'I started to walk away and he grabbed my arm, then that was it. He said what he had to say. Let go. I walked away.'

Michael swallowed beer and passed it back. 'You think he knows? That you've been seeing your mum?'

'I dunno, he didn't give anything away, but maybe he does. Yeah. I mean...that would explain it. Jesus Mike...' I sighed heavily, rubbed at my dry lips and then sloshed more beer down my throat. I was shaking hard and it was getting worse. I wrapped my arms back around myself, trying to hold still, trying to calm down. Michael kept shaking his head, his dark hair hanging over one eye, while the other stared out, solemn and afraid.

'He knows Danny, he must do, he must have found out! I swear I saw his car at Chaos that time, then Jake and Billy thought they saw him in that alley...'

I nodded at him. 'I know.'

'What're we gonna' do? He might have followed your bus here! He might know exactly where we live!' Michael leaned in the doorway and took the beer back from me. He finished it off in nervous little gulps. I stared at the floor and felt the strength leaving my legs, leaving all of me. I wanted to lash out suddenly. I wanted to smash in all the cheap flimsy cupboard doors, and swipe my arm across the manky pint glasses collecting flies on the draining board. I clenched my teeth together and tried to hold onto myself. Michael was watching me. I felt my legs weaken further. Any minute now I was going to hit the floor. 'Danny?' he asked me softly. 'You okay?'

'No!' I retorted, quickly and fiercely, looking up. 'He called me a good lad.'

'Did he?'

'Good lad, he said.'

'So?'

'I don't know...' I trailed off for a moment, not sure of what I meant, or how I felt, or anything, and I covered my face with my hands, and suddenly my knees dipped and I went down, my arse bumping into the floor and staying there. I buried my face in my knees, grabbed at my hair with my hands. 'Fuck! *Fuck*!'

Michael came forward. 'Mate?'

'I don't want to be like this!'

'Like what mate?'

'Like what he makes me! A victim!'

Michael crouched down slowly. 'You're not. You're not.'

'I am! I fucking am! That's what he makes me! That's how he makes me feel, now I feel like it all over again!' I rolled my head into the cup of one hand and stared at the floor. My feet twitched at the ends of my legs. I was remembering things I had fought so hard to forget. I wanted to fight back, I wanted to do something, I wanted to kick the place apart.

'He doesn't make you that Danny,' Michael was saying quietly. 'You're you, and he can't touch you now.'

'He'll do whatever the hell he wants.'

'We won't let him. We'll call the cops. We'll tell them everything.'

I just glared at the same grubby spot on the lino, until my eyes moved out of focus, and I was not sure whether it was tiredness or tears that blurred my vision. In my mind I saw myself crushed

The Boy With The Thorn In His Side-Part 2

down into the floor, a boot grinding into my neck, holding me in place, taking everything away.

'That's not who I am,' I murmured to myself. 'He made me like that, and that's not me, that's not me. I won't be like that again.'

'No way, I told you. Come on mate, up you get. Anthony will be home soon. He'll know what to do.' Michael nudged me, got to his feet and held his hand out to me. 'Come on,' he urged me. 'You're you. You're not whatever he thinks you are.'

'Good boy,' I muttered, distastefully, taking his hand and letting him haul me back to my feet. I held onto my head with one hand, followed Michael through the curtain and plonked myself down onto the bed. The springs sagged and creaked beneath my weight. Michael started to walk in small circles.

'We'll find another place to live,' he was saying quickly. 'We need to move again, that's what we need to do. Get out of here.' He stopped circling and looked at me. 'And please, *please* do not keep seeing your mum!'

I nodded silently from the bed. I had already decided that much myself.

'He's trying to scare you,' Anthony told me firmly, when he arrived home. He carried some bags of shopping into the kitchen, put them on the side and strode back out again. He regarded Michael and I with a stern expression. He kicked off his shoes and cracked his knuckles. 'Looks like he's succeeded too, so he must be one happy mother-fucker about now.' He placed his hands on his hips and looked at us, shaking his head. 'Look, he doesn't know where we live, that's why he went to your shop. He's just trying to scare you. Don't let him.'

'He must know I've been seeing Mum,' I spoke up dryly.

Anthony nodded. 'Yeah, probably. Or he's just bored and felt like stirring things up again.'

'But why now?' Michael questioned helplessly. 'It's been like ten months or something!'

Anthony shrugged at the pair of us. 'Who knows how his sick mind works? Maybe he does know about Danny seeing his mum. Danny, you should call her. See what she says.'

'What time is it?'

'After six.'

'Okay, pass me the phone.'

Anthony grabbed the phone and chucked it at me. 'I'm putting the kettle on, and a shit load of chips, anyone in?'

'We're both in,' said Michael. 'Did you buy any fish fingers?'

I dialled the number and got up from the bed. I stuck one hand into the pocket of my jeans and stalked restlessly around the room while it rung. It seemed to ring for a torturous eternity before finally she picked it up. 'Hello?'

I stopped next to one of the windows and pressed my forehead against the cool glass. 'Mum, it's me.'

'Danny! Are you all right?'

'Mum, listen, does Lee know anything? About us meeting? Or about you trying to leave him?' I gazed down at the street below. I watched a trio of young girls, dressed to kill and tottering on high heels towards the high street.

'Why?' her voice immediately lowered and hushed with fear. 'What's happened?'

'I just saw him today,' I told her, feeling the give of the glass under my head, knowing I would only have to apply a little more pressure before it cracked against my skin. 'He was outside my work. He spoke to me.'

'Oh my God honey! Oh God I am so sorry! As far as I know he knows nothing! But maybe he does...oh shit, how would he know?'

'I dunno,' I told her tersely, wanting to hang up. 'Just wanted to warn you. I won't see you again for a while Mum. I can't.'

'Okay, honey, I understand. Maybe we could arrange to meet somewhere else?'

'No. Not at the moment. I've got to go.' I hung up on her and turned around. Anthony was in the doorway, watching. 'Says she doesn't know anything,' I told him.

'Fair enough,' he nodded. 'But you see what he's done here, don't you? He's left you alone for nearly a year, let you settle into your life, and relax. It's almost like he *wanted* you to relax and enjoy yourself, 'cause then its' all the more fun when he pops back up again! He's messing with your head mate. Just don't let him.'

The Boy With The Thorn In His Side-Part 2

With that, he ducked back through the curtain and I was left staring. Easy for you to say, I almost called after him. Instead, I went back to the bed and lay down with the dog. My eyes jerked towards the door every few seconds. The spike of fear was sharp and turning within me. That night I drifted in and out of restless dreams, one half of me convinced that Anthony was right, that nothing was going to happen, and the other half of me dismally certain that Howard holding onto my arm in the alley way was just the beginning.

33

June 1996

I don't think they knew that I was watching. All the time, I was watching. They may have been keeping an eye out for my silver Merc, but that wasn't the only car following them. And when I couldn't follow them, I had Nick do it. They may have checking over their shoulders, staring into the shadows, but the funny thing was they missed me; they never knew I was there. I watched patiently from afar, and I found the patience soothing. It was all right to wait, you see, it was all right to bide my time and choose my moments. There was a delicious sense of regaining control, while they scrabbled about their untidy little lives, like rats abandoning a sinking ship. Their faces, panicked, pale. The girl did not go around again, maybe they had warned her not to. It was just the three of them, day in, day out, scuttling about with their eyes wide open, yet never seeing me.

I knew their routines. I knew their work hours and shifts. I knew that Anthony was scanning the newspaper for flats, for other places to live. I knew this because I often drank a pint in The Ship when he was not there. I found his rolled-up newspaper on the bar. He had a few lines of enquiry open, it seemed, a few options he was considering. Moving home was one. Numerous flats across the area were circled or crossed out. Question marks had been pencilled in next to a couple of old bangers in the car section at the back. I could see how his mind was working. Move further away, but buy a car so that they could still get to their jobs. Why, they had a dilemma on their hands, didn't they? Move away, run away and keep running, and lose their jobs, their income. Stay close, and run the risk of bumping into the bogey man on every dark street corner. It pissed me off, knowing what he was planning. He had no right, you see. Danny was not his son, not his anything. He had no right to take him further away from me.

Sometimes I parked the car on the road outside their building and just waited. I wanted to talk to them, to any of them. I wasn't sure exactly what I would say, but just the thought of engaging one of them in a meaningful conversation was a thrill stirring to life in my belly. I thought back to Danny, that day in the alley way. I'd felt so good afterwards. I'd consumed his stinking fear as soon as I'd opened the car door. I'd thought briefly about just grabbing him, just punching him in the head or something, taking him by surprise and slinging him into the boot of the car. I could drive somewhere and open it up and let him out, laughing. Just for the hell. Just for the kicks. Just to see the look on his face.

But this was more fun. The waiting, and the watching, and the observing. I felt calm again for the first time in ages. I felt like I had them all back in the centre of my palm, and their fate lay there, unsuspecting and blind. They knew nothing. They were rats in a cage, waiting for me to make my move. And here was one of them now. Anthony Anderson, leaving the building to make his early shift at the pub. I watched him push through the heavy metal door at the bottom. He stopped, work bag slung on one shoulder, and lit up a cigarette, blinking and wincing in the bright morning sun. He had not seen the car yet. He shoved his lighter into his back pocket and inhaled on his cigarette hungrily, as if he had been craving it for some time. Then he yawned and scratched at his head. He was wearing a t-shirt and jeans, and I could see the intricate tattoos winding up and down each forearm. What a tough guy, eh? What a piece of work.

He strode purposefully towards the crumbling brick wall that cornered off their crappy little piece of shit garden. He always walked like that. Fast and strong, his head held high, his eyes narrowing as he scanned the area, a ready smile on his lips, but not for me, not on that morning. He stopped when he saw the car. He lifted his cigarette to his lips and dragged long and slow, before flicking ash at the ground and stalking quickly around the wall.

'Fuck this,' I heard him mutter, as I rolled down my window to greet him. He walked along the side of my car and then aimed a kick at it, booting the back door as hard as he could. I merely shook my head and turned the engine off. 'Oi!' he called out, stopping at my window and bending down. His eyes; dark brown, raging and burning into mine. 'You lost or something mate?'

I stretched my arm out of the window, and tapped the ash from my own cigarette out onto the ground between his feet. Anthony looked me up and down and I could see his skin shaking, from anger, from fear, from barely contained disbelief. 'What the *fuck* do you want?' he asked, when I continued to smile up at him.

I tipped my head. 'Now that's friendly, all you boys are so friendly!'

'I asked you a question. What the fuck do you want?'

My smile stretched out across my clean-shaven face. I felt a little giddy and dreamy, as I looked up into his blazing dark eyes. 'Well, not that it's really any of your business at all, I wanted to have a quick word with my step-son again. Is he in?'

'No,' he snapped quickly, letting me know right away that he was. 'He's not. You stay the hell away from him, I'm warning you!'

I blew smoke up into his face and watched him pull back, his eyes fluttering in their sockets as he waved a hand in front of him. 'Well maybe you could pass a message onto him then, how about that? Maybe you could tell him that I dropped by to say hello, and maybe I'll drop by again another day, just for a chat, you know? Just to catch up and see how he's doing. I need to make sure he's all right, you know, living with you lot.' My grin crept upwards, my teeth shining out at him.

'Listen to me,' the boy snarled suddenly, pushing his face as close to mine as he dared to. 'You don't scare me, right? I see you for exactly what you are. I am telling you now. I am fucking *warning* you. Stay the hell away from us or I am calling the cops, do you hear? Danny wants nothing to do with you, not ever, so get that through your fucked-up head, and stay away!'

'Well listen, there's no law that says I can't drop by and say hello to my step-son if I feel the need,' I replied to him calmly. 'I've got something I need to talk to him about. I think he'll be interested, once he gets a chance to hear it. I've got a proposition for him that's far more attractive that smoking himself into oblivion with the likes of you.'

Anthony was shaking his head. 'You're unbelievable,' he breathed, pulling away from the window, as obvious sweat broke out across his frowning forehead. 'You're completely fucking insane if you think he wants to hear anything you've got to say! After what you did! Don't forget arsehole, me and Mike were there the day he stabbed your vile friend! We know how far you'll go to control and frighten

The Boy With The Thorn In His Side-Part 2

someone, and it turns my stomach, it makes me sick! I ought to go to the cops! You'd be finished if we told them everything!'

I could see he was hoping this would alarm me. But it did nothing of the kind. I was laughing so hard my shoulders were shaking with it. I looked up at his face and he stood back, straightened up and dragged on his cigarette. 'Go on get out of here,' he said to me coldly, flicking his head towards the road. 'You're vile. Get away from here.'

I leaned forward suddenly then, taking him by surprise and loving it. He was caught off guard by the ferocity of my movements and stepped back again, blinking, his lips pressed down over his teeth.

'Real tough guy aren't you?' I asked him, sneeringly. 'Yeah, look at you, talking to me like that, when you're the one who's done time. *Twice.* Very, very naughty boy, weren't you eh? Don't like the thought of going back there a third time, do you boy?' I raised my eyebrows at him and smiled slowly. He thought he was a big man, but I could see the truth. He was nothing of the sort. He was another scared kid, too big for his own boots, playing with fire. I nodded at him. 'Just pass the message onto him, or I'll go up there and tell him myself. Tell him I'm never very far away.'

'Well come on then!' he yelled at me, lifting his arms up to either side in frustration. He let his work-bag drop to the pavement and beckoned me. 'What are you waiting for? Come on! We're all just *dying* to know what you're gonna' do! Come on then! Why don't you take it out on me, eh? Try it on with me!' He nodded at me, daring me, sucking on his smoke and flicking ash at my car. 'Come on then,' he urged me. 'Take it out on me, take all your sick shit out on me, just you and me, right now, I fucking dare you! Get out of your shitty little car and try it on with me! Or do you only like your chances with little kids and women? Is that it? Hey?' He looked satisfied, and stepped closer to lean down towards me again. 'That's the truth of it, isn't it big man? That's the real truth, and it's exactly what I've always said about you...You're a big cowardly bully. You won't get out your car and take me on, will you? You had to get another cowardly piece of slime to do your dirtiest work for you, didn't you? How do you sleep at night? Really? How the fuck does someone like you sleep at night? You get your kicks controlling people, frightening people who are smaller, and weaker than you...burning them with cigarettes, for *fucks* sake! What the fuck is wrong with you, you evil mother-fucking bastard!'

I stared back at him and yawned. 'You finished?'

He shook his head at me. 'No. Come on, I'm serious. Get out your car and fight me. Show me you're not a coward and a bully, or I'll go to the police right now and tell them all about your drug dealing, child abusing ways!'

I offered him a knowing smile and a gentle shrug of the shoulders. 'Well I might have to drop a call to them myself,' I told him. 'Now that I know where my step-son lives. I better fill them in. How he's unfortunately got himself mixed up with a drug dealing ex-con. Still see Jaime don't you eh? Oh yeah, got tabs on you son. Got tabs on everyone. I just hope you don't have anything up there that might get you into trouble when the cops come calling. I think they'd send you down for a very long stretch, wouldn't they eh? And what would happen to your little brother then? No one else to look out for him, or so I hear. Hmm. I suppose I could keep an eye on him for you? See what he needs? What he likes?'

He threw his cigarette down and gripped the roof of the car, his head shooting in close to mine. I did not flinch. I considered a fast and brutal head butt; shattering his nose all over the pavement. 'We've got far more shit on you!' he snarled at me.

I laughed. 'Well fine, if you want to risk it. But if I was you I would make arrangements for Michael first. You know. You wouldn't want to leave him to fend for himself when the cops drag you away again, would you? Just something to think about.'

'I'm not scared of you,' he told me then. 'You disgusting slug. I'm not a sixteen-year-old kid. Does it make you feel good, does it? Scaring him? Fucking up his life again? Is that what makes you happy? You don't think you've tortured that kid enough? You can't just leave him the fuck alone?' He touched his head with his hands, shaking it in exasperation. 'It's not fair,' he started saying then. 'It's not fair what you're doing...just leave him alone why don't you? Just worry about your own life. After everything that you've done...it's just not fair...'

I could see what he was trying to do now. His tone had softened and his eyes were searching my face wonderingly. He was

The Boy With The Thorn In His Side-Part 2

trying something else. Seeing if there was another way he could get through to me. I looked past him, my gaze tracking up to the tall building behind him.

'I did everything I could to be a father and a good influence to that boy. I thought I'd done all I could and it was all too late. But it turns out it's not too late, you see. I can give him one more chance. I owe it to him to get him the hell away from you boys.'

'You're crazy,' he muttered, shaking his head. 'You're just crazy...leave him alone...he doesn't want to know you.'

'Well it's very honourable, all this care you show for him, but he's not your brother, is he? He's not your family, he's mine!'

'He's my friend!'

'Just tell him I want to see him,' I snapped, suddenly bored of all this, bored of his glaring, stubborn face, bored of going back and forth with him, not getting anywhere. I turned the key in the engine and he stepped back quickly. 'Just tell him we have unfinished business and he might as well talk to me and see what I have to say.' I checked the mirrors and slipped the car into gear.

'You shouldn't keep pushing him!' the boy was yelling at me now. 'He's on the edge after everything you've done! One of these days he's gonna' turn around and fight back, you know! He's gonna' stand up to you!'

I laughed out loud as I swung the car away from the kerb. I heard him yelling, and he kicked the car again as I did a three-point turn. I could let that slide, for now. He'd be paying for that before he fucking knew it. I drove off, casually, calmly, as if the roads were mine, as if I had not a care in the world, and really, I didn't. It was all coming together in my head you see. All of it.

I continued to circle the streets of Belfield Park in my car, like a low, sleek shark, moving in on its prey. I didn't want to go up to their crumby bed-sit just yet. That would be the last resort. I could be cleverer than that, and after all, at the end of the day, it was all for the boy's own good. There was a constant, warm and soothing calmness to my movements and to my thoughts. I had a feeling the boy would soon see sense. I had a good idea, a really good idea, and I just wanted to talk to him about it. I thought about the other two boys and rolled my eyes in impatience. They were like the fucking guards of filthy, shitty bed-sit kingdom. They were always there, weren't they? Interfering.

And so, whenever I had spare time to kill, I kept the car rolling, trundling around the block. I mostly felt at ease as I drifted around. The only thing that interrupted the relative tranquillity was the occasional grumbling and sniping that came from the voice at the back of my mind. The voice that poked and needled at me, reminding me that Kay was not to be trusted, reminding me that I was running out of time. There was a clock ticking somewhere and I could not afford to forget about it.

I parked the car in the darkness of the shadows and killed the engine. I kept my eyes on their scummy building. I sat slumped in the seat and chain-smoked cigarettes, keeping my eyes on the grotty looking people that came and went. It was twenty to eleven. I already knew Anthony was out. I had driven past The Ship to make sure. So, the younger boys were up there alone, and this excited me. I killed time imagining what their faces would look like if I marched on there, kicking down their door. What would they do?

I glanced up suddenly, using my elbow against the door to hoist myself up when I heard the heavy metal door clanging on the building. I could see Danny, just outside the building, lighting a cigarette while that little dog of his scampered about in the straggly grass. Wee wee time for the little rat, usually around the same time every night. I did not hesitate. I got quickly out of the car and strode towards him.

He was dressed in ripped black jeans which looked like they hadn't seen a washing machine in some time, and this baggy, shapeless grey hooded jumper. Before he noticed me, he was just smiling inanely at the dog as it squatted in the grass to take a shit. I held up my hands and approached him. When he saw me, his eyes widened like saucers, and the cigarette slipped through his fingers and landed smouldering in the grass, and then he turned in a panic and fumbled for the door.

'Hang on, hang on, wait!' I called out, still holding up my hands. 'I just want to talk to you a minute! Hold on!' I stopped walking and nodded at the ground under my feet. 'I'll just stop here yeah?'

He glared back at me. 'What now?' he growled, and I felt my skin prickling at the contempt in his tone.

'Just want a quick word, that's all,' I assured him. 'Just a quick word.'

'I don't want to talk to you, not ever. I want you to go away and stop hanging around here. Or I'll call the police. I've already spoken to them you know.'

I was intrigued. 'Really? Have you? What about?'

'About you!' he cried out. 'About you stalking us! I told them!'

'Oh,' I said, nodding and stroking my chin. 'Well that's the first I've heard about it. They haven't said anything to me yet. Maybe they're too busy out fighting real crimes, eh?' I watched his face crease up in dismay and confusion. 'Sorry,' I told him. 'I just want to talk a minute.'

'They said they can't do anything,' Danny told me, his eyes flashing with hatred. 'Until you've committed an actual crime, so why don't you get one with it then? Whatever you're gonna' do?'

'Well listen Danny, this is what I want to talk to you about, I just want a quick word then I'll leave you be.' I lowered my hands and chuckled softly. 'That's not too much to ask, is it?'

'Yes, it is,' he replied scathingly. 'I want you the fuck away from me. I've had enough.'

'Oh, calm down,' I advised him with a brief roll of my eyes. 'Stop getting your knickers in a twist and just listen. I have something to put to you, something to discuss. We can talk here, or we could go somewhere else if you like? Maybe a pub, or back at mine? It's up to you.'

He had one hand wrapped around the edge of the open door. His eyes drifted up and down me. 'You're crazy if you think I'm going anywhere with you.'

'We'll talk here then, fine,' I said amiably, stepping towards him.

'What is it?'

'Well, it's about Jack,' I started, and immediately I saw the alarm fill his eyes, and he shuffled closer to the door, pushing one side of his body through the gap and staring back at me with wary eyes. 'He was very handy to have around, you know. I sort of miss him now he's gone. He was my right-hand man, I suppose you would say. He took care of a lot of business for me. I haven't been able to replace him see, because there's no one I can really trust. So, I thought, I would offer you the job.'

He was shaking his head very slowly. His mouth was slightly open and his eyes were appalled. 'The job?' he uttered, as the little dog scuttled through his legs and into the hallway. 'Are you insane?'

I sighed, tiring slightly now. Why did everything always have to be such a fight and a battle with him? Couldn't he see a good opportunity when it was staring him in the face?

'Oh, don't be so melodramatic,' I said. 'It's not like you've ever been squeaky clean, is it? And I bet you're not now either! Jack had a job, didn't he? A position. Earned himself some good money too. I'm offering it to you Danny. You'd be great at it.' I pushed my hands into my pockets and shrugged my shoulders at him loosely. 'What do you say? You'd be rolling in it in no time. You wouldn't have to live in this shit hole. You could have Jack's place, all to yourself if you wanted.'

He just stared at me. 'You mean drug dealing?'

'Among other things,' I smiled. 'It's a colourful position, you wouldn't get bored. I thought you'd jump at the chance actually. Right up your street I should imagine.'

'You don't know anything about me!' he screamed at me then, his fingers clutching at the door, his eyes growing round and wild with a rage I could not fathom. The blueness of his eyes stood out all the more as his face drained of all colour. 'You never did!'

'What are you saying? You don't want to get rich? You don't want a stable job with good prospects? A nice place to live?' I clicked my tongue and raised my eyes up at the grotty hole they called home. 'Are you sure? Why would anyone want to live like this? Here? I don't understand you.'

'You...you...' the boy stopped and looked wildly around at nothing, as if he had lost the words he intended to speak. His chest was rising and falling at speed, his breathing had become laboured. 'You...you have no idea...' He pointed a shaking finger at me then. 'Why the fuck would I want to work with you? Do you think

The Boy With The Thorn In His Side-Part 2

I've forgotten what you did to me? Do you think I've forgotten about Jack?' His eyes bore into mine, heavy with a disgust that made me stiffen.

'Jack was a loose cannon in the end,' I tried to tell him. 'That's why I sent him away. He'd lost the plot. Couldn't control himself...But me and you, we could work well together Danny. Think about it. I'm giving you a chance here. You don't even really deserve one after all the shit you've put me through, but here I am again, trying *again*, trying to help you. I still hold onto hope that you'll listen to me!'

'No,' he was saying, looking away, shaking his head, 'no, no, no, just get away, just go away...' He pulled the door open, slipped through it and tried to close it on me, but I was too quick, shoving my foot and thigh into the space. His eyes met mine, dark with anger.

'Think about it carefully,' I warned him then. 'Don't make any more mistakes Danny. You've run out of chances. Don't fuck it up again. Think about what you are turning down. You don't want to regret it.'

'Anthony!' he turned and screeched into the hallway. I winced at the sound of his shrill tones, echoing up the stairwell. I felt my patience slipping and my calmness growing jagged.

'Fucks sake,' I muttered, leaning close. 'Don't be such a cry baby, he's not here, and I know he's not. I'm giving you an opportunity here! I'm giving you another chance to make amends!'

'*Leave...me...alone*!' He faced me and hissed it at me through the gap in the door, and then he jutted his face towards mine and spat a mouthful of gob out onto the ground. It landed between my feet and I stared at it and shook my head at it, at him. I looked up and smiled patiently.

'You really didn't want to do that little man.'

'What do I have to do to get it through to you?' he said to me, and his voice was this hard, brittle thing, rushing out between his clenched teeth. 'Leave me the fuck alone or I am going to kill you!' He yanked hard on the door, and I could hear voices reverberating up and down the stairs, people coming out to see what the noise was about, so I pulled my foot back and let him go. The metal wobbled and vibrated right in front of my stunned face. I was suddenly shaking,

305

fuming, boiling over with impossible heat. That ungrateful little shit had spat at me! He had threatened to kill me, he had spat at me, and he had slammed the door in my face! I stepped back quickly, panting. My tongue seemed to loll from my mouth as I struggled to breathe through the torrent of rage that rushed through me. This terrible, gut wrenching realisation was pounding at my head. He hadn't learnt a thing. Not one fucking thing. That defiant little shit. Nothing had worked. Nothing.

The Boy With The Thorn In His Side-Part 2

34

June 1996

It was only a matter of time. I told Anthony that, after he confronted Howard on the street that day. I just sat and took it all in, and I realised that in truth, it was what I'd expected all along. I wasn't really surprised or shocked. I had escaped. There had been a time when things were good. But now the hunt was on. I saw that I had two options. Run, or fight back. I could leave, and I could keep running. I would lose them all, because I would never be able to tell them where I had gone. The idea and the thought of being that alone in the world, made me want to fall to my knees and weep. I would hear Michael and Anthony discussing things in sombre, fear filled tones. Every now and then one of them would raise their voice in exasperation, or anger. I felt myself slipping away from them. I felt the distance imposing itself from within. I couldn't have stopped it if I'd tried. It was my problem, not theirs. Something would happen. One way or the other. I could run, or I could figure out a way to fight back.

The job offer was a joke. A way to taunt me. He was playing cat and mouse. I walked through the days that followed with the undeniable sense that everything was falling apart around me. I felt the distance stretch out between me and my friends. I felt it, like the unstable ground beneath my feet, stretched and flimsy, weakening as my mind drifted. I went about my business like a stiff little ghost. Around every corner, I fully expected to see the monster's face, preparing to eat me up. When I was alone, my mind echoed with the impossible loudness and clarity of the words I had spoken; *I am going to fucking kill you...*The words, they followed me to bed, and whispered softly into my ears. I awoke in the morning, with the force of them pounding at my head. When my friends spoke, I realised that I could barely hear them anymore and that their words meant nothing.

It was not their fault, but my heart was being wrung out by a pain they could never understand. I looked into the mirror and did not recognise the haunted face that stared back at me. I peered at my reflection and spoke the words, *I will fucking kill you...*The words occupied my mind. When I thought about the words, when I tested them out on my tongue, one by one, it was like laying out a plan, a proposition, and I felt better and the trembles eased. I felt a hardening inside of me and it gave me the strength to get up and go to work each day, always wondering if today would be the day. I held the words inside my chest like a weapon, like a shield. I aimed to build myself up, to stack up the hatred and the fury, brick by brick inside of myself. I thought about protection, and I thought about attack. I put the knife back in my pocket and kept it there.

When Lucy came to see me, she wanted to hold my hand and locate my softness, my warmth, but I had nothing left for her. Sometimes I looked at her face, and wanted to scream at her to get the hell away from me; I'll hurt you, I'll hurt you, one day I will really hurt you...She watched my rage erupt when I could not open a tin of beans, when the jagged rim bit into the skin of my thumb and sent blood drops scattering all across the kitchen floor. I felt like the rage inside of me was a black and bottomless pit. A torrent, a flood, with no end, no way to turn it off once it started. I watched her back away when I lost control and I saw the look in her eyes and it was the same look that my mother always had.

One day Anthony caught hold of my arm to make me listen. 'I've got an appointment with the bank manager,' he was trying to tell me. 'So we can apply for a loan, then we can afford to buy a car, and find a place further from here. Danny, you listening?' I wasn't listening. I pulled free of him and went back to kicking in one of the kitchen cupboards. It felt good, I reasoned. Maybe I was starting to see things from his side after all. Lashing out, striking something, feeling the wood give way and splinter under the force of my foot. Anthony attempted once more to pull me away, to make me stop, to make me listen. 'Danny, don't do this! We're nearly there! Just got to hold on a few more days! A week maybe, are you listening Danny? You've got to listen, you've got to let us in, if he does anything we'll call the police!'

I stopped the kicking. 'They won't care,' I hissed at him. I stared at the damage, my shoulders moving up and down breathlessly. I did not feel finished then and wondered what else I could attack. 'You'll see.'

The Boy With The Thorn In His Side-Part 2

'What will I see? What do you mean? Come on mate, pull yourself together. He's messing with your head and you're letting him!'

'It doesn't matter,' I told him, and I was right. 'Nothing does.' I pushed past him and lay down on the bed with my arms folded behind my head. My eyes moved up to find the yellowed ceiling. I found a crack, and followed it.

Saturday evening, and Anthony was at work. Michael and I were self-medicating our headaches from the night before, with carefully rolled spliffs and endless rounds of tea and biscuits. I ignored the phone ringing until Michael gave in, grunted and rolled from the bed to answer it. I opened my eyes and then closed them again. The familiar weight of dread and muted rage was pressing down on me, as it had done all day. Michael picked up the phone, rubbing at his red eyes under his hair, stretching out a yawn and mumbling his replies. Finally, he hung it up and swore.

'Been called into work,' he said to me, as I watched him. 'Bastards!' he expressed, and started to hunt for some clean clothes. I did not answer him. I had begun to view speaking as a mostly needless and pointless waste of energy. I listened to Michael stumbling around the room. 'Why don't they just hire more staff?' I felt the bed sag as he sat down on the edge to pull his legs through his jeans. 'It's not like there's a lack of people out there needing work! And then I could have my evening off, like I'd planned...'

He got up again, sighing wearily. I rolled over onto my side, away from him. Kurt whimpered and curled into a tighter ball beside me.

'You gonna' be all right?' he was asking me from the door. 'Anthony will be back in an hour or so. He won't be long.' I heard the rattle of keys as he grabbed his from the table next to the door. 'Danny?'

'Mmm?'

'I said, you gonna' be okay? If I go? I'd tell them to shove it, but Anthony reckons we really need the money, so...'

'Yeah, fine,' I muttered irritably. 'Just go.'

'All right, all right, sorry for breathing. I'll see you later okay?'

When I did not answer, he groaned and stormed out of the bed-sit. I opened my eyes and stared at nothing. I could hear the TV chattering in the background. The phone rang again, but I did not move. I closed my eyes and tried to find sleep. The smokes had removed me slightly from everything and that was a good thing. The rage was dulled for the time being, the fear and the panic held back. I would have to control them all until Anthony returned. I would have to keep my eyes closed tightly and tell myself that monsters did not exist. I missed Lucy's arms around me. It was like a knife to my heart every time I even thought about her, but I had told her to stay away. To be on the safe side, I had tried to tell her, but the grief and confusion in her eyes was hard to escape.

Why the fuck was the phone still ringing? I tried to sleep, but the phone would not stop screaming at me. It was making me feel rattled and caged in. I pulled my arms over my head and covered it. I squeezed my eyes shut. The phone stopped. I breathed in slowly, deeply, and exhaled it back out again. Sleep stole upon me.

I was torn back out from it just minutes later. The fucking phone again, ringing and ringing and ringing. I growled with impatience, sat up and lunged from the bed, and found the phone on the side table with everything else we needed in a hurry; ashtrays and lighters and keys and money. I picked it up and looked at it, and half considered hurling it through the window. Then I wondered if it might be Lucy.

'Hello?'

'Danny! It's me, Mum!' she sounded breathless with fear and something else. I leaned against the wall, and my head was spinning.

'Why'd you keep phoning?' I demanded. 'I'm trying to sleep.'

'Because it's important, that's why, I need to tell you something!'

'What?'

'I finally did it, I finally did something right.'

'What?'

'I called the police honey. Just now. I called them. I spoke to this really lovely female officer, and I said it's not an emergency, but she is going to come and see me tomorrow, when he's out.'

I pushed my hair from my face. 'Really?'

'Yes, really. I wanted you to know. I did it. I phoned them.' She seemed to catch her breath on the other side of the phone, and then went on. 'She talked me through everything. I have to press charges against him and then they can arrest him. They can even make him stay away from me while I get myself sorted. If he comes near me, he'll get arrested. Oh, she was so nice and helpful Danny.'

I breathed out through my nostrils. My mouth was clamped shut. My lips did not seem to be able to move, or open. Conflicting emotions rose up within me. Relief teased and taunted, daring me to believe in it, while resentment and darkness swirled so thickly inside my head I found it impossible to congratulate her. You don't know him at all, I wanted to say to her. Her naivety was astounding.

'Danny? Are you there?'

'Yeah.'

'Well what do you think?'

'Don't know.'

'Are you okay? Have you seen him?'

'Not for a few days.'

'Well you just hold on honey. You just sit tight. It will all be over tomorrow. Everyone will know the truth about him, and he will never be able to hurt either one of us ever again. Okay?'

I thought about what she was saying for a moment, turning the words over inside of my head. I wanted to believe her. I wanted to grab the light that she had held out to me. 'Okay,' I murmured.

'I'm sorry it took me so long.'

'Okay.'

'I'll call you tomorrow, after she's been. I'll have more to tell you then. I'll let you know what happens, okay?'

'Okay,' I hung up on her before she could say anything else. I wanted my mind to be free for a while. I turned off the TV, put a record on and went back to the bed. It was that old song, that song I had drifted towards at Billy's, all that time ago. I could see her in my head then. June Madison, her long blonde hair hanging down over one shoulder, as she swayed and moved to the music coming from her little battered radio on the kitchen window sill. My head sank into my pillow and I mouthed the gentle words as they came to me, as they filled my fading mind with sweetness and pain. It made me cry, and that was okay. I laid there and cried about it for a while, and then I curled around Kurt, and I slept.

The next time I awoke, it was because Kurt was whining. I could hear his little claws scraping at the door to get out. I rolled over in bed, groggy with clogged up dreams and stretching memories.

'You want a wee?' I asked him, rubbing at my face with one hand. He turned in a circle, tail wagging and eyes bright. He barked at the door and whined again. 'Okay, hang on, hang on.' I lowered my feet to the floor, grabbed my pack of cigarettes and lighter and stuffed them into my pocket to smoke outside. I opened the door and he scampered quickly through it on his squat little legs, and I smiled at the sight of his little white arse disappearing down the first flight of stairs.

I stepped through the door to go after him and was instantly startled by an enormous shadow coming from the right, smothering me in darkness. I backed up, shaking my head no, my eyes widening, as he filled the doorway, as he blocked out the light and the hope, and towered over me, with this strange and cautious expression on his face. He held up giant hands as if to soothe me.

'It's okay, don't freak out,' he said to me. 'I need to talk to you, it's about your mum.'

I glanced behind him. I could see Kurt out on the landing, hovering there with his small head cocked to one side and his ears aloft. I felt suddenly a million miles away from the outside world, and as the distance between Howard and me was swallowed up in huge strides, I knew that even if I did manage to get past him, I would not make it very far. I looked back at Howard and accepted this was it. I shrugged my shoulders.

'What about her?'

He looked pained, as if he might cry, and he wrung his big hands together. 'She's in the hospital,' he said. 'She took an overdose last night. I came back from work and found her. Called the ambulance just in time.'

The Boy With The Thorn In His Side-Part 2

'What?'

'She's okay,' he asserted quickly. 'They're taking good care of her. But she wants to see you. She asked me to come and get you, to go and see her there.' He made a small hand gesture towards the open door. I felt my skin crawl with knowing and I shook my head at him.

'Bullshit. I just spoke to her a while ago. You're lying. Get out.'

A different face fell over the one he had presented to me. His eyebrows rose slowly to meet his receding hairline. A calm smile tugged up the corners of his lips. 'I'm giving you a chance to do this the easy way,' he said very softly.

I felt cold with terror, like I had been wrapped in ice. 'My friends are back any minute.'

'Oh really?' he looked amused and rocked back on his heels. 'Is that why I saw one get on the bus not so long ago? And the other one is at work, because I checked, little man, I checked.'

My jaw was shuddering. My teeth clattered against one another. I watched the smile slide across his face, and I watched the small, stone like eyes gleaming at me with the satisfaction of victory.

'I've been watching you,' he informed me. 'I told you that once before, do you remember? After the wedding when you tried to run away? I also told you that *I'd* be the one to decide when you could leave. Didn't I? Do you remember that conversation? Anyway, I'm here to do you a favour. I'm your last chance mate. Your last chance to be a good boy. You get one last chance to get it right, to make amends and be part of a proper family.'

I backed up further. I reached out with one hand and made contact with the thin glass of the window. I felt nausea swimming to the surface. 'No chance,' I said, shaking my head, not taking my eyes from his face. 'I don't want it. I don't want anything from you.'

Kurt had edged back into the room. He was at Howard's feet, sniffing. I saw him pull his head back in confusion, before thrusting it forward to sniff again. Howard made his move quickly, letting out a hungry growl as he swept down with one arm and snatched the little dog up by the scruff of his neck. I stepped forward automatically, reaching for him.

'No! What're you doing?'

Howard held him up and looked him over. 'Ahh, what a sweet little thing,' he said. 'Sweet little rat! Yeah, I've seen you two going about together, makes me fucking sick!' He used his other hand to grab one of Kurt's wiggling back legs, then he let go of his neck and held him aloft by one leg. The dog cried out in pain and Howard jerked him behind, slamming him against the wall.

I ran forward. 'No!'

He laughed, shoved me back with a hand to the chest and I landed on my backside. Howard held the dog up higher, examining him as he twisted and yelped in his grip. I scrambled to my feet and rushed forward again, but he grabbed my t-shirt and held me back. 'Horrible little thing,' he mused. 'Look at it, nasty little rat!'

'Put him down you fucking arsehole!'

'I'll break his fucking legs,' he retorted and swung Kurt against the wall again. There was a horrible thump, and I felt desperate sobs rising in my chest. I struggled against his hand.

'*Please*!' I tried to reach for him, but Howard held him up higher and he was hanging limply now, breathing rapidly and looking dazed. 'Please stop it! Don't hurt him!'

'Come here,' Howard pulled me forward by my clothes and wrapped a firm arm around my shoulders. 'I ought to snap all his legs off and flush him down the toilet,' he sniggered into my ear. 'That's what I'll do if you don't behave yourself, right?' With my eyes on the dog, I nodded quickly. 'Good. Come here.'

I saw him drop the dog. I felt his hand snatching up my hair. I caught a glimpse of Kurt staggering off to hide under the bed, and then I saw the same wall, flying towards my face.

The Boy With The Thorn In His Side-Part 2

35

  I dreamed I was lying on my back, floating on a raft in the middle of a vast, black ocean. *I know it's over*, the words in my head...I could hear the fat man somewhere, mumbling and muttering, jangling his cashing up bags. But I couldn't see him...only darkness. Darkness, and The Smiths singing I Know It's Over. I was trying to get to sleep, but it felt like someone was trying to cut off my hands. I brought them up to my face and peered through them, looking for stars in the sky, but there was nothing. Just black. The ocean rocked beneath me, shushing and whispering, and the sky bore heavily down upon me. There was pain biting into my hands, my face, my head. I tried to call out, to call to Terry, if he was there, but I couldn't hear him now, he had faded away, and there was nothing, just darkness and an endless ocean and I was all alone. I know it's over, they sang, but it never really began I wanted to argue ...There was nothing. Just the lapping waves and the eerie dark, and The Smiths. I wondered if I was dead.

  I woke up to the sound of my own coughing. My throat was itchy and dry, coated with dust and stuffed tight with hot air. There was a massive pain in my head, right at the front and I screwed my eyes up against it, battling with the weight of it, wondering what it was. It throbbed relentlessly around my temples and my forehead, and there was another pain, a bitter stinging around my mouth and nose. I swallowed and tasted blood, tangy and metallic. I remembered, and the horror flooded me. I blinked faster and faster, trying to clear a space in the darkness that surrounded me. My eyes searched through it desperately, trying to work out where I was. Was I dead? If I were dead, how would I know? Maybe this was what death felt like. Just darkness and pain and confusion forever. I fought against the panic that was threatening to strangle me.

  I realised that I was in a small, tight space. My knees were right up next to my chin. When I moved my head back, I found a soft, yet unyielding surface right behind it. My face felt wet, but when I tried to wipe at it with my hands, I discovered they were tied together. I lifted them up slowly, gasping in pure terror, my mouth falling open, my heart thundering away under my t-shirt. I started to breathe faster and faster as panic set in. I looked up again. My eyes had adjusted enough to the darkness to make out a window, up and to the right of me. A car window.

Fuck. I was in Howard's car. I looked to the left and saw the other window. Straight ahead, the passenger seat. I was squashed down in the foot well. I didn't understand. I stared hard at the luxurious leather interior, at the green lighter lying on the driver's seat, and his pack of cigarettes resting in the space behind the gear stick. The engine was off and the car was cold. Howard's fucking car. It was dark outside. How long had I been out? What had happened? I clawed my way back through distorted memories to try to work it out. I could remember the phone ringing and Michael leaving, and Kurt scraping at the door to get out. I stared around, gulping and swallowing air, following the light that reflected from the leather seats. The light was coming from outside. It took me a few more moments to work out that it was coming from the moon, and when I stared harder at the passenger window, I could make him out, Howard. He was stood there, leaning against the door. I could even make out the grey swirls of smoke as they circled and rose into the air before him. I tried to lean forward, straining my ears to try to pick up any sounds that might tell me where the hell we were. I wondered if I could hear water running, or falling, but I wasn't sure.

Hearing a clock begin to tick inside my head, I looked back down at my hands. They were tied with some sort of wire. I lifted my wrists to my eyes to get a better look. I moved my palms against each other, back and forth, trying to loosen it, but it was wound too tight. When I moved my hands, the wire bit deep into my skin and I guessed that was the idea. I felt a huge sob lurching up from my chest and swallowed it back down. This was deep shit. This was worse than I had ever imagined. I listened to my breathing getting faster again. Panic was knocking really fucking hard. I stared back up at the window, at the outline of the man, still leaning and smoking casually against the car. He was just a man, I told myself. I would be able to get through to him. He was just trying to scare me. He would see sense and let me go, I knew he would. I'd do anything. I'd do whatever he wanted. I jerked my head to the left, but I was unable to tell if the door was locked or not. I couldn't make out if the knob was

The Boy With The Thorn In His Side-Part 2

up, or down. I tried to move around in the tiny space, but my body was taking up all of the room. As I stared at the door I knew it was my only chance of escape. If I could get out of the foot well, if I could get that door open, I could run, I could run and scream for someone to help me.

Just then, Howard moved from the door beside me. I saw him throw his cigarette butt down. I waited, fear gnawing at my guts, and then I saw my only escape route destroyed in a second, as he yanked open the driver's door and slid smoothly into the car. He slammed the door shut and our eyes met in the darkness, and I saw him smile, and I wondered how fucked I was. The moonlight snagged on his teeth, lighting them up in their small, neat rows. He rested one broad arm across the steering wheel, and shifted his weight to face me. I recognised the gloating, euphoric glint in his eyes, the look that reminded me of a junkie getting his fix.

'What are you doing?' I asked him, my voice a trembling disbelieving croak, as terrified tears rolled down my cheeks.

'Thought you'd fancy a drive,' came the smooth, controlled reply. He grinned at me as if we were sharing an inside joke.

I swallowed. 'Where?'

'At the beach,' he said with a small and casual shrug. 'Well the cliff top. You know the bit that's all roped off? They had a bit of erosion up here last week apparently. Big chunk of it fell off. Yeah. Fell right in. Splash.' His grin was bright and gleaming, his small eyes laughing in his calm face. 'Pretty deserted up here this time of night,' he added, with a slight nod. 'No one about for miles and miles.'

'Why?' My voice had crept higher, and quivered in terror. 'Why? What are you doing? What the *fuck* are you doing?'

He shifted a bit closer, leaning towards me as if to share a great secret. He pressed his finger against his thin lips. 'Shh,' he smiled. 'Keep it down little man. No need to shout. It's just you and me.'

'You're crazy,' I whispered, shaking so bad now I could barely think straight. I looked back at my hands and started trying to twist them free again. I could feel the wire eating into my skin, opening it up, and a warm sticky wetness spreading, but I did not care. 'You're completely insane,' I said, not looking at him. 'You can't do this, you have to let me go!'

'You're gonna' cut your own hands off if you keep doing that.'

'Let me fucking go!' I looked up and screamed at him. There was an explosion inside of me. I felt it and it was telling me to get out, to get far away, to not let this happen, to fight back. I struggled to get up, launching my body forwards and trying to use my elbows to hook into the seat for leverage. Howard just sat and watched me, with this sleepy and narrow eyed look of amusement on his face. Finally, he reached for me, grabbed my arm and hauled me out of the foot well.

'Been watching you for some time,' he announced brashly. I landed sideways on the seat and immediately tried the door handle with my hands, but it was locked. I brought my feet up instead and kicked the door, and then the window. I drummed my feet against them, while terrified tears squeezed free of my eyes. 'Okay, that's enough of that now, that's enough,' he said, pulling me back with my t-shirt and holding me in place with a hand to my chest. I squirmed and strained under it. I was in a state. Panicked, and out of control. I lurched against the hand, tried to knock it away, brought up my knees, tried to twist away from him. *'Calm down,'* he told me, 'that's enough of that! I'm talking and you should be fucking listening!'

I stopped struggling. I wasn't going anywhere. I stared at the windscreen breathlessly, with the weight of his hand on my chest making my guts wring out and forcing vomit up my throat. 'You're insane,' I panted. 'You've lost it. You can't do this. You can't do this to me.'

He pushed his hand into my chest. 'You better pipe down,' he said indignantly. 'You might have been gone for a while, but you should remember the rules. Shut the fuck up when I'm talking, or I'll break your fucking nose.' He stared at me. I stared at the windscreen. I saw him nod. 'Okay. I had to bide my time you see. Could have rushed in and taught you a lesson at any time. But you had all your homo friends swarming round you like fucking flies on shit. Had to be patient and wait for the right time.'

'They'll be worried about me by now,' I told him through my gritted teeth. 'They'll have called the police.'

The Boy With The Thorn In His Side-Part 2

'They'll probably think you're with your mum,' he said coolly, and our eyes met again. He nodded at me. 'Oh yeah, I know you've been sneaking around to see her for a while now. And I know what the bitch is planning too, thanks to you. Been putting ideas in her head, haven't you eh? Been trying to mess things up between me and her, yet again, haven't you eh?'

'Yeah, so what?' I shot back at him, pushing with my feet and shuffling my backside further back on the seat. 'She wants to leave you! She hates you, you stupid bastard! And that's nothing to do with me, it's 'cause of how you treat her! She contacted me, she *begged* me to come and see her, not the other way around!'

'Oh, is that so?'

'Yes!' I screamed, shifting to face him, easing my back up against the car door. He kept his hand on my chest. I couldn't get away from it. 'It's your fault! It's over!'

'Well,' he said, with a little tip of his head. 'You are right about that, anyway. It's over all right. Come on then.'

I shook my head at him, not understanding. 'What?'

'Come on! Look lively!' He sniggered, turned the key in the ignition and unlocked all the doors. He reached over me and opened the door I was leaning on. He used the flat of his hand to shove it open, and I nearly went with it, but moved forward just in time. 'Come on, out you get!' he laughed into my face. 'Can you hear that?' he asked, cocking his head to one side. I looked out of the door. I could hear the dark and lonely sound of the waves crashing violently against the cliffs. It was raining steadily. I looked back at him. His face had changed. There was no humour now. Only cold, dark malice. 'I knew you'd try to ruin things between me and her,' he growled and shoved me out of the car. I landed on my back, winded, but quick enough to roll over and get up onto my knees. He appeared behind me, grunting, like a living nightmare, wrapping his bear like arms around my middle and tearing me to my feet.

'*What are you doing?*' I screamed, thrashing wildly, kicking out with my legs, drumming my heels into his shins.

'Tried to ruin things from the start, didn't you?' he was growling, as he heaved me away from the car and towards the red and white tape I could see had been strung up along the footpath just ahead. He half carried, half dragged me, and I did all I could, bucked and strained and kicked and screamed, but there was no way out, no release from the massive arms that held me. 'They ought to put a proper fence up, eh?' he hissed into my ear as he hauled me along. 'Anyone could just drive up here and dump rubbish over the edge eh? Thorn in my side, that's what you've been since day fucking one!'

'What are you doing? You can't do this!' I tried to force my feet down into the ground, tried to plant them there and use the earth to hold me down, but he moved me on, dragging me closer and closer to the edge.

'Come on, come on, nearly there now, nearly there!' he was panting into my head. 'Then it will all be over Danny! You'll see!'

I didn't want to see. I twisted violently within his grasp. I made it as hard as I could for him to move me, scuffing my feet into the sand, turning and jabbing my elbows back into his body, but it made no difference. Finally, I opened up my lungs and screamed; *'Help! Someone help me! Help me!'* I could see the black waves down below, I could see them swelling and rising.

'No one can hear you,' he told me. 'We're miles from anyone. No one comes up here. I'd stop struggling if I were you, this is where the ground gave way, we might both go down together!'

He held me there. We were at the edge. His arms tight around my chest, squeezing the air from me. My feet dangled just above the ground, my toes scraping uselessly at the wet sand. I had no choice but to face the ocean. I could see the white froth down below, gleaming in the moonlight as it thrashed and hurled itself at the rocks.

'Time to pluck that thorn out,' he whispered into my neck. I heard him inhaling deeply and I knew what he was doing, breathing in my terror, sucking it into his rancid lungs. I tried to press my body back into his, tried to turn my head away from the blackness below.

'Don't do this, *please* don't do this,' I began to babble in a high-pitched sobbing voice. I couldn't understand, couldn't believe it had come to this...I stared at the sea and suddenly felt myself going, and a scream echoed from me, he had let me go, let me go, and I was falling forward, the big arms were gone, and he was laughing and laughing behind me. My t-shirt snagged up under my arm pits. I held. He knotted his hand in the material at the small of my back and that was all there was. That was all there was between me and falling. 'Oh my God, oh my God, oh my *God*, please, *please,* oh my God *please* don't let go, please, please, please, *whatta'ya doin' whatta'ya' doin...'*

'Do you want to die today Danny?'

'No! No! Please, please don't let go, don't let go...'

'It's about time you said please....'

'*Please!*' I screamed into the darkness. '*Please* Lee! Please don't do this!' I could not tear my eyes away from the angry black waves that rolled and crashed below us. The rain was falling heavier, plastering my hair to my skull, running in cold rivers down my back. My feet scraped pathetically against the fragile ground. My t-shirt was pulled tight around my neck. I could feel his fist there, warm and solid in my lower back, holding me. Oh God, oh God don't let me go, don't do it, don't really do it...If my t-shirt tore, or if he let it go, there would be no stopping me. There would just be falling and the cold whoosh of air and rain as I plummeted into the sea. 'Please,' I said it again, my teeth chattering together violently. 'I'm begging you, I'm begging you please, *please...*' There was a horrible and terrible pause, while I was forced to wait, and he didn't say anything, he just breathed heavily behind me, as if he was thinking it over. 'Please,' I whispered again, shaking so hard I could barely see straight. 'Please Lee...'

'You better let me hear some more of that,' he grunted finally and stepped back, yanking me with him. I closed my eyes, relief racking my body with an explosion of noisy sobs, as I felt myself tugged down to the ground. It shook through me, the disbelief, the horror, the fear...I felt like my mind was going to cave in, give up...I was on my stomach, my hands trapped beneath me, my face still just inches from the terrible edge, so I kept my eyes closed, not wanting to see the awful, hungry blackness any more. He was on top of me, his bulk pressing me into the sand. All I could do was sob and moan, and tremble, my eyes squeezed shut, my face against the sand, just desperate to block out the sound of the angry waves, just desperate to block everything out. Howard took me by the hair and pulled my head up. 'Look at that!' he snarled. 'Look at that there! You don't want to go down there, do you? *Do you*?'

'No,' I shook my head in his grasp. 'No, no, no, please no...'

'No one would ever find you down there, would they? You'd be lost forever down there, wouldn't you? You don't want to be lost forever down there, do you eh?'

I shook my head again. 'No, please, don't...'

'Well you have to be a good boy, don't you then?' He gripped my hair tighter, pulling my head up so hard and fast I thought my neck would snap. 'For once in your miserable little shit stained life, you have to be a good boy, don't you?'

I sniffed up my tears and snot. 'I will, I will, I will...'

'You've never been very good at it, have you?' he continued to rage on. 'Never been any good at doing what you're told, have you, you little bastard?'

'Sorry...I'm sorry...'

'You better be fucking sorry,' he pulled my head back even further, until all I could see then was the dense black sky. I closed my eyes before they filled with rain. 'You better be sorry, and you better start being a good boy, because this is your last fucking chance, or you're going down there, do you understand?'

'Yes!'

'You be a good boy or that's where I'll put you! You say sorry for trying to wreck things! For trying to get her away from me!'

'Sorry!' I screamed and sobbed. 'I'm sorry!'

He pushed his lips against my ear. 'She wants to leave me because of *you*, she's lying and cheating behind my back, because of *you*! She'll stop all that if you be a good boy! If you do what I say! If you do as you're told and be a good boy, she'll be all right again, won't she? We'll be a family, won't we? Are you gonna' do as I tell you and be a good boy?'

I swallowed. I opened my eyes and blinked in the rain, and in my mind, I saw the little bed-sit, with the bean bags, and the walls covered in posters, and the sagging bed, and the little tatty sofa that Anthony curled up on, and I nodded for him, I nodded. I felt my ribs groaning under the weight of him and I just wanted it to be over, whatever it was. 'Will you let me go?'

'I haven't decided yet. I might. If you're lucky. If you promise to be a good boy and if I believe you.'

'I will, I promise, I will.'

The Boy With The Thorn In His Side-Part 2

'Fucking say it!'

'I'll be good! I'll do whatever you want!'

'Yeah, that's right, you will, you'll be good and you'll take the fucking job I offered. You'll come and work for me and make amends. Last chance Danny!'

'I will, I will, okay...'

He finally let go of my hair and sniggered into my ear. 'Jack thought you were a good boy didn't he? He really did.' I felt the cold sand against my cheek again, and closed my eyes. If he didn't get off me soon, I would be dead anyway and nothing would matter anymore. 'He really liked you a lot,' he went on, slurring his words into my brain. 'If you're not careful, maybe I'll give him a call and get him to pay you a visit eh? You have no idea how much he'd like to get his hands on you.' He chuckled, and shifted his body against mine, as if to drum in the humiliation and he was laughing so softly, and I knew he would be licking his lips too, relishing every moment of the power he owned. 'I told you, didn't I? I told you not to leave. I told you I would find you, if you did. You should have listened to me, shouldn't you? You shouldn't have run off with your scuzzy friends. When you're part of a family, you don't do that sort of thing. You stick together and you're loyal. Like I am with my dad. You were a bad boy, doing that, weren't you? Naughty, naughty boy running off like that, weren't you eh?'

'Yes,' I replied quietly. 'I was.'

He laughed out loud, and finally eased himself off me and stood up. I could breathe again, but I was not entirely sure that I wanted to. I lay there, not moving, just breathing slowly in and out and questioning whether it was even worth it. He grabbed the back of my t-shirt and hauled me to my feet. I was soaked through. I just hung there, head down and eyes glazed and mind fogged with terror, and then he marched me back to the car with his hand around my neck. I had a feeling I knew what was coming and I was right. I didn't put up a fight and I didn't say a word. He opened the passenger door, pushed me down onto the seat and lifted my t-shirt up to my neck.

'Need to get you back in line,' he was grunting, and unbuckling his belt. I turned my face to the side while he chortled to himself up above. 'I'm gonna' fucking enjoy this,' he decided to tell me before the first strike came.

I closed my eyes, I braced myself for it, I arched my back and hissed the pain through my teeth each time I heard the belt cutting through the air behind me. Wow, I thought numbly, you mother-fucker, pulling out all the stops, all this, wow, what a show. I tried not to cry, but in the end it was too much to keep down, and the sound of my tears seemed to slow him down. I counted ten and then he stopped, turned me over and unwound the wire from my wrists. I just shook and tried to contain it all. I kept my eyes closed and when he slammed the car door on me, I curled into it and brought my knees up to my chin, and wrapped my arms around myself and refused to look. I didn't want to look, I didn't want to see, and I thought maybe if I stayed in a calm darkness, then none of this would be real, maybe it would all turn out to be just a nasty fucking dream.

The car rocked when he climbed in the other side. I wondered what was next. I wondered if it was over, or if it had just begun. I screwed my face up, burying myself in my arms, and the pain was getting worse, growing and swelling with every passing second, layers of hot, electric pain smothering my existence. He turned the engine on and pulled across his seat belt.

'Let's go,' he said. I kept myself turned to the window, my knees up and my head down. I recognised his voice. Calm, now all the anger had gone. He was like a junkie getting his fix, and now he was as high as a fucking kite on it all, until it started to run out again. We drove along in silence.

The Boy With The Thorn In His Side-Part 2

36

I didn't realise for a while where he was heading. I didn't realise until he swung his car into the road that led up towards Chaos. I remained pressed up to the window, too lost within the horror to realise where we were. On the drive over, I'd slipped into my own little world of grating pain and soothing music. I told you that before didn't I? That wherever I go, whatever I do, music is with me, drumming inside my brain, like a constantly changing soundtrack. I have no control over it, the songs just come, they make their own way in and out. I had Lithium in my head the whole time, while the car swerved corners and trundled across bridges. You might not know that song. You might not give a shit about that song. But it was there, so that makes it part of everything...When the car stopped, he killed the engine, and I moved my head slowly and rubbed at the steam on the window, and that was when I knew he had driven me home. I looked at the door handle and thought about wrenching it open, tearing down the road and screaming for help. But my body felt wrecked and ruined. My back screamed in agony with every muscle I twitched, and my legs didn't even seem to be with me...

There was a build-up of tears behind my eyes. I was too tired to give into them, and as I gazed through the hole I had rubbed on the steamed-up window, I felt sort of numb and detached from it all. I wondered blankly what would happen next. During the drive, I had felt the fear ebbing away. It broke up and floated away, because it didn't really matter anyway. It didn't really matter what happened next. Or who won. Nothing mattered. You lived, or you died. You took it, or you fought back. You cared, or you didn't. Now I knew where we were, I felt a little confused and uneasy, but at the same time, I felt the first tender sparks of anger, deep within my body. I turned my face slowly to look back over my shoulder at him. He appeared in a daze, staring straight ahead at the windscreen.

'So, what now?' I asked him. 'You're just gonna' let me go?'

'You need to get your stuff don't you?' he turned his head to look at me and his eyes looked glassy and strange.

'You really want me to work for you?'

He nodded slowly. 'That was the deal.'

The concept seemed to stun me for a moment or two. I just stared and blinked at him, open mouthed and teetering on the verge of nervous, disbelieving laughter. The sparks of anger gained a little more hold then. I could almost picture the match inside of me, sparks flying, the flame not quite taking hold, yet.

'But you actually want me to work for you?' I swallowed and asked. My mouth was paper dry, and I would have killed for a decent drink. He nodded at me, a slight crease appearing across his forehead.

'Hope you haven't forgotten our conversation already,' he said. 'It will do you good. I'm giving you one last chance Danny, that's what I'm doing.'

I ran my tongue slowly back and forth across my lower lip. I could taste tears and sand and blood. 'I'm just a bit confused,' I said softly, cautiously. 'You want me to work for you, when you hate me? When you've always despised everything about me? I would've thought you'd be happier with me gone.' His face darkened and his head lowered on his shoulders. I glanced at the door I was huddled against and then looked back at him. 'Come on,' I said. 'What the hell was all this? Missed having your favourite punch bag, did you? Punching Mum not quite the same for you? Scared you'd lost control? Had to come and show me who the big boss man is, all over again, right?'

'You needed showing!' Howard snarled, spittle flying from his lips as he thrust his big head towards me. 'Sneaking round to my house! Encouraging her to leave me!'

'And if I'd stayed away, you wouldn't be doing this now? It was her who begged to see me! I would have been happy never to set eyes on either of you again, to tell you the truth, but she begged Lucy, she told Lucy she needed to see me.'

With one meaty arm looped over the steering wheel, Howard leaned closer to me. 'You ought to be grateful to me,' he sneered. 'You ought to be grateful that I care about you! That I'm trying to help you!'

Again, I was stunned into silence. I opened and then closed my mouth. I shook my head as if to clear it. I didn't even know where to begin. The man was dangerously deluded. Did he truly believe he could be a force for good in my life? Or was he simply seeking ways

The Boy With The Thorn In His Side-Part 2

to justify his lust for constant violence? I lifted my bloodied hands and dropped them again.

'I'm supposed to be grateful?' I asked him. 'Really? I'm supposed to be grateful for what you just did to me? Grateful to you for dragging me away from my own life, and fucking it up all over again? I'd only just got you out of my head you know!' I stopped myself then, clamping my lips over my teeth, recognising the anger building in his face. But the thing was, it had to be said, and if I didn't say it then, when would I ever be able to say it?

'What have we just been talking about? Have you forgotten already? You said you were going to behave!'

I dropped my head into my hands. I didn't know what else to do. I felt so close to laughing at him it was scary. I scraped my fingers back through my hair, found my scalp and scratched at it viciously, whilst shaking my head from side to side.

'So, what're you gonna' do?' I asked, keeping my head down. 'Come and find me every time you wanna' beat someone up? Every time you wanna' remember how fucking big you are? Do you know how warped that is?' I looked up again, in curiosity. 'How do you know I won't go right to the police right now?'

Howard snorted in derision at the comment. 'You never have before, and besides, it's your word against mine. And if you behave like you are supposed to, there'll be no need for me to be tough on you! I've told you that so many times!'

I blew my breath out over my teeth, risked a smile and shook my head in pity. 'I ran away from you Lee. You should have just left me where I was.'

He leaned even closer, right over my seat, with one hand gripping the steering wheel. His breath was coming in short, furious bursts through his nostrils.

'I thought we just had this discussion Danny? Eh?' I looked him in the eye. I could feel the rage throbbing from him in waves, building up again steadily. As his face jutted closer, I moved back instinctively, only for his big hand to shoot out and grab hold of my face. I tried just once to wrench free and then I gave up. I had barely anything physical left to fight with, so I let my shoulders slump and stared back at him dully, while his fingers crushed my cheeks. 'You're

327

worrying me now,' he hissed, spit from his curled lips splattering my skin. 'I thought I'd got through to you back on the cliff. Maybe I ought to take you back up there? There are lots of horrible ways to die you know Danny. Throwing you off the cliff is only one idea. I've got lots more you know, because I think about it all the time. You said you were going to do what I told you, you said you were going to be a good boy, so were you fucking lying to me?' He let go of me, dropped his hands between his thighs and raised his eyebrows at me. 'Or maybe I should give Jack a call after all, eh? Shall I do that? Is that what you fucking want?'

'No, it's not what I fucking want.'

'I ought to call him right now, see if he wants to come back and have a date with you eh?'

I fixed him with a cold, hard stare. In that moment I understood that it was possible to hate someone so much that you wanted them dead. Stone, cold dead. Dead and in the ground. In the ground so I could piss all over his grave. I didn't just want him dead, I *longed* for him to be dead. I scowled at him.

'Why don't you save him the trouble and do it yourself? You obviously really get off on the idea, you dirty fucking bastard.'

He snarled and lashed out, his hand slapping my face so hard I fell back against the window. I laughed at him, I laughed at it all.

'What the fuck is so funny?' he bellowed at me.

'I'm tired of this...' I murmured, smoothing my hands out across my face and shaking my head behind them, as gentle, exhausted, close to hysterical laughter rocked through me. 'This has to end...one way or another...'

'I'll be the one who says when it fucking ends!'

'Control freak, aren't you?' I said from behind my hands. 'Is your dad like that too? Is that where you get it from? Are you trying to be like him all the time, and failing? Because one, I am *not* your son, and two, I fucking loathe you and nothing you can do or say will ever change that. You need help, you know. You really need help.' I moved my hands, and shrank slowly back against the car door, keeping my eyes on Howard. His face and neck had reddened to a dark shade of crimson and his eyes bulged out of his face. I sighed at him. 'You should have just left me where I was.'

The Boy With The Thorn In His Side-Part 2

'You're trying to help Kay leave me!'

'That's her decision!' I cried back. 'I'm not helping her do anything Lee. She wants to leave you because you've been beating her! Why do you do that?'

'Oh, I see the old you coming back now,' he grumbled, his top lip curling and his hands rolling into fists between his legs. His chest was trembling. It was all there, under the surface, the tumbling waves of violence, desperate to burst out. I watched his fists and knew I had to be careful. I didn't think I could take any more. 'Same as ever eh? One minute it's all please, please don't hurt me, I'll be good, I promise I'll be good! Then the next you're trying to fucking push me again! I think you like it, that's what I think. I think you enjoy winding me up. That's how it's been with you the whole time, isn't it? I've given you so many chances, and you fuck it up every time!'

I licked my lips. I wondered if I should keep pushing him. Let him do it. Let him kill me. Whatever. Did I give a shit anymore? Really, did I?

'I'm just wondering what the hell your parents did to you,' I said slowly. 'I mean, really, what did they do? To create this insane, delusional, monster, who can only see things his way. Come on,' I shrugged at him. 'You can tell me if you like. You can share it. Might make you feel better to open up. You think it was okay your old man hit you with a belt and shit, don't you? But it's not, it's not okay to do that to people...Did he burn you with his fags too? I'm just curious. Or is that your own little twist on things? Something you get a kick out of? And what about Jack eh? He's older than you, isn't he? Did your dad arrange that too? Did he get Jack into *your* life? Come on, you can tell me.'

'You better shut your mouth.' He could barely look at me. His face was going purple. The skin on his cheeks quivered. A massive vein was throbbing in his neck. I glanced back at the door handle. 'You didn't sound like this up on the cliff...'

I cleared my throat. 'Thought you were gonna' throw me off. I really did. But now I see you were just trying to scare me. Just playing games like always. Just getting that control back again, because it makes you feel so good. But maybe now I'm less scared, now I'm sat here with you. I remember exactly what you are.'

He leaned in dangerously close. 'I'll take you back up there you little shit!'

'Maybe I'd prefer that,' I shrugged again, eyeing him warily. 'That would be better than working for you. If that's the only choice I've got.' I shut up and waited. I expected his rage to erupt upon me once again, but he appeared frozen to his seat, his position solid and unmoving, his eyes fixed on mine. I watched his face carefully for a few moments, before pulling my feet slowly up onto the seat, and resting back against it. I lurched forward again as soon as I made contact, tears of pain springing into my eyes, swearing under my breath at the sting across my back. He chuckled at that.

'That'll teach you,' he said, like a child. He was one big fucking child. I winced and shifted my arse on the seat, holding myself in the centre of it.

'I could use a drink,' I said. 'Any chance of that?' I had just remembered my cigarettes and slid my hand into my pocket to retrieve them. The pack was squashed and soggy, but there were one or two smokes that appeared to be intact. I shook one out, stuck it between my teeth and lit it before he could react. 'How about it?' I prompted him. 'You got anything?' He grunted and his eyes shifted to gaze out at the dark street beyond the car. 'A nightcap, what do you say?' I urged him, almost desperate for one now. 'To toast this new *business* arrangement of ours? Then you know what? I'll promise to go home like a good boy and not say anything to anyone. I'll tell them I had another accident, how about that?'

He looked at me, his small eyes squinting down to slits. 'I don't think I can believe a word that comes out of your mouth.'

I laughed incredulously. 'Come on, what am I gonna' do? I can't even fucking walk! You're the biggest Lee, you remember? You'll always be the biggest. I'm not gonna' call the police, come on. I tried that a few days ago. They don't give a shit.'

'Jack Daniels,' he nodded abruptly at the glove compartment in front of me. He slipped his hand towards the gear stick and picked up his own cigarettes. I leant forward stiffly, pulled open the compartment and plucked out the bottle of whisky. I sat back, unscrewed the cap and lifted the rim of the bottle to my swollen lips. I took a long mouthful and closed my eyes.

'That's good,' I murmured, and drank some more. Howard gestured for the bottle so I passed it to him and sucked on my cigarette instead. I wrapped an arm around my knees and rested my chin on it while I smoked. The pain throbbed steadily across my back and in my head, in my brain and I just smiled at it. I still remembered how to claim it, how to make it mine, and not let it panic or consume me. I thought about my friends and wondered what they were doing up there without me. Would they even be worried? Would they just think I was at my mum's, or with Lucy? Howard nudged me and handed me the bottle. 'So, what're you gonna' tell Mum?'

'What?'

'What're you gonna' tell her? That you and me made up? That we're best of buddies now 'cause you had a little word with me?' I grinned at him, took another big swig of whisky that burned my throat raw and passed it back to him. ''Cause once she finds out how you got me to change my mind, she's gonna' be all over you like a rash, right?'

Howard glowered at me darkly. 'Always with the smart remarks eh?' he said, smoking with his elbow resting against the window. 'From day one. You know what I thought when I first met you? Arrogant, smart mouthed little shit. I thought there's a kid that needs taking down a peg or two.'

'Well yeah, you did that all right.' I took back the bottle and poured it down my neck. It was setting me on fire, but I loved it, I needed it. I swallowed and wiped my mouth on my arm, and it was like the whisky was fuelling the fire in my belly. I felt this strange sense of calm. 'So, couldn't you find anyone else to replace Jack?' I asked him.

'It's not just about that,' he looked at me and sighed. 'I've told you a million times Danny, I'm trying to *help* you. To give you an opportunity. We could run a family business if you play your cards right.' He was looking at me intently; his forehead furrowed with his own private frustrations. I didn't understand. I would never understand. I found it almost painful to look back at him. There was something in his eyes more disturbing than the blatant lust for violence I was so used to seeing there. He looked like a man torn between doubt and conviction, hope and frustration. And then he said something that chilled me to the bone. 'I could be a father to you Danny. That's what I've always wanted. We could put all this behind us. We could work together, and make the business a success.'

I felt choked with horror and disgust. I swallowed, but the lump in my throat would not budge. 'You really think I want to be like you?' I asked him. He jerked an angry thumb towards the darkened buildings outside.

'You really want to end up like your loser friends?'

'They're not losers,' I shook my head. 'They helped me get away from you. They're the only people who've given a shit since I was thirteen.'

'Yeah? Bunch of long-haired fucking druggies, drunks and ex-cons?' he replied distastefully. 'You'd be better off without them.' He lifted the bottle of whisky up to his lips and drank. His eyes appeared hooded and dark as he sloshed a double measure down his throat.

I opened the ashtray on the side of the door and tapped my cigarette into it. 'Let me ask you something.'

He looked my way. 'What is it?'

'When Anthony got arrested that time, when the cops raided their house? That was you, wasn't it? I mean, I've always known it, but how? How did you do it?' I smoked and kept my eyes on him. I watched his eyes widen and shine with a glitter of pride that sickened me. He snorted in reply.

'That was easy.' I waited for more. I could feel adrenaline moving through me and picking up speed. Something rearing up and stirring to life inside of me, and somehow the horrible pain was subsiding and the sudden and bloody desire for revenge was stamping all over the fear and making a mockery of it. 'Jack did it. Just broke in and planted it there.' He smirked a little at the memory and shrugged at me. 'Easy. The back door was knackered. I made the call. The punk deserved it for threatening me. Giving it the big I am.'

I nodded slowly and gazed down at the floor. 'So, you got Jack here on purpose? To do that for you?'

'He was at a loose end. Plus, he owed me.'

'Oh, I know why he was at a loose end. So, you got him here to get rid of Anthony?' I looked back at Howard and tried to determine

The Boy With The Thorn In His Side-Part 2

what I saw before me. A huge, physically dangerous man, who looked proud and arrogant, but at the same time nervous and twitchy. Did he feel guilt, I wondered? Did he ever feel sorry for the pain and fear he inflicted? 'Then Jack starts being nice to me,' I spoke up. 'At the club. Buying me smokes and drinks. I was lonely I guess. Staying away from my friends because I didn't want them to end up like Anthony. He started letting me go to his flat to get high. So, what was that then? Some perverse little favour you owed him?'

'No. He owed me, I told you.' He seemed to thrust his chest out a little then, drank more whisky and dragged a hand across his wet lips before breaking into a knowing smile. 'He owed me shit loads, let's put it that way. He owed me favours going back years. He owed me for every time I turned a blind eye to his sick little crushes. And believe me, he had plenty of them when he used to hang around my old man's gym! He even has a fucking type, you know? He has a type, and you were it.' He sniggered then, his eyes flicking all over me as I stared back at him in horror. 'He was pretty much in love with you, you know. Pathetic, eh?'

I finished my cigarette and stubbed it out in the ashtray behind me. 'So why didn't he try anything before?' I asked. I don't know why I asked the question, when the whole business was making me feel queasy in my stomach. I licked my dry lips, and then used my teeth to scrape at the dried blood I could feel on them. Howard was shaking with soft mocking laughter. He looked right at me, cocked his head and smiled.

'How do you know he didn't?'

'What?'

'Come on, don't make me laugh...all those times you were round his flat, off your fucking head? How do you know what he did, or didn't do? Could've dropped a fucking bomb on you sometimes and you wouldn't have woken up!' He was grinning at me like a shark, all small neat teeth and shaking shoulders, obviously finding this distressing scenario pretty amusing. I breathed in through my nostrils, felt the hatred pumping through me, and I exhaled it again slowly, steadying myself, staying calm.

'Pair of sad, sick bastards,' I whispered. 'Pathetic. Disgusting. You make my skin crawl. Pair of sad bastards who can only get their kicks torturing people who are weaker than them. And you! You are worse than him! And I am so fucking bored of all of this...' I turned my face to the window and sighed with exhaustion. I gazed at the dead street beyond the car, and I craved sleep and a chance to think...

'*Bored*? Bored are you?' I wouldn't look at him as he leaned over me again. 'I'll make sure you're not fucking bored! You brought it all on yourself Danny, you remember that! You made an enemy of me from day fucking one! You decided to mess with me, not the other way around! You tried time and time again to poison Kay against me. It would have been different otherwise, if you'd been a nice, normal kid! We could have been like father and son from the start!'

I puffed breath against the glass and shook my head. Then I turned my face and sneered back at him over my shoulder. 'Stop saying that. Do you know how fucking sick that makes me? It's a good thing you never had your own kids! You're a monster!'

His hand clamped down upon my arm. I felt the power like a shock wave, and my body wanted to recoil and shrink down to nothing. I looked into his eyes and they were ablaze with fresh anger.

'Maybe I've changed my mind,' he said to me. 'You don't really need your stuff. Maybe I better take you back to mine instead. Tell your mum I picked you up off the street, totally wasted.'

My eyes travelled down to the door handle. 'All right, I'm sorry.'

'You don't mean it. You're not sorry. You just say sorry when you have to. It doesn't mean anything.'

'I'll take the job,' I told him then. 'As long as you promise that's the last time you pull this shit on me?'

'I don't think I believe you.'

'We have a deal,' I gritted my teeth and told him. 'If you don't pull this on me again. I'm not gonna' work for you and be your fucking punch bag too. I mean it.'

'I wouldn't have to get tough if you behaved yourself.'

'Yeah, okay, I get it. I can get out here then.'

He looked like he was considering it. But his hand held tight. 'I don't know if I can trust you little man.'

'I'm telling the truth,' I urged him. 'I'll take the job. I don't have a choice, do I? I'll take it, I'll do it, I'll do whatever you want,

The Boy With The Thorn In His Side-Part 2

just as long as you keep your fucking hands and your fucking belt to yourself! That's the only way! The *only* way!' For some reason there were tears in my eyes again. I didn't feel sad though. Far fucking from it. But I was glad of the tears. They looked convincing and he fell for them.

'I'll have to trust you then,' he said slowly and thickly. 'One last time eh?'

I nodded. 'You can trust me. But that's the deal.'

He kept hold of my arm. I opened my mouth to breathe. The air in the car was stale and cloying. He reached out with his other hand, turned the key in the ignition and unlocked all the doors. I took a breath. I moved my free hand and tried the door handle. I pushed it down, and I felt the door give way, just a little, behind me. I looked back into his face, just inches from my own.

'I'll give you a few hours to get your stuff together,' he said to me softly. 'Then I'll be back out here to pick you up. And if you let me down this time, it's over little man, do you understand that?'

I nodded silently and pressed my tender back a little harder against the door. Howard kept hold of my arm and slipped his other hand inside the breast of his denim jacket. I watched him silently, as he pulled out a slick, shining blade. He held it up by the stubby wooden handle and then swished it dramatically through the air and I cringed away from it, just to please him, just to really knock him out. I could feel cool air teasing my skin from outside the car. I was so close to freedom, yet still locked in with a madman. He took the knife and pressed it up under my chin. I closed my mouth. I did not breathe. His tiny eyes were right in front of mine.

'This is the very last time I warn you,' he said to me. 'I won't be giving you any more chances little man. If you fuck this up, if you let me down, I'll come looking for you and I won't stop until I find you. You know what I'll do then?' I shook my head just a little. He growled very softly and pressed the knife harder into my skin. 'I'll take you home to your mother, and I will slice that bitch from her cunt to her throat and the two of us will sit and watch her bleed to death slowly. And then I will do the same to you. Because I am not going through this again, do you hear? This is it. *Final chance.*' He moved the knife away, dropped my arm and pushed the blade back inside his coat.

I lowered my feet to the floor and pushed the car open just a little. 'I think I get the message,' I told him quietly.

'Good,' he said. 'I'll come and pick you up in a few hours, do you hear? There is no time to mess about. That Lawler prick needs a kick up the arse to start with.'

I slipped one foot from the car, down to meet the road outside. The fresh air circled around my ankle, cold and soothing against the wet leg of my jeans.

'I need to call him actually,' I murmured wonderingly.

Howard leaned forward. 'Do it. Tell him he's working for you now and see how he likes that.' He laughed a little and put the car into gear. I lowered my other foot to the ground and eased the rest of my body out into the night. I felt odd. Dazed, and dreamlike.

'Yeah, I need something,' I said, and raised myself up onto my legs. They seemed to be able to hold me. I felt like I had climbed out of a hole. I felt the ground beneath my feet and tested it warily. I put weight down on them and straightened out my spine. My entire body began to shake violently in protest. I knew one thing. I did need to call Jaime. That was true. I needed to call Jaime and then I could get some sleep...and then...I looked into the car and my eyes met Howard's as they peered out at me.

I swear to God I felt it go. I felt it. Something grew hard and taut inside of me, and then snapped. I swear to fucking God I felt it happen. It's me or him, me or him, I know it, I feel it, it's me or him and I can't take it anymore...I can't...I turned away from him, shuffling footsteps like an old man, my feet unable to pick themselves up. I remembered all the other times both my mind and body had been crushed beyond repair. You could only pick yourself up so many times. You could only do so much with the damage before it got too late. It was too late. It's all right though, I told myself, glancing back one more time at the man who was responsible for all of it. The man who held the puppet strings. The man who was never going to let me fucking go. He stared back at me, hard slits for eyes, and a tight-lipped mouth turned up at the corners. He looked calm again, not twitchy anymore. He looked like he knew he had won. He nodded once, as if

The Boy With The Thorn In His Side-Part 2

everything was now well and understood, everything was as it should be.

'You've got two hours to get your shit together,' he called out to me. 'I'll be out here waiting, all right? Then we'll get you set up at the flat and talk properly.' He gave a strange little laugh and leaned across the passenger seat to yank the door shut. Then he put the car into reverse and screeched back down the road.

I remained on the pavement for some time, just staring. I was thinking about Howard rather calmly, and thinking that really it was all easy to understand, because we were all just humans and underneath it all humans are just animals. They fight and snarl and wreak havoc to get what they want, they destroy each other daily, so why be surprised by any of it? I realised then that my trouble had always been that I cared too much. I felt too much. People like Howard and Freeman, they did not care. They did not feel. They merely stomped through life like giants, stepping and stamping on anyone who got in their way, picking people up like toys, using them and tossing them away again. I turned and limped awkwardly down the road towards the phone box on the high street.

I went inside, lifted the receiver, found some coins in my pocket and fed them into the slot. I punched in Jaime's number and it rang six times before his groggy voice answered.

'Yeah?'

'Jaime. It's Danny.'

'Danny? What the fuck mate? Your friends have been out looking for you. They've called me like twenty fucking times!'

'I'm okay.'

'Where you been then?'

'With Howard.'

'Fuck! Shit! You okay mate?'

'Nah, not really. I really need something Jaime. Can you help me out?'

'Yeah, what do you need?'

'I tried coke a few times,' I remembered, pressing my aching head against the cold glass of the telephone box. 'Does it always make you feel really full of yourself?'

Jaime laughed at me. 'Yeah, basically, either that or it just makes you talk shit all night.'

'I need to feel really fucking full of myself, all right? I need to feel like king of this shitting world, yeah? I need to feel invincible.'

'Ah, are you sure you're okay mate?' he asked me then. 'You don't sound like yourself.'

'That's good, 'cause I don't want to be myself anymore. Can you help me out Jaime?'

'Um...' he sighed deeply on the other end of the phone. 'I dunno mate...I don't think your friends would be too happy with me, to be honest.'

'Don't worry about them! Come on man, I don't wanna' beg you. Listen, that bastard just totally fucked me up, and if I don't get hold of something to make me feel better about it, I'm gonna' do something stupid, I'm serious Jaime!' I paused and gulped, and stared through the glass at the deserted street beyond the phone box. All the shops stood in neat rows on either side of the street, black and silent and watching. 'I'm serious. If you can't help me out really quick, I'm gonna' go throw myself off a bridge or something...I really mean it Jaime.'

'All right, all right,' he said quickly, sounding alarmed. 'Calm down mate, just chill out a minute yeah? I get what you're saying. Look, I'll drive you over something to calm you down, yeah? Where are you?'

'I'm outside home. In the phone box. But I don't want something to calm me down Jaime, I want something to fire me up.'

'Right. Okay. Sorry. Just sit tight then mate? Don't do anything silly, okay? I won't be long.'

'I'll be here,' I replied and hung up. I felt my broken body weakening against the side of the phone box. I let myself slip slowly down to meet the floor. It reeked of piss and I could see a used condom in one corner, coiled and pink like a piglet's tail. I crossed my arms over my knees, rested my head down and closed my eyes as tightly as possible. I invited in and embraced the darkness, the ugliness inside of me, and I listened to the embers of the fire, crackling and hissing. The match had been struck, I thought to myself. I could feel it. I could really feel it. I could feel it burning. It

The Boy With The Thorn In His Side-Part 2

was burning, but I just needed a little more fuel to add to the fire...to keep it going.

I had no idea how much time had passed between my call to Jaime and the screech of tyres further down the road that let me know he had arrived. I lifted my head and squinted through the darkness. I could see his tall, gaunt figure loping up the street towards me, moving in that jerky, shifty way he had, his head held low, and yet whipping from side to side the whole time. I wanted to get to my feet to greet him, but I couldn't do it. My body felt like mush. He hesitated for a second outside, and then grabbed the handle and yanked the door open.

'Danny?' he sounded unsure.

I looked up at him and grimaced. 'You bring me something?'

He nodded, and crouched down beside me, a frown lining the face under the baseball cap. 'Bleedinghell mate, look at you.'

I nodded at him. 'I told you.'

'That insane bastard, what did he do?'

'He wants to own me. That's what it is. *Own* me.' I tried to shake my hair from my eyes, but it was all sticky and clumpy with blood, and rain, and sand from the cliff, and it wouldn't move. I lifted a hand and smoothed it to one side.

Jaime gasped. 'Your head's all cut mate. You should go to hospital!'

'He won't stop, you know, he won't ever stop. Not until one of us is dead. He thinks I work for him now. His fucking errand boy. If someone did this to you Jaime, would you do what they wanted?'

Jaime seemed to flinch and squirm at both the question I asked and at the state of me, slumped in front of him. He shrugged his bony shoulders.

'I dunno mate. I dunno what to say to you.' He shook his head and whistled through his grey teeth. 'Suppose that's up to you. Shit, I knew that bastard was nasty...whatever happened to Freeman, do you know? One minute he was here, barking orders at me, then suddenly he's vanished, and no one knows where the fuck he is!'

'I stabbed him, so he left town. That was ages ago.'

'Are you fucking serious? You *stabbed* him?'

'Yeah. Had to.'

'Jesus fucking Christ! Well you learn something new every day! Guess you had your reasons....are you okay mate? Can you get up? Shall I call Anthony and Michael down?'

'No,' I shook my head at him. 'I'll be okay in a minute.' I stared down at my trainers, sodden and crusted with sand. 'What did you bring me? I haven't got the money on me. It's up in the bed-sit.'

'Don't worry about it now,' he shook his head at me, dug around inside his tracksuit jacket and pulled out a plastic bag. 'Coke,' he told me. 'You sure you've done it before? It's a bigger deal than speed you know.' I nodded that I had. 'Okay then, here you go,' he placed the bag into my outstretched hand. 'I don't exactly feel good about giving you this, you know.'

'You're helping me out,' I told him, closing my fingers over the bag. My head felt so heavy and full, close to exploding with everything. 'If I don't get some way to feel strong right now, then that's fucking it, I'm done...I've had enough, you know. What's the point? What's the point in anything Jaime?'

Jaime just reached out and patted my shoulder clumsily. 'Don't ask me mate. I don't know a fucking thing about anything. You'll be okay. Take that and feel better then. Maybe call the old bill tomorrow, eh? That bastard needs stopping.' He got to his feet, stuffed his hands into his jacket pockets and glanced around him nervously.

'Yeah, he does,' I agreed with him. 'He needs stopping.'

He looked down at me worriedly. 'You're not gonna' sit in there all night, are you?'

I shook my head. 'Help me up?' I held up a hand, he took hold of it and pulled me to my feet. I closed my eyes against the pain, and my back took up its persistent drum beat once again. I stepped out from the phone box and leaned briefly against Jaime, took a deep breath, opened my eyes again, and felt ready. 'Okay,' I said. 'Thanks.'

'What the hell did he do to you anyway? Jesus!'

'Doesn't matter,' I breathed out heavily as we started to walk slowly and jerkily towards my building. 'Just listen, just don't ever mess with him Jaime.'

'God, I won't. I don't. Just keep my head down, I do. Do what I'm told.'

'Jaime, can I ask you something?'

'What is it mate?'

'When I first met you, you know, at the club?' Jaime nodded in reply. 'Was it Howard or Freeman who told you to deal to me? Who did it come from?'

'Freeman,' Jaime remembered. We had reached the building. I let go of Jaime and rested against the little red brick wall that cornered off our patch. I stooped slowly forward over my knees to catch my breath. Jaime brought out some cigarettes and offered me one. I took it and waited for the light. 'I met him there. Actually, he caught me dealing pills to some mates in the loos. Thought he was gonna' take me outside and give me a good hiding, but he was cool about it.' Jaime lit my cigarette, and then his own. 'He was pretty friendly. Suggested I went through him. He wanted a local bloke he could trust, someone who knew everyone I guess.' He shrugged loosely and puffed on his smoke. 'So, I said yeah. Made way more money through him. Heavier shit though. Always just sold grass and e's before then. That was it really. I did the dirty work. Made it easy for him.'

'He told you to deal to me?'

'Yeah, I knew he was mates with Howard. Thought they were like, I dunno, business partners or something. You could tell there was something going on between them. You wouldn't mess with either of them, you know?' He flicked ash behind him and peered at me curiously. 'Took me a long while to realise he was your step-dad though. That's when I realised how nasty he could be, I guess. Then Anthony shows up...starts sniffing around, asking me questions...Fuck, if they ever found out it was me who helped him...' Jaime shook his head and shifted uncomfortably from one foot to the other as he sucked on his cigarette. 'I don't exactly feel good about any of this,' he admitted. 'It's all totally fucked up.'

I blew smoke smoothly at the ground and looked up at him with a brave smile. 'You've done me a huge favour tonight,' I told him. 'So don't feel bad. They just used you, like they use everyone. I sorted Jack out, you know. Now I'm gonna' sort Howard out. I just needed this to help me feel better, you know? To help me feel strong. So I can fight back.'

Jaime frowned at me. 'Fight back?'

'Yeah, I have to. I'm not gonna' let him win. I'm not gonna' fucking work for him.' I took a few more drags then dropped the cigarette to the ground and stamped on it. I looked up at the building. 'I'll get that money to you tomorrow. Probably give it to Mike to give to you, okay?'

'Why? Where will you be? What're you gonna' do Danny?'

I turned away from him and begun to limp awkwardly towards the door. 'Fight back,' I called over my shoulder. 'You'll see.'

I did not look back as I arrived at the door. I realised then that I had no keys. I pressed the buzzer and waited. My head was pounding with the music, so I nodded along to it and thought it was okay, it was all okay, and I would just take it along with me, whatever I did, whatever happened, I would take the music with me.

The Boy With The Thorn In His Side-Part 2

37

From the bottom of the stairs, I could hear the music playing and that was the only thing that mattered. I grinned in relief, because it held a hand out to me and guided me up towards safety. Slide Away, calling out to me, echoing and dancing down the stairs, pulling me up, telling me to give it all I got...They were either side of me, Michael and Anthony, helping me up, and I think I was smiling and singing as we climbed up the stairs. I could feel the fire inside of me growing stronger and stronger. I couldn't believe it was happening, and it was making me feel so happy. The flames were inside of me, alive, and licking and reaching, and the heat was intensifying with every breath I took.

'I love this song! Come on...*listen!*' I was singing along, shouting it out, seeing Lucy's face shining back at me, and I was talking to her, begging her to let me be the one ... I felt like my head was on fire with it all, and my heart was pounding and leaping, fanning the flames inside my chest.

Once we were inside the bed-sit, Anthony closed and locked the door, and I pulled away from Michael to scoop Kurt up from the floor. 'Danny, you're bleeding...' Michael sounded like he was going to cry. I didn't look at him. I buried my face in Kurt's fur and he covered my beaten face in kisses.

'Mike, calm down...' Anthony told him. 'We found him hiding under the bed Danny...he's okay. Limping a bit. Where the hell have you been?'

I placed the dog carefully onto the bed and staggered towards the bathroom.

'Danny?" I heard Michael calling after me. He sounded awful, desperate and terrified. I couldn't even look at him. 'What the hell happened? What should we do?'

'In a minute,' I replied, in a flat tone. 'Roll me a fat one, would you.'

I slammed the bathroom door behind me, shutting them out. I faced myself in the cracked mirror that hung on the wall over the sink. I saw this strange version of myself snarling back at me. My hair, flattened by the rain at the cliff top, covered in sand and caked in blood along the hairline. There was a gash on my forehead and all the blood had run down onto my face, into my eyebrows and eyelashes, staining them all crimson. My nose and my lips were swollen and scratched from hitting the wall. I turned on the taps, staring back at myself. Then I grabbed the bar of soap and lowered my face into the flow of water. I used handfuls of soap and water to rub at my face, and I felt like I was rubbing it all away, and this time it would be gone, because it was never going to happen again. I washed until the water ran clear. Then I lifted my head, grabbed a towel and dried myself off. I examined myself again. I saw dead blue eyes glaring back at me. I saw a face that I wanted to pummel into mush. I saw a head that I wanted to smash against the wall until all the memories were gone. I put one hand into my pocket where I had stashed the bag from Jaime. I stared at myself, and listened as all the voices inside my head, as all their incessant and distorted chattering, finally began to join up and make sense.

Anthony had rolled the joint. Michael had just hung up the phone. He looked so miserable, so forlorn and childlike that I could not even bear to look at him, let alone talk to him.

'Lucy,' he told me. 'She's been worried sick. I just told her you're back.' I did not answer him, because the noise in my head was too loud. I did not look at them. I loved them, but I had to move away from them. It had to be done. So I climbed onto the bed and pulled the blankets over me and Kurt. I curled into a ball, rested my head on the pillow and I did not look at Michael as he cautiously approached the bed.

Anthony was sat on the sofa. 'Danny,' he said sombrely. 'You gonna' tell us what happened? It was Howard, wasn't it?'

Michael looked at his brother for a moment and then sat down warily on the edge of the bed, close to my feet. I could feel their eyes upon me, waiting. I put my hands together and rubbed one wrist against the other. I watched the dried blood flaking off. I used my nails to scratch away at it. It looked like rust red snow falling from my skin.

'What happened?' Michael prompted, when I did not speak. Anthony got up then, came to the bed, lit the joint and held it out to me. I took it down with me and smoked it like that.

The Boy With The Thorn In His Side-Part 2

'I'll call the police,' he offered, with this sad and shabby shrug. 'Whatever happened Danny, whatever he did, you can tell us. Tell us, and we'll call the cops right now.'

I took long, deep drags on the spliff, and felt my mind easing into a gently, cushioned state. The edges were softening and my heart was slowing down. I could hear my breathing getting slower and slower, and I could not prevent my eyes from closing.

'Danny?' I heard Michael saying again. 'Danny, what happened? Please tell us. Don't shut us out.'

'Talk about it tomorrow,' I murmured. 'Need to sleep.' I lifted the joint twice more to my lips before holding it out to Michael. I got hold of the blanket and tugged it up until it covered my face. There, I relaxed gratefully into the darkness and the silence, where I could hear my ragged breathing getting slower and quieter. My face ached against the pillow. My back burned and I was glad of it. There were voices taking up their chatter in my mind again, and I whispered back to them, colluded with them, agreed with them... 'Know it's over,' I muttered as the darkness began to carry me away. 'Know it...it's over.'

I slept deeply, for a while, and then I woke up and I was done with it. Michael and Anthony snored on, breathing, and twitching and murmuring in their sleep. The first glow of yellow sunshine stole in from behind the blankets pinned to the windows, which meant I didn't have much time. I stood up and walked slowly to the bathroom, the welts on my back stretching and screaming to life. I shut myself in, had a piss and then took out the little bag Jaime had given to me. I took the mirror down from the wall and balanced it across the top of the sink. I sprinkled two lines of powder onto it then used my fingertips to pinch them into longer, thinner lines. I stooped over, closed one nostril and sniffed them up. I blinked, rubbed my nose, sniffed again, and hung the mirror back up. I came out of the bathroom, found my old battered Nirvana t-shirt lying on the floor close to the bed and picked it up. It smelled. It smelled of old times. I pulled the blood stained one I was wearing up and over my head and tossed it to the floor. I pulled on the old one and noticed it was getting a bit small for me now, but it didn't matter, did it? Not today. I pushed through the beaded curtains and began to look for a knife.

Chantelle Atkins

The Boy With The Thorn In His Side – Part 2
Danny's Playlist

- The Boy With The Thorn In His Side – The Smiths
- Shoot You Down – The Stone Roses
- Safe As Milk album – Captain Beefheart
- Pablo Honey album – Radiohead
- Hot Rats album – Frank Zappa
- Parklife album – Blur
- Cigarettes and Alcohol – Oasis
- Fire and Rain – James Taylor
- Supersonic – Oasis
- Whatever – Oasis
- Live Forever – Oasis
- That Joke Isn't Funny Anymore – The Smiths
- Slide Away – Oasis
- I Am The Resurrection – The Stone Roses
- Break On Through – The Doors
- Up In The Sky – Oasis
- Sugar Cane – Sonic Youth
- For Tomorrow – Blur
- Come As You Are – Nirvana
- Animal Nitrate – Suede
- Should I Stay or Should I Go? – The Clash

Chantelle Atkins

- Panic – The Smiths
- Cry Myself Blind – Primal Scream
- The Bends – Radiohead
- Ruby Tuesday – The Rolling Stones
- Girl From Mars – Ash
- Breaking Into Heaven – The Stone Roses
- The Only One I Know – The Charlatans
- Bulletproof – Radiohead
- Only Love Can Break Your Heart – Neil Young
- Slide Away – Oasis
- Safe From Harm – Massive Attack
- Ten Storey Love Song – The Stone Roses
- Up In The Sky – Oasis
- Bones – Radiohead
- Movin' On Up – Primal Scream
- Champagne Supernova – Oasis
- Planet Telex – Radiohead
- Roll With It – Oasis
- I Know It's Over – The Smiths
- Lithium - Nirvana

The Boy With The Thorn In His Side-Part 2

About The Author

Chantelle Atkins was born and raised in Bournemouth, Dorset. She still resides there now, with her husband, four children and various animals. She is addicted to music and books and is on a mission to become as self-sufficient as possible.

Also By Chantelle Atkins;
The Boy With The Thorn In His Side – Part 2
The Boy With The Thorn In His Side – Part 3
The Boy With The Thorn In His Side – Part 4
The Boy With The Thorn In His Side – Part 5 – coming soon!
The Mess Of Me
This Is Nowhere
Bird People and Other Stories
The Tree Of Rebels
Elliot Pie's Guide To Human Nature

Please consider leaving the author a review on Amazon and Goodreads. Reviews really do help other readers decide whether or not to buy a book.
To find out more about Chantelle Atkins and her books, you can follow her here;

Facebook; https://www.facebook.com/chantelleatkinswriter

Twitter; https://twitter.com/Chanatkins

Blog; http://chantelleatkins.com/

Pinterest; https://www.pinterest.com/chantelleatkins/

Author Newsletter; http://eepurl.com/bVVbGD

The Boy With The Thorn In His Side-Part 2

Printed in Great Britain
by Amazon